You can never be
Or too we

Death, Taxes,

a rd Extra-

Hold

Hairspray

A Tara Holloway

Novel

Diane Kelly

"SMART, SASSY, AND SO MUCH FUN! Tara Holloway is
the IRS's answer to Stephanie Plum."—Gemma Halliday

Don't miss these other Tara Holloway novels
from Diane Kelly...

DEATH, TAXES, AND A FRENCH MANICURE

DEATH, TAXES, AND A SKINNY NO-WHIP LATTE

Both available from St. Martin's Paperbacks!

Praise for Diane Kelly's Tara Holloway Novels!

DEATH, TAXES, AND A SKINNY NO-WHIP LATTE

"Readers will find Kelly's protagonist a kindred spirit to Stephanie Plum: feisty and tenacious, with a self-deprecating sense of humor. Tara is flung into some unnerving situations, including encounters with hired thugs, would-be muggers, and head lice. The laughs lighten up the scary bits, and the nonstop action and snappy dialogue keep the standard plot moving along at a good pace."   —*RT Book Reviews*

DEATH, TAXES, AND A FRENCH MANICURE

"Keep your eye on Diane Kelly—her writing is tight, smart, and laugh-out-loud funny."   —Kristan Higgins,
New York Times and *USA Today* bestselling author

"A hilarious, sexy, heart-pounding ride, that will keep you on the edge of your seat. Tara Holloway is the IRS's answer to Stephanie Plum—smart, sassy, and so much fun. Kelly's debut has definitely earned her a spot on my keeper shelf!"
—Gemma Halliday, National Readers Choice Award Winner
and three-time Rita nominee

"The subject of taxation usually makes people cry, but prepare to laugh your assets off with Diane Kelly's hilarious debut."   —Jana DeLeon, author of the Ghost-in-Law series

"Quirky, sexy, and downright fabulous. Zany characters you can't help but love, and a plot that will knock your socks off. This is the most fun I've had reading in forever!"
—Christie Craig, award-winning author
of the Hotter in Texas series

MORE . . .

"With a quirky cast of characters, snappy dialogue, and a Bernie Madoff-style pyramid scheme—hunting down tax cheats has never added up to so much fun!" —Robin Kaye, award-winning author of the Domestic Gods series

"Kudos to debut author Diane Kelly, who brings a fresh, new voice and raucous humor to the market. I can't wait to read the next book in the Tara Holloway series!"
—Angela Cavener, Indie Book Award finalist and author of *Operation: Afterlife*

"Tara Holloway is Gin Bombay's BFF, or would be if they knew each other. Kelly's novel is smart, sexy and funny enough to make little girls want to be IRS agents when they grow up!" —Leslie Langtry, author of the hilarious Bombay Assassins mystery series

"This totally terrific debut is better than a refund check from the IRS!" —*Reader to Reader Reviews*

"Part romance, part thriller, and part comedic mystery, it's just the thing to help keep you warm on a chilly autumn night." —*The Maine Suspect*

"I was so delighted to stumble across *Death, Taxes, and a French Manicure* by Diane Kelly."
—CriminalElement.com

ST. MARTIN'S PAPERBACKS TITLES
BY DIANE KELLY

Paw Enforcement

Paw and Order

Laying Down the Paw

THE TARA HOLLOWAY NOVELS

Death, Taxes, and a French Manicure

Death, Taxes, and a Skinny No-Whip Latte

Death, Taxes, and Extra-Hold Hairspray

Death, Taxes, and a Sequined Clutch
(an e-original novella)

Death, Taxes, and Peach Sangria

Death, Taxes, and Hot Pink Leg Warmers

Death, Taxes, and Green Tea Ice Cream

Death, Taxes, and Mistletoe Mayhem
(an e-original novella)

Death, Taxes, and Silver Spurs

Death, Taxes, and Cheap Sunglasses

Death, Taxes,

and Extra-Hold Hairspray

DIANE KELLY

St. Martin's Paperbacks

This is a work of fiction. All of the characters, organizations, and events portrayed in this novel are either products of the author's imagination or are used fictitiously.

DEATH, TAXES, AND EXTRA-HOLD HAIRSPRAY

Copyright © 2012 by by Diane Kelly.
Excerpt from *Death, Taxes, and Peach Sangria* copyright © 2012 by Diane Kelly.

For information address St. Martin's Press, 175 Fifth Avenue, New York, NY 10010.

ISBN: 978-0-312-55128-5

Printed in the United States of America

St. Martin's Paperbacks edition / July 2012

St. Martin's Paperbacks are published by St. Martin's Press, 175 Fifth Avenue, New York, NY 10010.

10 9 8 7 6 5 4 3 2

To my Aunt Betty, who lost her fight with lung cancer. I know the margaritas are good and the slots are always paying off where you are now.

Acknowledgments

I owe many thanks to my wonderful team at St. Martin's Paperbacks. To my editor, Holly Blanck, who is so easy and pleasant to work with and whose insights and suggestions always make my work better. You rock! To Eileen Rothschild and Aleksandra Mencel for spreading the word about my books. To Danielle Fiorella and Monika Roe for creating such perfect covers for my books. And to everyone else who had a hand in bringing my books to readers, thanks for all you do!

Thanks to my agent, Helen Breitwieser, for your hard work, enthusiasm, and skillful guidance.

To authors Trinity Blake, Celya Bowers, Angela Cavener, Vannetta Chapman, Cheryl Hathaway, Angela Hicks, and Kennedy Shaw for your feedback, support, and friendship.

To Julia Hunter. Thanks for sharing your knowledge of firearms.

To my sister, Donna, for trying to teach me how to play craps. If not for the free drinks, I might have actually learned something.

To the clever and creative Liz Bemis and Sienna Condy of Bemis Promotions. I appreciate your hard work on my Web site and promotions.

To the IRS special agents who assisted in my research.

I'm in awe of what you do. Thanks for sharing your intriguing world with me.

And, finally, thanks so much to my readers. Enjoy your time with Tara and the gang. I hope this book brings you lots of LOL moments!

CHAPTER ONE

*T*his Is What Happens When Rednecks Have Too Much Time on Their Hands

"Damn." I dropped the phone back into its cradle on my desk. I needed help on a case, but it seemed no one was available this afternoon. I'd called every special agent in the Dallas IRS Criminal Investigations office.

Make that every special agent *but one*.

That one sat directly across the hall, his cowboy boots propped on his desk, his right hand rhythmically squeezing a blue stress ball as he eyed me. I sat at my desk, pretending not to notice.

Why didn't I want Nick Pratt working on this case with me? Because the guy had whiskey-colored eyes that drank a girl in, an ass you could bounce a quarter off of, and more sex appeal than George Clooney, Brad Pitt, and Johnny Depp combined.

I realize these factors might all sound like reasons *to want* to work with him. Problem was, I was in a committed relationship with a wonderful guy and, despite that fact, wasn't entirely sure I could resist temptation.

Better not put myself to the test, right?

My usual partner, Eddie Bardin, had received an unexpected temporary promotion to acting director three weeks ago when doctors found a spot on the right lung of our boss, Lu Lobozinski. Lu had taken time off for her chemotherapy treatments and recovery, appointing Eddie to take her place until she was able to return.

Eddie's temporary promotion left me to handle a buttload of cases all on my own. And not just any old buttload, but cases that had been purposely put on the back burner for years because each case was guaranteed to be a major pain in the ass.

One of the biggest of these cases involved an eighty-three-year-old chicken rancher who'd served seven consecutive terms as president of a radical secessionist group. Another involved a popular, charismatic preacher who financed a lavish lifestyle via his congregants' tax-deductible donations to his megachurch. It was almost enough to send me back to my boring old job at the CPA firm.

But not quite.

The phone on my desk rang. The caller ID readout displayed the name N PRATT.

Dang. No way I could ignore the guy now. It would be too obvious.

I looked across the hall as I picked up the phone. Nick looked back at me, one thick brown brow raised. How the guy could look so damn sexy in a plain white dress shirt and basic tan slacks was beyond me. Maybe it was the oversized gold horseshoe-shaped belt buckle that did it, drawing attention to his nether regions like a flashing neon sign that said WANNA GET LUCKY?

"Big Bob's Bait Bucket," I said in my best Southern twang. "We got whatcha need if whatcha need is worms."

You got me. I'm a bit of a smart-ass. But I had spent two summers in high school working for Big Bob. Minimum wage plus all the free nightcrawlers I wanted. Which was none.

Nick shot me a pointed look across the hall. "Why haven't you asked me to help you?"

Because you make my girlie parts quiver in a very unprofessional manner. But I couldn't very well tell him that, now could I? Better think quick, Tara.

"You looked . . . um . . ." *Gorgeous? Sexy as hell? Absolutely boinkable?* I went with, "Busy."

He grinned, flashing his chipped tooth, an imperfection that somehow only added to his primal appeal. "I fake it pretty good, don't I? That's how I got fast-tracked to senior special agent."

Nick's career as a special agent with the IRS had indeed been meteoric, at least until three years ago when he'd been forced to flee the country or die at the hands of Marcos Mendoza, a violent, money-laundering tax cheat.

Luckily for Nick, Lu had later assigned me and Eddie to renew the case against Mendoza. After the creep threatened Eddie and his family, I'd smuggled Nick back into the U.S. and the two of us had brought Mendoza to his knees. Literally. Hard for the man to stay standing after I'd shot off his left testicle. I'd considered taking the gonad to a taxidermist for mounting, but I doubted my mother would let me hang it over the fireplace back home next to Dad's sixteen-point trophy buck.

Nick sat up at his desk, his expression serious now. "You gave me my life back, Tara. I'll never be too busy for you."

Nick was directly offering to help me out. No girl in her right mind could say no to that, even if she had been avoiding him. There's only so much willpower to go around.

I hung up the phone. "Saddle up, cowboy," I called across the hall as I stood and grabbed my purse. "We've got a chicken farmer to check in on."

We snagged a car from the Treasury's fleet and drove for what seemed like an eternity through flat, dry country. The radio was tuned to a country station to combat our boredom and the air conditioner turned on full blast to combat the outdoor temperature, which had topped out at 103 degrees. That's August in north Texas. Brutal.

Nick had brought his stress ball with him and manipulated it in his right hand, slowly turning it and squeezing. His movements were oddly sensual and had me wondering how his hands might feel squeezing certain parts of me.

Splat.

We drove past a farmer driving a green John Deere tractor through a field, kicking up dust and scattering insects, most of which veered on a suicidal path toward the windshield of the car. I was glad I wasn't driving my precious red convertible BMW out here.

Splat.

Splat-splat.

Splat.

A colorful assortment of bug guts now decorated the windshield like miniature Rorschach ink-blot tests. One of the spots looked vaguely like our boss, who'd sported a towering strawberry-blond beehive since the sixties. Her hairdo had to be at least eight inches tall, held together by a thorough coating of extra-hold hairspray.

I pointed at the pinkish goo. "What's that look like to you?"

Nick squinted at the glass. "The Lobo."

"My thought exactly."

Nick glanced my way and my crotch clenched reflexively. He always looked hot, but he was especially attractive at the moment. He'd topped his stylishly shaggy brown hair with the white felt Stetson I'd bought him shortly after sneaking him out of Mexico. Yep, I had a soft spot for cowboys. Make that *two* soft spots—one spot was metaphorical, the other was between my thighs.

Nick flashed a mischievous grin. "You know what's the last thing to go through a bug's mind when he hits your windshield?"

I shrugged.

"His asshole."

I rolled my eyes and pulled to a stop behind another white government-issue sedan parked by a rusty gate. "Here we are. The middle of BFE."

A spray-painted plywood sign affixed to the barbed-wire fence read PROPERTY OF THE LONE STAR NATION. TRESPASS-ERS WILL BE VIOLATED.

Nick groaned. "You didn't tell me we'd be dealing with idiots."

"You didn't ask," I said. "And need I remind you that you volunteered for this assignment?"

"Next time I'll ask for more details before I commit," he muttered.

The Lone Star Nation was a separatist group, a bunch of antigovernment loonies who referred to themselves as "True Texans" and operated an unofficial sovereign state. For such a small organization they'd proved to be a huge pain in the ass.

The group was just one of several secessionist organiza-tions in the state. The largest group, known as the Republic of Texas, was the most notorious. The Republic had issued numerous bogus court summons and filed frivolous lawsuits with both the Supreme Court of Texas and the International Court of Justice at the Hague, challenging the annexation of Texas in 1845 by the United States.

That's what happens when rednecks have too much time on their hands.

After shootouts between federal agents and armed extrem-ists in Ruby Ridge, Idaho, and Waco, Texas, the government had received a lot of flack, virtually all of it from wack jobs and nearly all of it undue. There's no clean way to take down these types of people. They don't exactly think and act rea-sonably.

Government agencies had learned to be extra careful in handling interactions with members of such groups. In 1997, state troopers had negotiated a surrender with Richard McLaren, the former leader of the Republic of Texas, after he'd been accused of fraud and kidnapping. Still, two of the group's members had refused to cooperate and one of them had been shot dead after they'd opened fire on a police helicopter.

Thus, despite the fact that August and Betty Buchmeyer hadn't filed a tax return since Ronald and Nancy Reagan were bumping uglies in the White House, Lu had made a strategic decision not to arrest the couple. Rather, she'd instructed me only to see what we could collect from the elderly deadbeats, perhaps make an example of them to the dozen or so steadfast True Texans who stubbornly stuck to their beliefs.

Collections work was boring as hell, essentially standing guard while staff from the collections department seized any nonexempt assets. While most tax evaders cursed and glared, others moaned and sobbed, lamenting the loss of their RVs, their collection of mink coats, their limited-edition prints. But sheez, by the time it got to that point they'd been given ample opportunity to make payment arrangements and had stubbornly refused. It wouldn't be fair to honest, hardworking taxpayers to let scofflaws off the hook.

So here we were.

Nick and I climbed out of the car. The intense midsummer heat caused an instant sweat to break out on my skin. Nick shrugged into his bulletproof vest and a navy sport coat. I slipped my protective vest on over my white cotton blouse and secured my gun in my hip holster, covering them both with a lightweight yellow blazer. Standard precautions. After all, it wasn't likely a couple of octogenarians would put up a fight. Right?

A hundred feet inside the gate sat a weather-beaten blue single-wide trailer in a thick patch of weeds. The house stood slightly cockeyed from settling unevenly into the reddish soil. The metal skirting had pulled away in places and there was no telling what manner of vermin had made a home under the structure. An enormous, outdated satellite dish mounted on a sturdy five-foot pole stood between the trailer and a lone, misshapen mesquite tree that struggled for life in the bare, dry dirt. An ancient pickup with faded two-tone brown paint sat on the far side of the dirt driveway. Two rusted tractors, a dented horse trailer, and a broken-down trampoline, its springs long since sprung, littered the yard.

Fifty yards beyond the house stood a series of long metal barns. The hot breeze blew toward us, carrying with it the faint sounds of clucking and the stench of bird poop. Over it all flew the Burnet flag, an azure background with a single gold star in the middle, the last flag flown over Texas when it was still an independent country.

Nick gave a whistle. "Boy howdy. This is quite the presidential palace."

The collections agent stepped out of her car and met us on the asphalt. She was fortyish and slender, with short black hair. She wore a floral-print dress with sensible flats, and introduced herself as Jane Jenkins.

"This shouldn't take long," Jenkins said. "I'm not expecting to find much. Other than the trailer, twenty acres of scrubland, and the pickup, there's no property in their name."

"What about the chickens?" I asked. "They've got to be worth something." After all, a two-piece meal at KFC ran about four bucks. I should know. I'd had some extra crispy for lunch.

Jenkins shook her head. "We've got a strict policy in collections. We don't seize anything that eats and craps. Costs too much to care for animals."

Made sense. Better to wait for the owner to sell the birds then seize the resulting profits. Problem was, the IRS had levied the Buchmeyers' bank account years ago, garnering over six grand in one fell swoop just after the couple received a large payment from one of their customers. Since then, the couple had taken to operating on a cash-only basis.

Where the cash was being held was anyone's guess. With any luck, we'd find some in their trailer today, maybe under a mattress or in their toilet tank. Eddie'd once collected ten grand from a delinquent taxpayer who'd hidden large bills in his bowling bag, including stacks of hundreds stashed in his bowling shoes under a pair of Odor-Eaters. When Eddie couldn't find the cash he was sure the man had somewhere in his possession, he'd left the apartment and pulled the fire alarm at the complex. On hearing the alarm, the guy ran outside with the bowling bag. A dead giveaway.

Yep, sometimes being a special agent calls for creative tactics.

Nick, Jenkins, and I carefully stepped across the metal cattle guard and walked up to the gate. The opening was secured by two large, rusty padlocks joined with heavy-gauge chain thick enough to anchor an aircraft carrier.

I stepped forward and tugged on the locks. They didn't budge.

Jenkins frowned. "I called ahead and told them to unlock the gate for us."

It wouldn't be the first time a taxpayer refused to cooperate. Wouldn't be the last, either. For some reason, people didn't like turning over their sports cars, big-screen televisions, and jewelry collections to the IRS. Not that we were likely to find anything like that here. The Buchmeyers' profits had been modest. If they'd paid on time, their tax bill would've been paltry. But once three decades of interest and penalties were tacked on, those tiny tax bills had grown to over a hundred grand.

The three of us spent a few minutes searching for any keys that might be hidden about, turning over rocks, checking in and under the mailbox and behind the fence posts. We came up empty-handed.

I glanced back at the trailer. The faded blue and white striped bath towel serving as a curtain in the front window was pulled back, an older woman's face visible. She raised a gnarled hand and gave me the finger. Wouldn't be the first or last time that happened, either.

"Got their phone number handy?" I asked Jenkins.

She rattled it off and I dialed the Buchmeyers on my cell.

After five rings, someone picked up the phone. "Hello?" an old man's voice rasped.

"Mr. Buchmeyer, this is IRS Special Agent Tara Holloway. We need you to come on out here and unlock your gate."

An elderly man's face appeared in the window. "I ain't going to do that, young lady," he spat. "I don't recognize the authority of the United States government to tax me nor seize my property. This here place belongs to the Lone Star Nation. Didn't you see the sign?"

"The sign doesn't mean anything, Mr. Buchmeyer."

"Like hell it don't! If you all dare to enter my property, I'll be obligated to defend it. Now you go about your business and let me go about mine." With that, he hung up the phone and yanked the curtain closed.

CHAPTER TWO

$\mathcal{D}$eclaration of War

As well trained as we were, IRS special agents aren't equipped to act as a SWAT team. But even though this old man was clearly crazy and possibly armed, I couldn't bear the thought of having to drive all the way out here to BFE again later.

"Got any bright ideas?" I asked Nick.

"Let's get us a local yokel," he suggested. "Maybe they'll know how to handle this guy."

I telephoned the county sheriff's department for backup, explaining we were federal agents trying to get onto the property. Luckily, an officer was already in the area helping a rancher round up an escaped mule.

In minutes, a deputy drove up in a brown and tan patrol car and climbed out. He was tall and beefy with wavy brown hair. His bottom lip bore a telltale bulge of chewing tobacco.

He put two fingers under his junk and adjusted himself. Classy. "They said federal agents needed help out here." His eyes roamed over Nick and me, taking in our business attire, his expression skeptical. "You two feds?"

I whipped out my badge and held it up for him to see. "We're with IRS Criminal Investigations."

"IRS?" He gave a derisive snort.

Nick stiffened beside me, but managed to keep his cool. Nick might not look so tough in his business attire, but underneath his clothing he was one hundred percent pure badass. He stuck out a hand. "Nick Pratt, senior special agent."

The yahoo ignored Nick's outstretched hand, instead hooking his thumbs in his utility belt. "Special agent? Don't seem too special to me. Can't even get in a little ol' gate."

My jaw burned as my teeth clamped tight, holding back the words straining to spill out of my mouth. I was dying to tell the deputy off, but we needed him to get us onto the property. I glanced over at Nick. Rage burned in his eyes and a low growllike sound came from his throat.

The deputy reached in through the open window of his car and pulled out a bullhorn. "No need to get yourselves worked up. August Buchmeyer's a crazy old fart, but he ain't going to hurt nobody."

He put one foot up on the bumper of the cruiser as if posing for a stud calendar, gave his balls another adjustment, and raised the bullhorn to his mouth. "August, these people just want to take a look-see. If you don't let us in, we'll have to enter by force. Now get on out here and open your gate."

A few seconds later the front door opened and a thin, stooped man stepped out, brandishing a rifle.

"Look out!" Nick yanked Jenkins down behind our car.

I pulled my gun from the holster. Nick hunkered down next to me and jerked his gun from his holster, too. Our eyes met, exchanging unspoken messages. Slowly and carefully, side by side, we raised our heads and peeked over the hood.

The deputy glanced over at us crouching behind the vehicle and shook his head. "What a bunch of pussies."

I narrowed my eyes at him. "I prefer to think of it as being smart."

The deputy raised the bullhorn back to his mouth. "August, you get on out here and open this gate right now. I ain't gonna ask you again."

From the narrow porch, the old man made a show of shaking his head.

The deputy lowered the horn. "Guess I'll have to shoot the locks off."

He reached into the cruiser and pulled a gun from under the driver's seat. It was a small ornate pistol, obviously from the deputy's private collection. "Y'all didn't see this." The deputy beamed as if he were the first member of law enforcement to come up with the idea of using a personal piece to avoid the paperwork required when a government-issued weapon was fired.

We plugged our ears with our index fingers.

Bang-bang!

Two quick shots later the chains lay in a heap on the gravel, the busted locks resting on top.

The officer swung the gate open and turned to us. "See, I told you Buchmeyer's all bark and no bite."

The retort of Buchmeyer's rifle didn't meet our ears until after the deputy's windshield exploded into shards of glass showering down on the caliche.

The deputy shrieked like a schoolgirl and dove for cover in the small drainage ditch flanking the cattle guard. I crept to my front fender, took aim, and fired.

Blam!

Buchmeyer's rifle sailed out of his hands and into the dirt next to his pickup.

So much for avoiding paperwork. At the rate things were going, internal affairs would have to devote an entire filing cabinet just to my firearm discharge reports.

Buchmeyer threw two angry fists in the air. "Abuse of power!" he hollered. "Government oppression! Declaration of war!"

Apparently the exclamations were enough to tucker him

out. He plopped down on the top step of his rickety porch and crossed his arms over his chest like a pouting child.

Beside me, Nick shoved his gun back into his hip holster. "You beat me to the punch."

I flashed a smug smile. "Anything boys can do, girls can do better."

His eyes narrowed. "Is that a challenge?"

"It's a guarantee."

Betty Buchmeyer poked her head out the front door of the trailer. "Y'all might as well come in now," she called.

The deputy crawled out of the ditch on his hands and knees. Nick picked up the bullhorn from the asphalt where the officer had dropped it and stood over him. Pushing the talk button, he blasted the deputy with a hundred and fifteen decibels at point-blank range. "Who's the pussy now?"

The deputy's hands flew to his ears. Nick handed the horn back to him as he stood.

While the deputy dusted the burrs and dirt from his uniform, Nick, Jenkins, and I began to make our way up the short gravel drive. Seconds later, the deputy charged past us, took the two steps up to the front porch in one stride, and grabbed Buchmeyer by the front of his faded cotton shirt, lifting the old man off the ground. Buchmeyer thrashed and kicked his legs to no avail.

"You crazy coot!" the deputy shouted. "You could have killed somebody. I've got half a mind to haul your ass in for attempted murder." He let go of Buchmeyer's shirt and the grizzled man fell back to the porch.

Buchmeyer glared up at the deputy. "If I'd wanted you dead you'd be lying in a pool of blood on the road. But go ahead and charge me. The Nation will get me the best defense attorney money can buy. Besides, I'd be great in front of a jury. Watch this." August crossed one eye inward and grinned like an inbred, backwoods idiot. "I had no idea it was the sheriff and the IRS," he said in a feeble, shaky voice. "I'm eighty-three years old. I can't see more'n two feet in front of my face. All I heard was someone shooting at my gate. My poor wife and I thought it was one of them home invasions!"

Standing behind her husband, Betty Buchmeyer put on her best 'fraidy face and fluttered her hand at her chest, a performance worthy of an Academy Award. The two had their act down pat. Hell, if I hadn't witnessed the events myself I'd vote to acquit.

I whipped out my handcuffs, pulled the old man's hands behind him, and slapped the cuffs on. While the deputy kept an eye on August, Nick and I entered the trailer with Jenkins following. The air-conditioned interior felt like heaven compared to the relentless hell outside.

Nick stopped under an air vent, turning his face up to take full advantage of the cool air blowing out of it. His eyes were closed, an expression of ecstasy on his face. I imagined that's what he'd look like if he were having an orgasm. He opened his eyes and caught me watching him. Damn. I turned away, feeling the heat of a blush on my face.

Betty plopped down in a scratched wooden chair at the Formica dinette in the kitchen and picked up a can of store-brand grape soda from the table. "Been wondering when y'all'd catch up with us." She nonchalantly took a sip of soda, picked up a remote control, and tuned the TV in the adjacent living room to a *Bonanza* rerun.

I wasn't sure why August Buchmeyer had put up such a fight. From the looks of the place, they didn't have much to lose. The walls were thin, pressed-fiber paneling. Threadbare braided rugs covered dingy linoleum. The worn couch was a seventies-style tan and gold tweed, a foam square peeking through a split seam on one of the cushions. Plastic milk crates situated on either side of the couch served as end tables. The Buchmeyers had not only violated the tax code, they'd also violated every tenet of feng shui.

Nick and I stood on either side of the doorway while Jenkins sat down at the kitchen table with Mrs. Buchmeyer. "Where do you keep the silver?"

The old woman leaned to the side to keep an eye on the TV screen behind Jenkins. "Ain't got none."

"How about your jewelry?"

Mrs. Buchmeyer held up her left hand, showing us the tiny diamond chip and thin gold band on her ring finger. "This is all I got."

"Any furs?"

From her seat, Betty leaned over and opened a lower cabinet. She pulled out three tan pelts, each of which looked to be the size and color of a tabby cat.

I gasped. "Are those—"

"Squirrels." Mrs. Buchmeyer solved the mystery. "I make a mean squirrel stew."

Urk. My stomach seized at the thought.

Jenkins's gaze wandered around the room. "Any collectibles?"

"Not unless you count dust bunnies."

"Antiques?"

"Look around you," Betty said, sweeping her arm. "The whole damn place is full of antiques."

Jenkins ignored the jibe. "Cash?"

The old woman chuckled and shook her head. "Hon, any cash comes in goes right back out. The IRS ain't the only ones after us. We got no money. We keep telling everyone that but nobody wants to believe us."

"How do you afford the satellite TV?"

"Our son pays for that."

Jenkins stood up. "I'm going to poke around a bit." She motioned for Nick to follow her, leaving me alone with Betty.

The two of us sat in awkward silence for a few moments, the only interruption being the occasional sound of Jenkins pulling open a drawer or rummaging through a closet, searching for undisclosed valuables or cash.

Despite the fact that they'd neglected to pay their fair share to the government, my heart felt for the Buchmeyers. Obviously, they were barely getting by these days, any profits from their chicken-farming operation spent on basic necessities, yet here we were, snooping through their closets.

Mrs. Buchmeyer eyed the name badge on my chest, then looked up at me. "What do you carry, Agent Holloway?"

"Excuse me?"

She pointed to the bulge under my blazer. "Your gun. What kind is it?"

"Glock," I said. "Forty caliber."

"Long or short barrel?"

So the woman knew her guns, huh? "The twenty-two model," I said. "I like the longer barrel. It's more accurate." The longer barrel also made the gun somewhat heavier, which is why my workouts at the downtown YMCA always included several reps on the bicep and tricep machines.

Her gaze ran over my petite form. "I saw what you did out there, shooting that rifle out of August's hands. You're a good shot."

My eyes met hers. "They don't call me the Annie Oakley of the IRS for nothing." I didn't bother telling her the appellation had been recently replaced by a new one after I'd relieved Mendoza of his nut. My coworkers now deemed me the Sperminator.

Jenkins and Nick returned to the kitchen.

"Nothing in the house," Jenkins said. "Let's check the barns."

CHAPTER THREE

$\mathcal{P}$reparing for Armageddon

Nick, Jenkins, and I stepped outside to find Buchmeyer and the deputy sitting on the lowered tailgate of Buchmeyer's old pickup, both of them with a bulge of snuff inside their lower lips. His arms still shackled behind him, Mr. Buchmeyer aimed a stream of mucus-coated tobacco at our feet as we walked past. Fortunately none landed on my shoes. While I owned a pair or two of fuck-me heels, my work shoes were more of the fuck-you variety, leather loafers with thick soles and steel toes, perfect for preventing a stubborn target from shutting a door or for disabling an attacker with a quick kick to the nads.

I settled for shooting Buchmeyer a nasty look this time instead of a bullet and continued on. A duo of filthy but friendly coonhounds wriggled out from under the trailer, following as we gingerly picked our way to the chicken barns through a minefield of doggie droppings, some fresh, some dried.

Off in the distance, a cloud of dust rose as a pickup drove across the back of the property.

Nick must have noticed it, too. He turned to Jenkins. "Is there an easement on this land?"

She waved a pesky horsefly out of her face. "Not that I recall. There is a back gate, though. It exits onto a fire road."

We reached the first barn. A black-and-white-speckled chicken strutted up to the wire fencing and cocked her head, looking up at me with her innocent, shiny black eyes.

While Nick and Jenkins took a cursory glance inside the barns, I knelt down next to the fence. "Hey, there, little speckled hen."

She tilted her head to the other side.

"You're kinda cute."

She spread her wings and flapped them once, as if trying to communicate with me.

I made my best clucking sound at her.

She clucked back.

That was it. I'd never eat chicken again.

"Hey," Nick called. "Quit flirting with that bird and come here."

"I wasn't flirting," I called back. "It's a female bird." Not to mention that it was *a bird*.

Nick stood in front of the last barn. Unlike the others, this barn was closed up, no chickens in sight. The structure was surrounded by four-foot-high loops of barbed wire, a barrier clearly intended to discourage entry and one that just as clearly meant we had to take a look inside.

"We need wire cutters," Nick said.

Another pickup raised a dust cloud at the back of the property while I used my cell to call the Buchmeyers' house phone again. When Betty answered, I told her we needed to get into the back barn and asked if there were any wire cutters around.

"I plead the Fifth," she said.

"It's not illegal to own wire cutters," I told her.

She hung up on me. Not feeling so sorry for her at that moment.

I snapped my phone shut. "No luck on the wire cutters. But I can guarantee there's something in here they don't want us to find."

Ironically, the fact that Betty invoked the Fifth Amendment was an admission on her part. Whatever was stashed away in this barn, she knew about it.

Nick walked along the barrier, visually inspecting the coils until he found an end. Jenkins and I stepped back as he carefully reached in and grabbed the wire. He slowly pulled back on the fencing, emitting an occasional curse when an errant barb nicked him. Eventually, the sections of fencing separated and an opening appeared. The three of us stepped through and walked up to the door of the barn.

"Damn," Nick muttered.

My partner and I exchanged glances. Like the front gate, this door was secured with padlocks. And, like the deputy, both Nick and I carried a personal weapon in addition to our Glocks. But with Jenkins there as a witness, neither of us was inclined to use our private guns. I could justify my earlier shot at Buchmeyer, but no way could I justify discharging my Glock simply to disable a lock. Internal affairs would deem it reckless. Never mind that it would save us time. Safety over efficiency.

Jenkins opened her purse and fumbled around, whipping out a .38 special. "Can you two keep a secret?"

I raised my palms and looked around innocently. "Gun? What gun?"

Nick positioned the locks and stepped back. "Be my guest."

Bang. Bang.

Once again, two locks dropped to their deaths in the dirt. Score one for efficiency.

Nick pulled the chain off the door and swung it open. We

stepped into the barn, pausing for a moment as our eyes adjusted from the bright outside sunlight to the relative darkness inside the barn. When they did, we found ourselves surrounded by a dozen wooden pallets stacked high and covered with tightly lashed blue vinyl tarps.

"What have we here?" Jenkins wondered aloud as she stepped forward and worked at a rope securing one of the tarps.

Nick pulled a Swiss army knife from the front pocket of his pants and cut through the rope. Jenkins worked the rope loose so she could lift off the tarp.

Under the covering was case after case of Spam. Why the heck would anyone need so much canned meat?

Under the next tarp sat a tall stack of economy-sized cans of baked beans. The next tarp covered a pallet stacked with toilet paper. Gotta have TP if you're gonna have beans, right? Cases of bottled water were stacked on another pallet, while another supported radios, flashlights, and batteries, all still in boxes. Yet another pallet contained a dozen pup tents in nylon drawstring bags along with four propane-powered generators and several propane tanks.

"Reminds me of the seizures after Y2K," Jenkins said. "We had an entire warehouse filled with survival gear."

Nick cut the rope on one of the two remaining pallets and pulled the tarp away. "Whoa, doggie. We've hit the mother lode."

Box after box of ammunition stood in tall stacks on the pallet, everything from small-gauge shotgun pellets to cartridges for long-range rifles. Nick quickly sawed through the rope and pulled the tarp off the last pallet. Guns of every size, still in the manufacturer's packaging, lay stacked on the wood frame.

Nick's eyes met mine. "Looks like they've been preparing themselves for Armageddon."

We may have arrived just in time, which was something I didn't want to contemplate too intently. One on one, I had no doubt I could outshoot an opponent. But if we were outnumbered? The odds wouldn't be nearly so good.

Jenkins didn't bat an eye. She simply pulled her cell phone out of her purse and punched some buttons. "Send a truck."

CHAPTER FOUR

*M*y, What a Big Cock You Have

An hour later, a young male intern arrived in a rental truck, slowly making his way over the uneven terrain to the barn. Jenkins, Nick, and I helped the college kid load the boxes into the cargo bay, then crowded into the truck's cab to ride back to our cars at the front of the property.

The truck, now loaded with the spoils, bounced over the field, then rumbled slowly down the gravel drive, the loose rocks *plink-plinking* as the tires kicked them up against the undercarriage. As we drove past Buchmeyer's pickup, the old man made one last desperate stand, diving from the tailgate into the path of the moving truck.

The intern slammed to a quick, brake-squealing stop. "Is this guy crazy?"

"Six hundred pounds of Spam tell me yes." I opened the door to climb out.

Nick and Jenkins climbed out after me.

"You can't take that stuff," Buchmeyer yelled from his prone position underneath the truck's front bumper. "It don't belong to me. It belongs to the Lone Star Nation."

"Not anymore." Nick grabbed Buchmeyer's boots and dragged the old man out from under the truck's bumper and off the drive.

Buchmeyer rolled over onto his back in the weeds. He tried to sit up, but had trouble with his hands still cuffed behind his back. "You'll be sorry you messed with me." His narrowed eyes took each agent in turn. "Just you wait and see."

Vague threats. Not the first or last time for that, either.

Nick and I turned to walk back to the bug-splattered fleet car. We'd leave the old man there for the deputy to deal with. That'll teach the officer to question the capabilities of an IRS special agent.

Nick and I held the gate open as the intern drove the rental truck out. He gave us a honk and a wave before turning onto the county road. Jenkins thanked us for our assistance, then climbed into her vehicle and headed out, too.

Nick and I made our way to the car. He paused at the passenger door, his eyes focused on something off in the distance behind me. I turned to see what he was looking at. Though it was dusk now, it wasn't too dark for us to see another dark dust cloud being kicked up at the back of the Buchmeyers' place.

"Something's going on back there," he said.

Given that we'd just seized enough guns and ammo to arm a sizable battalion, I wasn't sure I wanted to go back there and find out what it was. Anyone there would likely be holding both a weapon and a grudge. But a girl's gotta do what a girl's gotta do if that girl's a federal agent on duty, right?

I put on my brave face. "Let's go check things out."

We walked back onto the property, stopping to speak with the deputy. He'd already secured August in the back of his cruiser, but he grabbed his rifle and joined us. Given that we'd seen at least three vehicles drive onto the property, he called for backup, suggesting his fellow deputies use the fire road for access.

"You're one helluva shot," the deputy said, cutting his eyes my way, his tone respectful now.

He'd underestimated me. Yet another event that had happened before and would surely happen again. I was tough, smart, and capable, but I came in a deceptively petite, benign-looking package.

"Where'd you learn to handle a gun like that?" he asked.

"My father taught me," I said. "He got me my first Daisy BB gun for my third birthday."

Dad was a gun nut and had taught all three of his children how to handle a weapon. He'd taken my brothers deer hunting on many occasions over the years, but settled to shoot skeet with me. I couldn't stomach the sight of a dead deer. I might be a tough federal agent, but I was still a girl at heart.

Darkness set in as we set out across the overgrown field. The deputy had a Maglite to light his way, but Nick and I had to pick our way in the dark. Too bad we hadn't had the foresight to snag a couple flashlights from the barn for ourselves.

Ahead we could see several more cars pull onto the property, their headlights sweeping across the pasture, illuminating the dust and people, who stood in a tight group. As we drew nearer, we heard whooping, catcalls, hollering. People raised fists in the air and jumped up and down. If I didn't know better, I'd think I was at a football game or a prize fight.

We finally made our way up to the edge of the noisy group. The people gathered around were so focused on what was going on in front of them they didn't even notice us.

I stood on tiptoe to see what had them so rapt. Then I wished I hadn't seen what I saw.

My hand went to my chest and I felt momentarily breathless. "Oh, my God!"

The people encircled a shallow pit in which two large, colorful roosters fought, running at each other, pecking and kicking and clawing.

A cockfight.

Another thing that happens when rednecks have too much time on their hands.

The deputy grabbed one of the smaller men on the outer loop of the ring and tossed him aside. He elbowed his way into the pit, raising his rifle over his head. "Don't none of you leave!" he shouted. "You're all under arrest!"

The crowd turned and scattered like fire ants from a mound, a couple of beer-bellied men nearly plowing me down. So much for not leaving.

The deputy fired his gun into the air and yelled, "Drop to the ground!" Nobody listened. Should've brought the bullhorn. Then again, it probably wouldn't have done much good. These people didn't look like the type who'd earned gold stars for good behavior in school. They didn't look like the type who showered on a regular basis, either.

Nick tackled a man half again his size, bringing him down and cuffing him in three seconds flat. I had to admit, his physical prowess was damn titillating.

While Nick wrangled with another man, this one a gangly guy with a ridiculous handlebar mustache, I held out my arms to block two chubby women in tube tops and blue jeans. Both had bleached-blond hair with jet-black roots showing at the part, sort of like inverse skunks. "Stop right here!"

"Who the fuck are you?" yelled the taller one.

"Federal law enforcement." I'd learned that saying "IRS" in such situations only served to confuse people.

The two exchanged glances, then turned to run in the other direction. I ran after them. I reached out and grabbed their ponytails, digging in with my heels and leaning backward, trying to pull them to a stop. Instead, the two dragged me along behind them, my heels digging trenches in the dirt as if I were a human plow. Still, they couldn't make good time with me weighing them down and, with their heads pulled backward at an odd angle, they couldn't see too well where they were going.

"Let go of me, bitch!" one of them yelled, turning and clawing at my wrist with two-inch acrylic nails. The other tried to twist out of my grip, failed, and backhanded me across the face. My cheeks burned with both the impact and fury.

So that's how they wanted to play this, huh?

Still holding on to their ponytails, I jumped into the air, coming down to the ground as pure dead weight, the force yanking them both backward onto their asses. The shorter one's left boob plopped out of her black tube top, her nipple pointing up to the sky like the lens of a telescope seeking the North Star.

I let go of their hair, leaped to my feet, and pulled my gun. Standing over them, I aimed the barrel first at one, then the other. "Don't either of you dare move." The nipple seemed to look at me expectantly. "Oh, for God's sake, put your boob away. But no funny business or I'll take you down."

Since I'd used my only pair of cuffs on Buchmeyer, I had to come up with a creative way to restrain them. I instructed them to sit back to back and quickly tied their ponytails together in a hopelessly tangled knot. Siamese twins joined at the stupid.

Engines roared and dust and rocks were kicked up as people attempted to flee in their cars. Luckily, backup had arrived and two county patrol cars blocked the back gate. The only exit was to drive directly through the fence. A pickup chose that route and a third cruiser took off after it, lights flashing, siren wailing in hot pursuit. The truck wouldn't get far. The barbed wire had punctured its tires and already they were becoming flat, losing traction.

The next few minutes were a blur of wrestling bodies, screams and shouts, along with dust in my eyes and nose. Finally things settled down. One of the cruisers had its bright headlights shining on a group of people sitting on the ground, their hands shackled behind them. Some sat slack jawed, while others cursed. There wasn't a full set of teeth among them.

In the pit, the two roosters continued to circle and lunge at each other. I ran to the pit and tried to shoo them apart.

Big mistake. My efforts only managed to infuriate the birds, who set their sights on a new target.

Me.

With one arm I covered my eyes lest they be pecked out. I whipped my other arm around, trying to scatter the birds. But these gamecocks had been bred and trained to attack and weren't about to back down.

Nick and the deputy jumped into the ring with me. While the deputy chased one of the birds, Nick quickly got hold of the other one, immobilizing the creature by holding its wings down flat at its sides. He held the struggling bird in front of his groin, a mischievous grin on his face. "I've got a large pecker here." He held the bird out to me. "Would you like to pet my cock?"

Before I could order Nick to behave, the loose bird fell out of the sky, flying right at me, the cruiser's headlights illuminating a bright flash of metal on its leg.

I fell back against the side of the pit and instinctively threw up my hands to protect my face. The next thing I knew, a three-inch metal gaff slashed through my pants and lodged in my upper thigh, mere inches from my girlie parts.

Holy hell, I'd never felt such sharp pain!

To make matters worse, the bird was still attached to the gaff, which was firmly embedded in my flesh. The rooster beat me with his wings as an involuntary scream tore from my throat, an elongated sound that basically ran through all the vowels, excluding the sometimes y. "Aaeeiioouu!"

Nick dropped the bird in his hands. It fluttered unhurt to the ground. He ran to me, grabbed the chicken that had stabbed me, and began to pull.

"Wait!" I barely managed, stumbling to hang on to Nick for support. "Don't remove the blade. Just get it off the bird."

I'd learned a few things about first aid in Girl Scouts and knew that removing an object could often be more dangerous than leaving it in. A person could bleed to death. The damn gaff could have sliced some important artery. For all I knew, the bird had damaged my G-spot. I'd never been sure exactly where the G-spot was, only that it was in that general area *down there*.

While I hung on to Nick's shoulder, he wrestled with the bird, finally removing the tie that held the gaff on the bird's leg. The deputy ran over with a small, open cage. Nick shoved the poor, terrified bird inside, and secured the door.

The deputy and the other bird now ran in circles around the pit. It was unclear who was chasing whom at this point, as this bird was outfitted with sharp, jagged blades on his legs. Nick managed to grab the bird as it circled by, tucking it under his arm where it couldn't escape. He quickly removed the razor blades.

I fell back onto the side of the pit, panting, trying to breathe through the pain. I tried that *hoo-hoo haa-haa* breathing technique that pregnant women used in TV shows and movies. I wasn't sure if the breathing method only worked on labor pains, but it was the only thing I could think of at the moment. My head felt light and fireflies seemed to be darting around my vision.

The deputy jumped out of the pit to retrieve the other cage and Nick shoved the orange and black bird inside.

He turned to me and scooped me up in his arms. "We've got to get you to a doctor. Fast."

CHAPTER FIVE

Medicinal Margaritas

Nick carried me in his arms as if I weighed nothing and rushed across the field toward the car. I cradled against his broad chest and tried to think happy thoughts. Not easy to do with a metal blade sticking out of your leg. Then again, I was pressed up against some pretty fine, rock-hard pecs. Under different circumstances, this could be fun.

When we reached the car, he set me down gingerly on the asphalt. I leaned against the fender and fished the keys out of the pocket of my blazer, tossing them to him. He bleeped the door locks open and helped me into the passenger seat, bending down to take a look at my leg in the overhead light.

"That looks deep," he said, noting that half of the gaff had disappeared into my leg.

I rummaged in the console and found some fast-food napkins another agent had left in the car, holding them around the cut and applying pressure. Nick hopped into the driver's seat and yanked out his cell to call 911 for directions to the nearest hospital.

I shook my head. "Take me back to Dallas," I gritted out between teeth clamped tightly shut against the pain.

"Tara, that cut looks—"

"Just get me the hell back to Dallas!" I shrieked.

Nick jammed the key into the ignition, gunned the engine, and took off like a bat out of hell, tires squealing.

On the way back to the city, my cell phone chirped. I checked the readout. Lu, our boss. I flipped my phone open. "Hi, Lu," I managed to grunt out.

"Did I catch you on the toilet?"

Ew. "No!"

"Why are you grunting, then?"

Thankfully, Nick took the phone from me. "Hey, Lu. You won't believe what went down."

"Don't tell her I got hurt," I whispered. With her lung cancer, the woman had enough to worry about without fearing for her agents' safety.

Nick lifted his chin in agreement and told Lu the rest of the story, leaving out the fact that a chicken had turned me into a human shish kebab. He flipped the phone closed. "She says 'good job.'"

Nice to feel appreciated. Of course Nick had also left out the part where I'd fired my gun, too. Lu might not feel so appreciative when she realized I'd be facing another internal investigation in what was already a long string of internal investigations.

In forty-five minutes we pulled up to the medical clinic where Dr. Ajay Maju worked. As many times as I'd been into the clinic to see him, the guy had practically become my personal physician. Driving all the way back to Dallas probably wasn't the smartest decision under the circumstances, but it would've felt like cheating to have another doctor treat me.

Leaning on Nick's shoulder, I hobbled into the lobby. He had one arm around my waist, and I tried not to notice how warm and strong it felt. The evening receptionist took one look at the bloody spot on my thigh and called a nurse, who led me to an examination room right away.

Ajay entered not ten seconds later. Ajay was short in stature but long in skill. He wore a T-shirt embellished with LET ME KISS YOUR BOO-BOO. Where did he find these things?

He stepped right over and looked at my thigh, his brows meeting in confusion. "What the heck is that thing in your leg?"

"We broke up a cockfight." I grimaced against the pain. "The idiots who fight them put gaffs and razor blades on the chicken's legs so that the fight is more violent and bloody."

Ajay shook his head. "There are a lot of sick fucks in this world."

And there'd be a lot of sick fucks spending the night in the county lockup. Neener-neener.

The doc grabbed a pair of scissors and, starting at the hem, cut all the way up the leg of my pants, stopping just past the gaff and just short of my panties. He pulled the fabric back to expose my bare leg. Good thing I'd shaved that morning. After injecting my thigh with a local anesthetic, he carefully began working the blade out of my flesh.

Oh, Lord. The fireflies were back.

"Look at me," Nick said, trying to distract me from what was going on. He took my hand in his and stared into my eyes. Under other circumstances, the interaction might have been romantic. But given that I was on the verge of puking, not so much now. Still, his golden-brown eyes proved to be a pleasant distraction.

Before I knew it, Ajay finished and held up the bloody gaff. "Mind if I keep this for my next medical conference? The doctors always meet in the bar for show-and-tell."

"It's all yours."

An hour later, Nick and I sat in a booth at a nearby bar with Ajay and Christina Marquez, a DEA agent with whom I'd worked on a recent case and who dated the doc. She'd also helped me smuggle Nick out of Mexico and back into the

U.S. Maybe one of these days I'd have the opportunity to pay her back for that favor.

Christina had the warm brown skin, bodacious body, and long legs of Salma Hayek, along with the kick-ass attitude of Angelina Jolie. The one thing she didn't have was a frozen margarita in front of her. She'd opted for a sparkling water.

"You've become a teetotaler?" I asked.

"I'm on a cleanse," she said.

I lifted my margarita glass. "Six or seven of these babies and, trust me, you'll get a cleanse."

This particular bar had a reputation for the strongest 'ritas in town. Rumor was the bartenders added a shot of Everclear. I didn't know if the rumor was true or not. At the moment all I cared about was dulling the pain in my leg. The anesthetic had begun to wear off, so I was self-medicating with a numbing agent of a more general, lime-flavored variety.

Ajay'd closed the wound with three stitches and covered it with a bandage. My boyfriend would be none too happy when he found out I'd been injured on the job, yet again. Time after time I'd told him how rare it was for special agents to fire their weapons, how infrequently agents were attacked or put in real danger. But time after time I'd had to shoot my gun and ended up at the medical clinic.

Even I didn't believe my spiel any longer.

Thankfully, my other pending case, which involved a nationally broadcast megachurch and its pastor, shouldn't pose any dangers. No real risk there other than the threat they'd try to convert me. I was plenty happy as a backsliding Baptist, thank you very much.

Nick rested his hand on the booth next to my bare leg, the warm skin of his fingers brushing against my thigh. I supposed I should've moved my leg away, but I wasn't sure Nick was even aware he was touching me and I didn't want to look like I was reading something into the touch that wasn't there.

There wasn't anything there. Right?

Christina tilted her head and looked at me. "How in the world did you get stabbed by a chicken?"

I told her the full story of the revenge of the birds.

She shook her head. "That kind of thing could only happen to you."

"I know, right?" I seemed to be a magnet for freak accidents.

"What's Brett going to think?"

My recurring injuries didn't just cause me physical pain, they were a sore spot between me and my boyfriend, too. Fortunately, he was volunteering tonight on a Habitat for Humanity project so I'd be able to put off sharing the news a bit longer. "Brett's not going to like it. That's for sure."

"Especially when he finds out you can't have sex for ten days," Ajay added.

My head snapped his way. "What? You didn't tell me that at the clinic."

Ajay shrugged. "I'm telling you now. That cut was deep. You can't risk straining the stitches. No physical exertion. That includes sexual activity."

Nick chuckled beside me as he took a sip of his beer. I shot him a frown.

Christina turned to Nick then. "How'd you know how to handle a rooster?"

Nick rested his bottle on the table. "My parents were farmers. I was in 4-H as a kid and a member of Future Farmers of America in high school."

I knew Nick had been raised a country boy in a small town outside Houston and that his parents had been farmers, but I hadn't realized he'd once planned to follow in their footsteps. "What changed your mind about becoming a farmer?" I asked.

He leaned back against the booth. "My mother and father weren't too happy about my plans. They wanted more for me and insisted I go to college. I decided to major in business because I thought it would help me run a successful farm later on." He took a draw from his beer before continuing. "When it came time to graduate, I realized I could either spend the rest of my life breaking my back to merely eke out a living or I could get a cushy job with some fancy corporation and make four times as much money, maybe buy a new car and a high-def television." He shrugged. "The decision seemed pretty simple."

"So?" I asked. "Which fancy corporation did you go to work for?"

He offered a sour grin. "Ever heard of a company called Enron?"

"Dude." Ajay cringed in sympathy. "Bad choice."

"No shit, huh?" Nick chuckled again, though this time it was mirthless. " 'Course hindsight's twenty-twenty. I had no idea what was going on there. I wasn't much more than a kid when I started, just one of the office grunts. I worked in payroll and employee benefits so I didn't get any inkling of what was happening until it was too late. Lost all of my stock, every cent I'd put toward retirement."

"That sucks," Christina chimed in.

Nick looked away for a moment, then turned back, his jaw set firm. "The worst of it was that my parents had invested in Enron, too, as a sign of their support. They lost more money than they could afford to lose. The bank ending up taking their farm. When I landed the job with the Treasury Department, I moved them up here to Dallas to help them out. My dad couldn't take it. It was too humiliating for him. He said he should've just let me be a farmer and none of it ever would have happened. He had a massive heart attack a year later, dead before he hit the kitchen floor."

Whoa. Nick had been through a lot. My heart broke for him. Clearly, he felt responsible for what happened even though there was no way he could have foreseen how things would turn out. But when I put a hand on his shoulder to comfort him, he instantly shrugged it off. I pulled back, surprised and, admittedly, a little hurt.

"Sorry," he said, apparently noting the wounded look on my face. "Didn't mean to throw myself a pity party. Must be the beer talking, making me all soft and girlie."

"Speaking of soft and girlie," Ajay said, "it's time for Christina and me to go." He gave her an exaggerated wink.

Nick and I sat in silence for several moments after they left. He'd exposed his vulnerable side and seemed embarrassed by it. Part of me was flattered he'd opened up to me, but another part knew the closer I got to Nick, the more dangerous things would become. And no matter how sexy Nick was, no matter how attracted to him I felt, he wasn't a sure thing. Brett was. And I wasn't about to risk what I had for something that might or might not ever be. Still, a part of me wondered where things would stand today if I'd met Nick first, before Brett.

Truth was, if I'd met Nick first, I'd have jumped in with both feet. I would probably never have gotten to know Brett. He would've been no more than an attractive ticket taker at the Arboretum's charity event.

But I *had* met Brett first, and he was a wonderful, caring, considerate guy. He made me feel special, made me happy. I'd be a fool to throw that away. When it got down to it, I hardly knew Nick. Still, I felt an odd connection to him, an instinctual understanding, as if the two of us connected on some primitive level.

Nick paid the tab and we left the bar. He drove the car to the federal building, parking it in the building's lot next to a hail-dented Chevy Silverado pickup. I'd bought the truck a few weeks ago to smuggle Nick out of Mexico. He'd later taken it off my hands as a sign of his appreciation, paying me every cent I'd dropped on the thing plus a ten percent markup. Nick might be a badass, but he was a good guy, too.

He made no move to get out of the car. Instead, he turned to me. "You and I make a good team."

"Sure. We're both skilled and well trained."

He tilted his head, eyeing me. "Maybe there's more to it than skills and training."

Uh-oh. Where was he going with this? And did I want to go there? I wasn't sure what to say, so I said nothing.

He didn't say anything, either. After a few seconds, he turned away, looking out the front windshield. "See you tomorrow." With that, he climbed out of the car, leaving the keys in the ignition and leaving me hot and bothered.

CHAPTER SIX

$\mathcal{H}$air Today, Gone Tomorrow

Friday morning, I drove to the Lobo's house, a green brick number with lavender shutters and trim. Needless to say, her neighborhood had no homeowners' association with a persnickety paint approval committee. Also needless to say, Lu had a style all her own.

I stepped to her door and rapped seven times in a quick beat. "Shave and a haircut, two bits."

After a moment, the Lobo opened her door.

I forced a smile. "Hi, Lu," I said. "You look great," I lied.

Bright orange go-go boots graced her feet, while a royal-blue minidress with a flared hem covered her pear-shaped body. The dress didn't fit as snug as I remembered, though, and her cheeks looked sunken, her skin dull. What's more, her always perky strawberry-blond beehive seemed to slump on top of her head. And was it just my imagination or was her hair thinner?

Although the tumor the doctors found on Lu's lung was small, its location near her heart made it inoperable. They'd decided to attack it with chemo. Today would be the Lobo's second chemo treatment.

Like Nick's mother, Lu was a widow. Her middle-aged son had taken her to the hospital for her first appointment, but he'd had an important business meeting today. Since she had no other family in the area, I'd offered to drive Lu to and from the hospital and she'd grudgingly taken me up on it. Lu had always been a strong, independent woman and the fact that a cancerous tumor had dared invade her body made her madder than hell. She didn't like being dependent on other people and she sure as hell didn't want them feeling sorry for her. She was like Nick in that way. No wonder the two of them got along so well.

Lu gripped a large purple can of extra-hold hairspray in her right hand. "I'm just finishing up." She held the can aloft and pushed the nozzle, spraying a large cloud of the sticky substance into the air. I took a step back, waving the fumes out of my face and coughing, wondering if it were possible her lung cancer was caused not by cigarettes but by hairspray fumes.

Her hair now glued in place, Lu plunked the can down on a table in the foyer. I picked it up and read the label. Well, the part I could read, anyway. The information on the label was printed in both poorly translated English and what appeared to be Chinese. The label proclaimed the contents capable of "make big hair not move" and deemed the product "much strong extra hold." Weapons grade was more like it. At the bottom of the label was a fire icon, the international symbol for flammable materials, as well as a verbal warning in all caps. "BE CAREFUL VERY! MUCH FLAMMABLE!"

"Where do you get this stuff?" I'd never seen this particular brand at the grocery stores or beauty supply outlets.

"My hairdresser, Ming Lai," she said. "She imports it direct from a factory in Shanghai."

I glanced back down at the can. The hairspray probably

contained a number of ingredients banned in the United States. But what the heck. It was a windy day. Might as well give the stuff a try, huh? I held my breath, closed my eyes, and sprayed a mushroom cloud of the stuff over my hair.

Lu grabbed her purse and house keys. After she locked up, we headed to my car and climbed in.

"Good job on the Buchmeyer case." She eyed me from under her thick false eyelashes. "That geezer's been thumbing his nose at the IRS for years."

"Well, he'll have to find something else to do with his thumb now."

She stared at me, unblinking.

"That didn't come out the way I intended."

"Lord, I hope not."

I backed out of the driveway. "I'm not sure how much money the Spam and beans'll bring in," I said, "but the guns have to be worth at least five grand." The Treasury Department held regular auctions to sell off property seized from deadbeats. A savvy buyer could find some pretty good deals. In fact, I'd phoned my father this morning to let him know about the guns. His current collection included over thirty weapons, but he was always looking to expand. Like I said, gun nut.

"Thank goodness you and Nick seized those weapons," she said. "There's no telling what that bunch of wackos might have been planning."

Probably more than a Spam cook-off.

After we'd driven a few miles and I'd shared the latest bits of office gossip, we reached the hospital. Lu and I sat in the waiting room flipping through magazines while waiting for her name to be called. Lu had settled on *Vogue*. Ironic, given that she'd bought no new fashions since the sixties. I opted for *People*. As expected, the issue featured several photos of Suri Cruise. That poor child couldn't take a dump without the paparazzi wanting to photograph it.

A nurse in blue scrubs stuck her head inside the swinging door. "Luella Lobozinksi?"

Lu tossed her magazine onto the table and stood to go.

I felt like I should say something but I had no idea what was an appropriate thing to say to someone heading into a chemo treatment. Best wishes? Break a leg? Mazel tov? I settled for giving her what I hoped was an encouraging smile.

She gestured for me to follow her.

"You want me to come?"

"I'll be hooked up to a drip for the next few hours. Misery loves company."

Lu was uncharacteristically quiet on the drive home. The strained expression on her face told me she didn't feel well. No surprise there. She'd spent the entire morning hooked up to an IV dripping poison into her bloodstream.

As she climbed out of my car, she turned and ducked her head back in. "Thanks for taking me to—"

Lu stopped speaking as a lock of her pinkish-orange hair fell from her head, fluttering like a feather to the seat. Even her contraband extra-hold hairspray was no match for chemo. The Lobo stared down at the hair lying lifeless on the seat. Tears pooled in her eyes, threatening to spill over her false eyelashes.

Oh, my God. I really had no idea what to do now. I was used to the Lobo barking orders, taking charge, bossing people around. This fragile, vulnerable Lu was a person I didn't recognize.

She put a hand to her head. "My hair." She looked at me now, desperation in her eyes. "How can I be me without my hair?"

"Come on," I said. "You'll still be you."

I was lying through my teeth. Lu's strawberry-blond beehive was much more than just a hairdo. It was her defining characteristic, a crown of sorts. The coiled fluff stood up on her head as if standing up to the world. The beehive was proud, rebellious even. Her do had both altitude and attitude.

Who would Lu be without her hair? Well, we'd never have to find out. Not if I had anything to say about it.

"I'll find you a wig," I told her. "One just like your real hair."

Her eyes lit up for the first time that day. "You'd do that for me?"

"Of course. You're the best boss I ever had."

It was true. Big Bob had made me mop the floor of the Bait Bucket, including his office, which was wallpapered with nude centerfold posters. Maybe if I'd taken a closer look I'd have learned where the G-spot was located. The partners at the CPA firm where I'd worked after college had been nice enough, but they'd measured my worth in billable hours. I'd been a replaceable cog in their moneymaking machine, nothing more. Lu was the first boss I'd had who appreciated me as a unique individual. The feeling was mutual.

Now, where in the hell was I going to find a strawberry-blond beehive wig?

CHAPTER SEVEN

$\mathcal{L}$ove 'Em and Leave 'Em

I spent the rest of Friday afternoon reviewing the case file for Pastor Noah Fischer and the Ark Temple of Worship. The audit department had already collected extensive evidence, including the church's travel expense ledger. The pastor might not worship a golden calf, but he was certainly using the church as his cash cow.

According to the records, Pastor Fischer had been quite the jet-setter in recent years, logging an average of fifty thousand airline miles annually, all of it on the Ark's dime. In the last quarter alone he and his wife, Marissa, had traveled to the Greek isles, France, and Tahiti, purportedly on mission trips for the church.

Smelled like bullshit to me.

Mission trips were normally to impoverished places like Guatemala or Haiti where people needed help, not to well-to-do countries that were also popular tourist destinations.

What's more, many of the expenses the church paid for had nothing to do with any type of religious activity. The church and its pastor could probably justify the visit to Notre Dame Cathedral, maybe even the visit to the Père Lachaise cemetery where Jim Morrison was buried. But I failed to see how a visit to the Louvre museum, a romantic boat ride along the Seine River, and tickets to the Folies Bergère could further any church-related purpose.

These expenses appeared to be nothing more than personal vacation expenses. As such, the church should have reported them as compensation to Pastor Fischer on his W-2. The pastor, in turn, should have reported the amount as wages on his individual return and paid the related income tax.

The church bookkeeper, the outside CPA, and the pastor had apparently forgotten one of the basic tenets taught in Sunday school. *Thou shalt not steal.*

The parsonage was another big issue. Although tax law allowed a church to provide a reasonable housing allowance or parsonage to its minister tax-free, the Ark's parsonage could hardly be deemed reasonable. At over eight thousand square feet with a heated swimming pool and Jacuzzi, high-tech media room, fully equipped fitness room, and gourmet kitchen, the place was a veritable heaven on earth.

What's more, the church had bought top-of-the line furnishings for the place, including custom-designed window coverings, imported Persian rugs, and the largest 3-D TV on the market. The Ark also paid for lawn and pool service, along with a full-time maid and cook. Heck, the Ark even provided Fischer with a limo and driver.

Several years ago, the Dallas county tax collector had deemed the parsonage ineligible for a property tax exemption because the home was far beyond what was necessary for use as a residence. The tax office had issued an assessment to the church, but the church refused to pay. When the tax collector pressed the county attorney to pursue the unpaid property tax bill in court, the county attorney had balked.

In Texas, as in many Southern states, a wide variety of

public offices are filled through elections rather than appointments. This system had been in place since just after the Civil War and was designed to keep power in the hands of the locals and prevent those pesky Yankees from appointing their cronies to office.

Problem was, the elected officials were now controlled by their financial supporters. In the case of the county attorney, a number of those who'd made significant contributions to his campaign attended the Ark Temple of Worship. Rather than risk alienating his supporters and losing his reelection bid, the county attorney wimped out and did nothing. Frustrated, the tax assessor had referred the case to the IRS, hoping the feds would take action.

After the case was referred, IRS auditors performed a thorough investigation and issued an income tax assessment of over five hundred grand to Pastor Fischer. Just as the Ark had ignored its property tax bill, Fischer refused to pay his federal income tax bill. Although collection action could have been taken, the head of the Dallas collections department realized he'd be in the hot seat if his department seized the pastor's assets. The buck was passed once again and the case was moved up the Treasury's chain to Criminal Investigations.

The case was sure to be a political nightmare for the IRS, just as the federal government's raid at the cult compound in Waco, Texas, years ago had caused untold amounts of grief for people at all levels of government, from low-level agents at the Bureau of Alcohol, Tobacco, and Firearms all the way up to then Attorney General Janet Reno. But unlike those who'd come before her, the Lobo didn't scare easily.

Neither did I.

The buck stopped here.

I reviewed the pastor's dossier next. Actually, it was just a bunch of copies of personal documents crammed into a reused manila folder on which another taxpayer's name had been crossed through and "Noah Fischer" written above it. But "dossier" sounds much more classy, doesn't it?

According to the information in the file, Noah Fischer

had been born in Dubuque, Iowa, and raised in government-subsidized housing. His father was a disabled Vietnam veteran, a former electrician for the Army Corps of Engineers who'd been injured in a fall and could no longer work. His mother was employed sporadically as a housekeeper. Their meager income was subsidized with benefits from government entitlement programs, including food stamps, Medicaid, and social security supplements.

Fischer had graduated in the bottom quarter of his high school class and engaged in no extracurricular activities, though he had been awarded an honorable mention in the school science fair his junior year for powering a low-watt lightbulb with an improvised potato battery. No doubt his father had helped with that project. Fischer's senior high school photo showed a scrawny, bucktoothed boy with white-blond hair and a disproportionately large nose.

During his late teens and early twenties, Noah had floated from one menial part-time job to another, flipping burgers, delivering pizza, detailing cars at a Cadillac dealership. A slacker. Not exactly the kind of background you'd expect of a guy who'd successfully built and led one of the largest churches in the metroplex and whose sermons were broadcast nationwide every Sunday morning to hundreds of thousands of viewers.

Things had seemed to suddenly change for Noah when he turned twenty-two. He began taking classes at the local community college, was later admitted to Iowa State, and went on to divinity school.

Had he found God then?

Maybe.

Or perhaps he'd discovered something else.

He'd married his wife, Marissa, a decade ago, when both of them were in their late twenties and Noah's career had just begun to take off. The couple had no children. Whether their childless state was by choice or due to fertility issues was unknown.

A recent photo of the couple from the Ark's Web site

showed that Fischer was indeed a much-changed man. Though he was still lean, he no longer looked scrawny. Gone, too, were the buckteeth and too-large nose, replaced by a perfect set of pearly whites and a schnoz in exact proportion with his other facial features.

Eddie Bardin, my usual partner, walked into my office. Eddie was tall and thin, with skin the color of black coffee. The guy was a sharp dresser with a sharp mind. Even his calculator was a Sharp brand model.

He plopped down in one of the two chairs facing my desk and grasped his head in his hands as if to prevent his skull from exploding. "Being director sucks."

Only three weeks ago he'd been thrilled when the Lobo asked him to fill her shoes—or should I say go-go boots?—while she'd be out for her cancer treatments and recovery.

"What's so sucky about it?"

"Everything!" Eddie rested his elbows on his knees now and slumped forward in the chair, his blue silk tie hanging like a cut noose from his neck. "I'm buried in paperwork, I rarely get to leave my office, and I have to listen to the staff whine all day about stupid shit."

"What kind of stupid shit?"

"The stupidest. Viola's on a rampage about parking. The new clerk in the records department has been parking in Vi's usual spot. I reminded Vi that parking isn't reserved, but she said she's parked there for thirty years, everyone knows it's her spot, and she wants me to do something about it."

"She's got a point," I said. "Thirty years is a long time."

Eddie frowned. "Whose side are you on?"

"Yours, buddy." I hooked my two index fingers together in a sign of solidarity. "Always yours."

He glanced at the clock on my wall, noted it was two minutes after five, and reached up to loosen his tie. "The second Viola left my office, Josh came in pitching a fit because someone stole a Twinkie from the box he keeps in his desk."

I grimaced. "Sorry, boss. That was me."

Eddie shot me a pointed look. "Tara, please. You know Josh gets his Underoos in a bunch when anyone touches his stuff. You can buy Twinkies from the vending machine in the break room."

"I know," I said. "But I was a nickel short." Plus it was kind of fun to put Josh's undies in a bunch. He could be a bit of a twerp sometimes.

Eddie pulled his wallet from his pocket, fished out a dollar bill, and laid it on my desk. "Do me a favor. Go buy him a Twinkie so he'll shut up."

"Will do." I slid the dollar into my pocket. "I guess this isn't a good time to tell you I had to fire my gun yesterday."

Eddie threw his hands in the air. "You're killing me, Tara."

"August Buchmeyer shot at us first," I said. "The hearing will be a slam dunk in my favor."

"Let's hope so." He stood to leave. "By the way, I assigned Nick to work with you on the Ark case."

My heart lurched in my chest. After the awkward conversation in the car last night, I wasn't sure it was a good idea for Nick and me to be alone together. In fact, I'd purposely avoided him all afternoon, waiting until I saw him walk into his office with his postlunch can of Red Bull before going to the kitchen to fill my coffee mug, timing my potty breaks just after his, keeping my door partially closed so our gazes wouldn't accidentally meet across the hall.

"Why Nick?" I asked.

"Pastor Fischer and the church won't go down without a fight," Eddie said. "It couldn't hurt to put more muscle on the case."

If it was muscle we needed, Nick was certainly the agent to turn to. Still, I was insulted. Lu had appointed me as the lead agent on the investigation. The least Eddie could have done was consult with me before assigning a secondary agent. I told him so.

"Nick asked to work with you. Said he thought you two worked well together."

Nick asked to work with me? Again?

Before I could fully process that information, Eddie turned and left.

After work Friday evening, I drove to Brett's house. He was already home and had left the door unlocked for me, so there was no need to use the spare key he kept hidden under the decorative birdhouse on his front porch. Brett smiled and waved to me from his kitchen as I stepped inside.

While Nick was tall, tan, and dark haired, Brett topped out at five foot eight, with sandy hair and green eyes. Nick's body was a weapon, carefully built and strategically sculpted with machines and weights, while Brett sported the lean, honest muscle that came with physical labor. Unlike Nick, who was all man, Brett had a sweet, boyish charm, like Brendan Frazier or Matthew Broderick. Not that I was comparing Brett and Nick. Oh, wait. I guess I was.

"Hey, Tara." Brett met me in his foyer, cupping his free hand behind my neck, giving me a warm kiss. As the kiss deepened, he twined his fingers in my hair, my stiff locks giving off an odd crunching sound. When he stepped back, he found his hand hopelessly stuck in my hair.

"What's so sticky?"

"Lu's extra-hold hairspray."

"Hairspray? Feels more like glue."

While he wiggled his fingers, trying to work them loose, I turned my head one way then the other, cringing as the action pulled at the sensitive hairs at the nape of my neck. He finally managed to free his hand from my hair. Thank God. I was beginning to think we'd have to use scissors.

A half hour later, Brett and I sat on his sofa, enjoying Indian takeout while watching back-to-back episodes of our favorite British sitcom, *Peep Show,* on the BBC America channel. Remembering the cute speckled chicken at the Buchmeyers' place, I'd forgone the tandoori chicken in favor of the channa paneer.

Brett wore his chili-pepper-print lounge pants and a green

T-shirt. I had slipped into the red satin spaghetti-strap nightie that made a home in Brett's top dresser drawer, next to his boxer briefs. Napoleon, Brett's furry black Scottish terrier mix, lay next to his master, his front paws and small head draped over Brett's leg. He watched every bite Brett put into his mouth, waiting for the nibbles he knew Brett would give him.

Brett's other dog was also black, but with an entirely different physique. Reggie, an enormous pit bull-Rottweiler mix, sat on the couch next to me, his brisket-sized head only inches from mine, his eyes on my mouth, his warm doggie breath on my cheek. With his square jaw and large teeth the dog looked mean as hell, but under Brett's constant doting he'd grown into one of the sweetest, most loyal dogs you'd ever meet. Of course the fact that Brett had relieved the dog of his pendulous nuts and the doggie testosterone they created may have contributed to the beast's new mellow temperament.

Reggie smacked his lips every time I took a bite. When I could take his stares no longer, I held out a big piece of bread to him. He grabbed the naan, hopped down from the couch, and lay down on the rug to eat it, thumping his tail against the floor in appreciation. *Thump-thump-thump.*

"How are things coming along at the Habitat house?" I asked Brett.

Though he'd grown up in one of the more exclusive parts of Dallas and had never wanted for anything, he was no spoiled brat. His parents supported several local charities and had instilled in him a sense of responsibility to his community and others. Brett had recently become involved with Habitat for Humanity, donating his landscaping design services, as well as grass, plants, and trees.

"The heat's been tough," he replied. "Not many people want to work in hundred-degree weather. We've had a hard time getting volunteers lately, but Trish has put some feelers out for new recruits."

At the mention of Trish's name, I felt my inner bitch rear her head. Trish worked as a reporter for a local television station. With butterscotch-blond hair, a bubbly personality, and equally bouncy, oversized boobs, she handled the happy-feel-good stories for the ten o'clock news. "Tune in for Trish at ten!"

Not long ago she'd done a piece on Habitat for Humanity. Brett happened to be landscaping the worksite when she arrived and she interviewed him for the piece, commenting in her airy way on the *size of his equipment* and *how skilled he was with his tools.* I might have been able to let her flirtatious comments go if she hadn't subsequently volunteered to work on the project with him, if I hadn't seen her hop into his wheelbarrow for a giggly, breast-jostling ride.

Although the exposure she'd given Brett had been great for his landscaping business, I sensed she had a few more questions she'd like to ask him, such as "Your place or mine?" and "Was it good for you, too?" Still, I didn't want petty jealousy to ruin my evening with Brett so I dropped the subject.

When we finished our dinner, Brett gathered up our plates and silverware while I collected the napkins, cardboard containers, and bags. I followed him to the kitchen and tossed out the trash while he rinsed our dishes and stuck them in the dishwasher.

He turned and leaned back against the counter. "I've got some news."

His posture was relaxed, but the fact that he'd waited until after dinner to tell me this as-yet-undisclosed information made me suspicious.

"Is it good news or bad news?"

"It's good," he said, but there was a slight hesitancy in his voice.

I stepped toward him, putting my hands on his chest and looking up into his eyes. "What is it?"

He grinned modestly. "I landed a new job today."

Brett was an award-winning landscape architect. His hard work and creative, distinctive designs had earned him quite a reputation. Each job he landed was larger, more prestigious. This guy was going places.

"That's great." I slid my hands up from his chest to encircle his neck. "Tell me all about it."

"It's a new country club," he said. "I'll be landscaping the clubhouse, pool area, and tennis courts. Around the golf course, too. They also want me to design an outdoor pavilion for weddings, that kind of thing."

"This sounds like a huge project."

"My biggest so far."

I still sensed the hesitancy. I slid my hands back to his chest. "What aren't you telling me?"

He exhaled slowly. "The job's in Atlanta."

That meant he'd have to travel. But when? And for how long?

These questions were quickly answered. "I'll be gone for a full month. I leave tomorrow."

"Tomorrow?" My hands dropped to my sides and I took a small step backward. My brain seemed to be spinning inside my skull. "How can they expect you to be there tomorrow when they just hired you today?"

Brett reached out and took my hands, pulling me back toward him. "I'm replacing the first guy they hired. He's tied up with another project, overbooked himself."

"But . . ." *But you can't leave me! I want you here! I need you here!*

As much as I wanted to, I knew I couldn't say such things. I had no right. I'd recently handled a very demanding, very dangerous case, a case that had left me little time to spend with Brett. He hadn't exactly been happy about it, but he'd supported me through the entire ordeal, even when it was clear it was the last thing he wanted to do. I owed it to him to provide the same support in return, didn't I? This project was big. A new country club in a rapidly expanding urban area. No doubt this would lead to more work, more projects.

Projects that might repeatedly take Brett away from me.

"But what?" he asked.

"But nothing," I said softly. "I'll miss you is all."

He pulled me full against him, kissing the top of my

head. "I'll miss you, too. We'll talk every day. And we can Skype, too, as often as possible."

My heart slumped inside my chest. This wasn't what I wanted at all. But there was no point whining about it, was there? Better to accept it and try to make the best of it.

I pushed my pelvis forward, grinding myself against him, and looked up at him with bedroom eyes. "If you're going to be gone for an entire month," I demanded in my best sultry voice, "you'd better give me a month's worth of loving tonight."

And he did.

CHAPTER EIGHT

$\mathcal{H}$ey There, Lonely Girl

Saturday morning, I woke to find Brett staring at me from his pillow. I wondered how long he'd been watching me, hoped I hadn't snored or drooled in my sleep.

He propped himself up on his elbow, looking absolutely adorable with his sandy bed head, his hair sticking up in crazy spikes. "Are you angry at me?"

Yes, I was. But I wasn't about to tell him that. I'd sound petty, hypocritical. It was ridiculous to be angry at him for taking on a project that would surely further his career. But emotions aren't exactly logical, are they? I decided to play dumb. "Why do you ask?"

"Because my balls feel bruised."

Not surprising. I'd insisted on being on top when we'd made love—against doctor's orders—for the second time last night. I'd claimed my superior positioning protected the injury on my thigh, but it was probably more a subconscious attempt to dominate him, bend him to my will, punish him for leaving me. I'd ridden the poor guy like a pogo stick.

I wasn't sure what to tell him, but figured I couldn't go wrong with, "Sorry about your balls. I couldn't help myself. You're so damn good in bed I lose all control."

His concerned expression melted into a grin. Sheez, men are so easy. "If you kiss them," he said, "it might make them feel better."

"Nice try." I threw back the covers. "No more nooky until I've had some coffee."

Later that morning, we drove out to a property Brett owned outside the city. He'd launched a landscape supply business there, though for all practical purposes he was his own silent partner. He'd hired a manager to take care of the day-to-day operations. Brett dropped by occasionally simply to check in on his investment.

The manager, a middle-aged guy named Dennis, did an excellent job. The place had been in business only a matter of weeks and was already breaking even. No doubt the enterprise would be well in the black before long.

Brett routinely took his dogs out to the nursery when he went, and the dogs and Dennis had become quite fond of each other. Dennis had offered to watch Napoleon and Reggie while Brett was gone to Atlanta. I would've liked to help out, but my busy and erratic work schedule would make it difficult to run by Brett's on a regular basis to check on his pets. I shared my townhouse with two cats, one skittish, the other intolerant, so taking the dogs to my place was out of the question.

I drove along the country road until we reached the white wooden fence lining the front of the property and turned in by the large sign that read ELLINGTON NURSERIES. Two king-cab dually pickups were parked in the small lot, the flatbed trailers attached to them loaded with drought-tolerant summer flowers. Petunias. Mexican heather. Dianthus. Yep, it was that time of year, when the flowers planted in spring had since burned up in the hot summer sun and fresh replacements were needed.

Dennis stood next to one of the trailers. He was stocky, with thick, reddish-brown hair and a matching, neatly trimmed beard. He placed a large flat of purple petunias on one of the trailers and waved a gloved hand in greeting. Brett and I raised our hands back at him.

The dogs hopped out of my BMW the instant I opened the back door. The duo ran over to Dennis, their tails wagging furiously. He knelt down to pet the two, pulling off his thick suede work gloves so he could give them a nice scratch under the chin. "Hey, boys."

Napoleon latched onto one of the gloves in Dennis's hand and yanked it free, holding it in his teeth and furiously shaking the glove back and forth.

"Give me that, you little troublemaker." Dennis chuckled as he gently pulled the soggy glove from the dog's mouth.

"Is everything ready to go to the Habitat house?" Brett asked Dennis.

Dennis nodded. "Got the delivery truck loaded and a driver lined up for later this afternoon."

"Great," Brett said. "Tell the driver to ask for Trish Le-Grande. She's got a copy of my landscaping plans."

I bet Brett's designs weren't the only thing Trish would like to get her hands on. "Why does Trish have a copy of your plans?" I asked.

"She's the coordinator for our latest project," Brett explained. "She keeps a copy of all the paperwork to make sure everyone's on the same page."

Hmm. What he said made sense. But just because it made sense didn't mean I had to like it.

So much for setting aside my petty jealousy, huh?

The dogs now situated, I drove Brett to the busy Dallas-Fort Worth airport. As we drove, a sense of emptiness and dread settled over me. The next month would be a long one without Brett.

I pulled to a stop at the curb in front of the noisy airport.

No sense in me going inside since I wouldn't be able to make it past security without a ticket.

I popped the back hatch, climbed out of my car, and stood on the sidewalk. Brett reached into the open trunk and pulled out his luggage and his golf clubs, packed in a hard-sided travel case. This month would be hell for me but for Brett it would be heaven. Though the country club in Atlanta had not yet opened, the course was already in place. He'd be able to play all the free golf he could find time for and never have to deal with a crowded fairway.

Brett set his stuff down on the sidewalk, closed the trunk, and stepped in front of me. "I'm going to miss the heck out of you."

"You better," I said, looking up at him.

He smiled down at me. "You better miss me, too."

I gave him a soft kiss followed by a tight hug, holding on as if I'd never let him go. "I already do."

Saturday evening I had dinner at an Italian place with my best friend Alicia and her boyfriend, Daniel.

"Working on any interesting cases?" I asked Daniel as I passed him the bread basket.

Daniel was an associate with a large, prestigious law firm. He focused primarily on commercial litigation—breaches of contract, trademark infringement, antitrust suits, that type of thing. His firm routinely hired CPAs from Martin and McGee to perform financial analyses for their cases, compute complicated damage amounts, and provide expert testimony in financial matters. In fact, Alicia and Daniel had first met when our boss at the CPA firm had assigned me and Alicia to review financial records in a court case Daniel was working on. For the two of them, it had been love at first *suit*.

An odd look passed between my two dinner companions before Daniel answered my question. "I've got one interesting case in the works," he said. "A big one. But it's not something I can discuss with you."

I raised a palm, letting him know I understood and took

no offense at his secrecy. "Client confidentiality. I get it." I was subject to similar restrictions.

We chatted amiably through the meal, the three of us sharing a cannoli for dessert.

Though I knew the two didn't mind having me along at dinner, without Brett I nonetheless felt like a third wheel, an intruder. When they invited me back to their downtown loft for a movie afterward, I begged off, instead going home to wallow in loneliness. Well, relative loneliness. My creamy white cat, Anne, was thrilled to have me all to herself and curled up, purring, in my lap. Henry, a robust and furry Maine Coon, maintained his usual post atop the armoire that housed my television, occasionally reaching out to swat at an errant fly that had sneaked into the house with me.

When the ten o'clock news concluded, I went upstairs to my room. I felt lonely in my bed, forlorn, forsaken. It was odd, really, given that Brett and I didn't spend every night together and I often slept alone. I guess there's a psychological difference between being alone by choice and having solitude forced on you.

Sheez. What a whiner, huh?

I turned off my lamp and turned onto my side, lifting up the patchwork quilt so Anne could climb under it with me. She tiptoed under the covers, turning to poke her head out the top, and lay down next to me. I cuddled her to my chest, the vibration of her purr against me a welcome comfort. Brett might be half a continent away, but I'd always have my Annie girl. I kissed the top of her milky head.

CHAPTER NINE

*G*et Me to the Church on Time

My landline rang at nine the next morning. Probably a tele-marketer. I put my pillow over my head and tried to go back to sleep. Seconds later, my cell phone bleeped from the night-stand. Dang. Whoever was trying to reach me knew my private cell number. Not a solicitor, then. I only gave my mobile number to a select group of people.

Without opening my eyes, I picked up the phone, punched the accept button, and held it to my ear. "Hello?" I croaked.

"You sound like a frog." It was Nick's voice. Why would he be calling so early on a Sunday?

"I was asleep. This better be important."

"Rise and shine, lazybones. You and I are going to church."

My eyes opened again and I sat up. "What are you talking about?"

"The Ark Temple of Worship," Nick said. "Let's go check it out. They've got a ten-thirty service."

Not only had Nick woken me up, he'd gotten my ire up, too. "The Ark is *my* case," I reminded him. "*I'm* the lead agent. *I* make the decisions."

"All righty, then. What say you and I head over there? Your decision, boss."

"I suppose it can't hurt." The guy may have pissed me off, but his suggestion was nonetheless a good one. Nick and I had a meeting scheduled for tomorrow afternoon with Pastor Fischer. It couldn't hurt to get a sneak preview of the man we'd be dealing with. Maybe we'd learn a thing or two to give us an edge tomorrow. It wouldn't be an easy meeting. We planned to take one last shot at securing the Ark's agreement to comply with their tax reporting requirements, to give Fischer a final chance to pay his long-outstanding bill. This game had gone on long enough.

"I'll swing by in an hour to pick you up," Nick said. "Make yourself purty."

The Ark Temple of Worship was a behemoth of biblical proportions, no pun intended. The church property fronted one of Dallas's many highways, stretching back a full half mile to encompass a sprawling parking lot as well as the extensive parsonage and grounds.

According to the information I'd read in his file, Noah Fischer had obtained the capital needed to buy the land and build the church from a wealthy elderly spinster whose soul Fischer allegedly saved mere weeks before her death. Perfect timing, huh? She'd revised her will to leave the bulk of her estate to Fischer's then-fledgling ministry.

The façade of the church building was designed to look like an enormous wooden boat. Though I understood the church was going for a theme here, I found the design to be a bit tacky. The place looked less like a place of worship and more like something you'd find in an amusement park. But who was I to say such things. *Judge not,* right?

Nick drove up and down the lanes, searching for an available spot. Several of the people making their way to the building did a double take as we passed. Nick's battered pickup didn't fit in among the luxury cars parked in the lot. The place was a virtual sea of Jaguars, Lexuses, and Mercedeses. Heck, I even spotted a Ferrari among the vehicles. This church certainly had an upscale clientele.

Nick pulled into a spot near the back of the lot and we climbed out of the car. Though it was only mid-morning the temperature was already stifling. The big boat was at least a quarter mile away. We'd have to make the trek in this heat. A glimpse into hell.

Nick had worn black boots and a bolo tie with a light gray western-cut suit. Cowboy chic. Today's belt buckle was a rectangular silver model with a bucking bronco embossed on it. He carried his jacket draped across his arm.

I'd thrown on a bright red cotton sundress and sandals, no panty hose for me on a hot day like today. Cleary I was underdressed. Each of the women I saw in the lot was dressed to the nines, maybe even the tens, in high heels and designer dresses, with carefully coordinated scarves and accessories. It was a parade of Prada, a vision of Versace, a deluge of Dior. I knew I paled in comparison to these women. Still, it would've been nice if Nick had commented on whether I'd succeeded in making myself *purty*. Or perhaps the fact that he'd said nothing was a comment in itself. Grr.

Chill, Tara. It doesn't matter what Nick thinks. You're in a committed relationship with Brett, I reminded myself. Then I argued with myself. *Shut up, bitch. You're a woman. Every woman wants to know whether a man finds her attractive.*

I looked up at the sky. Totally clear, not a cloud to be seen. That was a relief. Part of me feared that God might send a lightning bolt down on us.

As we neared the building, we discovered a six-foot-wide moat of sorts surrounding the structure, making it appear as if the boat actually floated on water. Pearlescent white koi swam in the man-made canal, their feathery fins like angel wings. Congregants entered the building up a series of wooden ramps that stretched over the shallow water.

Nick glanced around and snorted as we made our way up the ramp. "The only thing missing is a guy in a mouse suit."

"Mickey or Chuck E. Cheese?"

"Cheese," Nick replied. "Definitely cheese."

As we entered the building, we were met by a duo of grinning greeters, what would be cruise directors if this were a real ship. The two were a married couple judging from their name tags. GEORGE JOLLY and JUDY JOLLY.

The husband was tall and silver-haired, dressed in a tasteful navy suit. The wife's sleek platinum-blond bangs lay flat and smooth across her forehead, the rest pulled back in a tight French twist. She'd coated her bulbous, Botoxed lips with shiny, bright red lipstick. The combination gave her the look of a sophisticated sock monkey. Her fitted black Yves Saint Laurent number would have been appropriate for an art gallery opening but seemed a little much for a house of God. The plunging neckline framed a set of boobs too perky and perfectly shaped to be natural.

Judy took in Nick's getup then looked me up and down, too, forcing a porcelain veneer smile at us. "First-time visitors?"

That obvious, huh? I gave her my best smile in return. "Yep."

"Welcome to the Ark." She took my hand in both of hers. "So glad to have you with us today." She grabbed a bulletin from the stack on the marble-topped table behind her and held it out to me.

"Thanks." I took the pamphlet from her and glanced over it. The front bore a charcoal rendering of the Ark, while a series of business card ads filled the back cover. A probate lawyer. A dentist who specialized in cosmetic procedures, possibly the one responsible for Judy's veneers. A mortgage broker. Hmm. Maybe I should give the woman a call. Interest rates had declined since I'd bought my town house. Maybe I could save myself some money.

"Our annual women's retreat is next weekend," Judy said. "There's information in the bulletin if you're interested.

We're taking a charter bus down to the Hill Country Resort and Spa in Fredericksburg."

A sauna, facial, and massage? Yep, I'd call that a spiritual experience. "I'll look into it."

She gave us one last smile as we stepped away. "Have a blessed day."

"We damn sure will," Nick said.

The greeters' grins became confused.

I pulled Nick away, rolled up the bulletin, and smacked him with it. "Behave," I hissed. "God is watching you."

"I thought He loved me."

"He does," I said. "But He's keeping an eye on you, too."

"God sounds a lot like my granny."

In the center of the lobby stood an enormous cylindrical saltwater aquarium, extending upward the full three stories. Colorful angelfish and clown fish swam around a pastel-hued display of coral. A sizable sea turtle swam upward, its flat underbelly exposed as he climbed inside the tank. Children gathered around the base of the aquarium and watched the fish. Some of the kids were mesmerized by the animals' fluid movements, while others were more animated, pointing and pressing their faces to the glass. Around the perimeter of the lobby hung enormous, rough-hewn rope nets. A white nylon banner was strung across a wall, proclaiming I WILL MAKE YOU FISHERS OF MEN.

The smells of coffee and vanilla wafted through the lobby from a busy coffee bar and café across the way. A sign to the left caught my eye. GIFT SHOP. I jerked my head toward the store. "Let's check it out."

Nick groaned. "What is it with women and shopping?"

"Coming here was your idea, remember?"

"It might have been my *idea*," he replied, "but it was your *decision*."

"Oh, right," I said. "In that case just shut up."

We wound our way through clusters of chatting churchgoers and entered through the glass door of the shop. The gift shop featured a wide variety of Christian- and ocean-themed items, all of them overpriced. Ceramic angel figurines on white pedestals graced the entryway, welcoming shoppers with their beatific smiles. On the side wall hung crosses in copper, wood, and glass, something to match every décor. Rods and reels stood in a rack against the back wall. An assortment of colorful lures even Big Bob would envy hung from pegs to one side. A rotating glass case featured pendants, earrings, and charm bracelets shaped like starfish, sand dollars, seahorses, and crosses, some made with so much bling they were nearly blinding. A nearby shelf displayed fish-shaped car magnets in two sizes. Boxed starter sets of plastic Noah's ark toys sat on another shelf, pairs of the more exotic animals sold separately. A wooden bin overflowed with plush angelfish, sharks, and stingrays that could be purchased for twenty bucks a pop, a portion of the proceeds dedicated, of course, to funding the Ark's mission trips.

Nick and I stopped before the display of lures. Nick fingered several in the selection, eventually choosing one that resembled a small green and blue dragonfly. I selected a couple of colorful lures, too, and stepped up to the counter. The register was manned by an attractive brunette woman modeling some of the jewelry, Swarovski crystals refracting light from her ears, neck, and fingers. As she rang up my purchase, her jewelry sparkled in the lights, making her look like a human disco ball.

"You fish?" Nick asked me.

"Nah. They're for my dad."

Next to the cash register stood a display of hardback books, Pastor Fischer's face beaming from the cover. I had to admit, the guy looked angelic. From his shimmery, white-blond hair to his sky-blue eyes and perfectly proportioned, nicely tanned features, he looked like a modern-day Lucifer.

The title was embossed in gold lettering across the top of the book. *Toss Your Net*. Nick picked up a copy. "Let's see what this tosser has to say." He plunked the book onto the countertop along with the lure and addressed the cashier. "Add these to her bill."

I pushed the book and lure back at him. "Buy your own stuff."

Nick cut a grin my way. "This is *your* case, remember? I'm only along to help out."

Damn. My own words coming back to bite me in the butt.

I handed the cashier my credit card.

CHAPTER TEN

*N*o Old-Time Religion Here

The overhead lights flashed off and on twice as I paid the cashier.

"Power troubles?" Nick asked the woman.

"No," the woman replied. "The flashing lights mean the service will start in five minutes."

The service or the show? Though flashing lights were used in theaters to draw people back to their seats, I'd never seen the method used in a church.

I handed Nick the copy of Fischer's book and slid the small bag containing the lures into my purse. Nick and I continued on into the crowded sanctuary. Apparently you had to arrive early if you wanted a good seat. The first floor was packed wall to wall. Even the limited-view seats positioned behind the television cameras were full.

The ushers directed us up two flights of stairs, relegating

us to a back corner of the second balcony, what would be the cheap seats if this were a ticketed venue. Nick and I settled in.

"Nice," Nick noted, easing his seat back into a reclining position.

The chairs were indeed comfortable, slightly smaller versions of the seats at stadium-style movie theaters. No hard, butt-numbing pews for these well-heeled parishioners.

Nick rested his elbow on the armrest. I used my own to push it aside. "My case, my armrest."

He cut me a sideways glance and a grin. "Whatever you say, boss."

I looked down at the altar, which appeared tiny from our vantage point near the rafters. "If I'd known we'd be this far up I would've brought my binoculars."

"No need." Nick pointed across the cavernous opening to three jumbo-sized screens. One was mounted on the wall directly opposite us, while the others flanked it at slight angles like the three-way mirrors in the Neiman Marcus dressing rooms.

I glanced behind me to see a recessed pit of colored lights and the latest high-tech audiovisual equipment. A team of seven men sat at the consoles, headphones on their heads, ready to rock and roll. I hadn't seen such an elaborate setup since Lady Gaga came to town.

"Think they'll be serving drinks on the Lido Deck after the service?" Nick asked. "I could go for a banana daiquiri."

I elbowed him in the ribs.

Down below, the choir filed in, the members dressed in aquamarine robes the color of the Caribbean ocean. There had to be over a hundred singers taking places on the risers. An orchestra of near equal size filed in next, filling a wide pit in front of the choir. The musicians wore white shirts with aquamarine bow ties and vests. Not only did the group include the traditional brass, woodwind, and string instruments, but five electric guitars, three bass guitars, and two acoustic guitars were also in the mix. A shiny black grand piano sat off to the side, with two wide electronic keyboards situated next to it.

Once they were all seated, a dark-haired man stood from the front pew and made his way up the five steps to the podium, his movements tracked by several television cameras situated off to the sides of the sanctuary. Though he was a mere ant when viewed with the naked eye, he was a giant on the jumbo screen. He had a plain but friendly face, a trim build, and a slightly pensive demeanor. He wore a basic brown suit and tie, along with wire-rimmed glasses. I half expected him to direct us to our lifeboats to perform a muster drill.

He introduced himself as Associate Pastor Michael Walters, welcomed everyone to the service, and stated his hope that the service would be a source of inspiration and spiritual connection to a higher power. He quickly ran through a list of housekeeping items, asking the congregants to silence their cell phones and to shift to the inside seats to accommodate late arrivals waiting in the wings for an available place to sit. It was a full house today, a sellout crowd. "A great problem to have," he acknowledged with what appeared to be a sincere smile.

Walters led the group in a short, simple prayer, "amens" were murmured, and he left the podium.

The lights dimmed slightly and a spotlight shined on a man wearing black pants and a sport coat in the same greenish-blue as the choir robes. He made his way to the platform and stepped up to a podium that faced the singers and musicians. As he raised his conductor's wand, the musicians lifted their instruments into place, the percussion section holding their sticks poised over their drums.

The music director began moving his wand, mouthed "One, two, three, four," and the orchestra and choir launched into a modern, quick-tempo version of "Amazing Grace," the mix of classic and contemporary styles reminiscent of the Trans-Siberian Orchestra. Though the words were familiar, the normally solemn hymn now sounded upbeat, cheerful.

All around us the crowd rose to their feet, singing and clapping in rhythm to the music. So as not to be conspicuous, Nick and I stood, too. I had to admit, I found myself drawn to the joyful music, and my singing and handclapping were only partly to make sure I blended in.

The next song, ironically, was "Old-Time Religion." This megachurch offered anything *but* old-time religion. But from the size of the crowd, it was undeniable the Ark appealed to a broad market. People had grown tired of the stuffy, uncomfortable church environments of their youth, tired of the fire and brimstone, alienated from a God who'd smite sinners or send them wandering aimlessly around a desert for forty years without benefit of GPS, searching for the promised land. People wanted a more progressive, less regimented religion, a kinder, gentler, less demanding deity.

Churches across the metroplex had begun to market their services, and the Big Guy Himself, much differently. They offered a new way to worship, a new type of forum, a fresh take on God.

Some diehard traditionalists frowned upon the watered-down "religion lite" promoted by these churches. Others praised the ministers for keeping religion relevant in a world that posed so many new temptations, new ways to sin. When the popular *VeggieTales* show launched some years back, there'd been controversy whether cartoon vegetables were qualified to teach children fundamental biblical doctrines, just as there'd been debate whether the rise of Christian rock bands was good or bad. But for right or wrong, the Ark was packed to the rafters with worshippers.

After a couple more songs, the overhead lights went black, then colored lights began chasing each other over the audience and walls.

"What is this?" Nick said. "A circus?"

A booming male voice came from the speakers. "Ladies and gentlemen, boys and girls, put your hands together for the Ark Temple of Worship's very own Pastor Noaaah Fischerrr!" He drew out the last syllables like a cheesy game show announcer.

Around us, the audience roared with applause. Nick and I

exchanged glances. If we didn't know better, we'd think a rock star was about to take the stage.

The spotlight followed a fair-haired man making his way up the center aisle, smiling and waving to the crowd, stopping to shake hands with those on the aisle as if he were a glad-handing politician.

Noah Fischer.

In the flesh.

Fischer's black suit looked pricey and fit him perfectly. My guess was Armani. Underneath he wore a pink dress shirt with a white collar and a black tie with diagonal white stripes. I'd never seen a minister look so fashionable. Although not visible from our distance, a small bald spot on the back of the minister's head was revealed by the enlarged image on the jumbo screen, his virtually transparent blond hair encircling the bare skin and reflecting the spotlight like a hair halo.

He made his way up to the podium, waving first to those on one side, then the other, offering a thousand-watt smile to the deafening crowd. When the noise declined to a dull roar, he raised his hands skyward. "To God go the glory!" he cried.

"To God go the glory!" repeated the parishioners, following their proclamation with a fresh round of applause.

Eventually the pastor motioned with his hands for the congregants to take a seat. He leaned one elbow casually and confidently on the lectern.

"My, my," he said, grinning from ear to ear. "That was quite a welcome. Quite a welcome, indeed. It's wonderful to see so many faces out there, especially such good-looking faces."

The audience laughed, several around us turning to each other and grinning as if to say *We are good-looking, aren't we?*

Pastor Fischer raised his arm over his head and made a wide arc, waving to the television cameras. "Good morning to those of you all across our good nation who are watching from home today. Thanks for being with us this morning to share in worship and fellowship."

Yep, the Ark's services were broadcast throughout the United States, including Alaska and Hawaii. When I said this guy was popular, I meant *POPULAR*. Advertising rates for commercial spots before and after the service were among the highest for weekend programming.

Pastor Fischer stepped down onto the first step and looked out across the crowd. "Today we're going to continue our series of sermons on the seven deadly sins. Over the past few Sundays, we've covered gluttony, sloth, and envy. Today's sin?" A percussionist in the orchestra whipped his sticks in a loud drum roll and Pastor Fischer dramatically threw his arm into the air, pointing upward to the jumbo screens. On cue the word "Pride" appeared, flashing in bloodred letters against a black background on all three screens.

"Pride!" the audience shouted in unison as if controlled by a single brain. I found the groupspeak a little eerie.

Pastor Fischer's pointing hand clenched into a raised fist now. "You got it, folks. Today we'll be talking about the sin of pride."

He turned and walked to the other side of the sanctuary to address the people seated there. His voice was softer now, not much more than a stage whisper, and he leaned toward them as if sharing a secret. "Pride turned an archangel into the devil, folks. Pride is man's way of telling God—" His voice became a shout as he raised a palm toward the heavens in a sign of rejection. "We don't need You!"

The image on the jumbo screens changed, now featuring Proverbs 16:18 in glimmering gold lettering against the black backdrop.

Pride goeth before destruction, and a haughty spirit before a fall.

Prophetic words.

Pastor Fischer recited the Scripture and continued on in dramatic fashion, elaborating on the sin of pride, distinguishing it from mere confidence and self-esteem, both of which were apparently A-okay with the Creator.

At one point, Fischer's mouth continued to move, but no sound could be heard. When he realized his microphone had stopped working, he stepped back to the podium and spent a few seconds fiddling with the wireless system mounted there. In no time, he had the system up and running. Looked like his dad had taught him a few things about electronics.

"Sorry about that, folks," the pastor said. "Minor technical difficulties. But we're back in business now."

He stepped back out in front of the crowd and continued his sermon.

"All over America there are people who slept in this morning after a night carousing on the town. Those people were too proud to come to church today. Those lazybones, those sinners, they've got no use for God, no use for a savior." He stepped down another step, bringing himself closer to those seated. "But all of you," he said, sweeping his arm to include all of those in attendance, "you're better than that. You've pleased God by being here today. He's taken note and will reward you with great blessings."

At least a dozen shouts of "Amen!" echoed through the expansive chamber. Bring on the blessings!

Pastor Fischer flashed a gleaming grin. "The clock's ticking, folks."

The percussionist picked up a wood block and hit it four times with a stick, imitating the sound of a clock. *Ticktock, ticktock.*

Fischer swept an arm at the audience again. "You all have heard that ticktock and given your souls to God. You've made the smart choice, the right choice. God is saving a special place in his heavenly kingdom for each and every one of you."

More "amens" punctuated his words.

Ironic that the subject of the sermon was pride when Fischer was feeding their egos, making his audience feel superior to the heathen riffraff who'd failed to come to church

today, assuring the congregants they'd secured an eternal
home in the ultimate, most exclusive gated community.

Slick.

He concluded his sermon by noting that he'd cover the sin
of greed in his next sermon two weeks from now. Since many
of the women would be away the following weekend on the
women's retreat, he planned to let Associate Pastor Walters
lead next Sunday's service.

It was time for the offering. The lights dimmed slightly
and Pastor Fischer led the group in a prayer. "Dear Lord, let
us all show how much we need you. Let our offerings today
be a reflection of our faith and commitment to you. Don't let
pride hold us back from giving generously."

Salvation for sale.

Nick gave a small snort.

Pastor Fischer reminded those at home to join in by making an online donation—*right now!*—by simply clicking the
links on the Ark's Web site. He also reminded the congregants that they could set up an automated payment plan to
ensure timely payments in the event they missed a service
due to an illness or vacation. "With so many ways to pay,
we've made it easy for you to further the Lord's work here at
the Ark."

And easy for Pastor Fischer to finance his upcoming trip
to Aruba. According to the Ark's financial records, the plane
tickets had already been purchased and reservations secured
for an ocean-view suite at a five-star beachfront hotel. No
need for a manger, there'd be lots of room at this inn.

Fisher raised his arms again. "To God go the glory!"

And to Fischer go the cash.

As the collection plate headed our way, Nick nudged me
and made a writing motion with his hand, indicating he
needed a pen. He wasn't going to write a check to the church,
was he? It made no sense to line this shyster's pockets.

The mischievous grin on Nick's lips told me he had something else in mind. I dug through my purse, found a ballpoint
at the bottom, and handed it to him. Nick pulled out one of his

business cards and turned it over. On the back he wrote "Render unto Caesar."

The man sitting next to Nick passed the collection plate. The thing was nearly overflowing with checks and cash.

Nick plopped his business card on top of the pile. I dug through my wallet and added an expired coupon for fifteen cents off a can of cat food. I suppose I should've felt cheap, but no way was I going to support Pastor Fischer's lavish lifestyle. God would understand. Wouldn't He?

CHAPTER ELEVEN

$\mathcal{L}$ike Father, Like Son?

When the service concluded, Nick and I eased out of our seats and slowly made our way down the stairs. The crowd had thinned some by the time we reached the lobby, though a few of the choir members milled about.

Pastor Fischer stood at the open double doors next to his wife, Marissa. She was tall and thin, with the large brown eyes of a doe—a doe who'd spent a small fortune on eye shadow, liner, and mascara at the Lancôme counter. Copper and bronze highlights accentuated Marissa's naturally brown hair, which hung in loose curls down to her chest. She wore a sleeveless white chenille dress with a flowing hem and peek-a-boo collar, along with a gorgeous pair of genuine Jimmy Choo mock Mary Jane pumps.

Marissa's expensive wardrobe was yet another personal expense the Fischers had financed tax-free through the Ark's accounts. The shoes alone cost over eight hundred dollars. I should know. I'd ogled them at Neiman's just last week, even tried them on for grins. A perfect fit, leather soft as butter. But far out of my price range, dang it.

Thou shalt not covet, my inner angel reminded me. My inner devil scoffed in return. *My, aren't we a self-righteous nag?*

With their trim builds, perfectly proportioned features, and designer wardrobes, Noah and Marissa Fischer looked like a Hollywood celebrity couple posing on the red carpet. The two smiled and shook hands with those exiting the building, Noah occasionally reaching out to pat a parishioner on the back or tweak a child's chubby cheek. Marissa smiled down at the children but didn't touch them, instead clasping her hands behind her back and bending forward slightly to bid them adieu, as if she were afraid she'd catch cooties if she came too close to them.

"Check it out." Nick jerked his head almost imperceptibly to our right, where a towheaded toddler stood on a stepstool at the children's water fountain, getting a drink. The rump of the boy's navy blue elastic-waist pants bore the telltale bulge of a diaper. Looked like he wasn't yet ready for potty training. His fair hair had an unusual iridescent quality.

Standing next to him was his mother, a petite young woman in her early twenties with dark auburn hair that hung in a straight sheet halfway down her back. She wore one of the aquamarine choir robes, the front unzipped to reveal a fitted pink dress that stopped just above the knee. Though her hand was on her son's back to support him, her hazel eyes cut to the side, locking on Pastor Fischer and his wife, watching them intently as they continued their meet and greet.

The toddler turned around and looked up at his mother with sky-blue eyes.

"All done?" she asked, turning her attention back to him. She didn't wait for an answer before lifting the tiny boy off the stepstool, standing him on the floor, and taking his hand in hers. Forgoing the line of people waiting to congratulate

Pastor Fischer on his oh-so-inspiring sermon, the woman led her young son out through a side door.

"Keep your mouth shut and come with me." Nick grabbed my hand and pulled me along after him. Maintaining a distance of thirty feet or so, we followed the woman and child outside to the parking lot. Why, I had no idea. I only knew I felt a slight tinge of disappointment when Nick released my hand.

The Ark's pearlescent white limo sat idling at the curb, the air conditioner running to keep the interior cool, global warming be damned. A shark-fin satellite television antenna graced the top of the car, while two magnetic fish graced the back. The uniformed driver waited alongside the car, ready to open the rear door for Pastor Fischer and his wife once they'd finished their duties.

The auburn-haired woman stopped when she reached a silver SUV, opening the back door and lifting her son up to load him into the safety seat buckled inside. Nick's eyes registered the SUV's license plate as we continued past.

Once we were out of earshot, he once again demanded my pen. He wrote the woman's license plate number on the back of his hand and returned the pen to me.

"What are you doing?"

"You saw the kid, right?"

"Yeah."

"He look like somebody to you?" Nick held up his copy of *Toss Your Net* and pointed at the face of Noah Fischer on the cover.

Whoa. "You think Pastor Fischer fathered that kid?"

"Call it a hunch."

A hunch. Instinct. Intuition had served me well in this job. If there was one thing I'd learned since becoming a special agent, it was to never ignore my gut.

On the other hand, a gut was just that. A gut. A feeling, an emotion. Logic and reason had to be taken into consideration, too. Sure, the boy and the pastor shared similar coloring, but there were lots of blue-eyed blonds in the world, right? Heck, for all we knew Noah Fischer was sterile. He and his wife had been married for ten years but had no children. Still, if I had to hazard a guess, I'd say their childless state was by choice. *Marissa's* choice. She'd seemed almost repulsed by the children who'd passed through their receiving line. Her body language had belied the pleasant smile plastered on her face.

If the boy was Fischer's son, though, tax problems would be the least of the pastor's worries. The shit would hit the fan if word got out that Noah Fischer had had an affair with a member of the church and fathered an illegitimate child. *Thou shalt not commit adultery* was a black-and-white rule with no wiggle room. The guy would lose his ministry, his home, and his reputation, everything he'd worked so hard to build.

Given the potential consequences, would Fischer take such a risk? Was he that stupid? That ballsy? Heck, that horny?

I had a hard time believing he'd commit adultery. Then again, men with just as much if not more to lose had succumbed to this particular sin. Jim Bakker of the PTL television ministries was caught in an affair with the church secretary. The Reverend Jimmy Swaggart later suffered a fall from grace, admitting, among other things, to a sexual encounter with a prostitute in New Orleans. Bill Clinton's Oval Office blow job was no secret and, heck, Arnold Schwarzenegger had kept his love child under wraps for years while serving as governor of California.

Odd that infidelity seemed to be an almost entirely male-dominated field. Of course for all I knew Ruth Bader Ginsburg was a prowling cougar, boinking one of her interns at the U.S. Supreme Court, or maybe doing the nasty with fellow justice David Souter in his chambers. Still, I had my doubts. By and large, women were smarter than that.

Nick and I continued on through the oppressive midday heat to his truck. He opened his door and hung his suit jacket from the peg above the window. "I feel like I've been rode hard and put up wet."

Rode hard and put up wet. I really wished he wouldn't talk like that. It made a girl's mind go places it shouldn't.

We climbed into Nick's truck, rolling down the windows to let out the hot air that had accumulated inside. After a minute or two, the air conditioner caught up and we rolled up the windows.

"Let's check out the parsonage," I suggested.

Nick backed out of the spot and drove around the church to the curving, tree-lined driveway that led to Pastor Fischer's residence. After making our way down the long drive, we pulled up to a roundabout encircling a sizable fountain. Water spouted from the mouth of a large concrete fish in the center of the fountain. Though the driveway continued on from there to the house, a locked iron gate prevented us from going further. Too bad we didn't have the code for the security keypad.

The house sat a hundred yards beyond the gate, though "house" hardly seemed an appropriate term. "Mansion" was more like it. The place was a beautiful two-story plantation-style home, white wood with light blue shutters, a wide porch, and six oversized columns. Large terra-cotta planters sat on each of the brick steps leading up to the porch, all of them filled with colorful pink and blue hydrangeas. The grounds were well maintained, with vibrant flower beds of blue irises and white impatiens, as well as nicely shaped ornamental trees. Timeless, sprawling live oaks provided an abundance of shade.

I wanted to see more, partly out of professional curiosity, partly because real estate is like crack to women. "Let's park and take a look around."

"Anything you say, boss." Nick circled to the other side of the fountain and eased the truck to the edge of the driveway, leaving room for a car to pass if needed.

After we climbed out of the truck, Nick stepped up to the security keypad, used his index finger to punch in 666, and turned his head to watch the gate. Nothing happened. He shrugged. "It was worth a shot."

We walked along the iron fence that demarcated the

grounds. The enclosed yard was precisely one acre, a small acknowledgment of the state's property tax law, which imposed a one-acre limit on the exemption for a parsonage.

"This place is beautiful," I said.

"The Lord will provide."

I glanced up at Nick. "You sure know your Bible verses."

He shrugged. "Where I grew up there wasn't much to do in the summer other than attend vacation Bible school. For each verse you learned, you'd get a jelly bean."

"We got cupcakes at my church." What the Lord didn't provide, the church ladies would.

We continued on, waving away a swarm of pesky gnats that flitted around our faces. Too bad I didn't have any of Lu's extra-hold hairspray with me. That caustic stuff would've taken care of the gnats in short order.

When we rounded the back of the property, Nick stopped and whistled. "Boy howdy, take a look at that."

The back of the house was nearly all windows. Two sets of French doors opened onto an extensive covered patio, complete with half a dozen white ceiling fans and cushioned white wicker furniture. An enormous built-in red brick fireplace ran along one side of the patio, an outdoor kitchen, complete with a large propane grill and minifridge, along the other.

Crystal-clear water beckoned from a large swimming pool built in the shape of a cross, a diving board mounted where the crown of thorns would normally appear. A freestanding brick bathhouse sat at an angle at the top of the pool. An automatic vacuum with a long hose snaked along the bottom of the pool, leaving a small ripple in its wake. A covered hot tub sat between two trees off to the side.

Through the back window we could see a woman in the kitchen preparing lunch for the Fischers. Apparently the Sabbath wasn't a day of rest for her.

"Wow," I said. "Who knew there'd be so much money in being a minister?"

Nick's eyes narrowed. "I bet Noah Fischer knew it. He isn't

so much a preacher as a salesman. He's selling those people a version of God that requires little of them other than a big weekly contribution."

Not only did Nick have good financial and weapons skills, he also had a unique ability to read people. That skill had saved his life a few years ago, when Nick realized the target of an undercover mission had discovered his secret identity as a federal agent and determined to kill him. Before the guy could act, Nick confessed he worked for the IRS and offered to derail the investigation in return for a sizable payoff. As soon as he could, Nick double-crossed the murdering tax cheat and together he and I nailed the son of a bitch.

Maybe Nick was right. Maybe he and I did make a good team.

We continued on, eventually making our way completely around the perimeter of the parsonage and back to Nick's truck. I was sweaty now, my bra glued to my chest and back, my thighs sticky with perspiration. So much for feeling *purty*.

We climbed into Nick's truck and drove back down the driveway, passing the white limo as it headed to the house. Presumably Pastor Fischer and his wife sat inside, though with the dark tinted windows it was impossible to tell.

"Let's grab lunch," Nick said.

"How about Mongolian barbecue?" I suggested. "There's a great place near my town house."

Nick's lip curled up. "Barbecue sounds good, but not Mongolian. Let's get the good ol' American kind."

So Nick wasn't an adventurous eater. Hmm. Brett and I enjoyed making the rounds of local ethnic restaurants, sampling different cuisines. I'd been raised on a steady diet of Southern cooking and, though my mother was a good cook, her offerings were somewhat limited. It was always something fried in grease. She kept a tin can of recycled grease in the pantry, scooping out a spoonful to fry pork chops, eggs, what have you. She'd pour the leftover grease back into the can afterward, to be used again at the next meal. Heck, I bet there was some grease in that can from the first dinner Mom had fixed Dad after they'd married.

Nick and I stopped at a barbecue joint off the highway a few exits down. As I perused the menu, I wondered what Brett was having for lunch today halfway across the U.S. of A. My heart sagged. He'd been gone only twenty-four hours, but it had been a long twenty-four hours.

One day down, thirty more to go.

A waitress arrived to take our order. Nick chose the chicken, but after the moment I'd shared with the hen at the Buchmeyers' barn I just couldn't do it. I opted for a veggie plate. Better for my heart and arteries anyway. Better for my ass and thighs, too.

CHAPTER TWELVE

*T*hat's Not What Jesus Would Do

Nick eyed me across the table. "If you'd put up more of a fight, I might've agreed to eat that mongrel barbecue."

"Mongolian," I said, "not mongrel."

"I know." He cut a grin my way. "Just yanking your chain."

When Nick finished his lunch, he wadded up his napkin and dropped it onto his empty plate. "Got your Glock with you?"

"Of course." I never felt fully dressed without a gun.

"Let's hit the range," he said. "I'm rusty."

Mexican law forbade citizens from owning guns. Nick had been without a piece for the past three years while he'd been in forced exile south of the border. It couldn't hurt for him to sharpen his skills. I, on the other hand, was the best marksman in the office, probably even the entire IRS. Who better to help retrain him?

An hour later we stepped into position in adjacent spots at

the firing range, protective earmuffs on our heads, goggles over our eyes, loaded guns in our hands. We faced paper targets hanging from an overhead pulley.

Nick counted down. "One. Two. Three. Go!"

We unloaded our clips as the pulley quickly drew the targets away from us.

Blam. Blam-blam. Blam-blam-blam-blam-blam.

Guns now empty, we retrieved our targets from the pulley and compared them. As expected, each of my bullets hit the paper target square in the heart. Nick's shots were more sporadic. Though three had penetrated the heart and one had hit the target in the head, several missed the dark human outline entirely and pierced the paper on either side.

Nick emitted a frustrated grunt. "I've got some work to do."

"Don't be so hard on yourself," I said. "You did fine."

"Fine's not good enough." Nick shoved another clip into his gun. "Let's go another round."

After the second round, Nick held back, watching me as I fired alone. He yanked the target from the clip when I finished. He eyed the target—all shots square in the heart, as always. "This is a thing of beauty."

He was impressed. I was flattered.

He joined in with me again, and we fired several more rounds. Soon my forearms, elbows, and shoulders began to ache. Holding a heavy gun in place for extended periods of time wasn't easy and the recoil was a bitch. "I'm out."

I packed up my gun, then stood back and watched Nick as he shot several more rounds. "Squeeze the trigger faster," I advised, "and loosen your grip a little."

"Fast and loose, huh?" His next three shots found their mark. He glanced back at me. "Whaddya know. Your advice worked."

I shrugged. "I know my guns."

"You may be a weapons expert, but I'm an expert in other areas." A sly smile slid across his lips. "I'd be happy to return the favor, show you a thing or two."

No doubt about it now. The guy was flirting with me.

"I'll take that under advisement."

Talking with Brett via Skype Sunday night was a poor substitute for seeing him in person. No shoulder rub, no snuggling on the couch, no nooky.

Waah.

I told Brett about my visit to the Ark, but chose not to mention that Nick had attended the service with me. Why ask for trouble, right? Brett would be none too happy if he knew I'd be working closely with Nick, but there was nothing I could do about it. Sure, Nick was hotter than a jalapeño pepper, but I was beginning to see beyond his yummy exterior to the man underneath. And while I respected Nick's take-charge style, I didn't so much appreciate it when the thing he was taking charge of was my case. Then again, he did have more experience than I did. Maybe I should set aside my simmering resentment and appreciate his help. He could be a good mentor.

"I shot a 78 today," Brett said, a grin spreading across his face.

"That's wonderful." I assumed it must be a good score since he seemed happy about it, but honestly I had no idea. I'd never played enough golf to learn much about the game. "I shot ninety-nine percent at the firing range." It would've been perfect had Nick not bent over that one time. His ass had been quite a distraction.

"Looks like it was a good day for both of us."

Oh, yeah.

We chatted for a few more minutes, then wound up the conversation since it was growing late.

"I'll call you tomorrow night," he promised from my laptop's computer screen.

"Nighty night." I raised my sleep shirt and flashed my bare breasts at the Webcam.

He groaned and sat back, crossing his arms over his chest. "That was really unfair."

"Just wanted to remind you what you're missing."

* * *

I stopped by the doc-in-a-box Monday morning. My stitches had pulled loose, and the area had become pink and puffy and oozy. Ick.

Ajay frowned when he looked at my thigh. "You had wild monkey sex, didn't you? Against my direct orders?"

"No," I lied.

He gave me a stern look under his dark brows while he injected a local anesthetic. He removed the original stitches, cleaned the area with antiseptic, and stitched me back up. He handed me a prescription for an antibiotic and told me to come back in two weeks to have the stitches removed. "No lollipop today. You've been a bad girl."

Darn. But at least I wouldn't have to worry about the new stitches coming loose. With Brett off in Atlanta, I wouldn't be getting any sex, wild monkey or otherwise.

When I arrived at work, I passed Josh's office. He stood in front of his bookshelf, carefully positioning what appeared to be a hardback copy of *The New English Dictionary* between volumes of the *Internal Revenue Code*. I slowed and glanced into the trash can by his door. Sure enough, there was an empty box in the bin, one for a nanny cam designed to look like a book. He was bound and determined to discover who'd been stealing his Twinkies. Looked like my days of pilfering snacks from his desk were over.

I continued on to my office, took a seat, and pulled the church bulletin out of my purse. The note about the women's retreat was tempting. I sure could go for a day of whirlpools, aromatherapy, and a mani/pedi. But the trip cost $750 per person. Out of my price range. I wondered if I could sell Eddie on the idea, convince him the retreat would somehow help me with the case and that the IRS should fund it. Probably not. The guy wasn't stupid. He wasn't a pushover, either, except where his wife and twin daughters were concerned.

I flipped to the back of the bulletin and placed a call to the mortgage broker who'd posted her ad there. After holding for a minute or two, her secretary put me through. I introduced myself and she asked me some questions about my existing mortgage loan and credit history.

"Current rates for someone with your good credit would be a percent and a half less than what you're paying now." She quickly ran some figures. "Refinancing would reduce your monthly payment by roughly a hundred dollars."

"Let's do it." Who couldn't use an extra hundred bucks a month? I grabbed a pen to make notes. "What do you need from me?"

She ran through a list of documents for me to fax to her. Last year's tax return, account statements, my latest pay stub. "Once you get the documentation to me, it'll take only a day or two to get the loan paperwork ready."

Nick walked into my office as I ended the call and ceremoniously plunked a stack of papers on my desk. "Check these out."

I quickly riffled through them. A vehicle registration. A birth certificate. A marriage license. A final order in a paternity suit. A divorce decree. A photocopy of someone's ass.

I held up the ass. "Yours?"

"Nope. I found it on the copier."

"It's a white butt," I said, "so we can rule Eddie out. But other than that I don't have a clue."

"It looks like a female ass to me. My guess would be the new clerk in the records department."

"The one who keeps parking in Viola's spot?"

Nick nodded.

I turned the copy one way then the other. Was I looking at a G-spot and just didn't know it? "Maybe this is actually Viola's butt and Vi's trying to frame her, get the girl fired."

"I wouldn't put it past her. Viola's damn upset about that parking spot."

"So I hear." I crumpled up the paper, tossed it into the wastebasket, and turned to the other documents.

Nick slid into one of my chairs. "The auburn-haired choir girl from the Ark is Amber Hansen," Nick said, providing a quick Cliff's Notes version of the paperwork. "Amber was married briefly to a marine named John Vincent Hansen. Got herself knocked up while her hubby was serving a tour of duty in the Persian Gulf."

"So much for keeping the home fires burning."

Nick pulled his stress ball out of his pocket and began working it. "According to the court documents, Amber claimed she got pregnant when her husband was home on leave, but the timing didn't jibe. When her husband returned, he moved out of their house and filed a paternity suit. The DNA evidence proved he wasn't the biological father."

"Hence the divorce."

"You got it."

I glanced at the birth certificate. Although the child's name was listed as David Jacob Hansen, the space for the father's name was blank.

"Are there any other records?" I asked Nick. "Maybe a subsequent paternity suit filed by Amber?"

"Nothing."

So Amber's little boy could, in fact, be Pastor Fischer's. Or he could be someone else's. There had to be thousands of blond men in the Dallas area, after all, men with much less to lose than Pastor Fischer.

"I'm surprised Amber didn't file for child support." After all, it wasn't cheap to raise a kid these days, even with the dependency exemptions and tax credits for child care costs.

Nick cocked his head. "I'm thinking she didn't pursue financial support because this dirty little secret would get the father in trouble."

"Or maybe she doesn't know who the father is. Maybe she had a one-night stand with a guy she met at a bar."

Nick rolled his eyes.

"I'm just saying we can't be sure of this. We need to tread carefully."

Because when you didn't tread carefully, it was easy to step in it.

* * *

I sneaked out of the office just past eleven to meet my best friend, Alicia, for an early lunch. As always, Alicia was impeccably dressed. She wore sling-back heels with a colorful, embroidered Asian-style dress, complete with a high collar and buttons in the form of small fabric knots. She topped off today's look by pulling her short blond hair into a small bun bisected by black lacquer chopsticks that formed an X on the back of her head.

Yep, Alicia was a master fashionista. I was more of an apprentice, with less of an eye for detail and a smaller budget. But I'd befriended a salesgirl with an inside track to the Neiman's clearance rack and thus managed to hold my own.

Alicia and I had met as accounting majors at the University of Texas in Austin years ago and immediately hit it off. We'd roomed together during college and, after graduation, had both taken jobs at Martin and McGee's Dallas office. While working at the CPA firm was the perfect fit for Alicia, the job proved to be less than perfect for me. I'd grown up a tomboy in the open spaces of east Texas and didn't cope well with prolonged periods of confinement. I simply wasn't cut out for the cubicle world. Nevertheless, I'd maintained my close bond to Alicia even after I'd left the accounting firm to take the special agent job with the IRS. She was a true friend, someone I could always count on. And today I needed her help.

After a quick bite at a sandwich shop, we made our way to a downtown wig store, two women with a mission—find a strawberry-blond beehive wig for my boss. We stepped inside and surveyed the room. The wigs were arranged in a veritable rainbow that spanned from one side of the boutique to the other. Blonds lined the wall on the left with reds in the center, giving way to brown and black wigs on the right.

We headed down the middle aisle. The wigs were displayed on two-tiered shelves and perched on white ceramic head-shaped figures that resembled decapitated albino aliens.

Alicia leaned into me and whispered, "This place gives me the creeps."

I had the same feeling. "Yeah. It's like Jeffrey Dahmer's freezer in here. Except warmer."

We stopped to look at three models on an upper shelf.

Alicia tilted her head, considering. "What about one of those?"

"Nope." I pointed at each wig in turn. "Too dark, too orange, too straight."

Alicia pointed her finger in my face. "Too picky."

"It has to be just right," I said, "or Lu won't be happy with it. Her hair means a lot to her."

Alicia picked up one of the heads from a lower shelf and turned it to face me. "What about this one? It reminds me of Debra Messing." Alicia had been a huge *Will and Grace* fan. She'd cried when the show ended.

I shook my head. "Too curly. Lu would look like Little Orphan Annie in that thing. Or Shaun White. Or Carrot Top."

"Okay, okay. I get it. No curls." Alicia put the head back on the shelf.

An older clerk approached us. Given that her hair was a natural wiry gray, she apparently didn't take advantage of her sales position to wear the merchandise. "May I help you ladies find something?"

"We're looking for something in a strawberry blond," I said.

"I think we can help you out." She slid a pair of glasses onto her nose and gestured for us to follow her. "This way."

She stopped on the next aisle in front of a straight pale blond wig with slight undertones of red. She gestured with her hand. "Here we go. Strawberry blond."

The color was closer to Lu's shade, but we weren't quite there yet. "Got anything that's a little heavier on the strawberry?"

The woman took a few steps forward and bent down to pull a display head off the bottom shelf. This wig was redder than the previous selection, but still too light. Lu's color was a unique shade of pinkish-orange that was apparently one of a kind. We moved forward a few feet and she picked up another. Still not quite right.

I reached into my purse and pulled the lock of Lu's hair from the inside pocket where I'd stashed it. Fortunately, her industrial-strength hairspray had held the sample together. "I'm trying to match this."

The woman took the strands from me. "Is this from a doll? Or a stuffed animal?"

I shook my head. "No. It's from a real person. My boss. She has cancer and her hair's falling out."

The woman ran her thumb over the hair. "Why is it so stiff and sticky?"

"She uses a special type of extra-hold hairspray," I explained. "It's imported." Without the sturdy stuff her beehive could never have maintained its height.

We made our way down the aisle, the saleslady holding up Lu's lock to each of the wigs. We must've looked at a dozen of them before she proffered one cut in a stylish shag. It wasn't Lu's color exactly, but it was likely the closest the store had.

"Do you have that same shade in a beehive style?"

The woman shot me an incredulous look. "Your boss not only has pink hair, but she wears it in a beehive?"

I nodded.

The woman tucked the head under her arm. "Honey, my family has owned this store for more than fifty years. The last beehive I remember seeing in here was in 1972."

I sighed. Looked like I'd have to forgo the style and hope Lu would at least be satisfied with the color. "I'll take it."

I insisted on driving to the meeting at the Ark. Nick had offered to take his truck, but I felt that if I drove perhaps it would be a subtle reminder to him that this was my case and he was only along as backup. I had no problem with him providing some muscle if needed, but I wanted to be the brains of the operation. Besides, Lu had assigned this case to me, not Nick. It wasn't fair for him to swoop in and start taking over.

On the drive to the church, Nick chugged a Red Bull while I ran down the strategy I'd planned. "I'm going to play the publicity card, remind them of the potential consequences if word got out that the church and Pastor Fischer were allowing the Ark's funds to be spent improperly. The parishioners would be enraged, demand changes."

"That tactic won't work."

My simmering resentment began to boil now. "Why not?"

"You saw those people yesterday, giving the guy a standing ovation, saying 'amen' to everything that came out of his mouth, standing in line for half an hour to shake his hand. They think Pastor Fischer walks on water. They're not blind, they see that huge house back there, they see the limo. They think he deserves those things. They like having a celebrity pastor. It makes them feel important to be part of a popular church. They're perfectly fine with things the way they are."

Okay, maybe he had a point. These types of financial indiscretions were often overlooked. The public hardly batted an eye when Martha Stewart was convicted of insider trading, and they'd eagerly welcomed her back on television after her brief stint in the pokey. Money crimes seemed deceptively victimless and many people weren't sophisticated enough to understand them. Thus, they were quickly forgiven and forgotten.

"What would you suggest, then?"

"Beat them at their own game," Nick said. "Point out that failing to properly report earnings and pay taxes is tantamount to theft, that misreporting is not"—he formed air quotes with his fingers—"*what Jesus would do.*"

Now it was my turn to point out the flaws in his plan. "That's not going to fly, either."

Nick crushed the now-empty can of Red Bull in one fist, squeezing his ever-present stress ball in the other. "Oh, yeah? Why not?"

"The guy obviously has no conscience or none of this would have happened in the first place."

He grunted, which I supposed was his way of acknowledging my argument might have some merit, too. "There's always plan C."

"Which is?"

Nick pulled his handcuffs from the pocket of his jacket. "Say nothing, slap cuffs on him, and haul his hypocritical, tax-cheating ass off to jail."

CHAPTER THIRTEEN

*T*urning the Tables

Only a dozen or so cars were parked in the Ark's lot today, and we were able to snag a spot not far from the doors.

Nick leaned forward, looking up at the Ark through my front windshield. "Watch out, *Titanic*," he said. "Here comes your iceberg."

We climbed out of the car into the scorching heat. An iceberg wouldn't last a minute out here.

"What did you think of Fischer's book?" I asked Nick as we walked toward the building.

"*Toss Your Net*? It made me want to toss my lunch. It wasn't about saving souls. It was about recruiting more members for the church, more pockets for Fisher to pick." Nick gave a snort of disgust. "Fischer stole his tips from those multilevel marketing gurus. Except instead of promising financial rewards here on earth, he claims the recruiters will be rewarded in the hereafter."

Nick held the door for me and we stepped into the foyer, finding it dim today, no grinning greeters to welcome us. The turtle continued to slowly circumnavigate the aquarium, while the fish alternated between floating serenely on the current and darting in crazy paths through the water.

We made our way past the tank today, following the hallway back to the administrative wing of the church. Double glass doors etched with EXECUTIVE OFFICES led to a waiting area. The receptionist sat on a high-backed leather chair behind an expansive mahogany desk, sorting through a stack of mail and dividing it into piles. She looked up as we came in. Before I could speak, Nick handed her his business card and informed her we had an appointment to meet with Pastor Fischer at three o'clock.

"Please have a seat." She picked up her phone and dialed an extension. "The pastor's three o'clock is here."

I glanced at my watch. It was 2:57. Shouldn't be a long wait.

Nick and I sat in silence. We couldn't exactly discuss the case in front of a church employee and, frankly, I wasn't much in the mood for idle chitchat. I was miffed Nick had rejected my plan. He seemed to think he was smarter than me. *Grr.* This was my case and I was going to attack it the way I thought best. And if he didn't like it, well, to hell with him.

After a few minutes of waiting, I became bored and looked over the selection of magazines on the coffee table. No *Vogue*. No *People*. And, of course, no *Cosmo* with its standard fare of sex tips. All of the offerings were religious in nature. *Christianity Today*. *Guideposts*. And, ironically, *Men of Integrity*.

I picked up *Guideposts* and flipped through the pages, stopping to read a piece about a woman who'd dedicated her life to helping abandoned children living on the streets of Romania. She embodied the true Christian spirit in action. I made a mental note to send her organization a contribution. They'd benefit from the funds and I'd benefit from the tax deduction. Win-win.

My phone vibrated in the pocket of my blazer as a text

came in. I pulled out the phone and checked the readout. The message was from Nick.

BTW you looked mighty purty yesterday.

I felt a warm blush on my face. I felt Nick's eyes on me, too. Not looking up, I hit the delete button and replaced the phone in my pocket, returning my gaze to the magazine even if my attention was now hopelessly elsewhere.

Nick stood and began to pace. The guy couldn't sit still. He was like a fidgety child with ADD.

"Maybe you should cut back on the Red Bull," I suggested.

Nick ignored me, instead stopping in front of the receptionist's desk. "We've been waiting half an hour," he said, more than a hint of irritation in his voice. "How much longer is he gonna be?"

The woman gave Nick an icy smile. "Let me check for you." Nick hovered over her while she dialed Fischer's office again. "Can you tell me when Pastor Fischer might be ready to meet with Mr. Pratt and his assistant?"

Nick's assistant?

Ooh, that did it. Hot and bothered now, I stood, slapped the magazine back on the table, and walked over to take a place next to Nick in front of the desk. I could stare down the receptionist just as well as he could. Heck, even better. I had the added benefit of mascara.

"Thanks," the woman said into the receiver before hanging it up. She looked up at us. "His executive assistant is on his way now."

A side door opened and a fresh-faced guy in his early twenties poked his head in. "I can take y'all back now."

We followed the guy to a door marked CONFERENCE ROOM. He opened it for us and gestured for us to step inside.

I took three steps in and instinctively took one back, stepping on Nick's boot, my back colliding with his rock-solid chest.

Holy moly.

The room contained a virtual horde. Seated at the table

were not only Pastor Fischer and Associate Pastor Walters, but also Scott Klein—the managing partner of Martin and McGee and my former boss—Alicia's boyfriend Daniel, and five other stern-looking men in business suits, one of whom was Tim Haddocks, the pinched-faced former attorney general for the state of Texas.

Daniel offered an apologetic smile. I knew now why he'd declined to discuss his work with me at dinner the other night. This case was apparently the big one he'd alluded to. I had no problem going head to head with him. I knew we could both maintain our professionalism and not let the case interfere with our friendship.

My former boss gave me a respectful nod. Haddocks merely glanced up briefly before looking back down at the cell phone in his hands. He resumed typing on the tiny keyboard with his pudgy thumbs. The other suits bored holes in us with their eyes.

Nick put a strong hand on my back to steady me and stepped to my side. Given the unexpected squad of suits, I had to admit I was glad Nick was there with me. Still, we were outnumbered four and a half to one.

"Didn't realize we'd be having a party here." Nick smiled and stuck his hand across the table to Noah Fischer. "Senior Special Agent Nicholas Pratt."

Pastor Fischer stood. The gray suit, white shirt, and red tie he wore today were more demure than the attire he'd worn during the church service yesterday, but I doubted they were less expensive. His flashy Cartier watch caught the light as he extended his hand to Nick. "Pleasure to meet you, Nicholas."

Pleasure? As if.

"You can call me Special Agent Pratt." Nick's tone made it clear Fischer could also kiss his ass.

Nick had put the pastor in his place by refusing to accept the first-name familiarity. Yep, the guy played hardball. The strategy could be a good one, though occasionally a softer touch led to better results. As my mother always said, you can catch more flies with honey than vinegar. But Fischer was more a vulture than a fly, feeding on the church as if it were a rotting carcass. He hadn't exactly played nice so far, had refused to pay both the county and federal tax assessments sent to him. So, yeah, hardball was probably the way to go here.

A patronizing smile played across Fischer's lips as his gaze locked on Nick's. "Certainly, sir. Special Agent Pratt it is."

I introduced myself next, noticing a chunky gold bracelet slip out from the cuff of Fischer's suit jacket as he shook my hand. I also noted that his fingernails appeared to have been professionally trimmed and buffed. Cleanliness is next to godliness, as they say.

"Nice to see you again, Mr. Klein," I said, moving on to my former boss and shaking his hand.

"You, too, Tara."

It was odd to face my previous employer now as not only an equal, but also an adversary. Ditto for my best friend's live-in boyfriend.

Daniel extended his hand to me. "Agent Holloway."

"Mr. Blowitz." I gave his hand a soft squeeze as I shook it, letting him know I bore him no ill will. He was only doing the job that had been assigned to him. Still, I felt a little shaky. I was a smart, savvy agent. But Daniel was no shirk, either. If there was any legal way to get Pastor Fischer and the Ark off the hook, he'd find it. He hadn't lost a case in years.

Yep, Daniel was a workaholic, doggedly determined and ingenious, not to mention relentless. But so was I. And I hadn't lost a case since I'd joined the IRS, either. Still, there was no way both of us could come out on top. One of us would suffer a blow.

Fischer introduced the rest of those at the table. In addition to the church's bookkeeper, Associate Pastor Michael Walters, and the former state attorney general were the Ark's outside CPA and two more attorneys. One of the attorneys was a partner with Benson and Brubaker, otherwise known as B and B. The other was a partner at Gertz, Gertz, and Schwartz, the firm where Daniel worked as an associate and one which routinely hired CPAs from Martin and McGee to serve as consultants on cases requiring financial expertise. The firms were two of the largest and most prestigious law firms in Dallas. Also the most expensive. The ten seconds spent on handshakes had likely cost a couple hundred bucks.

The B and B attorney indicated he represented Pastor Fischer, while the partner from the Gertz firm said they represented the church. Due to ethical rules, an attorney could not represent both parties since there could potentially be a conflict of interest between the church and its pastor.

I looked at the former AG. "Whom do you represent, Mr. Haddocks?"

He glanced at me, then exchanged looks with the other attorneys. Sheez. The guy didn't have a clue whether he represented the Ark or its pastor. Clearly he'd been hired onto the team merely as an intimidation tactic, another warm body to sit at the table, another waste of the Ark's, and its members', money.

Nick emitted a soft snort. "The name on your retainer check might give you a clue, Mr. Haddocks."

"He represents Pastor Fischer," spat the partner from B and B, shooting Nick an eat-shit-and-choke-on-it look.

Technicalities aside, all of this splitting hairs was silly, really. In actuality, the church and its pastor were virtually one and the same, the tax issues and their funds inexorably intertwined. Fischer sat at the table both as the pastor of the church and in his individual capacity as a taxpayer. Or should I say *non*taxpayer?

Nick and I took seats on our side of the table, flanked on each side by several empty chairs. But what the IRS team lacked in head count, we made up for in determination.

I figured I'd better jump in before Nick could completely take over. With so many people on the other side of the table, I wasn't quite sure whom to address, but I figured I couldn't go wrong with speaking directly to the pastor.

"Pastor Fischer," I said, using what I hoped was a certain but reasonable tone. "Your outstanding tax bill with the IRS is now well over half a million dollars, with interest continuing to accrue daily. The government has been more than patient with you and the Ark, but we simply can't let this go on any longer. When one taxpayer fails to pay their fair share, the burden falls on other taxpayers. It's tantamount to stealing."

Nick cut his eyes my way. Ha! I'd stolen his argument and, thus, his thunder.

"The time has come for you all to do the right thing," I added, "and take care of this bill. Let's get this settled today, shall we?"

When one of the attorneys down the table began to speak, Fischer silenced him with a raised hand. He then raised a white-blond brow at me and, though responding to my words, stared intently at Nick. " 'Render unto Caesar,' you mean?"

Nick chuckled. "Found my card, did you?"

The brow lowered as Fischer's eyes narrowed. He turned his focus back to me. "We beg to differ, Miss Holloway. We believe the time has come for the federal government to do the right thing and stop harassing this ministry. Those in power are clearly trying to restrict the practice of religion and the fundamental freedoms on which this country was based. That, Miss Holloway, is tantamount to oppression."

Wow. Pastor Fischer was a master of spin. His bullshit sounded almost rational. No doubt his attorneys had spoon-fed him these responses, and no doubt much of the public would be swayed by this rhetoric.

As much as I hated to admit it, Nick had been right. The soft sell didn't work with these people. Well, it might work with the associate pastor. His expression seemed more concerned and conciliatory than defensive.

Nick jumped in now and, damn me, but I was grateful. "You've taken a number of extravagant vacations on the church's dime, Pastor. Spent the church's funds on a luxury mansion and limousine and servants. 'For where your treasure is, there will be your heart also.' "

I wondered what flavor of jelly bean Nick had received for learning that verse.

Fischer blinked several times in quick succession. "None of these expenses are unusual or unreasonable for an operation with the size and resources of the Ark."

"Well, now it's we who must beg to differ," Nick replied. "Most churches do not operate this way."

It was true. Despite the rise in nonprofit fraud over recent years, the vast majority of tax-exempt religious organizations were legitimate and spent their funds on appropriate programs.

"How do you think the people in your congregation would feel if they knew how their hard-earned money was being spent?" Nick was offering my arguments now, playing the publicity card as I'd suggested.

The sound of birds chirping and a pig oinking came from the former AG's phone. Looked like he'd finished his texts and moved on to playing Angry Birds. I surreptitiously tossed a glance in Daniel's direction. He discreetly rolled his eyes, letting me know he agreed the AG's presence was pointless.

Fischer leaned forward, glancing down the table at his extensive legal team before continuing. "The Ark is transparent. We review our financial statements in detail at our biannual business meetings. Not a single person has expressed concern about how the Ark chooses to allocate its funds."

"And just how many people attend those meetings?" I asked, knowing full well that only a handful of parishioners bothered to show up. In this busy day and age, who had the time? Besides, most people avoided any discussion of numbers like the plague. Budgets, balance sheets, and profit-and-loss statements were indecipherable to most people. They trusted those in charge to do the right thing. In this case, however, their trust was misplaced. And the few who might have concerns about Fischer's expenses were probably too intimidated to rock the boat. Questioning a beloved pastor, a purported man of God, could result in alienation or worse.

"You can't deny that my salary is reasonable," Pastor Fischer said, ignoring my question and going on the offensive now.

"True." Nick dipped his head in agreement. "Problem is, the Ark is covering personal expenses you should be paying out of that salary."

Nick noted that, in addition to paying for the extravagant vacations and covering the wages of the domestic staff, the Ark paid the utility, insurance, and repair bills for the Fischers' residence. Because the Ark covered many of the Fischers' personal expenses, the couple had been able to accumulate quite a nest egg. Not only had they made the maximum contributions to their retirement accounts, they'd amassed a portfolio of stocks and bonds with a market value in excess of two million dollars. According to the Bible, a camel would have an easier time passing through the eye of a needle than the Fischers would have getting into heaven.

Fischer gave Nick a patronizing smile. "Surely you can understand that having a household staff frees more time for Marissa and me to pursue God's work. Besides, the parsonage is used for church purposes. It's not only our home, Mr. Pratt, it's an extension of the Ark's facility."

"Not buying it, Mr. Fischer," Nick replied. "The documentation collected during the audit clearly showed that the vast majority of the Ark's functions were held here in the church building. In fact, the only church-related events you've hosted at the parsonage were Christmas parties for the Ark's major contributors."

Three thousand dollars' worth of Cristal champagne and two grand in caviar had been enjoyed last year alone, every ounce on the Ark's tax-exempt dime. The events were essentially a taxpayer-subsidized cocktail hour for the wealthiest church members.

"Those contributors are critical to the Ark's success," Fischer admitted. "Without their funds, we wouldn't have this beautiful facility for our congregants to worship in. I assume you saw the huge crowd we drew at yesterday's service?"

"It was a boatload," Nick said.

I tried not to groan at his lame pun.

"Then you saw the success the Ark is having," Fischer

said. "We're giving people hope here, Agent Pratt. Hope helps them manage in what is otherwise a dark, scary world."

The guy had a point. Disregarding the fact that Fischer had screwed the federal government out of half a million in tax revenue and was living high on the hog thanks to his parishioners, he had managed to draw a large number of people into his ministry. Though I didn't necessarily agree with his methods, he made people feel good about the world, happy, optimistic.

"The Ark's members have completed some very worthwhile projects," Fischer continued. "The youth group has implemented an after-school peer tutoring program in several of the inner-city schools. The men's club recently performed much-needed repairs at the downtown women's shelter. A team of women from the Ark regularly serves meals at a facility for the homeless." He raised his hands and eyes to the heavens. "To God go the glory." His focus returned to us. "I've provided the leadership that made these things possible."

According to the documentation I'd reviewed, Walters was the one who engaged in the hands-on ministerial work. He'd helped organize the volunteers, made arrangements with the schools and shelters. He was the one who deserved the credit. "Wasn't it Associate Pastor Walters who led these projects?" I asked.

"Michael took care of some of the details, but he did so under *my* direction," Fischer insisted.

Though Walters remained quiet, a subtle shadow seemed to cross his face.

Nick switched tactics, seeming to realize the current course of the conversation would lead only to further argument. "May I ask when and how were you saved, Mr. Fischer?"

I wasn't expecting that question. Apparently neither was the pastor. He glanced at his attorneys, all four of whom exchanged glances and shrugged. Fischer seemed to mull the question over in his mind, realizing that refusing to answer the common question would be suspicious. However, he was clearly suspicious why the question had been asked.

Noah turned back to Nick, his expression wary. "I was saved when I was in my early twenties."

"When you worked for the car dealership in Dubuque, right?"

"That's correct."

Nick shifted in his seat, leaning back and draping his right arm over the back of the chair next to him, giving the illusion he was relaxed and comfortable. But I knew better. His left hand was tucked into the pocket of his suit jacket, squeezing the bejeezus out of the stress ball hidden inside. "A minister came to the dealership and you washed his car, right?"

That tidbit came directly from Fischer's file, from an interview printed a year ago in *USA Today*. I remembered reading it. But I wasn't quite sure where Nick was going with this line of questioning.

Fischer nodded tentatively. "I come from humble beginnings. I wasn't too proud to wash cars for a living, just as Jesus washed the feet of those he ministered to."

Squeeze. Squeeze. "You didn't just wash the cars, you detailed them, right?" Nick asked.

"That's correct."

"Wax included?"

Fischer nodded.

"Vacuum?"

Another nod.

Nick made a wiping motion with his right hand. "Wipe down the tires and interior with polish?"

"What the hell does any of this matter?" spat the attorney from B and B, who'd momentarily forgotten he was in a house of God, representing its minister.

"I'm happy to answer." Fischer shot the attorney a warning look, then turned back to Nick with a smile. "Yes, sir. Tires and interior were included. I did a good job, too."

Hmm. Did I detect a hint of pride there?

Nick continued his questions. "You attend church with your family back then?"

"No. I'm sorry to say my parents weren't religious."

Squeeze. Squeeze. Nick pursed his lips and looked up as if grasping for straws but, again, I knew better. Whatever he was about to say, he'd thought out well in advance. "So you found out that a car you were detailing belonged to a minister and, just out of the blue, you asked him about God?"

"Yes. The Holy Spirit moved me." Fischer looked upward now, raising his palms as if to acknowledge God before turning his attention back to Nick. "I'll never forget that day as long as I live. The best day of my life was when I was born again. It was when my life truly began."

Puh-lease. Even for a Holy Roller, the guy was laying it on a bit thick. Listening to him was like trying to swallow a mouthful of peanut butter.

"You'll never forget that day, huh?" Nick cocked his head. "What was the minister's name?"

"The Reverend Alton P. Rogers."

"What church was he with?"

"First Methodist of Dubuque."

Nick gave a whistle. "You weren't kidding. You do have quite a memory."

Noah offered a half smile. "God gives us all gifts of one kind or another."

"That He does," Nick agreed. "He hung me like a horse and for that I'll be eternally grateful."

Daniel barked an involuntary laugh, then tried unsuccessfully to mask it with a cough. His boss rebuked him with a stern look.

"First Methodist of Dubuque," Nick repeated. "That was a big church, wasn't it?"

"The largest in town."

"Rogers was quite a successful man, wouldn't you say?"

"Indeed I would. The Reverend Rogers saved thousands of souls before he retired."

"Sounds like business was good." Nick paused a moment before cocking his head. "So, Mr. Fischer, what kind of car was the successful Reverend Alton P. Rogers driving?"

Fischer's face flared red, his hair looking far more white than blond in contrast to his pink skin. Clearly Nick had struck a nerve, backed Fischer into a corner. The man couldn't pretend not to know what kind of car the minister owned after saying he'd never forget that day and had been bestowed by God himself with the gift of good memory.

Fischer shifted in his seat, crossed his arms on the table in front of him. "An Eldorado."

"What color?"

"White."

"Six or eight cylinder?"

Fisher exhaled slowly before replying. "Eight."

"Fully loaded, I bet."

Fischer offered no response. Then again, Nick hadn't phrased his words in the form of a question. If this were *Jeopardy!* his response wouldn't count.

Nick rephrased. "Was the car fully loaded?"

"Yes."

Nick chuckled. "If I were a minimum-wage grunt washing cars and discovered I could get myself a big ol' Cadillac by becoming a preacher, boy howdy, I reckon I'd see the light, too."

CHAPTER FOURTEEN

$\mathcal{E}$at, Pray, Love, Post Bail

Fischer's face blazed but otherwise he maintained his composure.

I jumped in now. No sense letting Nick have all the fun. "So after you met the Reverend Rogers, you decided to go to college, correct?"

Fischer nodded.

I pulled his personal file out of my briefcase and riffled through the contents, pulling out a sheet of paper and pretending to peruse it. The paper had nothing to do with his college attendance, but he couldn't tell that from his vantage point across the table. "Who paid your tuition and expenses?" I was operating on pure gut instinct now.

"I received a number of scholarships," Fischer said.

"Based on your family's income, I presume?" I said. "Given your lackluster academic performance in high school I can't imagine you were a contender for merit scholarships."

It was more a statement than a question. A statement meant to bring the pompous ass down a peg or two.

He offered a smile. "You are correct, Miss Holloway."

I glanced back down at the paper. "You received grants, too, didn't you?"

He nodded.

"Federal government grants, right?"

He nodded again.

"Free money, that you didn't have to pay back?"

The smile remained on his face, but his eyes were aiming poison darts in my direction. "That's correct."

I was getting to him and, God forgive me, but I was enjoying giving the pastor a little hell. "You know where the federal government gets the money to fund those grants, don't you, Mister Fischer?"

When he didn't respond, I supplied the answer for him. "From honest taxpayers who pay their fair share. People like me and Senior Agent Pratt." I looked down the table and gestured at the men seated there. "People like your accountants and attorneys and Pastor Walters."

I'd dug into Walters's tax filings, too. The guy was squeaky clean. He'd taken no extravagant vacations on the Ark's dime nor financed any personal expenses from the church collection plates. Heck, the guy had even reported the six bucks he'd earned serving a day of jury duty.

Still Fischer said nothing.

"You owe the taxpayers and Uncle Sam a big 'thank you.' " I left it there. I could've pointed out that his mother currently lived in a Medicare-subsidized nursing home, but if I pushed any harder, his attorneys might raise a stink.

"This is your last chance, Fischer." Nick sat up straight in his chair. "You gonna pay up or not?"

Fischer's eyes narrowed into little slits. "I am not."

"All righty, then." Nick stood. "Noah Fischer, you have the right to remain silent. Anything you say can be held against you in a court of law."

Wait. Nick had launched into the Miranda warnings. Nick

was arresting him? Taking Fischer to jail had been the plan if he refused to cooperate, but *I* should be the one reading Fischer his rights, not Nick. This was my case, dang it! And if anyone would be reading Fischer his rights, it would be IRS Special Agent Tara Holloway.

I leaped to my feet, placed my palms on the table, and leaned forward. "You have the right to consult with an attorney." Duh. He had a whole slew of them at the table, including the pinched-faced former AG who'd done nothing the entire time but send text messages and play games. The next warning also seemed nonsensical under the circumstances, but nevertheless we were legally required to state it. "If you cannot afford an attorney—"

"Just get your church to hire a whole team of lawyers for you." Nick grinned at the legal team across the table.

I looked up at Nick and shot him a shut-up look. I turned back to Fischer. "If you cannot afford an attorney," I repeated, "one will be appointed for you."

Fischer slowly stood, his eyes burning with fury, his blue pupils virtually crackling with flames. Clearly he hadn't anticipated being arrested. He'd probably thought his team of high-priced lawyers would scare us off as they'd successfully done with other government officials in the past.

Neener-neener.

Nick and I didn't scare easily. We'd faced tax cheats far more formidable than Pastor Fischer in the past and lived to tell about it.

Nope, Fischer's legal team hadn't done jack crap for him today. But really, what could they do? No matter how good they were at lawyering, the IRS clearly had probable cause to arrest Fischer. We'd had it for years. The best they could hope for was to spring the pastor on bail and somehow convince a judge and jury that his personal vacations and living costs were valid church expenses.

Good luck on that one.

Then again, it wouldn't entirely surprise me if a judge or jury let this guy off the hook, regardless of how many tax laws he'd violated. Fischer was a celebrity in local circles and if there was anyone America worshipped it was their celebrities. Seemed if you were famous enough and rich enough in America, you could buy your way to freedom no matter how guilty you might be, or at most receive a slap on the wrist. Americans continued to buy Chris Brown CDs after he beat the crap out of Rihanna. When Charlie Sheen's boozing put an end to his role on a hit TV show, they still paid a pretty penny for tickets to see the guy make an ass of himself on stage. Any lame excuse was acceptable. No one was held to account for their sins anymore.

Don't get me wrong, I was all for second chances. But not at the price of justice.

Oh, well. No sense worrying about something that wouldn't be my problem, right? Our job was essentially done now. When this case went to court, Nick and I would be mere witnesses, though critical witnesses. It would be up to the lawyers at the Department of Justice to see that Pastor Fischer received the sentence he deserved.

Walters stood. "Just a moment, please. Can't we work out some kind of settlement here? Maybe pay the taxes out over time?"

Nick threw his hands in the air. "Hallelujah! Finally someone on your side of the table is showing some sense."

"No!" The lawyer from Benson and Brubaker jumped from his seat. He shot a warning look at the associate pastor. "Sit down, Michael. And don't you dare say another word!"

Sheez. They spoke to Walters like he was a disobedient child when, in fact, he was the smartest guy on that side of the table. If they'd let him speak, if they simply worked out a deal with us today to pay the taxes and straighten up their act, Fischer could avoid going to jail. We didn't really want the hassle of sending anyone to the klink, especially someone who was sure to generate a backlash against us. We just wanted to collect what was owed and ensure they'd play fair in the future.

Once the associate pastor had taken his seat, the lawyer

turned his attention back to Nick. "Walters doesn't speak for the church."

"Neither do you." Nick quirked a brow at the lawyer from B and B. "You represent Pastor Fischer, remember?" He pointed to the other attorney. "He represents the church." He pointed at Haddocks next. "And the former AG will let us know who he represents once he checks his bank statement." Nick chuckled again.

Daniel bit his lip to fight a smile. I fought a smile myself. The relationship between the pastor and the church was so entangled even the attorneys couldn't keep it straight.

The Gertz partner addressed Walters now. "Please remember, Pastor Walters, that you are here only as an observer."

"And now, Mr. Walters, you can observe my partner and me taking Noah Fischer off to jail." Nick pulled back the flap of his jacket to retrieve his handcuffs from the inner pocket, making sure to pull it back far enough so that all of those at the table could see the gun holstered at his hip.

Oh, no he didn't. If anyone was going to haul Fisher off to jail in handcuffs, it would be the lead agent on this case—me. I shot Nick a pointed look. "My case, my cuffs."

He shrugged. "Suit yourself."

I reached into my purse to retrieve my cuffs, rummaging around in the various pockets when I failed to find them in their usual spot. Pulling my purse open, I looked inside. No cuffs. Then I remembered. I'd used my only pair of handcuffs a few days ago on August Buchmeyer, after he'd shot at us. Stupid old fart.

Nick raised a brow when I came up empty-handed.

"Buchmeyer," was all I said. But he understood.

"You only had the one pair?"

"Yeah." After all, it wasn't like I was going after armed gangs on a daily basis.

Nick turned his attention back to Fischer and dangled his cuffs from his index finger. "Do I need to put these on you, Mr. Fischer? Or will you be a good little boy and cooperate?"

While part of me admired Nick for his ballsy style, another part of me worried that he came on too strong, that agents like him gave the IRS a bad name. Then again, other than Walters, Daniel, and Scott Klein, these guys were a bunch of assholes. Who cared whether we offended them?

The B and B attorney said, "My client will come willingly." He turned to Noah. "Don't worry. We'll have you out of jail by the end of the day. You won't have to spend the night there."

I pulled out my cell phone. "I'll call the marshals to come pick him up." We couldn't exactly put Fischer in the backseat of my BMW.

"No need," Nick said. "I already put in a call. A marshal's outside waiting for us right now."

Grr. Once again, Nick had usurped my position as the lead on this case. But I had to admit it would be nice not to have to wait for a patrol car to arrive.

I led the way outside with Nick taking up the rear like a cattle driver ready to round up any mavericks who tried to break loose from the herd. The marshal leaned against the front fender of the car. The back door hung open like an invitation to which any sane person would respond with regrets.

Fischer slid his designer sunglasses onto his face and slipped gracefully into the backseat as if taking his place in his limo.

Nick put a hand on top of the marshal's car and leaned in. "Just a suggestion, Pastor Fischer. If you feel the need to pray in jail, I'd advise against getting down on your knees."

CHAPTER FIFTEEN

Wigging Out

Nick and I watched as the marshal drove away with Fischer in the backseat. The attorneys hopped in their cars and followed after them.

Although I was glad that our investigation was over, the whole thing seemed a bit anticlimactic, especially compared to the previous cases I'd handled. I hadn't been slashed with a box cutter, or shot at, or attacked by a chicken. It just didn't seem right to go home without some type of war wound. Dr. Ajay would wonder why I hadn't been to the clinic lately.

"See?" Nick said, as we made our way back to my car. "I told you we make a good team."

Things had turned out well, there was no denying that. And with Nick's badass attitude and my less confrontational approach, we had a good cop/bad cop thing going. Still, I had conflicting feelings. Part of me appreciated his help, but I couldn't quite let go of my irritation that he'd overshadowed me. Add that to the growing attraction I felt toward him and it became a game of emotional pinball with my feelings bouncing back and forth all over the place.

"Want to grab some dinner?" Nick asked.

It was close to five by then, and I was hungry. But I needed to get away from Nick, to sort through the events of the day, to try to put things in perspective. I simply couldn't think straight around him. Not when he drove me so crazy in so many ways. "No, thanks. I can't tonight."

"Plans with Brat?"

"His name's *Brett*."

"Oops," Nick replied, a mischievous grin quirking about his lips. "My mistake."

"Brett's out of town."

Nick cocked his head. "Oh, yeah?"

"Yeah. He got hired on a project in Atlanta. A big country club."

"How long is he gone for?"

"A month."

"Good to know." A voracious smile crept across Nick's face now and he looked intently into my eyes.

"Why's that good to know?" I think I knew why. But, God help me, I wanted to hear Nick say it.

His eyes flashed. He lowered his voice to a seductive whisper. "You going to keep pretending there's not something between us?"

My heart thudded against my rib cage and a warmth spread up my neck and cheeks. Heat spread down my body, too. I looked to the side, downward, anywhere but at Nick. I'd wanted to hear him say he was attracted to me, but now that it was out in the open, I realized it may have been a mistake. With it out in the open, it would have to be faced, dealt with, resolved. "There isn't anything between us." My voice was soft, shaky, utterly lacking in conviction.

Nick reached out a finger, putting it under my chin and lifting my face, forcing me to look into those whiskey-colored eyes. "There could be, Tara."

I shook my head, shaking his hand free, and stepped back, out of his reach. I could still feel the warm spot on my chin where his finger had been. "It would be a mistake. We work together. Besides, we're too much alike."

It was true. We were both type A personalities. Two type As in a relationship was a recipe for disaster, right?

Nick eyed me, his gaze assessing. "And, of course, there's Brett."

Oh, yeah. How could I have forgotten him? "That, too."

He backed up a step now, too. "Well, darlin', when you change your mind, just say the word."

My mind was on mental overload Monday night. Too much had happened that day. Fischer's arrest. Nick's come-on. It was too much for a girl to deal with. And when I felt like I had too much to deal with, I did what I always did. I phoned my mother.

"Hey, Mom."

"Hi, there, honey! It's good to hear your voice."

Aren't mothers great?

I told her about Brett leaving for Atlanta. She extended the proper amount of pity, promised to send me a tin of her pecan pralines, and suggested that with Brett gone it might be a good time for me to come home for an extended visit.

"I'll think about it," I said. "Hey, I went to this church yesterday—"

"So glad to hear that, sweetie. It's been a long time since you've been to church, hasn't it?"

Okay, maybe sometimes mothers weren't so great. "Well, yeah, but—"

"You ought to join a church out there," she said. "The way things are going with you and Brett, you might be needing an aisle to walk down sometime soon."

Mom knew good and well that when I got married it would be at the family church back home in Nacogdoches. Her comment about me finding a church here was simply her way of steering the conversation, trying to find out more about the status of Brett and my relationship. Maybe she'd stop that habit if I mentioned I'd bruised Brett's balls riding him like a pogo stick.

Mom wasn't subtle, but she wasn't wrong, either. Brett and I had arrived at a critical dating juncture. We'd made it through the honeymoon phase and were beginning to settle into the relationship. Things had reached a point where we could evaluate our connection more objectively. We'd soon reach that make-or-break point.

Would we make it? Or would we break up?

Though I was crazy about Brett, enjoyed spending time with him, and felt a strong sexual attraction to him, I couldn't say with absolute certainty that I'd fallen in love with him—at least not yet. But if I wasn't yet falling, I'd definitely tripped in that direction and was still stumbling headlong that way. Even if we did fall in love, though, I knew love wasn't all that was needed to have a successful, long-lasting relationship. A person could love someone who wasn't right for them. Still, even though I wasn't yet sure he was *The One,* he'd been the first guy I'd dated who'd made it onto the short list.

But with Nick in the mix now, I felt less sure about Brett. Though I hardly knew Nick, I seemed to innately understand him, to identify with him. It was as if we shared some type of instinctual link.

Then again, it could simply be primal lust.

I told Mom about Pastor Fischer, about the Ark funding his vacations, about the limo and the designer wardrobe and the eight-thousand-square-foot house and the domestic staff and the hot tub and the cross-shaped swimming pool. Whew!

"Well, now, that just seems wrong," she said. "A man of God shouldn't be so greedy."

The parsonage at our church back home was a second-hand double-wide mobile home that looked out over the city landfill. Not exactly lavish. Yet our pastor hadn't once complained about his modest digs.

Mom and I chatted for a few more minutes before I ended the call. It was time for a scheduled Skype with Brett.

I went to the bathroom and freshened up my makeup, even spritzed a little jasmine-scented body spray on my wrists. Silly, I know. It's not like he'd be able to smell me through the computer and the picture quality wasn't all that great, either. Nonetheless, I wanted to look my best for my man.

I logged on and attempted to call him, staring expectantly at his photo icon with a ready smile on my face as my computer attempted to establish a connection. When there was no response, the screen displayed a message.

Call failed.

My spirits sagged in disappointment. I waited a few minutes, sniffing my wrists and getting high on jasmine fumes before trying again. Still no response. I checked my e-mails. Yep, sure enough, there was one from Brett sent earlier in the day telling me he wouldn't be able to talk tonight. The manager of the country club had invited him out for dinner and drinks. He wouldn't be home until late.

Dang!

Being stood up long distance sucked. I had so much I wanted to tell him. Plus, after Nick's not-so-subtle proposition, I'd wanted to connect with Brett, get a read on my feelings. Guess it would have to wait until tomorrow.

I replied to his e-mail with a cyber raspberry.

Pfffft.

Tuesday morning, I stopped by Lu's house on my way to the office. When she answered the door, she looked even more pale than before and had clearly dropped more weight. Her hair looked thinner, too. She'd lost another inch of her beehive.

I held up the wig and forced a smile I didn't really feel. "Ta-da!"

She reached out and took the wig from me. "The color isn't right."

"It was the closest the wig store had."

She turned and I followed her into her foyer. She stopped in front of a mirror mounted over a small table and slid the wig onto her head, tugging it down tight.

When she finished, I said, "It looks nice." And it did. The shag framed her face well and the warm color of the wig made her skin look less sallow.

But it wasn't the beehive we'd all come to know and love and sometimes fear.

Lu reached up and fingered the wig. "I doesn't feel like my hair."

"It'll just take some getting used to."

Lu picked up a teasing comb from the table and began back-combing the shaggy do, trying her best to form it into her signature beehive. Unfortunately, the hair wasn't long enough to reach such heights and ended up sticking out on the top and sides of her head in triangular spikes, like a manga character's hair.

She grabbed the can of extra-hold hairspray and pushed the nozzle, releasing a mushroom cloud of hairspray fumes. She waved the can around, coating the wig, and me, with spray.

When she finished, she set the can down. "At least now it smells like my hair." She eyed herself in the mirror, turning her head from side to side. "What do you think?"

What did I think? I thought she looked like Elmo, that's what. But I didn't have the heart to tell her she resembled the giggling Muppet. "It's cute," I offered. "Sassy."

She sighed in resignation. "I guess it'll have to do."

I couldn't stand the dejected expression on the Lobo's face. "I'll keep looking, Lu," I said. "There are a couple other wig stores I can try. Maybe one of them will have something better."

She turned to me then and put her hands gently on my shoulders. "I'm sorry to sound disappointed. I really do appreciate your getting this wig for me."

"The lady at the wig store said that wigs made of real human hair can be dyed and styled. I could get you one of those."

Lu cringed. "I suppose wearing someone else's hair wouldn't bother some folks, but it's a little too *Silence of the Lambs* for me."

"I understand." I'd found the concept a little creepy, too. What if the wig started channeling the other person's thoughts or something?

She released my shoulders. "Got time for a quick cup of coffee before you head into the office?"

"Sure," I said, following her to her kitchen. "Just don't tell my boss. She can be a real bitch."

She glanced back over her shoulder. "Always a smart-ass."

Over coffee, I told Lu about the preceding afternoon's events, how Nick and I had arrested Pastor Fischer. Of course I left out the part where he'd propositioned me.

"Hot damn, girl." Lu raised her coffee mug in salute. "But watch yourself. There's sure to be some backlash."

"I can handle it."

Lu smiled her first sincere smile of the day. "That's the spirit."

At the office later that morning, I stood at the table by Viola's desk, faxing my tax return, bank statements, and W-2s to the mortgage broker's office.

Vi's phone rang. She picked up the receiver. I could only hear her side of the conversation. It was three "Yes, sirs" in a row. After she hung up, she hiked a thumb toward the conference room. "You've got a hearing on the Buchmeyer shooting in five minutes."

"Piece of cake." These internal affairs hearings used to terrify me. But once I'd survived several of them, not so much. "Can you round up Nick for me? I'll need him as a witness."

A few minutes later, Nick stepped into the conference room where I sat waiting for the director of field operations to arrive. He gripped a small paper bag in his hand and held it out to me. "For you."

I took the bag from him, opened it, and looked inside. At the bottom of the bag was a new pair of handcuffs to replace the pair I'd used on Buchmeyer. But this pair came with fuzzy red covers on them.

"Good for all kinds of situations," Nick said with a grin.

I shook my head. "You are absolutely shameless."

"Just figurin' that out, are ya'?"

The words he'd said yesterday echoed through my mind. *Just say the word.*

Lord, it was tempting. I could imagine several situations in which Nick and I could put the handcuffs to creative use.

"If I get you off the hook," Nick said, his tone deep and sultry, "you'll owe me. Just so you know, I'm open to various forms of payment."

My face burned. I'd like to say the blush was caused by embarrassment but more likely it was pure lust. "If you *don't* get me off the hook," I said, cutting my eyes his way, "your nuts will be in the Ark's collection plate next Sunday."

Nick slid me that chipped-tooth grin and I nearly turned into a puddle of goo in my chair.

The DFO arrived and held out his hand. I took it in mine and shook it. There was some slight resistance when he pulled his hand away.

His upper lip curled back. "You're sticky."

"Sorry, sir. It's extra-hold hairspray."

"You might want to cut back."

No sense explaining that it was Lu who'd unintentionally doused me with the stuff. "Yes, sir."

The hearing lasted all of thirty seconds. Nick told the DFO that Buchmeyer shot out the window of the deputy's cruiser and that all I'd done was shoot the rifle out of the old fart's hands to disable him and protect ourselves and the collection agent. Buchmeyer hadn't been hurt, other than his pride, perhaps.

"I'll rule this shooting justified," the DFO said, though he gave me a pointed look. "But for the love of God, Agent Holloway, could you try to get through an investigation without using your weapon?"

"I'll try my damnedest," I promised.

In the late afternoon, Ross O'Donnell stopped by my office. Ross was an attorney for the Department of Justice who represented the IRS on a regular basis. His demeanor was so laid-back I sometimes felt tempted to check him for a pulse.

Despite his relaxed manner, he was a bright guy, a methodical thinker, and a persuasive arguer. With Ross assigned to the Ark case now, the judge was sure to rule in favor of the IRS. With a court order, we'd finally collect the long-overdue taxes. Fischer wouldn't go scot-free, either, though as a first-time offender he'd likely receive probation only. Okay by me. We weren't looking to ruin the guy, just to ensure he and his church played by the rules.

The fluorescent light reflected off Ross's shiny, balding head. "Got the Ark files for me?"

I picked up a cardboard banker's box from my desk and offered it to him. "Right here. Enjoy."

It felt good to get the box out of my office. One less case to worry about.

"I'll walk out with you." I grabbed my purse from my bottom desk drawer. It was four o'clock. Close enough to quitting time, especially since I'd worked extra over the weekend. Besides, Nick had headed out early to hit the firing range. No sense being the last schmuck at my desk.

Ross and I headed down the hall to the elevator, making small talk about his kids, my cats, the cold spell we were having. Yep, the temperatures had hovered in the low nineties the past few days. We Texans feared frostbite from this prolonged cold spell.

We pushed open the double front doors and stepped outside. There, on the steps, stood a woman in a black suit and high-heeled pumps. Though she faced away from me, I'd recognize that butterscotch-colored hair anywhere, even if it was uncharacteristically pulled back into a tight bun. Trish LeGrande.

Trish normally wore casual clothes on her job, so I wasn't sure why she wore a business suit today. She waved a hand when she noticed me coming out the door and clacked across the concrete steps in her stilettos, a cameraman jogging along behind her. Three other reporters noticed Trish coming my way and began making a beeline for me, too.

WTF?

"May I have a word with you, Agent Holloway?" Trish said in her typical girlie, breathless fashion. She shoved her microphone in my face, practically knocking out my front tooth.

"About what?" I asked.

"About the Ark case. Pastor Noah Fischer?"

How did these reporters know about the case? Nothing had yet been filed with the court. Then again, there was always a rookie reporter or two hanging out at the jails, hoping to be the first to catch the arrest of a serial killer or celebrity.

The other reporters had reached us and now four microphones were shoved in my face. Looked like the extra-hold hairspray wasn't the only sticky situation I'd face today.

Ross looked my way and gave a small shake of his head, telling me to keep my mouth shut.

"I'm sorry. I can't discuss confidential taxpayer information or pending cases."

Trish put the microphone back to her own frosty pink lips now. "So you're refusing to tell us anything, Agent Holloway?"

The microphone returned to my chin. "I'm not refusing, I just can't—"

A dark-haired female reporter elbowed Trish aside, jockeying for position. "The Ark's attorneys claim this case is the government's attempt to restrict religious freedom."

The Ark's attorneys are a bunch of dumb asses, I wanted

to say. Instead, I gave them, "No comment." I tried to move
to the side, but they moved with me, a mirror image, as if I
were an aerobics instructor and they were students in my
class. "Excuse me, please."

They didn't excuse me, continuing to block my path.

"Pastor Fischer says the government is trying to reduce
the deficit by wrongfully taxing churches and nonprofits.
What do you say to that?"

So Fischer had taken a preemptive strike and put his own
perverse spin on the story, huh? His arguments were ridiculous. The government wouldn't go after legitimate churches
and charities in order to balance the budget. The reason charities and churches were given tax-exempt status in the first
place was because they stepped in where government did not,
providing services like literacy programs and low-cost health
care, protecting children and animals and the homeless.
Charities and churches saved the government money by sup-
plementing federal programs. Imposing taxes on these groups
would be entirely counterproductive.

Fischer's argument made no economic sense. Which probably meant the public, who didn't understand economics,
would fall for it.

Hook.

Line.

And sinker.

"Any response, Agent Holloway?" the reporter demanded.

What part of "no comment" did these people not understand? "No comment."

I finally managed to get around the group by faking right,
then rushing down the stairs to the left. Junior high flag
football had taught me some important skills.

A high-pitched shriek came from behind me, and I glanced
back to see Trish falling to her hands and knees. She'd tripped
over the last step. *Neener-neener.* While her cameraman
helped her to her feet, the other reporters continued to tail me
to the parking lot. With their equipment, though, they couldn't

quite keep up. I managed to hop into my car and start the engine before they could reach me.

Tires squealing, I floored the gas pedal and drove away, angry and frustrated.

Still sticky, too.

CHAPTER SIXTEEN

That's News to Me

After a few deep breaths, I calmed down. I shouldn't let a few pushy reporters upset me. I was bigger than that, right?

Sure.

But they were still stupid, stinky doo-doo heads.

I made my way slowly through the developing Dallas rush hour gridlock to another wig store. This one had a more limited selection. Nearly all of the wigs were blond and nearly all of them were long. I had a feeling this store didn't cater so much to women who'd lost their hair as to women who were into sexual role play.

The drive over had taken nearly an hour, though, so I wasn't about to return home empty-handed. I chose both a golden-blond bob and a longer dirty-blond model for Lu. If nothing else, they would give her some variety.

* * *

I heard the answering machine clicking off as I walked in my door. My home phone began ringing again immediately.

I tossed the wigs and my purse onto the kitchen counter and picked up the receiver. "Hello?"

"Tara Holloway?" asked a woman's voice.

"Who's calling, please?" Never admit who you are until you're sure it's not a salesman, right?

"You should be ashamed of yourself!" screamed the woman on the other end. "How dare you go after a man of God!"

Wow. Word travels fast, huh?

"You're not worthy to walk this earth!" she continued. "You'll get yours in the end!"

Seriously?

"Do you mean the end of time?" I retorted. "Or are you referring to my butt? Because suggesting sodomy is downright sinful of you. Pervert!"

I had to admit, it felt good to let loose. That whole "no comment" business had left me feeling emotionally constipated. I was willing to obey the rules on the job, but this was my personal phone line, in my private home, and this was America and, by God, I was going to exercise my First Amendment right of free speech and let loose all my pent-up anger on these buttheads.

As my grand finale, I inserted my thumb and index finger in the corners of my mouth and let loose the same shrill, earsplitting whistle I'd used as a girl to round up my brothers from the back forty for dinner.

THWEEEEET!

I hung up the phone.

Earlier I'd felt like Pastor Fischer's arrest had gone too easily, had been anticlimactic. I supposed I'd asked for this, huh?

The LED call counter on my answering machine flashed

"99." I had a sneaking suspicion the call count exceeded the two-digit readout, but 99 was as high as the counter could go. I poured myself a full glass of sweet moscato wine, steeled my sphincter, and pushed the play button.

Most of the messages were similar to the call I'd just taken, but a few used surprisingly un-Christian language. One caller said I deserved a good, hard spanking, while another suggested I should be lynched. I was called a Jezebel, which didn't seem quite apropos, as well as a she-devil, a minion of Satan, a plain old bitch, and, my personal favorite, Uncle Sam's whore. I had trouble seeing Uncle Sam as a pimp. Then again, he did wear the bright clothing and funky hat pimps were known for.

Where did these people come up with this stuff? It was like they were speaking in tongues.

Religious zealots. Yep, for better or worse there were plenty of them in the Southern Bible Belt. They often had knee-jerk reactions, such as the group who'd gotten up in arms when one of the suburban school districts sought a federal grant to implement an Arabic studies program. Though the program was designed to give students the opportunity to learn about a language and culture with increasing relevance in today's world, perhaps even give the students a highly marketable job skill given the scarcity of Arabic speakers in the U.S., ultra right-wing parents were sure the program was the district's attempt to convert their children to Islam. For such a small group they raised a mighty big stink and the program was never implemented. But give these same people a devastating natural disaster like a flood or tornado and they responded with equal fervor, organizing food and clothing drives, providing shelter and comfort to those affected.

I'd questioned their ways, arrested their pastor. Yep, I'd sure enough asked for trouble. I was beginning to have a better understanding why the other government agencies wimped out on pursuing Pastor Fischer and the Ark, why Lu had sat on this case for years. But frankly, I was more than a little miffed that here I was, taking all kinds of shit, when

Nick had virtually stolen the case from me. Some of this shit belonged to him. It wasn't fair.

After I listened to all the messages, I went into my living room. Henry lay sprawled on top of the armoire, his eyes at half-mast. I patted his furry head and grabbed the remote to turn on my television. I plopped onto the couch with my wine to watch the six o'clock news. Annie crawled out from under the couch and jumped up into my lap where she turned in a circle twice before settling in.

The arrest of Noah Fischer was a top story on the evening news, not only locally but nationally. Video footage showed the pastor walking out of jail yesterday. He was flanked by his four attorneys as if they were bodyguards protecting an innocent victim. On screen, Trish asked him about the criminal tax evasion charges.

Fischer flashed his best angelic smile. "Our Savior was wrongfully persecuted, too," he replied. "These trumped-up allegations are the government's attempt at a modern-day crucifixion." He looked directly into the camera now. " 'Forgive them, for they know not what they do.' "

Ooh. Them's fighting words.

The screen changed to a close-up of my face from earlier today. Compared to Trish, I looked washed out. If I'd known I was going to be on camera I would've put on some lipstick.

My name appeared in white print over a blue banner on the bottom of the screen. IRS Special Agent Tara Holloway. Sheez, why didn't they just print my address and social security number while they were at it?

"No comment," my bare lips said on the TV screen.

Damn. I appeared annoyed, evasive. Of course I had been annoyed and evasive so it only made sense.

I picked up the remote and flipped through the channels. There I was. Again, and again, and again.

No comment.

No comment.

No comment.

My phone rang once more. I tossed back a good chug of

wine and picked up the receiver. "Uncle Sam's Whorehouse," I said. "She-Devil speaking. And, just for the record, I need no forgiveness for I know exactly what I'm doing."

"Tara?" It was Brett. He sounded confused. Understandable. I'd be worried if he actually thought I was making sense. Maybe I was the one speaking in tongues now.

"Hey, Brett."

"Did you say 'Uncle Sam's Whorehouse?' "

"Yep." Another chug of wine made its way down my throat. "It's been a hell of a day."

I told him all about the arrest of Pastor Fischer the previous day, about Trish and the other reporters accosting me on the front steps of the federal building earlier today.

"Trish mentioned she was filling in for a reporter who's on maternity leave," Brett said. "Funny that her first story involved one of your cases."

Funny?

FUNNY?

Had Brett gone nuts?

There was nothing at all funny about the Ark investigation, nothing funny about reporters making me, and the entire federal government, look bad. And there was nothing funny about the fact that my boyfriend seemed to keep tabs on a bosomy cheesecake reporter. "You and Trish best buddies now?"

"No," Brett said, his tone wary. "She just happened to mention it last time I saw her at the Habitat house."

"Is there something going on between you two?" I was in a totally pissy mood now. Might as well get this subject out in the open.

"Of course not, Tara." Brett's voice was surprised, indignant. But it was a bit tentative, too, wasn't it?

"You sure seem chummy."

He was quiet a moment. "Where is this coming from?"

It hit me like the two o'clock freight train from Shreveport. This was coming from the fact that I could be totally crazy about Brett, maybe even be falling in love with the guy, yet still be hopelessly attracted to Nick. Truth be told, if there was some way I could have them both, I'd do it in a heartbeat. And if I could feel this way about two men, what was to prevent Brett from feeling the same way about two women?

I was in a love triangle. Or, since there were four of us involved, perhaps a rectangle was the more appropriate analogy. But since the connections between the parties were not equally close, that really made it more of a trapezoid or rhombus. Some type of relationship quadrilateral. Hell, I didn't know. It had been a long time since I'd taken geometry.

Tears pricked at my eyes. The last few days had been emotionally draining. I'd been angry, aroused, frustrated, worried, horny, and relieved, then angry all over again. My emotions were all over the place, out of control.

I did a horrible thing then. I betrayed all of womankind by playing the PMS card. "Sorry, Brett. I must be hormonal." It was no more than a convenient, bullshit excuse, a placeholder in the conversation until I could sort out my feelings. *If* I could sort out my feelings. Logical things could be sorted. But trying to sort something illogical, like emotions, could prove impossible.

Time to change the subject. "How was dinner last night?" I closed my eyes and held my fingertips to my lids, forcing the tears to stay in the ducts.

"Dinner was great. The restaurant had the best peach cobbler I've ever tasted. Their chef is incredible. You would've loved it."

I inquired about Napoleon and Reggie next. Dennis had reported they were doing fine. "I don't think the dogs even miss me," Brett said.

"I'm sure they do," I said. "I know I do." Sort of. I'd missed him a whole lot more before this conversation. Now I was just . . . confused. Normally Brett offered a welcome, calm respite from my crazy world, but tonight he'd only added to my stress level. And he wasn't even here for me to use his body to work off the stress.

After we ended the call I unplugged the cord from the

jack. Any idiot who tried to call me now wouldn't be able to get through.

I pulled my cell phone out of my pocket and dialed Nick. Maybe it was the wrong thing to do, but I couldn't help myself. Brett had left me feeling alone and abandoned and vulnerable. And the callers had left me feeling royally pissed off.

"You suck!" I shouted in the phone when Nick answered.

He was nonplussed. "And this is about . . . ?"

"I came home to ninety-nine phone messages from people accusing me of being the Antichrist."

"Seriously?"

"Seriously."

"How did they get your number? Isn't it unlisted?"

"Maybe it was written on a bathroom wall." More than likely it was on the Internet somewhere. Probably a high-school reunion list or the Junior League cookie committee roster. The World Wide Web made it virtually impossible to keep anything secret. Damn Al Gore to hell for inventing the thing.

Nick's tone bore concern. "Did any of the callers threaten you?"

"Not directly," I said. "They seem to believe God or Satan will give me my due." I wasn't sure which would be worse, being smote down or tossed into a lake of fire. Six of one, half a dozen of the other, I guess.

Nick was quiet a minute. "I don't like this, Tara."

"Really? Because it's loads of fun for me." Whoa. I was being superbitchy, wasn't I? Then again, it was refreshing to feel that I could totally be myself, superbitch or not. With Brett, I tended to be more reserved, on my best behavior. With Nick, though, I felt more free to let loose.

Nick let my snarky comment slide. "I don't trust those kooks. You shouldn't stay alone tonight."

"I've got an alarm system." It was an older system, a basic one that had been installed when my town house was originally constructed years ago. Though it lacked the interior motion sensors common in the more modern systems, it would sound both an audible alarm and send a signal to an offsite monitoring company if any of the exterior windows or doors were breached.

"The average response time for Dallas PD is twenty minutes," Nick said. "A lot can happen in twenty minutes."

He had a point. It didn't even take twenty minutes to bake a frozen pizza. And I couldn't count on my neighbors, either. False alarms were routine in the neighborhood. Nobody paid much attention to the alarms anymore.

"By the time the security company or police respond to an alarm," Nick said, "it could be too late. It's not enough to keep you safe. I'm coming over there."

I wasn't sure it was safe to have Nick here, either. As emotionally confused as I felt I was likely to do something stupid, like boink his brains out. That was a complication I didn't need. "I'm not sure that's a good idea."

"I didn't ask what you thought."

Damn me again, but my nether regions fluttered. I found his alpha male style to be both titillating and irritating at the same time. What's a girl to do? I'd just as soon slap him across the face as tackle him to the ground and have my way with him.

"I'll be there in half an hour. Call the cops and tell them what's going on."

With that, he was gone.

And on his way here.

CHAPTER SEVENTEEN

My Boinkable Bodyguard

Nick banged on my door. The noise scared Annie and she darted under the couch to hide. My girlie parts whimpered.

I walked to the door and opened it.

Nick barged past me, a small black duffel bag hanging from his right shoulder, the handle of a blue dog leash and a cardboard six-pack container of Shiner Bock in his left hand. He'd changed out of his work clothes and wore a pair of faded jeans, tan ropers, and a light blue western shirt, untucked. Damn, but he looked absolutely boinkable. His fluffy golden-haired dog followed him in, tail wagging.

I knelt down to greet the dog. His orange snout bore the telltale white hair of a canine entering his twilight years, his eyes the cloudiness of cataracts. He appeared to be part golden retriever, with some mixed lineage tossed in. I let him sniff my hand and, when he'd become acquainted with me, gave him a two-handed scratch behind the ears. "Hey there, old boy. What's your name?"

"Nutty," Nick replied for the dog.

"Is that a comment on his character?"

"No," Nick said. "It's short for Sir Nutlicker of Butt-munch."

"Ew." I scrunched my nose and looked up at Nick. "That's disgusting. What were you thinking?"

"Give me a break. I was eighteen when I got him."

"Guess I can't fault you too much," I said, standing. "We've got a barn cat back home named Pukey."

Nick unclipped the dog's leash and hung it from the door-knob. "He can't see too well anymore, but his hearing's as good as ever. If anyone tries to sneak in here, he'll let us know."

I wasn't sure the old dog would be much help, but if nothing else maybe an intruder would trip over him.

Nick slid the duffel off his shoulder and tossed it onto my couch. "I want to hear those messages. Where's your answering machine?"

Nick's half-blind dog stopped in front of the TV, raised his snout in the air, and sniffed, trying to locate the source of the cat scent. Henry stood up from his perch atop the armoire, arched his back, and hissed down at the dog.

"Mind your manners, Henry," I admonished my cat as I stepped past. "Nutty's our guest."

I led Nick to the kitchen. He twisted the top off one of the bottles of beer and stowed the rest in the fridge. Nutty toddled in and snuffled around the perimeter of the room, eventually finding Henry and Anne's food bowl on the mat by the sink. He helped himself to a snack, crunching down the kibble. Henry had climbed down from his perch and sat in the door-way now, a death glare locked on the dog. Nick and I stood at the counter for the next few minutes, Nick sipping his beer, me sipping a second glass of wine, both of us listening to a bunch of ranting lunatics review a litany of my alleged sins.

When they were done, Nick turned to me. "Uncle Sam's whore?"

I raised a palm. "That's me."

"This is bullshit," Nick said, putting a hand to the back of his neck. "Complete and utter bullshit."

"You didn't get any calls?"

"Not a one."

Not surprising, I guess. His face hadn't been splattered all over the news and, besides, the guy lived with his mother and didn't have a landline in his name. He'd done some house hunting since he returned from Mexico, but hadn't yet found the right place. He didn't seem to be in a hurry. Having been in forced exile for three years, he was making up for lost time with his mom.

"I called the police like you said," I told him. "They're going to have a patrol come by every hour or so."

"Good." Nick unplugged my answering machine. "I'll drop this by the district attorney's office tomorrow. I don't think any of the messages are threatening enough for them to take action but they should know this is going on."

"I'll call the phone company tomorrow and have the line disconnected, too." I used my cell phone almost exclusively these days. I couldn't think of any good reason to keep the landline.

Nick jerked his head to indicate my living room. "Mind if I turn on the Rangers game?"

"Suit yourself. I'm going to soak in a bath."

A sexy smile spread across his lips. "Want some company?"

"No, thanks."

"Some whore you are."

"I'll work on it."

Nick reached out and cupped my chin in his hand. I tried not to notice how warm and strong and reassuring his touch felt. He lifted my face, forcing me to look at him, at the worry in his eyes.

Worry about *me*.

His voice was soft now. "You okay, Tara?"

My eyes began to tear up. I closed them and nodded.

With Nick there, I was more than okay.

"Your guest bed still lumpy?"

"Yep. Sorry."

"Darn."

He'd stayed at my place the first night after Christina and I smuggled him out of Mexico.

He'd complained about the mattress then, too, though then his solution had been to climb into my bed with me during the night. Nothing had happened between us. I'd been so exhausted I hadn't even realized I wasn't alone until I awoke the next morning and found his warm, muscular body glued to my back, his morning wood giving new meaning to the term "rise and shine."

The memory had me feeling warm all over. Better make this bath a cold one.

Annie summoned all her courage, darted out from under the couch and past Nutty, and trotted up the stairs with me, following me into the bathroom. I turned on the water and dumped a large capful of gardenia-scented bubble bath into the tub. Using the cheap plastic lighter I kept stashed in the drawer, I lit the three scented pillar candles on the countertop. After I undressed, I pulled my hair up in a ponytail, turned off the lights, and eased myself into the hot, steamy water.

The soft light and warm bath felt so luxurious, so relaxing, I could almost forget about the pushy reporters, about the nasty names those people had called me, about the love rhombus I was involved in.

But I couldn't forget about the luscious, brown-haired cowboy on the couch downstairs.

If those religious zealots ever dared lay a hand on me, they'd be sorry. But I wouldn't mind a good, hard spanking from Nick.

Just say the word.

Ugh.

When the water grew cold, I climbed out and slipped into

my ratty gym shorts and LONGHORN T-shirt. I was tempted to lock the door to my room, to put another barrier between me and Nick to help prevent us from doing something stupid, but I had to leave the door cracked so Henry could get to the litter box if needed.

God help me if Nick came into my room tonight. Under the circumstances, I wasn't sure I'd be able to resist him. The guy could be damn irritating, but he seemed to know what I needed and gave it to me willingly. Still, I had to be careful what I took from him.

I turned on my bedside lamp, climbed under the covers, and picked up a paperback from the nightstand. Hmm. It seemed a little dangerous to read a sensuous romance at the moment, especially when this particular author's sex scenes were so hot it's a miracle her books didn't self-combust. I returned the book to the table and chose the thriller instead. Nothing sexy about a psychopathic hot dog vendor who laced his sauerkraut with cyanide, right? Then again, the book contained a few too many references to foot-long wieners, references which got me wondering whether what Nick had said at the church about being hung like a horse was true.

Sheez. I was hopeless, huh?

I turned out the light and snuggled in, Anne lying curled in a ball against my side.

I slept surprisingly well and awoke the next morning with a warm body pressed against my back.

Nick had done it again, climbed into my bed uninvited, though I'd have to plead the Fifth if asked whether the intrusion was unwelcome. At least he wasn't spooning me and poking me in the back with a stiffy this time.

He gave a soft snore, which I found endearing. I lay quietly for a moment, feigning sleep while secretly enjoying the feel of his body pressed against mine.

He shifted in his sleep, and had apparently turned his head, his warm breath now feathering the back of my neck, sending a sensual shiver down my spine. Lord help me, but I felt my body respond, my nipples hardening, a pleasant tingle erupting lower down.

He sighed and stretched behind me, apparently waking up. The next thing I knew a warm, wet tongue licked the back of my neck. *Mmm.* But as good as the sensuous touch felt, he'd taken things too far.

"Stop, Nick. Please." I sat up and turned to face him.

But it wasn't Nick. It was Nutty.

Urk! I'd been turned on by a dog!

There was a knock at my bedroom door and Nick pushed it open. He was dressed in navy pants and socks, his starched white dress shirt buttoned but not yet tucked in.

I felt a little exposed in my threadbare tee, especially since I wasn't wearing a bra, but this wasn't the first time Nick had seen me in my night clothes.

"Up and at 'em, lazybones." He bore a cookie sheet loaded with a bowl of Fruity Pebbles and a glass of orange juice. He glanced down at the tray. "I'm not much of a cook."

"Good enough for me." It was the gesture that counted, not the cuisine. My guess was this breakfast was his way of apologizing for taking over my case, for leaving me holding the metaphorical bag with all those callers yesterday.

I propped my pillow against the brass headboard behind me and pulled the patchwork quilt up to cover my chest.

"I couldn't find a tray," he said, carefully settling the cookie sheet on my lap.

"This was sweet of you." It almost made up for the fact that I'd taken all the heat for Noah Fischer's arrest.

"Sweet? You best keep your mouth shut, woman. I can't have word getting out that I'm sweet. It'll ruin my badass reputation."

I gave him a conspiratorial smile. "Your secret's safe with me."

He sat down on the bed next to me, stretching his long legs out in front of him. Nick smelled of the citrus soap I kept in the guest bathroom and his hair was still damp from the shower. I fought the urge to reach out and touch a wet tendril that had curled up behind his ear.

"Did I hear you talking to Nutty before I came in?" he asked.

I spooned up some cereal. "Yeah. He licked the back of my neck."

"He's a romantic, like me. I've taught him my best moves."

I rolled my eyes. "Maybe you should consider getting yourself neutered, too."

He chuckled but cut serious eyes my way. "I'm going to stay here another night or two. Until we're sure none of Fischer's followers is going to do something crazy."

"No need," I told him. "I think those people are all bark and no bite. Besides, I can stay at Brett's place."

The thought hadn't occurred to me last night. But I realized now that Brett's house would be the perfect place for me to hide out temporarily. I knew he wouldn't mind and I'd have no trouble getting in. I could use the spare key he kept hidden under the birdhouse on his porch.

Nick slid his legs off the bed and stood, his posture rigid. "All righty then. Sounds like you've got it all worked out and don't need me anymore."

I'd thought Nick would be relieved that he could go back home tonight but he seemed insulted, hurt even.

I climbed out of bed and grabbed his arm as he headed out of the room. "Nick, wait. I need to thank you. I don't know what I would've done without you last night."

That little comment seemed to do the trick. His shoulders relaxed. His whiskey eyes bored into mine. "Anytime you need me, Tara, I'm just a phone call away."

He chucked my chin and was gone.

CHAPTER EIGHTEEN

God's Pep Squad

I stopped for gas in the morning, eyeing the self-service newspaper stand as my tank filled. Fischer's arrest was front-page news. The cover bore a full-color close-up of his face under the headline "They Know Not What They Do." He'd managed to give the photographer his best tolerant-despite-unrighteous-persecution smile. I fought the urge to kick the machine.

It was ten minutes after nine when I turned onto Commerce Street.

Holy.

Moly.

Not only were there a dozen reporters in front of the federal building today, but there were also at least a hundred people carrying signs, marching back and forth on the sidewalk. Their mouths were moving, but with my Kenny Chesney CD playing I couldn't hear what they were saying.

I jabbed the button to turn the music off, grabbed the golden-blond bob wig from the bag on the passenger seat, and plunked the wig on my head. The last thing I needed was these people recognizing me and running into the street, surrounding my car, maybe flipping it over with me in it or setting it on fire. With a full tank of gas it would burst into flame lickety-split. Okay, maybe I was being paranoid, but I didn't know what these people were capable of. I certainly hadn't expected this kind of demonstration.

I put on my Brighton knockoff sunglasses for extra anonymity and drove slowly by. A large wooden cross on wheels had been erected in the center of the sidewalk. Have cross, will travel.

I took in the slogans scrawled on the signs the protestors carried.

IRS = INHIBITING RELIGIOUS SERVICE.

Puh-lease.

DON'T TAX OUR PROPHETS!

Okay, even I had to admit that one was clever.

UNCLE SAM—KEEP YOUR HAND OUT OF OUR COLLECTION PLATE!!!

I eyed the woman holding that sign, wondering if she was the overzealous congregant who'd called me Uncle Sam's whore. If the three exclamation points were any indication, I'd say she was. While her mouth screamed the chant, the tight skin on her face screamed plastic surgery.

Another woman wearing a short skirt with a matching sleeveless sweater put a megaphone to her mouth and yelled, "What do we want?"

The crowd responded at the top of their lungs. "Religious freedom!"

"When do we want it?"

They raised their fists in the air. "Now!"

This mantra was repeated ad nauseam as my car crept slowly forward in the heavy downtown traffic.

I rolled my eyes. Nothing we'd done infringed on their right to worship as they pleased. All we'd done was try to make sure their pastor wasn't using the church as his own private ATM. We were trying to protect the church's coffers, make sure the money was spent where it should be, on religious programs. Heck, we were trying to keep contributors—and God himself!—from being ripped off.

But they'd never see it that way. Pastor Fischer had pulled the wool over the eyes of his sheep.

Oh, dear Lord. I was closer now and recognized the woman with the megaphone. It was Judy Jolly. She'd seemed so sweet last Sunday. Today? Not so much. The benign sock monkey had become a rabid gorilla.

Judy changed chants now, moving on to, "We've got the holy spirit, yes we do, we've got the holy spirit, why don't you?" At the "why don't you," the crowd pointed up at the federal building.

Several Dallas police officers were making their way up the sidewalk. Ever since the bombing in Oklahoma City, law enforcement had been extra vigilant about protecting federal buildings. Such a large group of protestors would never be allowed this close. Clearly, these churchgoers were picketing without a permit.

I parked in my usual spot in the lot and hurried into the building, noting a lime-green VW Bug parked near the doors in the space historically occupied by Viola's white Chevy Malibu. I left the wig and sunglasses on in case any of those loonies had managed to get inside.

The sheriff's deputy working the security screening stopped me as I attempted to go through the expedited employee lane. He'd seen me nearly every weekday morning for several months now, but he didn't recognize me today in my getup.

"It's me, Special Agent Holloway," I whispered, lowering my sunglasses. I jerked my head toward the crowd outside the front windows. "I didn't want them to recognize me."

"Gotcha." He winked at me. "Don't worry. They'll be out of here soon." His eyes flicked to the wig again. "You look good as a blonde."

What was it with men and blond hair?

I rode the elevator up to my floor. Viola, Eddie, Nick, and Josh stood at the window near Viola's desk, looking down at the crowd picketing below. Josh pulled something small and black out of his pocket and held it up to his eyes.

Nick glanced over at him. "Those some kind of miniature binoculars?"

Josh nodded. "They've got a built-in camera, too."

The guy was a regular Inspector Gadget.

I stepped up beside them. They all did a double take when they noticed the blond wig.

"It's for Lu," I said. "I'm still trying to find a strawberry-blond beehive, but I thought this might hold her over."

The new clerk from the records department walked up, a stack of files in her arms, a bright pink feather weaved into her black-dyed hair, skintight leggings hugging her slender thighs. I couldn't say much for her choice of office attire, but given that she'd managed once again to snag Viola's choice parking spot, the girl must be responsible enough to get to work early.

The clerk ignored the hairy eyeball coming from Vi and looked at me instead. "You going for the Gwen Stefani look? Christina Aguilera? Pink?"

"No," I said. "Just trying not to look like me."

"Whatever," she tossed over her shoulder as she continued down the hall. "It looks hot."

"Thanks . . . I think." Was it good to be complimented when you didn't look like yourself? Not sure about that one.

Eddie looked down at the mob on the sidewalk. "Can you believe this?"

Viola shook her gray curls. "In all my years with the IRS I've never seen anything like it."

Below, an officer had hooked his hands under the armpits of Judy Jolly, who'd gone limp and was being dragged to the paddy wagon. A couple other protestors had taken a similar tack and lain down on the sidewalk. The cops paired up to deal with those people, one picking up the person's arms, the other grabbing the person's legs. Meanwhile, the reporters and cameramen caught it all on tape. No doubt the arrests would be the top story on today's newscasts.

Eddie put a worried hand on the top of his head. "This is out of control. The police are arresting those people."

"It's their own damn fault," Nick said, squeezing the stress ball in his hand. "The cops told them to leave and they didn't do it."

Eddie's hand slid down to his forehead. "Barely nine o'clock and I've already got a migraine."

Poor guy. His temporary promotion was causing him headaches of both the figurative and literal variety.

I reached into my purse and retrieved a small plastic bottle of aspirin. "Here you go, buddy."

"Thanks." He shook out two tablets and returned the bottle to me.

I walked to my office, stowed my purse in the desk drawer, and settled into my seat. The first thing I did was call the phone company to have my home landline service disconnected. The second thing I did was check my voice mail. Fortunately, there were no hate messages here. The Treasury Department's automated call routing system was virtually impossible to navigate. For the first time ever I was glad about that.

There was, however, a cryptic message from the mortgage banker. "Call me. I've got some bad news about your refi."

I dialed her number. "This is Tara Holloway. You called about my loan?"

"Sorry, Miss Holloway. I'm going to have to reject your application."

"You can't do that," I said. "You can't discriminate against me just because I've gone after the Ark Temple. That's a violation of the equal lending laws."

"What are you talking about?"

I figured she'd seen my pay stub from the IRS and put two and two together, realized I was the one who'd arrested her beloved pastor. But when I explained, she was nonplussed.

"I'm a Lutheran," she said. "I don't attend the Ark. I only advertise in their bulletin. It's cheaper than advertising in the newspaper and reaches a lot of rich holy rollers."

Her words illustrated the point Nick and I had been trying to make. Big churches sometimes became big businesses. And when they did, they should be taxed as such.

"What's the problem then?"

"The title company says there's a lien against your home. We can't make a loan on a property with an outstanding lien."

Lien? What was she talking about? When I'd bought the place a few years ago, the title company had done a thorough search of the property records and come back with a clean report.

"What kind of lien is it?" I asked.

"Not sure," she said. "I'll have the title company fax you a copy."

Probably the whole thing was some type of administrative error that could be easily cleared up. I hoped it wouldn't take long, though. Rumor had it interest rates would soon be back on the rise.

An hour later, Vi stepped into my office and plunked a fax in my in-box.

"Thanks." I picked up the two-paged fax and flipped the cover page over to read the attachment. Across the top of the document was the seal of the Lone Star Nation, complete with the oversized five-point star the state of Texas was known for. The title of the document was "Judgment Lean and Arrest Warrint." Jeez. They couldn't even spell "lien" or "warrant" correctly.

The language claimed that a duly appointed judge for the Nation had found me guilty of damage to and theft of government property. The property value and purported criminal fine together exceeded a quarter of a million dollars. The document further ordered my immediate arrest if I ever again dared to set foot on Lone Star Nation soil.

Found guilty in absentia without prior notice or a chance

to defend myself? Apparently those jackasses didn't believe in due process. I should've known they'd try something like this. Was there no end to the bullshit I had to endure?

I carried the fax across the hall to Nick's office. He sat back in his chair, his boots propped on his desk. Today's belt buckle was an enlarged silver dollar. Appropriate for a guy whose job it was to collect funds from deadbeats.

"Get a load of this." I handed the paper to him.

He quickly glanced over it. "Hell's bells, woman. You're getting it right and left, aren't you?"

"Yep."

He stood and grabbed his cowboy hat. "Let's go see Ross. Since this is related to your job, he'll handle it for you."

Good. At least I wouldn't incur any legal fees.

Eddie spotted us as we made our way to the elevator, calling out to us from Lu's office where he sat behind her enormous, paper-strewn desk, his dark face sagging with exhaustion. "Where are you two going?"

"To see Ross O'Donnell," I called back, holding up the piece of paper. "The Lone Star Nation filed a lien on my house."

"What?" Eddie stood and grabbed his jacket from the back of the chair. "I'm going with you."

"No need," Nick said, holding up a palm. "We've got this."

Neither his words nor his gesture stopped Eddie, who virtually sprinted toward us.

"I've got to get the hell out of here," Eddie whispered, glancing guiltily back at Viola, who stood at a filing cabinet trying to wrangle a folder into the tightly packed drawer. "I feel like a caged bear."

I knew just how he felt. I'd experienced that same sense of entrapment when I'd worked at the CPA firm. One of the perks of being a special agent was that our work took us out and about. We weren't forced to stay inside and ride a desk all day. Since Eddie had been filling in for Lu, though, he'd been stuck at the office, buried in paperwork. Poor guy.

As the three of us rode the elevator down, I slid back into

the blond bob wig and sunglasses just in case any stragglers remained outside. I lucked out. By that point, all of the protestors had either left voluntarily or been hauled off to the city jail. In all likelihood a jailer was giving Judy Jolly a body cavity search about now. I hoped she was getting hers *in the end*.

Nick and I waited on the sidewalk as Eddie made a quick run into a nearby coffee shop. As tired as he looked, he clearly needed an extra-large cup. I couldn't blame him for bypassing Viola's bitter brew back at the office. That stuff was nasty.

I looked up at Nick. "What do you think of me as a blonde?"

He cocked his head one direction, then the other, considering. "It ain't bad," he said. "But it ain't *you*." He reached out and pulled it off my head, gesturing for me to tuck it into my purse. "I happen to like you just the way you are." He paused a moment before adding, "Even if you are stubborn and ornery."

"Hey!"

Eddie returned with his coffee, offering the first smile I'd seen on his face in weeks. I hoped Lu would recover soon, not only for her sake but for Eddie's as well.

The three of us continued on to the Department of Justice office, making our way inside and up to Ross's office on the fifth floor. He sat at his desk perusing case law online.

He looked up when I rapped on the door frame.

"Got a minute?" I asked.

"Sure. I was just about to call you anyway." He motioned for us to come in.

Once we were all seated, I explained the situation and handed the fax to him.

"Don't worry," Ross assured me. "The judges are familiar with these secessionist folks. It won't be any problem getting an order removing this lien from the deed records."

"Great."

"We do have another problem, though." He laid the lien

aside and picked up another document, a thick one, and held it out to me. "There's been a major development in the Ark case."

I looked down at the first page of the document. Nick and Eddie leaned in from their seats on either side of me to take a look, too. Centered across the top was the caption "*U.S.* v. *Noah Fischer and the Ark Temple of Worship,*" along with the assigned criminal case number and court reference. The title underneath read "Motion to Dismiss." I didn't bother reading the document, knowing it wouldn't make sense to me anyway and that Ross could give us the gist without all the incomprehensible legalese. I did, however, flip to the last page.

"Respectfully submitted, Daniel Blowitz."

"Damn." This didn't bode well at all.

"Damn, indeed," Ross agreed. "The Ark's attorneys were well prepared. Apparently they figured a case might eventually be filed and they'd already done the legwork to develop a defense."

"Defense?" Nick snorted. "What kind of defense can they have?"

"Yeah," added Eddie. "The expenses were clearly extravagant and personal."

"That's not the issue."

Nick's brows drew together. "Say what?"

"They're going the constitutional route, invoking the equal protection clause. They claim that the Ark and Pastor Fischer have been singled out and denied equal protection of the laws because the IRS hasn't pursued other churches and pastors in similar circumstances. They've put together a list of over thirty megachurches across the United States that provide similar housing and benefits to their ministers. They've verified that the IRS hasn't pursued any of them for taxes."

Ross pushed a piece of paper across the desk to Nick. Eddie and I read it over his shoulder. It was a printout listing the other churches, as well as the names of their pastors and an accounting of the salaries and benefits paid to them. Given that tax-exempt organizations were legally required to allow the public access to their financial records, such information could be easily obtained.

A notation on the spreadsheet indicated it had been compiled under the direction of Scott Klein, managing partner of Martin and McGee. The CPA who'd prepared it was none other than my best friend, Alicia Shenkman. The spreadsheet was well organized and detailed. I'd expect nothing less of Leesh. When we'd lived together she'd been invariably anal, maintaining a joint calendar on the fridge so that we'd know each other's whereabouts, sorting the bills by due date and filing them in neatly labeled manila folders, making grocery lists divided into separate columns for "fresh," "frozen," and "other."

Sure enough, like the Ark, the other churches on Alicia's list had paid an exorbitant amount in personal expenses for their celebrity pastors. And, likewise, none had reported the expenses as taxable income, nor had their pastors paid any income tax on the veiled compensation.

With limited staff and tight budgets, IRS Criminal Investigations simply couldn't go after everyone who failed to pay their taxes. The director of each region was forced to pick and choose which tax evaders to pursue. In all likelihood, the directors in the other regions let the churches slide to avoid the type of repercussions we'd experienced the last couple of days. But Lu had bigger balls than the other directors— metaphorical ones, that is.

"Just because other churches and ministers are getting away with not paying their taxes," Eddie said, "it doesn't make the Ark and Noah Fischer innocent."

"No, it doesn't," Ross agreed. "But it means I've got one hell of a legal battle ahead of me. They've not only filed this motion to dismiss the criminal case, but they've also sought an injunction to prevent the collections department from seizing Fischer's assets. There's a hearing on the injunction Friday afternoon. If the judge rules that the income taxes were not legally assessed, the criminal case will be thrown out. If there was no tax legally due, then there was no tax to evade."

Nick and Eddie both glanced at me, anger burning in their eyes. Heck, I felt the same way. None of us liked being made fools of.

I gestured toward Ross's computer. "Have you found any cases in our favor?"

"I'm working on it."

"And?" Eddie asked.

"It's not looking good."

CHAPTER NINETEEN

$\mathcal{A}$ttack from All Sides

On our way out of the building, I texted Alicia and Daniel. *Saw your spreadsheet and brief. U 2 suck.*

Alicia came back with *Sorry! Still BFFs, right?*

Daniel's response was more pragmatic. *Just doing my job.*

As we headed down the sidewalk, Nick exhaled sharply. "Lu's going to be damn disappointed if we lose the hearing on Friday."

"Don't remind me," Eddie said. He momentarily closed his eyes and pinched the bridge of his nose, his migraine apparently making a comeback.

Even though Eddie wasn't working the Ark case himself, the case was being handled under his watch. Clearly, he felt responsible for how things turned out. I didn't want to disappoint Lu, and I didn't want to let Eddie down, either. Guilt and frustration battled inside me.

Eddie opened his eyes, his gaze locking on mine. "I know you two will do the best you can."

Nick and I *would* do our best. No doubt about that. But would our best be enough? I didn't mind putting time and hard work into a case and I could even get past the offensive phone calls, but I couldn't face it all being for naught. That just didn't sit well with me, what with my being a type A personality and all.

Apparently it didn't sit well with Nick, either. As Eddie headed on down the sidewalk, Nick stepped in front of me, blocking my path, and put his hands on my shoulders. He looked into my eyes. "We can't let them get away with this, Tara. If we don't win in court we've got to find another way to bring Fischer down."

"How?" I suppose I should've been asking myself that question. I was the lead agent on the case, after all. But if the law wasn't on our side, I had no idea what to do next.

"If we can't attack from the outside," Nick said, "we'll have to bring him down from the inside."

"What do you mean?"

"If Fischer's willing to cheat the government," Nick said, "I'd hazard a guess he's involved in some other shenanigans, too."

"What kind of shenanigans?"

Nick shrugged and dropped his hands from my shoulders, leaving two warm, lonely spots behind. "I don't know. I still think there may be something between Fischer and Amber Hansen."

I yet harbored doubts, but I wasn't willing to throw in the towel until we'd explored all of the options. We owed it to the honest, hardworking taxpayers who were subsidizing Fischer's luxurious lifestyle and personal round-the-world tour.

"It's Wednesday," I noted. "There'll likely be some mid-week church activities going on tonight. Want to meet at six o'clock to do a little spying?"

"It's a date."

* * *

Nick and I caught up to Eddie at the corner and continued on back to the office. As the three of us approached the federal building, we noted yet another horde of people gathering out front with signs, though this was a much smaller horde. Unlike the well-heeled Ark members from earlier that morning, this group was dressed in jeans, boots, and matching blue T-shirts with a gold star in the middle. But these weren't Dr. Seuss's Star-Bellied Sneetches. Nope, these were True Texans from the Lone Star Nation.

Their signs, though plentiful, lacked proper spelling, grammar, and punctuation.

UNCLE SAM STOLED OUR SPAM!

Not quite as catchy as "green eggs and ham," but as far as rhymes go it wasn't half bad.

NO TAXATION, WITH OUT REPRESENTATION!

Betty Buchmeyer was in the bunch, wielding a piece of poster board on which she'd written THE IRS SHOT MY HUS-BAND!

That was a lie. I'd only shot *at* him. And, besides, he'd started it.

"Twice in one day?" Eddie muttered. "You've got to be kidding me." He pulled me into a doorway where we wouldn't be visible while Nick dialed 911 to summon local police. No sense in us facing those crazies head-on.

We peeked around the wall, watching as a Dallas police car pulled to the curb moments later. The group scattered like billiard balls, disappearing before the police could get their hands on them. Perhaps they weren't quite as stupid as they looked.

Once the coast was clear, we emerged from our hiding place in the doorway and continued on toward the building. Seconds later, a rumbling, mud-coated pickup truck pulled out of an alley and approached us. Two men sat in the cab, both wearing blue T-shirts with gold stars, both looking our way as they passed us. In addition to the Lone Star Nation tee, the driver sported a handlebar mustache.

When Nick noticed them, he stepped between me and the truck, a protective gesture that gave my heart a little flutter.

"Shit," he said. "I can't read the license plate. It's covered with mud."

No doubt mud created from the sovereign soil of the Lone Star Nation.

I left work early and stopped by Lu's on my way home to take her the blond wigs.

When she answered the door, she looked even more pallid and drawn. Patches of her pale white scalp were clearly visible through her thinning hair now. She wore only a faded yellow bathrobe and house slippers, no jewelry or makeup, not even her usual false eyelashes.

Not a good sign.

Lu's normal clothing might be hopelessly out of date, but she nonetheless took pride in her appearance and normally coordinated her outfits and accessories carefully. The fact she hadn't bothered to dress today worried me.

I held the long-haired wig out to her. "I know it's not right, but I'm still looking for a wig that looks like your hair. I thought this might be something different to try in the meantime." I forced a jovial tone into my voice. "You know what they say. Blondes have more fun."

She looked down at the tangled mess in my hands. "That looks like a rat's nest."

"Sorry," I said. "My cat got a hold of this one." Henry had shredded the darn thing to bits. I'd found clumps of synthetic hair all over my kitchen and living room this morning. I shoved the long-haired wig back into my purse and offered her the golden-blond bob.

She shot me a skeptical look as she took the wig from me. She stepped to the mirror in her foyer and slid the hairpiece onto her head. She took a moment to properly position the wig, then picked up her teasing comb and did her best to fluff it. She grabbed her can of extra-hold hairspray and gave it a thorough shellacking. With all the spray Lu used, I was beginning to think she'd single-handedly caused the hole in the ozone layer.

The blond bob wasn't Lu, of course, just like it wasn't me. But it wasn't bad, either. She looked like an updated and more sophisticated version of herself, a version that might drink Grey Goose martinis and shop at Nordstrom's and belong to a book club that read critically acclaimed literary fiction.

She stared at herself in the mirror.

"Well?" I asked hopefully. "What do you think?"

She turned one way, then another. "I'm not having more fun yet."

Strike two. Darn. No sense getting her more upset. I decided not to tell her about the development in the Ark case, that they planned to present the equal protection defense in court on Friday. Stupid Constitution. I'd have liked to kick the Founding Fathers in the seat of their breeches about then. But I suppose it didn't really matter. Nick and I were bound and determined to bring Fischer down, one way or another.

"I'm not done looking, Lu. I promise I'll find you the right wig."

Lu retrieved a second can of her contraband hairspray and held it out to me. "Here's some for you. I had my stylist order extra."

"Gee," I said. "Thanks."

I took the can from her, though I had no intention of using the stuff on my hair. It was much too caustic and sticky. Still, it might come in handy if I ever needed to install wallpaper or stop a lynch mob in their tracks.

I turned the sharp corner onto my street. *What the hell?* In the front yard of my town house stood a metal red and white sign reading FOR SALE BY OWNER.

I parked in the driveway, climbed out of my car, and made my way across the grass to the sign. What was this thing doing in my yard? If it had been a professional Realtor's sign, I might've thought that one of the agent's staff had gotten an address wrong and put it in my yard by mistake. But FOR SALE

BY OWNER? I was the owner of this town house. And I sure as hell wasn't selling it.

It took some wrangling to pull the metal prongs loose from the soil, but I finally managed to yank the sign out of the lawn. As I was on my way to stow it in the garage, a fluttering to my left caught my eye. A piece of paper had been taped to the glass of my front door.

Lugging the cumbersome sign with me, I went to the porch and snatched the paper from the glass. Across the top of the page was an embossed Lone Star Nation logo. For a government that didn't legally exist, they sure spent a lot on stationery.

The title of the document read "Fourclosure Notice and Order to Vacate." The paragraphs below informed me that the Nation had exercised its right to seize my property and was hereby notifying me that I had three days to vacate the property or I would be removed by force.

Was there no end to their dumbfuckery?

I found myself glancing up at the sky, beseeching God to tell me just what I had done to deserve the nonstop hassles that had confronted me over the last few days. I was a sinner, sure. I engaged in premarital sex, used foul language on occasion, and hadn't set foot in a church, other than the Ark, in several months. Still, I wasn't truly a bad person, was I? I contributed to charities, worked hard, used my turn signal as a courtesy to other drivers. So why did it seem like karma was out to kick my ass?

Maybe I was paying now for something I'd done in a former life. Perhaps I'd been a hooker in a saloon in the old west or stolen precious jewels from an Arabian princess for whom I'd served as a handmaid in the Middle Ages.

Or maybe shit just happens.

Given that I planned to stay at Brett's for the time being, the notice to vacate was not only illegal but also moot. They couldn't very well remove me if I wasn't here, right?

But what if they tried to get into my place? I phoned Ross O'Donnell. He instructed me to fax him the notice in the morning. He'd take the notice to court and obtain a restraining order for me.

I stashed the FOR SALE sign in the garage and carried my purse, Lu's hairspray, and the notice inside. After changing into jeans, tennis shoes, and a dark tee, I packed a few days' worth of clothes into a suitcase and rounded up my toiletries, leaving the extra-hold hairspray behind on the bathroom countertop. I also gathered up the cat food and bowls, the litter and litter boxes, and loaded everything into my car.

I hadn't originally planned to take the cats with me to Brett's place, but the sign in the yard and the bogus foreclosure notice had me rattled. I didn't trust the religious fanatics from the Ark at all, and I trusted the wack jobs from the Lone Star Nation even less. If they'd fight roosters to the death, they probably wouldn't hesitate to cause me or my cats bodily harm.

Annie was easily coaxed into her plastic pet carrier but Henry put up his usual fuss, spitting and clawing and hissing until I finally managed to shove his fat, furry ass into his crate. I pointed a finger at him through the metal bars of the cage. "I'll have no more of your crap, sir." The ungrateful beast responded with both a growl and a scowl.

I swung by Brett's place and dropped off the cats and my suitcase. I texted Brett a simple message, *Working tonite. Let's talk tomorrow.* I didn't bother telling him I'd be staying at his house tonight. He wouldn't mind me squatting and there was no sense typing a long and detailed text message when I could just tell him tomorrow. Besides, this was simply a precaution. I didn't want to cause him unnecessary worry.

The worry would be unnecessary, right?

I headed out to meet Nick. We met at a burger joint one exit down the freeway from the Ark and left Nick's truck there, figuring we'd be less conspicuous at the highbrow church in my BMW.

Nick's long legs preceded him as he slid into my passenger seat. Damn, but the guy could fill out a pair of jeans. He pulled the brim of his white cowboy hat low to shade his face and slid on his sunglasses. I put on my sunglasses, too, though I opted to disguise myself by pulling my hair up into a ponytail. It wasn't much, but we weren't exactly going undercover here. We were just trying to be inconspicuous.

We drove to the temple and circled slowly through the parking lot. The crowd entering the church tonight was predominantly female, mostly choir members attending practice and mothers bringing their youngsters to the weekly children's program.

I pulled into a shady spot under a tree and parked. We rolled down the windows and sat for a few minutes, watching the activity.

"Well, well. Look who's here." Nick jutted his chin to indicate a silver SUV driving by.

Amber Hansen was at the wheel, her young son strapped into his seat in the back. She pulled into a nearby spot and cut the engine. Nick and I watched as Amber unloaded her son, grabbed her purse and a diaper bag from her front seat, and took her boy's hand to lead him inside.

The evening sun glinted off the boy's white-blond hair as he jumped with both feet, hopping over the cracks in the sidewalk. He was a lively, cute kid. But was he Noah Fischer's? Short of a DNA test, we'd never be able to prove it. And we had no legal basis for demanding a DNA test. Whether he'd fathered this kid or not had nothing to do with the taxes we were trying to collect.

We slunk lower in our seats as Fischer's white limo pulled to the curb near the main doors. The driver climbed out to open the door for the pastor and his wife. Both were as impeccably dressed as they had been on Sunday, though their clothing tonight was more casual. Noah sported gray pants with a striped dress shirt, no tie or jacket, while Marissa wore a white lacy blouse, baby-blue Capri pants, and a cute pair of wedges. Noah spoke briefly to the driver, then put a hand on his wife's back to guide her inside.

The flurry of activity subsided, but Nick and I continued to sit and watch the building. What we were waiting for, I wasn't sure. But whatever it was, it didn't happen. An hour later there was another flurry of activity as the people left.

"Let's come back Friday evening," Nick suggested, "when the women will be leaving for the retreat."

I wasn't sure the surveillance would get us anywhere. But with Brett out of town it wasn't like I had anything better to do on Friday night.

When Pastor Fischer and his wife returned to their limo, Nick let out a long huff of air. His eyes locked on the back of the car as it drove out of the lot.

"Enjoy your taxpayer-subsidized limo while you can, Noah Fischer. Your empire won't last much longer."

I wished I could say I was feeling as confident as Nick, but I wasn't. Pastor Fischer just might end up being the one that got away.

CHAPTER TWENTY

*I*ntruder

When I arrived at Brett's, it was growing dark. A woman pushing a baby in a stroller was heading down the sidewalk in front of the house, so I bypassed the driveway and parked at the curb.

Though the streetlights were flickering on in the dusk, I'd forgotten to leave the porch light on for myself and had to fumble under the birdhouse for the spare key. I let myself in, checked on the cats, and got ready for bed. It had been a long day and I was pooped.

It felt strange climbing into Brett's bed alone without him here. The place felt too quiet, too empty. I traded the pillow on my side of the bed for his, resting my head on the soft fabric of the cover, smelling the scent of him on it. It made him seem close, yet far away at the same time.

I'd been asleep only a short while when a soft rumble and

vibration woke me. Brett's garage door opening. I glanced at the clock. Twelve-thirty.

I scurried to the front window and looked outside. There was no moon and the porch light didn't reach the driveway. All I could see was a dark car backing into his garage.

Holy crap! He was being robbed!

I rushed to the kitchen, grabbed my Glock from my purse, and snatched Brett's cordless phone from the wall. I had just finished dialing 911 when the door from the garage to the kitchen opened. All I could see was a dark human form silhouetted against the light of the garage.

I dropped the phone so I could hold the gun steady with both hands. "Freeze, fuck face! Or I'll blow your head off!"

The figure emitted a high-pitched, breathless cry and shrieked, "Please don't shoot me!"

I felt around for the switch and snapped the kitchen light on. There, standing in the doorway, was a bosomy, butterscotch-haired bimbo.

Trish.

What the hell?

A voice came from the phone on the floor. "Nine-one-one. What's your emergency?"

Trish waved a frantic hand at me. "Could you please put that gun down?"

I still had my weapon trained on her. Old habits are hard to break.

I lowered the gun and returned it to my purse, then picked up the phone from the floor. "Sorry. False alarm," I told the operator. I clicked the button to terminate the call, plunked the phone into its cradle, and turned back to Trish.

"What are you doing here?" the two of us said in unison.

"You first," I demanded, crossing my arms over my chest.

She shot me a nasty look and her tone was no more pleasant. "I'm returning some tools Brett left for the volunteers to use at the Habitat house. He left me his garage door opener and a key so I could bring them back."

Her explanation was logical. Not that it pleased me one bit, but still, it wasn't totally out of line for Brett to give another woman his garage door opener under those circumstances, was it? But why had he given her a key, too? Hell, I was dating the guy and I didn't even have a key to his place. I had to use his hidden spare.

"If you were only dropping off tools," I asked, "why did you come inside?"

"I offered to check on things for him. Bring in his mail and water his plants."

Heck, I hadn't thought twice about his mail or plants. Some girlfriend I was.

"It's late," I noted, pointing out the obvious.

"I work on the late news. 'Tune in for Trish at Ten'. Remember?"

Oh, yeah. How could I forget?

She crossed her arms over her substantial chest now and gave me an icy stare. "Brett didn't mention you'd be at his house. Does he know you're here?"

Trish was questioning *me*? How dare she! I had far more right to be here than she did, didn't I? Brett was *my* boyfriend, not hers.

Then again, Brett had given her a key. He had no idea I was here. Technically, I was trespassing.

"I'm on confidential IRS business," I said.

"Right." Her tone was scoffing. She twirled Brett's spare key ring around on her finger. "As long as you're here, you can water the plants then."

I nodded. I didn't like taking orders from her, but I didn't want this discussion to develop into a brawl, either. Well, truth be told I kind of did. Taking the bitch down would be pretty damn satisfying. But Brett wouldn't like it.

"How long will you be staying here?"

"A couple of days," I said. "Ring the doorbell first next time."

With an exaggerated eye roll, she flounced back through the door.

I locked it behind her and went back to Brett's bed. But I couldn't get comfortable. I felt like an intruder, like I didn't belong.

Like I hardly knew the man whose bed I was sleeping in.

CHAPTER TWENTY-ONE

You've Got Mail

In the morning, I took the cats and my stuff back to my town house before heading to work. I doubted the lunatics from either the Lone Star Nation or the Ark would make a move in broad daylight. And, after my run-in with Trish last night, I didn't want to stay at Brett's place again. Rather than making me feel safe and secure, I'd only felt more ill at ease there. I'd ask Nick to come stay with me again. After all, he'd offered. He was only a phone call away. Heck, he was right across the hall.

Just say the word.

One of the young men from the mailroom entered my office, followed by the new file clerk, whom he'd apparently enlisted to assist him. Both had large canvas bags slung over their shoulders.

"What's that?" I asked.

"Your mail," he said.

The two of them upended the bags over my desk, letting loose a cascade of envelopes of various shapes, sizes, and colors that quickly covered my desk, some of the mail falling off onto the floor. It was like the scene from *Miracle on 34th Street* when the post office staff brought Santa Claus bag after bag of undelivered mail that had been addressed to him.

Their task completed, they left the room.

I grabbed a couple envelopes off the top of the pile and eyed the return addresses. One was from a Ricky Don Dupree, General Delivery, Lone Star Nation. The other was from an Elizabeth Beardsley at a Dallas address. I opened the letters. Ricky Don's letter was written in barely legible chicken scratch and contained a verbal barrage of accusations against me, ranging from tyranny to illegal imperialism. Elizabeth's letter was written in precise, flowing handwriting, accusing me of essentially the same things but for different reasons.

Eddie passed by my office but then retreated a few steps, doing a double take at the pile of mail on my desk. "What's all that?"

"Love letters from the Lone Star Nation and the Ark," I replied.

He put a hand to his forehead. "I feel another headache coming on."

"Don't worry about it," I said. "I'll handle it."

My cell phone chirped and I pulled it from my purse. The readout indicated it was Brett. Thank goodness. I could use some moral support. I pushed the button to accept his call. "Hi, Brett."

"You pulled a gun on Trish last night?" he said. "And called her 'fuck face'?"

No "hello"? No "good morning"? No "how are you"?

"I thought Trish was an intruder," I replied. As for "fuck face," well, that was simply false bravado mixed with alliteration.

"She was only returning some tools, Tara. You could've shot her!"

"I wouldn't have pulled the trigger until I identified

whether she was a threat," I said. "Besides, how was I supposed to know it was her? You didn't tell me she was coming to your house."

"You didn't tell me you'd be in my house, either."

"It was a long story. I figured I'd tell you all about it today, when we had more time to talk." Wait. Why was I the one defending myself here? This didn't seem right.

"What's going on?" Brett asked, finally expressing some concern about my welfare.

I told him about the phone calls, the foreclosure notice, the FOR SALE sign, the big-ass stack of hate mail staring me in the face.

"I can see why you might have been feeling on edge." His voice softened a little. "Why is it you always get assigned the cases with the nut jobs?"

"Just lucky, I guess."

He was quiet a moment. "Look. I'm sorry I jumped on you. It's just that Trish called me this morning freaking out. You scared her half to death."

What was I supposed to say to that? Was he expecting me to apologize? I wasn't quite sure I was in the mood for that. I settled for, "It was just a little misunderstanding. All's well that ends well, right?"

He hesitated a moment before saying, "I guess so."

I was hot and bothered by that point, but I could feel Nick's gaze on me from across the hall and didn't want to take this unpleasant discussion any further in front of him. I forced a smile onto my face. "I've got to be somewhere," I said into the phone. "Can we talk later?"

Brett let out a long sigh. "Okay."

I hung up and gently slid the phone back into my purse, fighting the urge to hurl the thing against my wall. Nothing in my life seemed to be going right at the moment. Not work. Not my refinance. Not my personal life. Hell, I'd even woken up with an unsightly sty in my eye this morning. The thing hurt and itched and had tripled in size already, threatening to take over my entire face.

My desk phone rang then. I picked it up without checking the readout. "Agent Holloway."

"Trouble in paradise?" It was Nick.

I looked up and my gaze met his from across the hall.

I turned away. "I don't want to talk about it."

"Brett's a pretty boy, Tara. He's not man enough for you."

I didn't much appreciate Nick insulting my boyfriend but, at the moment, I was inclined to agree with him. So I'd pulled a gun on someone. Big deal. Nothing Brett should have gotten himself so worked up about. Still, I said nothing.

"For now," Nick continued, "Brett thinks it's cool dating a federal agent. But as the reality sets in, things are going to fall apart. I guarantee it."

I turned back, glaring at him across the hall, shooting daggers at him with my eyes. "What makes you such an expert?" I spat.

"Been there myself," he said matter-of-factly. "This job cost me a fiancée."

"You were engaged?" My rage was instantly replaced by a surge of pure jealousy at this unknown woman, then anger at myself for feeling it. I had no right to feel possessive of Nick. He wasn't mine.

Just say the word.

"It was a while back," he said, "before Mexico." He failed to elaborate further on his derailed nuptials and I didn't push him. No doubt it was a sore subject. "Not everyone can handle a relationship with someone like us, Tara. It takes a very independent and brave person."

"Brett's brave," I replied. "When I was stuck in a hole being shot at, he snuck up on the shooter and whooped the guy upside the head with a pipe."

Nick raised a brow. "No shit?"

"No shit."

"Guess I'll have to give him some credit, then. Still, I don't think he's got what it takes for the long haul. He doesn't get why you do this, does he? He doesn't understand you."

It was true. Though Brett respected my work, he'd never

understood why I was willing to take the risks I took for my job.

But Nick understood.

Fully. Completely. Intimately.

I felt my throat grow tight. "Please don't do this," I whispered, my voice high and squeaky.

"Don't do what? Tell you the truth?"

Exactly. Nick was putting into words the fears I now realized I'd harbored in the back of my mind all along.

When I failed to respond, Nick asked, "What do you see in him?"

What did I see in Brett? Lots of things. He was a nice guy, sweet, thoughtful. I admired his work ethic. But, admittedly, one of the things I liked was that he was generally an easygoing, undemanding guy. Our relationship didn't take much effort, on my part at least. "He's an easy guy to be with."

"Easy?" Nick emitted a snort of derision. "Since when does Tara Holloway take the easy way out?"

"I get enough challenges every day on the job," I replied. "I don't need my personal relationships to be work, too."

My intercom buzzed. I pushed the button and Viola's voice came over the speaker. "Your parents are here."

"Thanks," I told her. "Gotta go," I told Nick.

He skewered me with a pointed look. "This conversation isn't over."

I hung up my phone. The conversation might not be over, but it had concluded for now.

CHAPTER TWENTY-TWO

Outbid

I met my mother and father in the building's foyer, giving them each a big hug.

My dad was a weatherworn, broad-shouldered man, old-fashioned and no-nonsense. If someone were to be cast as my dad in a movie, the role would have to go to Tommy Lee Jones. Mom, too, was a bit old-fashioned, chestnut-haired and petite like me. Though she was down-to-earth, she appreciated the finer things in life, too. Reba McEntire would be cast in her role.

Dad wore his best pair of cowboy boots, a pair of starched and ironed jeans, and a classic white button-down. Mom had dressed in a blue A-line dress and low heels, sophisticated enough to fit in here in the somewhat pretentious city of Dallas, but comfortable enough for the six-hour roundtrip drive they'd make today. My hometown of Nacogdoches lay three hours to the east, in the piney woods, not far from the Louisiana border.

They'd made the trek for this morning's government auction, but couldn't stay the night. Dad had a load of hay to deliver to a horse-breeding facility first thing tomorrow morning.

Mom put a hand on each of my shoulders and squinted at my face. "What's wrong with your eye?"

"It's just a sty, Mom. No big deal."

"It looks horrible."

"Gee, thanks."

"You're not getting enough sleep, are you?"

"I'm sleeping fine." *Liar, liar, pants on fire.*

"You should come home for a nice, long visit. Get some rest."

"I will," I promised. "As soon as things slow down." Heck, I'd love to go home and let Mom take care of me for a few days.

"Put a warm teabag over your eye," Mom suggested. "That'll get rid of the sty."

The last home remedy my mother had suggested was to coat my hair with mayonnaise to get rid of lice I'd contracted from trying on a hat at a thrift shop. While her advice had worked, my greasy hair had induced a large hunting dog to knock me down and lick my head. The beast had nearly given me a concussion.

We made our way out to Dad's pickup and loaded in. As I had since I was a little girl, I sat between my mother and father, where I'd be both safe and in easy reach should I smart off and need a corrective smack. I'd never actually received the threatened smacks, though I'd had a hostile finger pointed in my face a few times. I was much too old for insincere threats or finger-pointing now, but old habits die hard.

I gave Dad directions to the auction site, which was at the livestock barn on the Dallas fairgrounds. We arrived twenty minutes later and parked. The enormous, permanent Ferris wheel loomed motionless over us as we walked through the lot into the sprawling metal building.

During the annual state fair, the building housed everything from pigs, to cows, to llamas, to ostriches. Today, though, the space housed an assortment of items seized from deadbeats who hadn't paid their taxes. Though the stalls had been hosed down, the place retained the faint, earthy smell of farm animals.

The Treasury Department hired a local auction service to conduct the sale. While the fast-talking auctioneers were more used to negotiating the sale of steers and sows, they did a fine job with the assorted electronics, jewelry, and tools that made up much of the seized inventory.

Dad filled out the requisite paperwork, obtained a paddle bearing his assigned number—362—and led us to three seats on the second row. As we sat, I spotted Betty Buchmeyer across the aisle. With her was a fiftyish man that must be her son. He was the spitting image of his father, both figuratively and literally. He held a paper coffee cup to his bulging lower lip, but rather than drinking from it he expelled a glob of tobacco into the makeshift spittoon. August Buchmeyer wasn't in attendance. According to information we'd received from the district attorney, Buchmeyer had accepted a plea bargain and was serving six months in a psychiatric facility.

I glanced around the room. Several country-looking folks were seated about, but without the Lone Star Nation T-shirts there was no way to tell whether they were also members of the group. The last thing I wanted was to be ambushed. Maybe they wouldn't recognize me with the unsightly bulge on my eyelid. Or maybe they'd think I suffered from a contagious disease and keep their distance.

We waited while the auctioneers sold off a numbered G. Harvey print, followed by a first edition of *Elmer Gantry* by Sinclair Lewis. The first went to a woman in a gauzy and colorful bohemian dress, probably an art dealer. The latter went to a stooped man with round-framed spectacles, probably a retired librarian or English professor.

Some odd things made their way onto the auction block. A canoe that had been fitted with wheels, a motor, and a steering apparatus. A half-dozen naked male mannequins. A neon sign that read GIRLS! GIRLS! GIRLS! Although the Buchmeyers' chickens had been seized by the sheriff's department after the cockfighting incident, the birds wouldn't be on the auction block today. They'd been rescued by an animal welfare organization and would live out their lives strutting and pecking dirt at a sanctuary. I was glad to know the speckled hen I'd befriended wouldn't end up on someone's dinner plate.

When the cases of Spam came up for auction, Betty Buchmeyer engaged in a brief bidding war against an Asian man wearing white pants and a white T-shirt, his clothing spotted with food stains. A fry cook, perhaps? After a bit of back and forth, the man gave up and the canned meat was once again the property of the Lone Star Nation. With any luck, clogged arteries would prevent the secessionists from launching any violent takeover they might have planned.

Finally, it was time for the guns.

The auctioneer started with the lower-ticket items, used guns in varying, and sometimes questionable, condition. Once those were out of the way, he began to peddle the brand-new guns that Nick, Jenkins, and I had seized at the Buchmeyers' place. He began with a semiautomatic shotgun, starting the bid at a bargain price of fifty dollars. The gun retailed for twelve hundred.

Dad raised his paddle, along with a dozen other men, including the Buchmeyers' son. After several rounds of bidding, Betty reached out a hand to hold her son's arm down. Either they'd replaced the guns already or they'd run low on cash and couldn't bid any higher. I was hoping it was the latter.

The group dwindled down to Dad and a deep-voiced man at the back holding paddle number 437. The man's voice seemed oddly familiar. Was it one of the men who'd been arrested the night of the cockfight? Hard to tell when he issued only clipped bids and not complete sentences.

When the price reached eight hundred, Dad bowed out. "Too rich for my blood."

The man with the deep and oddly familiar voice won the bid at $815.

Though Dad lost this initial battle, he later managed to snag both a short-range rifle and a handgun for rock-bottom prices. All in all, not a bad morning.

When we went to claim Dad's new guns, I was surprised to see Nick at the front of the line. He doled out a stack of cash, signed the paperwork, and turned around, his new semiautomatic shotgun in his hands. No wonder that deep voice had sounded familiar.

Despite our earlier unpleasant conversation, Nick's face brightened when he saw me. "Hey, Tara."

Mom took one look at Nick, grabbed the paddle out of Dad's hand, and began to fan herself with it. "Boy howdy," she whispered under her breath. "Something's giving me one mother of a hot flash."

That *something* headed our way, stopping when he reached us. I introduced him to my parents, noticing my mother blush when Nick flashed his chipped-tooth smile at her.

Dad eyed the shotgun in Nick's hands. "So you're the one who outbid me."

"Sorry, sir," Nick said. "But I've got something very precious to protect." He glanced my way.

I tried not to swoon.

"We were heading out to lunch," my mother told Nick. "Would you like to join us?"

Nick glanced my way again, but ignored the shake of my head. "That's mighty nice of you, Mrs. Holloway. I'll take you up on that offer."

We headed out to the parking lot, Mom and I walking ahead of the men, who were discussing the weapons they'd just picked up.

Mom looked back at Nick. "He sure is one good-looking cowboy," she whispered. "I can tell he's sweet on you, too. He lit up like an offshore rig when he saw you."

I shrugged. Whether Nick was sweet on me or not was irrelevant. So why did the thought give me such a thrill?

"I'm in a committed relationship with Brett, remember?" A troubled relationship at the moment, but committed nonetheless. "Just a few days ago you were suggesting I scout churches for our wedding."

"Perhaps I was a bit hasty," Mom said, taking another glimpse back at Nick and fanning herself again. "It never hurts to play the field before you settle down for good."

True. But that strategy could backfire, too. If I slowed things down with Brett to give Nick a try, I could end up losing both of them.

A few minutes later, my parents, Nick, and I were seated at a booth in a nearby café. Mom and Dad sat on one side, Nick and I on the other. Nick's arm was draped across the top of the booth behind me, a casual yet familiar gesture that caught my dad's eye. He shot me a questioning look. I pretended not to notice. Heck, I had a lot of questions myself. One of which was, how much longer could I resist this sexy cowboy's charms? Just having him sitting beside me had my girlie parts on alert.

Nick and Dad talked easily. Not surprising, I suppose. They'd had similar upbringings. Both were farm boys, both were former high school linebackers, both were diehard Cowboys fans. Just three weeks until the preseason games. Not to mention the cheerleaders in their skimpy halter tops, hot pants, and white go-go boots.

Mom asked Nick about his family. Nick noted that he lived with his mother but was looking for a place of his own.

"'Course I haven't been in too much of a hurry," Nick said. "It's nice having someone to clean up after me and do the cooking. My mother makes the best chicken-fried steak in Texas."

Dad set his tumbler of tea back down on the table. "That's pure blasphemy, son," he said jovially. "Tara's mother makes the best chicken-fried steak in the Lone Star State."

"It's true," I said.

Nick's gaze locked on my face. "Well, then. You'll have to come over for dinner, judge for yourself."

Backed myself into that corner, didn't I?

"Mom's been wanting to meet you," Nick added. "To thank you in person for what you did for me."

Dad sat up rigid in his seat. "And what was that, exactly?" He looked from Nick to me, waiting for an explanation.

I'd told my parents that I'd driven to Mexico to retrieve an agent who'd been stranded down there. But I hadn't exactly told them I'd smuggled the guy back across the border in the toolbox of a pickup truck. They knew I did some crazy things, but risking jail time to transport a wanted fugitive went beyond my usual level of crazy.

I tried to send Nick a telepathic message with my eyes.

Fortunately, the guy could read me like a book. "She gave me a ride when I needed one," he said simply.

Dad's expression was skeptical, but he didn't push the matter further.

Nick, however, didn't stop pushing me. "You don't have plans for Sunday night, right? I'll tell her we'll come for dinner then."

Before I could protest, my mother chimed in. "That would be lovely."

I shot my mother a look across the table. She responded by batting her eyes at me and fanning herself again with the paddle.

After lunch, Nick offered to give me a ride to the office so my parents could head on home to Nacogdoches without having to backtrack through Dallas traffic.

I gave each of my parents a hug and kiss on the cheek. Dad gave Nick's hand a shake, as did Mom. She tossed me one final raised brow as she and Dad climbed into their truck.

Nick opened the passenger door on his pickup and held out a hand to help me inside. He made his way around the bed, climbed in the driver's side, and stuck the keys in the ignition, but he didn't start the engine. Instead, he glanced over at me. "Think I passed muster?"

"What do you mean?"

"With your parents. Did they like me?"

He'd passed with flying colors. Heck, I think my mother had a crush on the guy. Still, whether my parents liked him or not didn't matter, did it? "What's it matter?"

"It would be nice to know they've got no objections to me," he said, "seein' as how I'm bound and determined to make you my woman."

An instant blush warmed my face. "They liked you just fine." I turned away, away from his sexy grin, away from those soulful, whiskey-colored eyes. "I really wish you'd stop talking like this. It makes me uncomfortable."

"Why?"

I turned back. "You're trying to get me to cheat on my boyfriend. What does that say about you, Nick?"

He was the one who blushed now, but it was with red-hot anger. "Is that what you think I'm doing?"

"Isn't it?"

"No," he said adamantly. "I'm not trying to get you to cheat on Brett. I'm just trying to make you realize there might be someone better suited for you."

"You, you mean?"

"Maybe," Nick said. "Maybe not. Hell, you won't know unless you give it a shot, will you? But Tara, whether things work out with us or not, I still think Brett's the wrong guy for you."

"Can we stop talking about this?" I shouted, angry now, too. "My personal life is none of your damn business!"

Nick looked taken aback. "All righty, then. Does this mean I shouldn't ask what the hell's wrong with your eye?"

"No!"

We drove back to the office in silence.

CHAPTER TWENTY-THREE

*M*y Human Security Blanket

Ross faxed me a copy of the restraining order later that afternoon. Another copy was on its way to the Buchmeyers' place, along with instructions for copies to be distributed to every member of the Lone Star Nation. None of them was to come within three hundred feet of me. Little consolation given that many rifles had a range much longer than three hundred feet. But maybe it would scare off any crazy True Texans intent on invading my home.

Brett and I talked via Skype Thursday night, but the conversation felt awkward and strained. Not surprising. My feelings were all over the place. Why had Brett agreed to let Trish pick up his mail and water his plants? Didn't he realize that was inappropriate? Or was I being too old-fashioned, assuming a man and woman couldn't be just friends?

Who was right and who was wrong?

I had no idea.

Things with Brett used to seem so simple. Now our relationship felt as confusing and complicated as the tax code.

"Any chance you could take a day or two off from work and fly out to Atlanta?" Brett asked. "There's a beautiful rose garden in Fernbank Forest. You'd love it."

As much as I'd love to see Brett in person and try to get things between us back on track, the timing wouldn't work. "I wish I could," I said, "but I can't. Work's too busy right now."

His brow furrowed and he stared at me from the screen for a few seconds, concern in his eyes. "Okay," he said finally. "I miss you. A lot." He reached a hand out to touch his screen, as if attempting to connect physically with me through cyberspace.

I returned the gesture, but all I felt was the cold, hard surface. "I miss you, too."

When we ended the call, I sat for a moment with my eyes closed, willing things between me and Brett to return to normal.

Nick phoned at ten to let me know he was in the driveway. "Didn't want to scare you by knocking on the door unannounced."

I went to the door and let him and Nutty in with only an angry glance. Make that an angry *one-eyed* glance. I'd affixed a warm, moist teabag over the other with gauze tape. Still, as mad as I still was at Nick for questioning my relationship with Brett, I had to admit it was nice to have a bodyguard in case the kooks from the Ark or the Lone Star Nation tried to pull anything tonight. I had no doubt Nick could dispatch any intruder in short order. His presence made me feel more relaxed, too. He was like a human security blanket.

"What's that on your eye?" Nick asked.

"A teabag," I said. "My mother says it'll get rid of the sty."

"Lord, I hope so. That thing's hideous."

I knew his jibe was a joke, his way of trying to force me to engage with him. But I refused to jump to the bait.

We sat at opposite ends of the couch with Nutty lying

between us. Nick unpackaged his new shotgun and looked it over as I watched the news in silence. An armed robbery at a convenience store in south Dallas had left the clerk with a bullet in the leg but, fortunately, he was expected to make a full recovery. The Dow-Jones Industrial Average was down nine points. Another bomb exploded in the Middle East.

Trish's usual happy-feel-good segment came on near the end of the newscast. She offered a brief live introduction from her seat in the studio, then the image cut to footage filmed earlier today. In the recorded clip she wore a frilly pink apron over a pink top and white jeans. Small, giggling children flanked her on both sides. Apparently, she'd spent the day baking carrot cupcakes with a local kindergarten class learning about nutrition. They'd topped their healthy cupcakes with natural honey instead of frosting.

I fought the urge to heave a lamp through the television screen.

Trish knelt down, put an arm around the tiny pigtailed girl next to her, and smiled at the camera. "As you can see, the cupcakes aren't the only sweet things around here." She gave the viewers an exaggerated wink with an overly made-up eye.

I couldn't take it anymore. I stood and made my way to the stairs.

Nick's voice came from behind me, soft but sure. "You should've shot her while you had the chance."

I didn't dare turn around, knowing he'd be able to read my mind from the expression on my face.

He'd said just the right thing.

God help me, I could fall hard for the guy.

An hour later, I was still awake, lying in my bed, trying to count sheep but instead distracted by the confusing mess my life had become. Work sucked. I wasn't sure where Brett and I stood. And my swollen eye itched like crazy. Damn sty. The teabag hadn't helped a bit.

A creak sounded from the stairway. The third step making its usual protest as Nick climbed the stairs.

I heard him in the hallway outside my bedroom, then the noise stopped. I opened my good eye just a tiny slit to see him standing in my dark doorway. He said nothing, probably assuming I was asleep by now. He stood there for several seconds, watching me, before finally heaving a sigh and turning to go into the guest room.

A low growl woke me at three A.M. Nutty. It sounded as if he were downstairs.

I grabbed my Glock from my nightstand, climbed out of bed, and tiptoed into the hallway, nearly running into Nick, who'd come out of the guest room to investigate. He wore nothing but a pair of plaid boxers, but he held the shotgun in his hand.

"Go back to your room," he whispered. "I'll check things out."

"No!" I whispered back. "I'm coming with you." I wasn't about to cower in fear from crazy rednecks or religious zealots. Of course I might not have felt so courageous if Nick wasn't there with me.

Nick let out a frustrated huff. "At least stay behind me then, okay?"

Not a bad idea. Big as he was, Nick would make a darn good human shield if anyone opened fire.

He flattened himself against the wall and tiptoed down the stairs. Instinctively, I put a hand on his shoulder. I wasn't sure if it was for reassurance or simply to help guide me down the stairs, but either way his warm, muscular shoulder felt nice under my fingers.

Creak. The third step from the bottom gave a bit under his weight.

A couple more steps and we were on the ground floor. By then, Nutty was scratching at my back door, his loud growls interspersed with woofs.

We crept through the kitchen in a crouch. Nick pulled back the curtain at the window over the sink and looked outside. The back porch light was on, but the far corners of my small yard were in shadow. It took a few seconds for our eyes to adjust. When they did, I could just make out a face above the metal utility box in the corner, eyes shining.

"Oh, my God!" I gasped. "There's someone back there!"

Was it someone from the Lone Star Nation?

Nick dashed to the back door, threw it open, and aimed the shotgun at the would-be intruder. "Put your hands up!"

Nutty scrambled out the door, stopped to sniff the air, then ran to the box, leaping up on it and barking to raise the dead.

I went to the back door. My next-door neighbor flipped on her floodlights and we could clearly see the prowler's face now. He had beady eyes, a pointy nose, and long whiskers.

A possum.

Sheez.

"Holy hell," Nick spat, lowering his gun. "It's just a varmint."

The possum blinked his eyes. For a flea-bitten rodent, the thing was actually kind of cute.

My neighbor came to the fence and stuck her head over it. "What's going on?" Her eyes went from me to Nick. They stayed on Nick.

"We thought someone was prowling around back here," I told her. "Turns out it was just a possum."

The poor creature was terrified, frozen in position on top of the metal box. Luckily it was too high up for Nutty to quite reach him.

"Sorry to wake you," I apologized to my neighbor.

"No problem." She took one last, longing glance at Nick before heading back into her town house.

Nick grabbed Nutty by the collar and dragged him back inside. I followed them.

Despite his age and poor eyesight, Nutty'd proved to be a darn good watchdog. I gave him a slice of bologna to reward him.

"What about me?" Nick asked. "Wasn't I a good boy, too?"

I tossed him a slice of bologna, too, and headed back to bed.

Nick had already left when I woke Friday morning. I knew I shouldn't have been disappointed by that fact, but I was. At least the sty was gone, too. Thank heaven for small favors.

I showered, put on my makeup, and dressed in my best black pantsuit with a red silk camisole and a red and black polka-dot scarf knotted loosely around my neck. It was stylish, yet professional, the perfect outfit for the courtroom showdown scheduled for the afternoon.

As I pulled the hot rollers out of my hair, the can of Lu's contraband hairspray beckoned from my bathroom countertop. I hadn't planned to use the stuff, but why not? The spray might be excessively sticky, but I wouldn't have to worry about my hair losing its sassy curl for court and maybe it would give me some of Lu's kick-ass attitude.

Annie watched from her perch on the toilet seat while I fluffed my hair, picked up the can, and aimed it at my head. I held my breath, closed my eyes, and pushed the trigger. *Psshht.*

A cloud of the stuff hung in the air. My poor cat leaped off the toilet seat, sneezing three times in quick succession before bolting from the room.

I returned the can to the countertop and touched my hair. My chestnut locks were frozen in place. Not even hurricane-force winds could move them now.

Nick left me alone at work that morning, going so far as to close his office door so that our eyes couldn't meet across the hall.

I was the one who'd pushed him away.

So why did it hurt so bad that he was shutting me out?

Men were nothing but trouble. I wasn't sure they were worth it. Maybe I should consider switching teams. We had a couple of lesbian agents. They could probably give me some pointers.

I sighed. Nope, it wouldn't work. I was hopelessly heterosexual. As infuriating as men were, I preferred a sexual partner with guy parts.

I spent part of my morning sorting the pile of mail I'd received the day before into two separate stacks, one for mail from Ark members, the other for mail from the self-proclaimed True Texans. The clerk brought me another bag of letters, though today's take was significantly smaller. Maybe things were looking up for me.

"Did you see your new Facebook page?" the mail clerk asked.

"What are you talking about?"

He stepped around my desk and began typing on my laptop's keyboard, pulling up the Facebook site. He angled the laptop so I could view the screen. "See?"

The page was titled "Tara Holloway Stinks." As if the title weren't bad enough, they'd posted a very unflattering photo of me from my days as a member of the NRA chapter at the University of Texas. My eyes were crossed, my tongue hanging out. I held a rifle in one hand, a bottle of beer in the other. The beer bottle was empty, though you couldn't tell that from the photo. The snapshot had been taken as a joke after I'd led a workshop on gun safety. Talk about taking something out of context. Hell, I looked as crazy as the kooks from the Lone Star Nation.

Stupid Internet. Nobody could have any secrets anymore.

Seven hundred and eighteen people had "liked" the page, and nearly as many anti-Tara comments had been posted. Most were the incoherent, rambling rants of Lone Star Nation members, but a few members of the Ark had discovered the site and chimed in, too.

A pox on the infidel who dares to steal our meat and guns! The True Texans shall triumph!

Tara Holloway must be stopped!

Repent now, Tara, or live forever in hell!
Damn. My enemies had joined forces.

On the bright side, I'd gone viral and achieved a level of popularity I'd never managed to muster in high school.

CHAPTER TWENTY-FOUR

$\mathcal{C}$ourting Trouble

At two o'clock, Nick opened his door and stepped across the hall, leaning against my doorjamb, arms crossed over his chest. He said nothing, just flicked his eyes to the clock and back.

Time to leave for the hearing on the Ark case.

I grabbed my briefcase and slung my purse over my shoulder. Together we headed down the hall.

"Sorry I jumped on you yesterday," I said, keeping my voice low as we passed the other offices. No sense giving our coworkers any grist for the gossip mill.

Nick kept his eyes locked straight ahead. "It was my fault. I come on a little too strong sometimes."

"A little?"

"Okay, a lot. Sometimes I'm a big old jackass."

"A jackass who's hung like a horse?"

He cut his eyes and a grin my way. "Yeah."

We rounded up Eddie and headed to the courthouse. Twenty minutes later, the three of us made our way past a crowd of Ark members in the hallway. Some of them held the signs they'd carried at the earlier protests. What the heck did they think this was, a football game? They were arguing with deputies, upset that they'd been denied seats in the courtroom.

"Full is full, folks," the deputy said. "You can't be standing out here in the hall. I'm going to have to ask you to head on out." He spread his arms and walked slowly forward, effectively herding the crowd back into the elevators.

We walked into the loud, packed courtroom. Members of the Ark crowded butt cheek to butt cheek along the wooden benches, talking animatedly among themselves. As we headed up the center aisle, a woman's voice hissed from behind us. "Jezebel!"

I turned and scanned the faces. Judy Jolly glared at me from a couple rows back. I fought the urge to respond with, "Takes one to know one, bee-otch!"

"Who's that?" Eddie asked.

"Judy Jolly," I said. "She's one of the Ark's greeters."

"I'll get in touch with the audit department," Eddie said. "I'll make sure she's greeted with an audit notice ASAP."

We continued to the front, taking seats at the counsel table with Ross O'Donnell. Fischer and his team of lawyers crowded around their table ten feet away, heads down in a huddle as they consulted. Former Attorney General Tim Haddocks was at least going through the motions today, his cell phone tucked away in the breast pocket of his suit jacket.

I pulled out my cell and sent a text to Daniel. *Nice tie.* I'd bought him the darn thing for his birthday.

When his phone vibrated, he pulled it out of his pocket and read the message. He sent a discreet smile my way.

I eyed Ross. No need to ask him how things looked for us. The death pall on his face said it all.

I glanced back at the crowd. Behind us sat a pack of reporters from the local television stations and newspapers, including one from the local weekly alternative magazine who sported three silver nose rings and shoulder-length blondish dreadlocks. Trish sat on the front row, dressed in a pink suit, her legs crossed, her short skirt riding up on her thighs. She was gazing in my general direction, though not directly at me. Her face bore an expression most accurately described as predatory.

I followed her line of sight, realizing she had her eyes on Nick. He was looking over the case file and hadn't noticed her. Thank goodness. I scooted my chair back, blocking her view. If that bitch thought she'd sink her teeth into Nick, too, she had another think coming. Nick was mine. Well, not mine, exactly. But I was holding him in reserve.

Trish looked up at me. I forced a smile at her and raised a hand in greeting. She simply quirked her brows at me, then made a notation on the small pad of paper in her hand. I supposed it said something like "Die, Tara Holloway. Die!" Well, two could play that game. I uncapped my pen and wrote "butterscotch pudding sucks" on my legal pad.

Eddie cast a glance at my note, his brow scrunching in confusion.

"All rise." The bailiff instructed us to stand as the judge came through the private door that led from her chambers into the courtroom.

Judge Alice Trumbull was one of the few liberal judges in Dallas. In her sixties now, she had the round body, loose jowls, and demeanor of a bulldog. Also a tendency to snap and snarl. She bounded up to her bench in her black robe, motioning for those in the room to sit once she'd taken her seat.

Her clerk handed her the case file. As crowded as the court schedules were these days, it was likely the first time she'd seen the paperwork.

Trumbull glanced down at the counsel tables. She nodded in greeting to Ross before turning to the defense. "Awfully crowded over there, isn't it?"

The men looked up at her, Noah Fischer offering his most angelic smile.

Trumbull pointed a finger at him. "You're that guy from television."

Fischer nodded, beaming with pride. "Yes, Your Honor."

"From that commercial, right? How in the world did you manage to turn all those cartwheels in that taco costume?"

Fischer's expression turned from proud to perturbed. "Actually, I have a television ministry," Fischer corrected her. "The Ark Temple of Worship. We're on Sunday mornings at ten-thirty."

"My mistake." Judge Trumbull shot our table a wink before looking back down at the file. Apparently she knew exactly who Noah Fischer was. And, just as apparently, she wasn't impressed. But impressed or not, the legal doctrine of stare decisis would require her to follow established law. Her personal feelings couldn't enter into the equation.

Too bad.

She pulled out the documentation and scanned it over. "An injunction. Okeydoke." She looked back at the defense table. "I don't want to hear a bunch of squawking. Which one of you is going to argue?"

Daniel stood. "That would be me, Your Honor. Daniel Blowitz with Gertz, Gertz, and Schwartz."

"All right, Danny boy. Let's hear what you've got." She sat back, her hands folded over her plump stomach, as Daniel eloquently argued the case, beginning with the purposes of the equal protection clause, summarizing the relevant case law, then offering defense exhibit number one, Alicia's spreadsheet that listed the other megachurches and the salaries and benefits offered to their ministers.

Judge Trumbull took the document from Daniel and glanced down at it. "Numbers? I hate numbers." She tossed the spreadsheet onto the desktop in front of her. "Tell me in words what this document says, son."

"Yes, Your Honor," Daniel said patiently. He continued on,

summarizing the data on the spreadsheet, carefully choosing his words to make it sound as if the Ark were doing nothing unusual or inappropriate. "There are thirty-four churches in the United States with congregations and annual revenues similar to those of the Ark Temple of Worship. All of them provide benefits to their pastors similar to what the Ark has provided to Reverend Fischer and his wife. However, not a single one of these churches or their ministers have been pursued for taxes, nor have any of them been threatened with revocation of their tax-exempt status."

When Daniel finished, the judge said, "You've certainly done your homework, Mr. Blowhard."

Daniel didn't bother correcting the judge on his name.

She turned to Ross. "I hope you've got something good for me, too, Mr. O'Donnell."

Ross stood and did his best, offering some information that Nick had pulled together about the number of large churches who did not provide excessive benefits to their ministers. "Clearly, not all large churches divert such enormous sums to their minister's personal living expenses," Ross offered. "Only a very small number of them are misusing their funds this way."

The judge waved her arm dismissively as Daniel stood to rebut Ross's argument. "I know what you're going to say. Those churches are irrelevant because they're doing the right thing with their money rather than using it to pamper their pastor, and therefore they're not quote unquote 'similarly situated' to the Ark."

Daniel glanced back at the other attorneys at his table as if unsure how to respond. "That's not precisely how I would have put it, Your Honor," he said tentatively. "But yes, the churches noted by Mr. O'Donnell should not be taken into consideration because they do not have similar spending patterns to the Ark."

Trumbull shook her head before looking down at Ross. "I gotta give 'em that one, Ross."

Strike one.

Ross tried another tack now, noting the number of churches that had had their tax-exempt status revoked after they'd engaged in proscribed political activities. Though these churches had lost their tax exemption for reasons different than our reasons for pursuing the Ark, I hoped the judge would make a broad interpretation of the law and use these churches as a basis for finding in favor of the IRS.

"Tax-exempt status is intended to be a very limited privilege," Ross argued, "offered only to those organizations and entities that are willing to comply with the attendant restrictions, Your Honor. When a church allows its leader to use its resources for personal luxuries, those restrictions have been violated, just as those churches that have engaged in political activity have violated the legal restrictions."

Ross called me to the witness stand. As I stood from the government's table, both Nick and Eddie whispered words of encouragement, though Eddie's "go get 'em, tiger" held far more decorum than Nick's "give the bastard his due."

All eyes were on me as I walked across the courtroom. When I climbed into the booth, Judy Jolly jumped from her seat, pointed a finger at me, and shrieked, "Whore of Babylon!"

Trumbull banged her gavel. *BAM!* She eyed her bailiff and jerked her head toward Judy. "Get that woman out of here."

Judy Jolly struggled to pull free from the tight grip the bailiff had on her arm as she was led from the courtroom. "Get your hands off me!"

Her words only enticed a second bailiff to grab hold of her.

Once the doors closed on Judy, Trumbull pointed her gavel at the gallery. "If anyone else pulls a stunt like that, you will find your butt in jail quicker than you can say 'Hail Mary.' Got that?"

CHAPTER TWENTY-FIVE

*T*estify

At the bailiff's instruction, I raised my hand and swore to tell the truth, the whole truth, and nothing but the truth. I looked straight at Pastor Fischer and loudly vowed, "So help me, God."

From the counsel table, Ross asked me to list Fischer's personal expenses that had been paid for by the church and given rise to the IRS investigation. "My pleasure, sir," I said to Ross.

I raised the thick, stapled document in my hand so that those at the defense table, the reporters, and the Ark members could see it. The document was two hundred pages thick, documenting each and every personal expense the Ark had paid on behalf of Noah and Marissa Fischer over the past few years. Luckily for Nick and me, Viola could type a hundred and twenty words a minute and had assembled the document for us. Eddie had to promise her an extra vacation day in return, but it was worth it.

The attorneys at the defense table had been huddled, whispering. Daniel stood now. "Your Honor, we object to this testimony. The case law involving churches that lost their tax-exempt status for violating the restrictions on political activity are not comparable to the Ark's situation. The issue is covered at length in our brief." Daniel motioned to the file sitting in front of Judge Trumbull. "If you'd like to take a look, you'll see that the law is well established."

Judge Trumbull's jowls tightened as her jaw tensed. She said nothing for a moment, simply staring at Pastor Fischer. Clearly, she didn't like the man. But just as clearly, she recognized the law was in his favor.

"Good idea," she said finally, turning her attention back to Daniel. "I'll take a gander at your brief while Special Agent Holloway tells us about the personal expenses the Ark paid for its pastor. If I decide her testimony about the expenses is irrelevant, I'll instruct my court reporter to strike it from the record."

The angry faces at the defense table made it clear they didn't like her decision. But there was nothing they could do about it.

Ross stood again. "Agent Holloway, could you please read into the record a description of each personal expense that the Ark paid for Mister Fischer, as well as the amount?"

"Gladly," I replied. I looked down at the document. "Item one. Dinner for Mister Fischer and his wife at Bijoux restaurant. Three hundred eighty-four dollars and sixteen cents." I looked up and shot a pointed look at Fischer. "Including the six-dollar tip."

Trumbull looked down at the pastor now. "You stiffed the waiter? That doesn't sound like the Christian spirit to me."

Silly that he'd been so cheap, really, since it wasn't even his money he was using to pay the food bills.

"Perhaps his Christian spirit had been dulled by the spirits he had consumed," I offered. "The bill includes a charge of ninety dollars for several glasses of single-malt scotch."

Trumbull glanced down at the defense table and raised an eyebrow.

Daniel stood. "The small tip was likely a math error, Your Honor."

"Not likely at all," I replied, looking over at Fischer. "The list will clearly show that Mister Fischer routinely left far less than the standard tip, even when the restaurant receipts showed no charge for liquor and he was presumably sober."

Daniel sat back down, realizing that pushing the issue would only make his client look worse.

I continued on, the court reporter typing along on her machine as I spoke. "Item two. Two La Perla bra and panty sets purchased at Neiman Marcus. Two hundred sixty-seven dollars and thirteen cents."

The judge looked down at Fischer again. "Suffering a gender identification issue, Mister Fischer?"

The reporter from the alternative paper snickered.

Fischer's face blazed, though his eyes remained icy. "That purchase was made by my wife, Your Honor."

"She can get a three-pair package of panties at Wal-Mart for $4.99," the judge said. "That's where I get mine. They cover my bum pretty darn well, despite its size."

Fischer didn't respond, realizing the judge was goading him. I'd never seen Judge Trumbull act like this. Judges normally tried to appear as unbiased as possible. Then again, her salary was paid by federal tax dollars. She probably didn't appreciate it when people failed to pay their due.

While the court reporter typed her fingers to the bone, I continued on, ad nauseam, for nearly three hours, noting each and every personal expense the Ark had paid on Fischer's behalf. Initially, Daniel objected to my testimony regarding a number of the expenses, arguing that some of the meals were church related since members of the congregation had dined with the pastor. But after I pointed out that only the Ark's largest contributors had been invited to the dinners and Judge

Trumbull overruled his objections, he eventually gave up and let me ramble on uninterrupted.

Several of the Ark members in the gallery eventually left the room. Apparently my litany wasn't nearly as fascinating as the self-serving sermons and laser light shows put on by their pastor every Sunday. But, then again, not all of us were born for show biz.

A few of Fischer's supporters who had openly glared at me when I'd taken the stand now bore bewildered expressions, apparently shocked to learn the full magnitude of personal expenses their church had paid for its pastor. Maybe next time they'd attend the Ark's business meetings, they'd make sure they were better informed before jumping to the conclusion that the government was the enemy and their pastor was a saint. Still, I doubted whether any of them had the guts to take a stand on the issue, to rock the boat and risk ostracism or retaliation. Yep, it would take a very brave person to point out that their beloved emperor wasn't wearing any clothes—or, in this case, that he was wearing clothes paid for with misappropriated funds.

When I finally finished, the judge, who'd been working a seek-n-find puzzle on her desk, asked if the defense would like to pose any questions to me. When Daniel declined, I climbed down from the witness box and returned to my seat at the counsel table

The judge looked down at her court reporter, giving her an apologetic look. "Strike Agent Holloway's testimony from the record."

The court reporter heaved a heavy sigh.

Trumbull looked from Ross to Daniel now. "I've read over your brief, Mr. Blowitz. You win this one, too."

I wasn't entirely surprised, despite the fact that Judge Trumbull had let me go on for so long. Ross had told us the argument was weak, the case law by far in Fischer's favor.

Strike two.

"Anything else?" Trumbull asked Ross.

Ross slowly stood and shook his head. "No, Your Honor."

"Mr. Blowfish?"

Daniel stood. "No, Your Honor."

Trumbull looked down at Fischer, simply staring at him a few moments before speaking. "In all my years on the bench," she said finally, "I have never been more sorry to issue a ruling than I am today. I agree with the IRS that all of these expenses were personal and should not have been paid by the church. But I'm sworn to uphold the law, even when I don't like the results. The case law interpreting the Constitution is clear. The IRS has violated the equal protection clause by singling out you and the Ark when they haven't pursued those other naughty pastors and churches, too." She banged her gavel once. *Bam.* "Injunction granted."

The gallery erupted in shouts of "Hallelujah!" and "Amen!" Some of the people stood and high-fived each other. Associate Pastor Michael Walters was not celebrating, though. He sat quietly on the aisle of the fourth row, his expression troubled.

Bam! Bam! Judge Trumbull banged her gavel again. "Quiet!" she hollered. She waved her gavel at the now silent gallery. "You people should expect more of your pastor. Why you let him get away with this behavior is beyond me."

Why did they let him get away with it? Because many of them, too, had benefited. Those in the room were the best heeled of the Ark's well-heeled parishioners, the elite few whom Fischer allowed into his inner sanctum, the indulgers in the Christmas Cristal and caviar. Many had attended the expensive dinners with the Fischers at the city's finest restaurants. Fischer's exoneration probably gave them a sense of relief, too. Still, I was pleased to see that not all of them appeared jubilant.

Tim Haddocks stood. "With all due respect, Judge, it's not appropriate for you to make such comments."

Trumbull's eyes narrowed at the former AG. Her nostrils, on the other hand, flared. "Are you telling me how to behave in my own courtroom?"

Haddocks opened his mouth as if to say something else, then thought better of it and sat down. "No, Your Honor."

"I didn't think so. Only an absolute moron would do that." The judge looked down at her desk, signed a document, and held it out to me. "This is probably little consolation, Miss Holloway, but here's the order to have the lien removed from your house."

I walked to her bench and took the paper from her. "Thanks."

"I've got to go pee now." With that, she left the bench.

Nick, Eddie, and I exchanged frustrated glances.

At the defense table, Fischer stood, turned around, and raised his hands to silence his congregants who'd begun chattering again the second the door had closed on Judge Trumbull. "The judge's decision wasn't just a victory for the Ark Temple," Fischer said in his best pulpit voice, "it was also a victory for God. Let's bow our heads and thank the good Lord that justice was done here today."

I felt like I was going to be sick.

Once the prayer had ended, Daniel stepped over to our table. "No hard feelings?"

I looked up at him. "You were just doing your job," I said. "It's just too bad you do it so well."

He gave me a wry smile.

Fischer walked over to our table then, smiling. "I'd like to offer a sign of peace," he said, holding out his hand to Nick, his chunky gold bracelet reflecting the overhead light. "All is forgiven."

Nick stood and took Fischer's hand. "Is it, now?"

Judging from the grimace on Fischer's face, Nick had taken a fairly firm grip. The two men shook hands, a glare of pure hatred like a laser firing from Fischer's eyes despite the forced smile on his lips. The pastor nodded curtly at Eddie and me. "God be with you." He returned to his counsel table, gave a quick wave to his team, and headed out the door.

As the courtroom emptied, Ross quietly gathered up the documentation and packed the documents in his briefcase.

Eddie stood, his cell phone in hand. "I'll call Lu."

I looked up at him, grateful he was willing to take the heat. "Thanks."

He headed out of the courtroom to find a quiet spot from which to phone our boss.

I sat with my eyes closed, trying to calm myself. I didn't like losing, especially to such a flagrant scofflaw. Justice had not been served today. The Lobo wouldn't be happy we'd lost the case. And I doubted God was pleased, either.

You're not happy about this, are You? I silently prayed. *I know You work in mysterious ways and all that, but how could You let this happen?*

A deep voice whispered in my ear. "This isn't over."

Was it God?

No, it was only Nick.

"What else can we do?" I asked, opening my eyes.

Before he could answer, something pink with butterscotch-colored hair appeared in my peripheral vision. I looked up at Trish, fighting the urge to wrap my polka-dot scarf around her neck and strangle her with it.

She looked down at me for a quick second, then tilted her head, smiling at Nick, and holding out her hand to him. Was it just my imagination, or did she also push her breasts forward? Her watermelons loomed over me. Oh, yeah. She'd definitely stuck out her chest.

"Hi, there. Nick Pratt, right? I'm Trish LeGrande. From the ten o'clock news?" The lilt in her tone meant she expected Nick not only to acknowledge her minor-celebrity status, but to be impressed by it, too.

Nick didn't stand but he shook her hand, simultaneously shaking his head. "Sorry. I don't watch the local channels much. I get my news on cable."

Ha! He'd slammed her. For me, I suspect. Yep, if I wasn't careful I could fall hard for this guy.

Cameras hadn't been allowed in the courtroom, so Trish held out a tape recorder. "Any comment, Tara?"

How about "Shove it up your ass?" I shook my head. "Nope. No comment."

She shrugged. "Whatever." She slid the tape recorder into her purse and pulled out her cell phone. She offered another smile, the expression more a challenge than a friendly sentiment. "Do you want to let Brett know how things turned out, or should I?"

She may not have hit me, but she'd dealt me an enormous emotional blow. I felt myself slump involuntarily.

Strike three.

Nick draped a protective and reassuring arm across the back of my chair. "Tara and I have some important things to discuss," he said, looking up at Trish. "So if you've got time to contact Brett, I'm sure she'd appreciate it."

Trish tossed her head, looking from Nick to me and back to Nick, her eyes assessing the two of us. "Okay. See you."

When Trish had gone, I looked Nick in the eye. "Thanks for that." My voice sounded as weak as I felt.

"She's not half the woman you are, Tara."

I held my palms in front of my chest, fingers splayed. "She's four times the woman I am."

"Her chest, you mean?" Nick leaned closer in to whisper, "I'm an ass man, myself. You've got her beat in that department." He pushed my raised arms back into my lap. "Hands down."

CHAPTER TWENTY-SIX

When God Closes a Door, Somewhere He Opens a Window

Defeated and furious, Nick, Eddie, and I walked back to the office.

"How'd things go?" Viola called from her desk as we stepped off the elevator.

"We lost," Nick spat.

"Damn," Viola said. "How'd Lu take it?"

"Not well." Eddie shook his head. "I hated to disappoint her in her condition."

"It's not like you had a choice," I said.

"Maybe you could shoot the guy," Viola suggested to me.

I must've hesitated just a second too long because Eddie turned to me, put his hands to his head, and hollered, "Don't shoot anybody!"

"I'm not shooting anybody! Sheez!" Not that the thought hadn't crossed my mind. "Who wants to hear Vi complain about the paperwork?"

Nick and I headed on to my office. I plopped into my desk chair while he took a spot at the window, looking out on the late-afternoon traffic downtown.

"What now?" I asked.

"I don't know about you," Nick said, "but I could go for a beer or two. Or ten."

"Did I hear you say you're going out for drinks?" Josh appeared in my doorway, his expression hopeful.

Nick looked from Josh to me then back to Josh again. "Yeah. And you're the designated driver."

Despite the fact that he'd have to refrain from alcohol, Josh's face lit up. "Really?"

"Bring all your gadgets," Nick instructed him. "We may do some spying later."

"Cool!" Josh scurried off to gather his stuff.

"You sure you want him tagging along?" I asked Nick. The last thing I wanted to do on a Friday night was spend time with Josh. Sure, the guy's technical skills came in handy now and then, but overall he was still an annoying little twerp who never offered to share his Twinkies. He seemed to think Nick hung the moon, though, like a kid brother who looked up to an older sibling.

Nick shrugged. "Josh is harmless. Besides, we might need him for tech support."

Our coworker returned with his keys and a box full of spy equipment.

"Don't you have some work of your own to do?" I asked Josh, making a last-ditch effort to exclude him.

"Nothing I can't work on later at home." As the office's reigning computer geek, Josh was primarily assigned technical tasks, such as decrypting files, which could be done after hours and gave his schedule some flexibility.

Looked like I was stuck with the guy for the time being.

We bade Viola and Eddie good-bye and made our way out to the parking lot. After Josh bleeped the door locks, I climbed into the back of his tiny silver Honda. Good thing I was short. The backseat had little leg room.

Josh thrust the box at me. I took it and set it on the seat
next to me, sorting through it. The box contained the minibinoculars he'd used to zero in on the protesters, a sporty black
wristwatch with a built-in camera for still shots, and a writing
pen equipped with a video camera and audio recorder. I also
found a small GPS tracking device that was less than an inch
square, a body wire, and a micro ear device that, according to
the box, would allow the wearer to clearly hear conversations
taking place in a whisper up to thirty feet away.

None of the equipment was government issued. Then
again, we weren't exactly on an official government mission
anymore, were we? Nope. We were like the Blues Brothers.
On a mission from God.

After everyone was settled, Josh asked, "Where to?"

Nick glanced back at me. "What do you say we see the
women of the Ark off for their weekend retreat?"

I shrugged. "Why not?" It might be overstepping after
our loss in court today, but what the hell. With Brett in Atlanta, it wasn't like I had anything better to do tonight.

We swung by a convenience store, where Nick picked up
a six-pack of Shiner Bock for himself and a four-pack of
wine coolers for me. Josh settled for a root beer.

Nick gave Josh directions to the Ark. Half an hour later,
we were sitting in the lot, strategically parked between two
other cars a few rows back where we wouldn't be as notice-
able. I'd removed my scarf and blazer and put on my sunglasses and the shredded blond wig. Nick, too, had donned
sunglasses and removed his jacket. He'd also slipped on his
white cowboy hat.

Three charter buses lined the front curb. Dozens of women
milled about with their suitcases and overnight bags, looking
for seatmates, their excited chatter carrying across the lot. I
recognized a few of them from the courtroom. The bus drivers helped the women load their bags into the cargo bays
on the sides of the buses. I envied them, going away for a relaxing weekend. I could hardly remember the last time I'd had
the chance to unwind.

We saw Amber Hansen among the throng, her fair-haired son in the arms of an older woman with auburn hair the same color as Amber's, presumably her mother. Amber gave the woman a kiss on the cheek, her son a dozen smooches all over his face. He squirmed and giggled. Whether or not he was Noah Fischer's son, I had to admit the kid was adorable.

Judy Jolly had the megaphone in her hand again, calling out instructions to the crowd. "Get your luggage stowed, ladies, so we can be on our way!"

The Ark's limo rolled up then, the women turning and applauding as Pastor Fischer and his wife stepped out. He raised a hand. "Now, now," he scolded playfully. "I'm just a mortal man. Let's save our praise for God."

What a bunch of hooey. The guy clearly loved the attention.

The limo driver removed two Louis Vuitton suitcases from the trunk and loaded them onto the first bus. Pastor Fischer gave his wife a hug and a quick kiss before holding out a hand to help her climb into the bus. No easy feat in her four-inch Prada peep-toe pumps.

Thou shalt not covet, I reminded myself yet again.

"Do you think we should be doing this?" I asked. "We haven't been authorized to continue the case."

"We haven't been told not to, either," Nick replied.

"True. But I'm sure Eddie and Lu assumed that the case was over once we lost in court today."

Nick shot me a pointed look. "Since when did you become so concerned about following the rules?"

Okay, I admit. I haven't always followed the letter of the law. Such as when I'd smuggled Nick, who at the time was a wanted fugitive, into the U.S. Still, I only went rogue when the situation demanded it. Nick had been the key to bringing a murderer to justice. I'd had to bring him back across the border to prevent the deaths of more innocent people. The ends justified the means.

But Fischer? He wasn't a murderer. He was greedy, sure. An egotist with a strong sense of entitlement. Maybe even a con artist. But it was only money at stake here, not lives. And given that he'd apparently complied with current law, screwed up though it was, I wasn't entirely sure I was comfortable following him around like this.

"I'm just wondering if we're taking this too far," I said. "Maybe taking it too personally, too."

Nick frowned. "You wimping out on me?"

"No!" Tara Holloway never wimps out.

Finally, the buses were loaded. The limo pulled away, turning down the long drive to the parsonage, while the buses eased away from the curb and headed toward the freeway entrance ramp.

"That was a waste of time," I said, downing the remains of my second wine cooler.

"I think it's too soon to tell," Nick said. He held Josh's miniature binoculars to his eyes, watching the parsonage. "While the cat's away, our little church mouse may decide to play."

"His plaything is on the bus with the cat," I reminded Nick. "We saw Amber get on."

Nick removed the binoculars and glanced back at me. "Maybe he's got more than one toy."

Josh looked from me to Nick. "What are y'all talking about?"

Nick voiced his suspicions about Amber Hansen's son.

"Really?" Josh said, his blue eyes wide. "You think Fischer cheated on his wife?"

"We may never know for sure," Nick said, "but it's worth keeping an eye on him, for a little while longer at least. If he does something stupid, we may be able to use it to our advantage." Nick put the binoculars back to his eyes and aimed them again at the parsonage. "Bingo. The garage door is opening. Looks like our tomcat is going on the prowl."

In the distance, Fischer's white Infiniti M56 coupe eased through the tall iron gates that surrounded the parsonage. The car continued on, pulling down the long drive and onto the street.

"Follow him," Nick told Josh, "but hang back a bit so he doesn't catch on."

Josh pulled onto the street, following Fischer at a distance as he eased onto the highway. Fischer continued on, eventually merging onto Interstate 20, heading east. We kept after him, even when he left the city limits, passed the extensive suburbs, and kept right on going.

"Where do you think he's headed?" Josh asked.

Nick shrugged. "We'll just have to wait and see. How are we on gas?"

Josh glanced down at the gauge. "Half a tank."

I knew this stretch of highway well. This was the very road I took when I went back home to Nacogdoches to visit my mom and dad. Several towns lay ahead, mostly small ones. But a few larger ones sat out this way, too. Tyler. Longview. Shreveport, Louisiana.

I couldn't think of any obvious reason Fischer would be heading in this direction. It was possible he was planning to spend the weekend at one of the lakes in east Texas. They were popular vacation spots for fishermen and families looking for an inexpensive getaway. Some of the smaller towns out this way were known for their antiques shops. Shreveport offered several casinos and drew a sizable number of Texans across the border into Louisiana every weekend.

I began to squirm in my seat. The two wine coolers had filled my bladder to capacity. But I knew we couldn't stop or we'd risk losing Fischer's trail. I crossed my legs tight and tried to think dry thoughts.

We continued on for three long hours and drove past the tourist information center that sat on the other side of the highway, welcoming visitors from Louisiana into the Lone Star State. A quarter mile later, we passed the sign that read WELCOME TO LOUISIANA, the sentiment expressed a second time just below in French. BIENVENUE EN LOUI-SIANE.

"How far does I-20 go?" Josh asked.

"South Carolina," I replied, praying Fischer would stop

before then. If he didn't, I just might have to throw myself from the car.

I was in luck. Shortly after we reached the Shreveport-Bossier city limits, he took an exit. We followed him more closely now, not daring to risk losing him after coming so far. It was after eight o'clock now, dusk setting in. Josh kept his car lights off as long as he dared, but finally had to switch them on.

Fischer continued down a major north-south thoroughfare. He slowed as he drove past a construction site where an older building had apparently been razed, then turned down a side street that flanked the fenced-in building zone. He pulled to a stop just after he turned. Nick and I ducked down in our seats as Josh drove past him.

Josh pulled into the parking lot of a doughnut shop a block down and cut his lights and engine. Nick and I sat up and looked back at Fischer's car. The interior light came on as he opened the door and stepped out. He walked over to the construction site and stopped, looking in the fence.

"What's he doing?" Nick asked.

"Heck if I know," I said.

Josh shrugged.

Fischer continued walking along the fence, eventually disappearing from our sight when he rounded the corner. I debated running inside to use the restroom, but I was afraid Fischer might return quickly and I'd be left behind. I crossed my legs in the other direction to see if that would help. It didn't.

A few minutes later Fischer came back around the corner and returned to his vehicle. Josh started his car and we eased onto the road, following Fischer again. We passed the construction site.

A large white sign was posted on the fence. FUTURE HOME OF THE ARK TEMPLE OF WORSHIP—SHREVEPORT.

CHAPTER TWENTY-SEVEN

$\mathscr{C}$hecking In

"Another Ark?" Nick spat. "What's Fischer doing, selling franchises?"

So the Ark planned to further expand its reach and potential resources. Noah Fischer was building himself quite an empire, his own earthly kingdom. The sky was the limit.

Fischer returned to I-20, heading east again, though he drove only a couple of miles before exiting again. We followed him as he turned into the front drive of the luxurious Horseshoe Hotel and Casino.

"A casino?" I asked. "Isn't gambling supposed to be a sin?" In fact, greed was one of the seven deadly sins, the focus of Fischer's current sermon series. Yet here he was at a casino. Then again, the Horseshoe boasted one of the nicest hotels in town. Maybe he planned to use the hotel facilities only and forgo the gambling.

We held back and watched as Fischer pulled into the valet

area. The car's trunk popped open like a gaping maw, revealing a Gucci overnight bag. A uniformed valet opened the driver's door and took Fischer's keys, while a bellhop removed his luggage from the trunk. The pastor headed inside. The bellhop followed with his bag. Poor guy. Given the expensive luggage, he'd probably be expecting Fischer to bless him with a generous tip. He was in for a rude surprise.

"What should I do?" Josh asked.

"Grab your spy gear," Nick said, "and follow him."

I handed Josh the wristwatch and writing pen, but left the remaining items in the box. The micro ear would be too obvious and, since Josh wouldn't try to engage the man in conversation, there was no need for him to strap on the wire.

Josh slid the pen into his breast pocket, clipping it in place, checking to make sure the tiny camera lens was facing outward. He fastened the watch on his wrist. "Ready."

"We'll park in the garage," Nick told Josh. "Call or text us and let us know what's going on."

Josh hopped out of the car and headed down the sidewalk and into the building. Nick climbed out of the passenger seat, circled around the back of the car, and slid into the driver's seat.

"You okay to drive?" I asked him.

"Yeah," he said. "I've only had half a beer. Once Fischer was on the go, I figured it was best for me to stay sober." He'd been much smarter than I had.

Nick pulled into the parking garage, circling up and then back down until we had a choice spot near the exit where we could see the main doors into the lobby and also leave quickly in case we needed to follow Fischer again.

"I've got to run to the ladies' room," I told Nick. My bladder had reached critical mass.

"Make it quick," he said, "and make sure Fischer doesn't see you."

"Got it." I reached into Josh's box of tricks and picked up the tiny GPS device, noticing it had a magnet on the bottom.

"Should I sneak into the valet area and put this on Fischer's car?"

Nick dipped his head in agreement. "Sounds like a plan."

First things first. I hurried up the concrete ramp and through the doors that led from the parking garage into the casino's small array of shops. Luckily for me, there was a women's restroom nearby. I ducked inside and quickly did my business.

While I was washing my hands, I received a text from Josh. *Checked into hotel and went to room.*

I texted him back. *Keep an eye on the elevators. He may come back down.*

I returned to the parking garage and glanced around. The valet parking area was on the first floor where cars could be retrieved quickly for guests. I headed toward the area, keeping my head down as if looking for something in my purse to avoid eye contact with any of the young men parking the cars.

Fischer's Infiniti sat at the end of the row. I ducked between his car and the Mercedes parked next to it, lying down on my back and shining the flashlight app on my cell phone underneath the car to find the best spot to place the GPS. I tucked the device between two pieces of metal where it would be less likely to be dislodged should he drive the vehicle through a car wash or accidentally hit a curb.

"Can I help you, ma'am?"

Busted! I looked up to find a young man in a valet uniform standing at the front fender, looking down at me.

"Um . . . I dropped my lipstick," I said. "I thought it rolled under this car, but I can't seem to find it." Pretty quick thinking for a girl who'd drunk two wine coolers, huh?

The young man got down on his hands and knees and looked under the car. "I don't see anything."

"Silly me," I said, whipping the lipstick out from my purse. "Here it is!"

Before he could think too much of my odd behavior, I stood, thanked him for his help, and scurried back to Josh's car on the other side of the garage. This time, I took a seat up front.

Nick and I sat quietly for a few minutes, listening to a country-western station on the radio and watching the lighted, scrolling sign in front of the casino.

SHREVEPORT'S BEST BUFFET.

LOOSE SLOTS—98% PAYBACK.

$5 BLACKJACK.

Too bad we couldn't go inside and sample the buffet, maybe play a little Texas hold 'em.

"You think we'll learn anything that'll help the case?" I asked.

Nick glanced my way. "You never know."

"I hope we don't end up working on a Friday night for nothing."

He glanced my way. "Is this so bad?"

Honestly? It wasn't. But I couldn't very well admit to Nick that I enjoyed his company, could I? I chose to ignore his question. "You gamble much?"

"Occasionally," he said. "Been to a few bachelor parties in Vegas. Always end up losing my shirt."

Lost his shirt, huh? I wouldn't mind him losing his shirt right now. I'd seen what was underneath his shirt up close and personal when I'd first met him in Mexico. He'd been wearing nothing but a tiger-striped Speedo and a sexy grin. The guy had pecs like Rambo. Yummy.

"What about you?" Nick asked.

"What about me what?" Visions of Nick's naked pecs had mentally derailed me.

"Do you gamble?"

"Just slots and poker," I said. Alicia had once tried to teach me how to play craps, but I couldn't quite grasp the concepts. Of course, the five free drinks I'd downed made it hard for me to grasp much of anything, including the drinks. I'd ended up down fifty bucks and with amaretto-sour-soaked shoes. Since then I'd stuck mostly with the one-armed bandits. The machines were no-brainers and if I dropped my drink while seated on a stool, the only thing that would get soaked was the carpet.

Nick and I sat in companionable silence for a while, the windows down, listening to the soft rush of cars driving up and down the ramps of the garage, the occasional chatter of casino patrons making their way through the garage, and the chirp of a nearby cricket. At least I hoped it was a cricket and not the first in a plague of locusts about to descend on us.

Nick reached across the gearshift and palmed my knee, wrapping his fingers around my kneecap and squeezing.

"What are you doing?" Not that I minded. *At all.*

"I forgot my stress ball. I need to work off my tension."

His touch might have relieved his tension but it only made mine worse.

He squeezed once more. "Your knee's awful hard. What else you got?"

Oh, I could offer him some soft things to squeeze. But that would be wrong, right? I pushed his hand away. "Just deal with your stress the way the rest of us do."

"How's that?"

"Develop an ulcer."

A half hour later, Nick and I were sitting in the front of Josh's car, waiting for word from our coworker, when Fischer's Infiniti drove by right in front of us.

"That's Fischer!" I cried.

Nick cranked up the engine, waited for the exit gate to close behind Fisher's car, then eased out. "Call Josh. Let him know what's going on."

I dialed Josh's number and told him we were following Fischer.

"That can't be him," Josh insisted. "There's only one elevator bank that goes from the lobby to the rooms. I've been watching it ever since he went up and he hasn't come back down."

"Maybe he came down the stairs," I said. "I don't know. All I know is his car just drove by and Nick and I are going to follow him."

"What should I do?"

"Get out here!" I cried. "Now!"

Nick eased out of the garage, proceeding cautiously. Fischer's car was stopped at the end of the exit drive, waiting for the traffic signal to turn green. Nick pulled to the curb to wait. Josh stepped out of the casino, spotted us, and ran down the sidewalk toward us. He jumped in the backseat just as the traffic signal turned green and Fischer made a left turn onto the street. Josh barely had time to close his door before Nick floored the gas pedal and blew down the drive. The light ahead turned yellow.

"Hurry!" I cried. We'd tailed the guy for four hours. We sure as hell didn't want to lose him now.

CHAPTER TWENTY-EIGHT

Where's James Bond When You Need Him?

Nick turned left onto the street, tires squealing, just as the traffic signal cycled back to red once more. Luckily for us, there were no cops in sight.

Fischer took another left and pulled onto the bridge that crossed the muddy Red River. Once over the bridge, he took a right turn and continued on a couple of blocks before pulling into another parking garage, this one servicing Sam's Town Casino.

Nick pulled into the garage, tugging his white cowboy hat even lower on his head. Given that it was a Friday night, the garage was nearly full. Fischer had to circle up several levels before finding a spot. Josh and I ducked down and Nick punched the gas as we drove past Fischer's parked car. Nick pulled into an open spot near the end of the same row and quickly cut the engine.

In the backseat, Josh raised his head and peeked over the windowsill.

"Can you see anything?" Nick asked.

Josh glanced back at us, his brow furrowed. "A man just got out of Fischer's car," he said, "but it's not Fischer."

"What?" Nick leaned into the backseat, craning his head to get a look. I couldn't see anything but the pickup parked next to us. I grabbed the minibinoculars, stepped out of the car, and held them to my eyes as I peeped over the bed of the truck.

The guy walking away from Fischer's car was the same height with the same trim build as the pastor, but rather than Fischer's thinning white-blond hair, this guy had thick, dark hair and wore plastic-framed glasses. He was dressed in jeans, casual loafers, and a blue and white striped polo shirt.

What the heck?

I was confused until the man went to slide his keys into his pocket. The light in the parking garage glinted off a chunky gold bracelet on his right wrist. His left arm bore what appeared to be the same flashy Cartier watch he'd worn the day of our meeting. It didn't have a built-in camera like the spy watch Josh was wearing, but I bet it had cost twenty times more, at least.

I slid back into the car. "That's him!" I hissed. "He's wearing a toupee and glasses to disguise himself."

The toupee actually looked pretty good. I wondered where he'd bought it. Maybe the place would have a strawberry-blond beehive wig for Lu.

Josh watched through the back window of the car. "He's heading for the sky bridge."

"Go after him," Nick ordered.

Josh climbed out the car and hurried across the parking lot after Fischer. Nick and I watched as Fischer made his way down the glass-enclosed walkway that spanned the side street, leading from the garage to the casino. Josh followed forty feet behind, cleverly glomming on to a group of young guys to make it appear as if he were with them.

Ten minutes later, Nick received a text from Josh. *Fischer is playing slots. What should I do?*

Nick rolled his eyes. "What a newb." *Try the machines nearby,* Nick suggested. *Take some photos.*

A few minutes later, Josh texted again. *Free drinks!*

Josh seemed surprised by the casino's purported generosity to its players. What he didn't seem to realize was that the casino was playing him, plying him with drinks so he'd be looser with his money.

Shortly thereafter, we received another text from our coworker. *He's playing blackjack now.*

Join the table, Nick replied.

Josh texted back. *Don't know how to play.*

Nick groaned. "We've sent a boy to do a man's job." He sent another text to Josh. *You try to get cards that add up to 21. Follow the others.*

Nick and I sat for another half hour, waiting. The night had grown fully dark by then.

We sat silently side by side. I wondered if he was as acutely aware of me as I was of him. I noticed his smell, crisp deodorant soap and a hint of boot leather. I noticed the soft sound of his breathing, the rising and falling of his chest. I noticed the manly five o'clock shadow that had formed on his cheeks and jawline. God help me, I ached to touch it, to feel the roughness on my skin.

Guilt sliced through me. I was in a committed relationship with Brett. We'd agreed to date exclusively. It was wrong for me to have these feelings for Nick.

It was wrong, sure. But wasn't it also natural? Nick was good-looking, well built, masculine. What woman wouldn't be attracted to him?

But it was more than that, wasn't it? Nick and I connected on a deeper level. We both had an inner rebel, an almost insatiable ambition, an innate drive to right wrongs. I'd have these same feelings for Nick even if he weren't so physically attractive. The rock-hard pecs, the sexy grin, the whiskey-colored eyes . . . all of those things were really just a bonus, weren't they?

Brett and I appeared well matched, too, but on a much more superficial level. The things we shared—a love of ethnic foods, a fondness for British television, a strong sexual attraction—those were the icing on the cake. But I began to fear that there wasn't much cake underneath that icing. And I still wasn't certain whether there was anything between Brett and Trish. He'd denied it, of course, but maybe he just hadn't admitted it to himself yet. Or maybe he'd flat out lied to me.

I glanced over at Nick again.

He glanced back, removing his cowboy hat from his head and fanning himself with it. "What's the matter?"

Sheez. Could the guy read my mind? "Nothing."

"Liar." He placed the hat on the dashboard. "You're upset."

I frowned at him. "How would you know?"

"You chew on the inside of your cheek when you're upset."

Now that he'd mentioned it, I noticed the inside of my cheek felt raw.

I said nothing. He continued to eye me, but said nothing, too. He must've sensed that the thing upsetting me was a subject he shouldn't bring up. The guy really could read my mind.

"This is boring," I said. "Let's go inside and have some fun."

"What the hell," Nick said, pocketing Josh's keys. As we climbed out of the car, he reached out and snatched the scraggly blond wig off my head, putting it on his own, pulling it down over his ears.

"How do I look?" he asked as we headed across the parking garage.

"Like you should be touring with Metallica."

He held up his right hand and formed the devil's horns with his fingers. "Rock 'n' roll!"

We made a quick stop at the gift shop in the casino's lobby. Nick selected a Saints baseball cap and tee for himself, while choosing a black tank top with LADY LUCK spelled out in gold sequins for me. From a display near the register he grabbed a purple sequined eye mask and a green and purple jester hat complete with jingly bells, no doubt items left over from the spring's Mardi Gras festivities. Nick paid for the items with his credit card and we slipped into the nearby restrooms to change.

I emerged from the ladies' room with my work top stuffed into my purse. Nick shoved his dress shirt into my purse, too. The thing bulged, the seams threatening to split.

Nick had put the ball cap on sideways over the snarled wig and slid his sunglasses back on. Though I barely recognized him, the ridiculous look hardly made him inconspicuous. In my mask with my hat jingling every time I took a step, I wasn't exactly subtle, either. When I pointed this out to Nick, he said, "Ever hear of hiding in plain sight?"

We made our way down the colorfully carpeted hallway to the casino, the sounds and lights growing more vivid with each step. The burly guy working the entrance asked for my identification, ordering me to remove the mask so he could compare my face to the photo on my driver's license. Getting carded was one of the hazards of being short.

Once I passed muster, Nick and I continued on into the smoky, noisy casino.

The place comprised three floors, with gaming tables in the center of each floor and slots around the perimeter. We spotted Josh and Fischer at a table and quickly turned tail and headed up to the next level.

Nick steered me toward a craps table where a boisterous crowd was gathered. The group was an interesting cross section of society, including an older Asian couple in matching track suits, a stylish young black man in an expensive silk shirt, a heavyset middle-aged woman in a gauzy batik dress, and two thirtyish white men in jeans and casual golf shirts. One of the white men glanced over at Nick, a condescending smirk on his face as his gaze roamed over the wild hair and sideways hat.

Nick laid two twenties on the table, one in front of himself, the other in front of me. "My treat," he said.

"Thanks."

The dealer exchanged Nick's bills for colored chips, setting one stack in front of Nick, another in front of me. Nick picked up his stack and placed several chips on the felt. The other players likewise placed their bets. When I failed to place a bet, the dealer looked at me expectantly.

I looked up at Nick, holding a small stack of chips in my hand. "What should I do?" I'd never played craps before. The numbers and words on the felt were incomprehensible. *Field? Pass Line? Don't pass bar?* What the heck did they mean?

Nick guided my hand to a rectangle in which the word "Come" was written. He leaned down and whispered in my ear. "When a lady's with me, she's sure to come."

I didn't doubt his words for a second. I dropped my chips where he'd indicated.

One of the other players rolled the dice. When the dice stopped rolling, the people surrounding the table cheered. I had no idea what had happened, but when the dealer set another stack of chips next to mine, I realized I'd won and cheered, too.

A waitress stepped up to the table. The low-cut bodice of her skimpy black uniform left little to the imagination. "Cocktails?" she asked, offering a flirtatious smile to the male players at the end of the craps table.

Nick waited his turn while the other players, including me, placed their drink orders. He'd just opened his mouth when the waitress turned and walked away, tray held aloft.

"Wait!" Nick called after her. "You didn't get my order."

She kept on walking.

Nick turned to me, an expression of disbelief on his face. "What the hell just happened?"

Clearly, he wasn't used to being ignored by women.

"It's your disguise," I said. "You look like . . ." An idiot is what he looked like, but I couldn't very well tell him that, could I? I settled for, "Like you'd be a lousy tipper."

We played for several more minutes, every come bet I placed paying off. Nick hadn't been kidding.

The waitress returned with the drinks. When she handed me my red wine, Nick plunked a five-dollar tip on her tray, buying her attention.

"Gosh, thanks," she said, smiling up at him. "Can I get you something?"

I took a sip to hide my grin as Nick ordered a bourbon.

Fifteen minutes later, I was up by two hundred dollars but Nick had run out of chips. I tried to split my winnings with him, but he refused.

"You won it fair and square," he said, pushing my hand away, refusing the bills I'd offered.

"But I was betting with your money. And you told me what bets to place."

"True." He cocked his head, his eyes intent on mine. "So, you going to start doing everything I say now?"

"Hell, no."

"I didn't think so. Not sure I'd want you to." He shot me a wink. "Let's try the slot machines."

"My treat this time," I insisted, pressing a twenty-dollar bill into his palm.

The place was packed now. We wandered through the smoky haze, making our way up and down the aisles, having difficulty finding any available machines. We finally spotted a quarter slot along the back wall. The stool in front of it was unoccupied. Nick gestured for me to take the seat.

I stepped over to the machine, Nick trailing me. Just as I was about to sit down on the stool, the bald, elderly man seated at the adjacent machine stuck out a wrinkled, liver-spotted hand to block me, nearly burning me with the cigar stump gripped between his fingers.

"Back off," he spat. "I'm playing that machine." He jammed the button with his crooked index finger, ash falling from the cigar onto the seat of the stool. While the reels spun, he turned to the machine in front of him and punched the button to activate that device, too.

A sign on the wall overhead noted that the casino reserved the right to limit play to one machine per person. Still, the machine didn't seem to be paying off and I wasn't sure I wanted to sit next to someone smoking a stinky cigar anyway. Besides, thanks to August Buchmeyer, I'd had my fill of crotchety old men lately.

I let the old coot keep his precious machine, but I treated him to a raspberry. *Pfft.* He gave me one right back, nearly losing his dentures with the effort.

"Jackass," Nick muttered as we stepped away.

A woman playing a dollar machine three seats down pushed the button to cash out.

"Give it a whirl," Nick said.

I slid onto the stool as soon as the woman's butt cheeks vacated it, the pad still warm from her body heat. Nick stood behind me to watch.

After inserting a single, I reached up and pulled down on the arm. The machine emitted a loud *rat-a-tat-tat* as the reels spun, the images a blur before us.

The first line clicked into place. A red 7.

The second line clicked into place. Also a red 7.

I held my breath.

The final line clicked into place. Another red 7.

A loud buzzer sounded and a light on top of the machine began to spin.

"Holy moly!" Nick hollered. "You won twelve hundred dollars!"

The old man looked our way. The buzzer was too loud for me to hear what he was saying, but judging from his lips, he'd formed a string of curse words. I waggled my fingers at him.

Nick glanced his way and chuckled. "You reap what you sow, dude."

A uniformed attendant came over, congratulated me on my win, and led me to the cashier's cage to collect my payout. The cashier asked for identification and handed me a pen and a form to fill out.

"You'll owe taxes on your winnings," she said. "You know how the IRS is." She rolled her eyes.

"Yes, Marlene," I said, reading her name from the tag on

her chest. "I know exactly how the IRS is." I pulled one of my business cards out of my wallet and handed it to her.

She read the card and turned red, all business now.

I completed the form, turned it over to her, and collected my check.

Nick pulled his vibrating phone from the front pocket of his pants. Another text from Josh. Nick held his phone up so we both could read it.

Fudher id leavinf thw casini.

"What the heck does that mean?"

"Fischer is leaving the casino," Nick translated. "It also means Josh had one too many free drinks."

We headed downstairs and made our way up the ramp to the exit. Half a minute later, Nick's phone rang. Nick answered, putting it on speaker so I could hear, too.

"He's walking somewhere," Josh said, his voice slurred. "He's not going back to the parking garage."

"Keep following him," Nick said, "but for God's sake, don't let him figure it out."

We waited a few more minutes, then received another text from Josh. *He wenr in Hustlr clib.*

Despite the misspellings, it was clear what Josh meant. Fischer had gone into the Hustler Club, a topless bar a block away.

"I was wrong," Nick said. "Fischer's not a church mouse or a tomcat. He's a horn dog."

I smiled. "This was almost too easy."

CHAPTER TWENTY-NINE

$\mathcal{L}$ ike a Virgin

Keep following, Nick texted back to Josh.

As long as we were at the casino, we figured we might as well enjoy the buffet. We feasted until we risked a stomach rupture, then returned to the car, moving it to the parking lot of the Hustler Club where we could keep an eye on the front door. Flowing in and out was a steady stream of men, ranging from groups of fresh-faced college boys to solitary gray-haired geezers.

I put a hand on my too-full tummy. "I don't think I'll ever want to eat again."

"'All you can eat' is a marketing ploy," Nick teased, "not a challenge. I told you that second dessert was a mistake."

I hadn't been able to decide between the bread pudding and the chocolate pie, so I'd tried both. In retrospect, that may not have been a wise decision. The waistline of my pants now dug into my extended belly.

A half hour later, the doors flew open and two enormous bouncers with buzz haircuts tossed Josh outside. Josh stumbled forward, falling to his hands and knees in the entryway, a goofy smile on his face despite the manhandling he'd received. A group of businessmen walked up and one of them helped Josh to his feet.

Josh gave him some type of awkward salute in thanks.

"Josh!" I called out the window, waving my arm. "Over here!"

Josh looked our way and raised a palm in acknowledgment. He staggered to the car, pausing every few feet to put a hand on a fender to steady himself.

"Uh-oh," I said. "He looks wasted."

Josh fell against his car, then yanked the back door open. "Hey!" he hollered into the car. He fell into the backseat, his usual stiff movements now loose limbed. It took him three tries to close the door. The first time his hand slipped off the handle, the second time his leg was in the way. On the third attempt, he finally managed to get the door shut properly.

He stuck his head between the front seats, putting a hand atop each seat to support himself. "There were boobies everywhere!"

"Boobies?" I repeated, shooting him a stern look. "Seriously?"

Josh ignored me. "When you pay them money, the girls will dance at your table and bump up against you and you can see their boobies up close!"

I looked at Nick. He was fighting a grin.

"But you can't touch them," Josh said, holding up his hands as if to demonstrate, "or the bouncers will throw you out!"

"I take it you learned that the hard way," I sniped. "Really, Josh. You're what, thirty? You act like this was the first time you've seen breasts."

"It was!" Josh cried. "I'm a virgin!"

Nick lost the fight with the grin. "A virgin, huh? That explains so much."

"It certainly does." I turned back to Josh. "Did you get some good photos and video of Fischer?"

He gave an exaggerated nod, then lurched forward and made an odd sound. *Urp.*

Nick leaped out of the driver's seat, opened the back door, and pulled Josh across the seat and out the door again just in time for Josh to empty his stomach onto the parking lot.

"Lovely." I turned my head away, but unfortunately it didn't drown out the retching noise. Thank goodness he'd only had drinks and hadn't joined us at the buffet.

Several minutes later, when we were convinced Josh had completely emptied his stomach and perhaps even coughed up part of a spleen, Nick helped him back into the backseat, sliding the seat belt across him and clicking it in place. Josh promptly wriggled until the belt loosened a bit. He lay down across the seat. "Night-night."

Nick climbed back into the driver's seat and turned to me. "What now? Should we head back to Dallas or get a hotel room?"

I wasn't sure I was up for a three and a half hour drive back to Dallas. After sitting most of the evening, first in the car and then in the casino, my butt was asleep and my back was sore. But I wasn't sure a hotel was a good idea, either. I didn't have a toothbrush or makeup with me, let alone a clean pair of panties to put on in the morning. But I did have a spare toothbrush and panties at my parents' house, which was only an hour and a half drive away. Besides, my mother had been begging me to come for a visit.

"We can stay the night with my parents," I said. "Head west. I'll show you where to turn."

I hoped my mother had taken her estrogen pill today. Seeing Nick might send her into another hot flash.

Josh snored in the backseat as Nick ditched the wig, I ditched my hat and mask, and we headed out toward Nacogdoches.

"What're you going to do with your winnings?" Nick

asked. "Buy yourself some diamond earrings? Put a hot tub on your patio? Maybe take a vacation in Hawaii?"

"Nope, nope, and nope." I told him I planned to donate the funds to the animal welfare group that was taking care of Buchmeyer's chickens. "And maybe call a handyman out to fix my creaky stair."

Nick eyed me for a moment, a soft smile playing about his lips. "You and that chicken had something real special, didn't you?"

The low-gas warning light came on. Nick pulled into a Texaco station and filled the car.

Josh raised his head. "Are we there yet?" He put his head back down and was asleep again before I could answer.

Gassed up now, we turned down the highway that led to my hometown. As we approached the northern outskirts of Nacogdoches, the lights of a roadside honky-tonk shined up ahead. Judging from the number of pickups in the parking lot, the joint was jumping tonight.

When we reached the entrance of the gravel parking lot, Nick turned in, raising a cloud of dust behind us. "I want to celebrate," he said. "Let's go scoot our boots."

I wasn't wearing boots. Besides the sequined tank top, I was still dressed in my suit pants and business loafers. But properly dressed or not, Tara Holloway was no party pooper.

Nick grabbed his cowboy hat from the dash and we climbed out of the car, making our way under the Christmas lights that were strung from the metal roof of the prefab building to a nearby oak tree. The sign on the side of the building indicated the place was currently called the Bar None, but in earlier incarnations it had been known as Uncle Rowdy's, Junior's Gin Joint, and Nasty Nellie's. I'd drunk my first beer here. Tasted like bull piss. My brother happily took it off my hands and bought me a margarita instead.

Nick handed a ten-dollar bill to the man at the door to pay our cover charge and we headed inside. Despite the fact that the place bore a new name outside, the inside hadn't changed much over the years, if at all. The same band graced the stage, performing the same songs they'd played thousands of times. The same scarred wooden tables sat scattered haphazardly around the room, the same mismatched chairs surrounding them. The same mechanical bull stood in the corner. The same rednecks and roughnecks milled about. The place smelled the same, too. A mix of beer and sawdust, like the cage of an alcoholic hamster.

Nick and I found a table near the bar and staked our claim.

"What are you in the mood for?" he asked.

If we were in Dallas, I'd order an appletini. But place an order like that here and you were likely to get your ass kicked. "Margarita, on the rocks with salt," I said, ordering the most exotic drink the place offered.

As Nick stood at the bar, the horrendous wig now gone, several women glanced appreciatively his way. Who could blame them? A tall woman in tight jeans with breasts nearly tumbling out of her halter top sidled up to him, put a hand on his shoulder, and whispered in his ear. He gave her a smile, but shook his head. He said something I couldn't make out and jerked his head my way. The woman looked me over, quirked her brows to indicate she wasn't much impressed, and walked away.

Skank.

Nick returned with our drinks. I sipped at my margarita. Not bad.

Nick took a pull at his beer. "I can't wait to see those photos," he said. "Fischer's going to shit a brick."

I ran my finger around the rim of my glass, collecting large grains of salt. "What do you think will happen?"

"Gambling and ogling titties?" Nick said. "At worst, we'll put an end to his good times. At best, the guy will be seen for the fraud he is and removed from his position as pastor."

CHAPTER THIRTY

*E*ight Seconds to Qualify

A young guy who appeared barely old enough to drink climbed onto the mechanical bull in the corner. His friends gathered round the makeshift pen, urging him on, while the operator handed him a clipboard and a pen. A full release and waiver, no doubt. You break your neck, don't blame us.

We watched as the operator started the bull. It began to move up and down slowly, regularly, hardly more than a person would experience on a trail ride. The boy motioned with his hand for the operator to up the pace. The bull now bucked in an irregular rhythm, turning first one direction then the other. The kid made a decent showing, hanging on for a good five seconds before losing his balance and being thrown to the padded mat on the floor.

Nick turned to me. "You ever ride a mechanical bull?"

"Hell no."

He cocked his head. "I thought you were fearless."

"I am," I lied. "I just don't invite trouble." My thigh bore the wide, pink scar from my recent adventures in cockfighting. I didn't want to take on another animal, real or otherwise.

"Give it a try," Nick said, his eyes narrowed at me in challenge.

"Nope." I took another sip of my drink.

"I dare you," Nick said.

"Nuh-uh."

"I double dog dare you," Nick said.

"Yeaaah, no." I shook my head.

Nick leaned toward me, his face only inches from mine. "I triple dog dare you."

Just like the young boy in the beloved movie *A Christmas Story* who was dared by his friends to lick a frozen flagpole, I knew that backing down in the face of a triple dog dare would forever brand me as a wuss. "A triple dog dare? Well, now, that changes everything. You're on."

I downed the rest of my drink, mustered up my courage, and stood from the table. Nick followed me over to the bull, even paid the cost of my ride and intertwined his fingers to form a step for me to boost myself onto the automated beast.

After signing the waiver, I closed my eyes in quick prayer, grabbed the rope with both hands, and tried to relax. I'd attended enough rodeos to know that the best way to stay on a bull or bronc was to become one with the animal, to go with its flow.

A few people gathered around, mostly men.

"Twenty bucks says she falls off in under three seconds," a man said to Nick.

Nick looked my way and shot me a wink. I was on a roll tonight. Nick just might win this bet. He turned back to the man, opened his wallet, and laid a twenty on the wooden rail surrounding the bullpen. "You're on."

"Ready?" the operator asked.

"Ready as I'll ever be," I replied.

I took a deep breath as the bull kicked on and began to dip forward. I leaned back in response, rolling forward as it reversed its motion. It was a bit like riding a teeter-totter. Of course the last time I'd been on a seesaw I'd been seven years old. A girl can forget a lot in twenty years.

Nick raised his white hat over his head and shouted, "Ride 'em, Tara!"

Encouraged both by Nick and my success thus far, I let go of the rope with my left hand and raised it above my head, pro rodeo style. "Crank it up!" I hollered to the operator.

The guy tipped his hat, called out, "You asked for it!," and turned the machine up higher.

The bull began to shift from left to right, then back again, sometimes faking one direction, then doing a three-hundred-and-sixty-degree turn in the other. While the operator eyed his stopwatch, I hung on, trying not to anticipate the bull's moves lest I be wrong and lose my delicate balance, letting myself rock and roll with the haywire actions of the machine.

I tried to count as the bull spun, and bucked, and gyrated under me.

One second.

Two seconds.

Three.

I felt like one of those inflatable figures that waved in the wind, bending first one direction then another as the bull maneuvered chaotically under me. I stayed on only by the grace of God.

Clang! Clang! The operator rang the cowbell that hung from a post nearby. "You got your eight seconds!"

The crowd cheered. All but the guy who'd placed the bet with Nick, that is.

"Woo-hoo!" Nick hollered, waving his hat in circles over his head before pocketing the twenty bucks he'd just won.

Eight seconds was the benchmark for qualifying in an actual rodeo and it was more than enough for me. I motioned for the operator to turn the machine off. It slowed and rocked to a stop. When I slid off the bull, Nick entered the ring and gave me a high five.

I looked up and poked a finger into his chest. "Your turn, buddy."

"Uh-oh." He grimaced. "I should've thought this through first."

I took his hat and his spot at the rail.

Nick signed the release and swung his long leg over the bull, shifting a bit as he settled himself. I watched as the bull began bucking. Nick moved with the bull, rhythmically undulating, his chest rising up and falling back, his back arching, his pelvis moving back and thrusting forward. Damn if it wasn't one of the sexiest things I'd ever seen a man do. The motion had me wondering how it would be to have him riding me, whether the expertise he showed riding this beast translated to the bedroom.

The crowd whooped and hollered as the intensity and action ratcheted up, yet Nick held on like a pro on the rodeo circuit. When his eight seconds were up, Nick kept right on going. I wasn't sure whether he was trying to show me up or show off for me, but I didn't much care. I was having a hell of a time just watching him ride.

"Shee-it," said the cowboy next to me, taking a drag from the cigarette in his hand. "That boy's got some talent, too." He turned to me. "You two are a matched set."

When the bull failed to throw Nick after thirty seconds, the crowd turned on Nick and began to root for the bull. There is such a thing as being *too good* at something.

When the bull executed five quick circles in a row, Nick began to tilt precariously to the outside and had trouble righting himself against the centrifugal force. The bull continued to spin, and Nick was eventually thrown clear. He somehow managed to land on his feet, but he was bent over, momentum carrying him forward. He staggered as he tried to right himself, moving closer and closer to the edge of the bullpen until he collided facefirst with the wooden rail.

A sympathetic "Oooh!" came up from the fickle crowd, which was on Nick's side once again.

I ran into the ring and over to him. He stood, his hand

over his nose, a trickle of blood running down his bristly cheek. A drop fell from his chin onto his shirt.

The woman in the halter top appeared with a stack of napkins and handed them to Nick. "Much obliged, ma'am," he said.

"Much obliged?" I rolled my eyes. "What is this, the old west?"

We left the ring, heading back to our table. We sat there for a few minutes, Nick tilting his head back and holding the napkins to his nose until the bleeding stopped.

"You think it's broken?" I asked Nick as he wadded up the napkins.

He shrugged. "Wouldn't be the first time."

CHAPTER THIRTY-ONE

$\mathcal{B}$oot Scootin'

Nick went to the men's room and cleaned himself up, returning to the table just as the band launched into their rendition of the electric slide. The chairs emptied as everyone hit the floor.

Nick held out his hand and cocked his head in the direction of the dance floor. "Let's go."

I probably should've resisted, but in Texas refusing to dance the electric slide was akin to refusing to say the Pledge of Allegiance. Besides, what could it hurt? It wasn't like we'd be dancing together. Line dancing was a group activity.

I took his hand and he led me onto the dance floor.

We began dancing the standard moves side by side, occasionally bumping elbows as the crowd closed in around us and we were forced closer and closer together. Nick had just as much rhythm on the dance floor as he'd shown on the mechanical bull.

It was very late by then, only an hour until closing time, and many of the patrons had left sobriety behind hours ago. While their drunken state made them less inhibited on the dance floor, it also made them far less graceful and less able to keep count or remember which direction they were headed next. A tall cowboy near the stage shuffled left when he should've gone right. He knocked into the woman next to him, who ricocheted off the woman next to her, who grabbed the shoulder of the man in front of her in an attempt to regain her balance. After downing untold pitchers of beer, the man could barely keep himself upright, let alone help the woman hanging on to him. His body buckled and he fell backward into her. The two of them went down hard. Without any means of escape, the tight crowd began to fall like dominos, people pushing and shoving, trying to remain on their feet but having little luck.

It was a country-western cluster fuck.

The crowd surged toward us like a wave. I looked around, but we were surrounded on all sides. There was no way out.

Nick wrapped an arm around my waist and pulled me tight against him. "Hang on!"

I latched on to Nick, hanging on for dear life lest I be crushed by the human tsunami rushing our way. He spread his legs slightly, bracing himself, swaying backward but somehow managing to stay on his feet when everyone around us fell. He held me upright, too.

Around us, people slowly pulled themselves to their feet, most laughing, a few others angrily pushing and shoving. Someone hollered "Catfight!" We turned to see Miss Halter Top and a shorter, pudgy woman, both on their knees in the middle of the crowd, engaged in a hair-pulling, face-clawing, cheek-slapping bitch match.

Classy.

A few people gathered around to cheer them on, while Nick and a couple other men made their way through the crowd to pull the women apart. When the woman in the halter top realized it was Nick who'd locked his arms around her and was dragging her backward off the floor, she smiled up at him and bellowed, "Hey, cowboy! Wanna get lucky?"

Nick deposited the drunk woman at a table with her friends and returned to me.

I looked up at him. "Gonna take her up on that offer?"

"Not even tempted."

I turned to head back to our table.

A warm, strong hand on my forearm stopped me. "Where you going?"

I looked up into Nick's eyes. "Back to the table."

"Come on, Tara," he pleaded. "I haven't been dancing in forever. Stay out here with me."

I looked away, knowing I'd have no chance of resisting him if I kept looking into his eyes. Unfortunately, my eyes now met those of the drunk but determined woman in the too-small halter top. She'd left her table and hung strategically nearby, like a wolf circling a sheep, clearly hoping to sink her teeth into Nick. I couldn't very well let that happen, could I? For his sake, mind you. Not mine. I looked back up at him. "Okay."

We danced a two-step, a lively polka, and a classic waltz, keeping a respectable distance between our bodies. Still, we were connected at three points—where my right hand rested in his left, where my left hand arced over his strong, muscular shoulder, and where his right palm cupped my hipbone.

My body ached for more contact, but my heart ached with indecision.

Should I keep things moving ahead with Brett?

Or should I give Nick a chance?

Even if I decided to give Nick a chance, the right thing to do would be to discuss things with Brett first, let him know I wanted to slow things down, keep my options open, see other people. It would be unfair to start something with Nick before extending Brett the courtesy of letting him know where I stood.

Did the fact that I was thinking this through mean I was seriously considering giving Nick a shot?

Hell, I didn't know. It could be the margarita talking.

Nick expertly maneuvered me around the dance floor. I tried to avoid eye contact with him, but it wasn't easy when he spun me around and I instinctively looked up at my partner to keep myself oriented. Each time I looked up, he was looking down at me, an expression on his face that was equal parts desire and pent-up frustration.

Just say the word.

The band played another two-step. Nick pulled me into a three-turn spin, then drew me back toward him, noticeably closer than before. Our knees and thighs bumped lightly as I tried to keep pace with his longer strides. I could feel the heat from his body against my chest, feel my nether regions swell with need.

He pulled me closer still, until I felt the hardness of his belt buckle pressed against my stomach. There was another hardness not far below, a long, thick hardness pressed firmly against my abdomen. The guy hadn't been kidding. He *was* hung like a horse.

Hi-ho, Silver!

Just say the word.

The band picked up the tempo, issuing a musical challenge. Nick, likewise, picked up the pace. I was virtually running backward now. No easy feat. When the band upped the tempo once more, several couples left the dance floor, unable to keep up.

"Come on, Tara!" Nick urged, smiling down at me. "We can do it!"

"I can't go any faster!"

"Oh, yeah? Well, I can!" Nick's hand moved from my waist to cup my rear as he hoisted me onto his hip.

Laughing, I wrapped my legs tightly around his hips and my arms around his neck, pressing my body to his chest and holding on for dear life as he spun around the dance floor with me clinging to him like a baby monkey. I felt the rumble of his chuckle in his chest, the stimulation causing my nipples to harden into almost painful points against him.

Laughing, I threw my head back. "I'm getting dizzy!"

He smiled down at me again. "You can do it!" He spun me around again.

With a final burst, the song ended. Nick came to a stop, but momentum carried me around a few inches before my body stopped moving. My breasts were now pressed directly against his chest, my legs wrapped around his back, my crotch now directly aligned with his.

I looked up at him, at those eyes that could drink a girl in, at the manly scruff on his cheeks, at those soft, warm lips that figuratively and literally begged to be kissed.

"Kiss me, Tara."

I couldn't help myself.

I closed my eyes.

I raised my lips to his.

And, at the last second, I turned my head.

Nick buried his face in my hair, groaning in my ear and pulling me even tighter against him, so tight it seemed he'd never let me go. "You're killing me, woman."

He pulled his head back, put his fingers on my chin, and turned my face to his.

Our lips were mere inches apart.

And he was closing in.

If he kissed me now, I'd kiss him back. I wouldn't be able to resist. It had taken everything in me to turn my head away from him a moment before. "Please, Nick," I whimpered. "Don't."

He emitted a sound that was half moan, half sigh.

I felt as if I were going to be ill.

I put my hands on his chest and pushed him away. He loosened his hold on me and I slid down his body to stand in front of him.

I couldn't help myself this time, either. I balled my hands into fists and banged them once against Nick's chest as hard as I could. A first kiss was supposed to be something special, not something that made a person feel sick with guilt and shame and remorse. Not that we had actually kissed. But we'd come close.

Too close.

How could I have let this happen? How could I have done this to Brett?

I was a skank. A slut. A whore. No better than the woman in the halter top who'd all but thrown herself at Nick and was now watching us with an amused smile on her face.

I turned and stormed toward the door, running away from Nick, away from my feelings.

Nick was hot on my heels. "Tara, wait." He reached out to grab my arm but I jerked out of his grip. I headed out the door and into the parking lot. Nick grabbed my arm again, more forcefully this time, pulling me to a stop. He stepped in front of me, holding me by the forearms, pinning them to my sides.

"Tara, I'm sorry. I didn't mean to—"

"Don't! You . . . you don't owe me an apology."

What had happened wasn't Nick's fault. Well, not entirely. Whether he'd intended to or not, he had seduced me. Slowly, subtly, and successfully. But I hadn't exactly resisted. I'd been weak.

He released my arms and stepped back. "Please look at me."

I turned my head up to face him, though he was a kaleidoscopic blur through the tears forming in my eyes.

He emitted a mirthless chuckle. "Now I know how Georgie Porgie felt."

"Who?" I croaked, my throat tight.

"Georgie Porgie, puddin' and pie. Kissed the girls and made them cry." He used his warm thumb to brush away a tear that had escaped my eye to run down my cheek.

I smiled, despite myself, and looked up at him. "We didn't kiss."

"Trust me," he said. "I'm acutely aware of that fact." He tilted his head and looked at me. "Would kissing me have been so bad?"

I shook my head. "It would probably be wonderful," I said, feeling myself choke up again. "That's the problem."

Nick pulled me to him and I rested my head against his chest, my eyes closed, listening to his strong, fast heartbeat. "What do you want, Tara?"

"Honestly?" I whispered, my eyes still closed. "I wish I could have you both. At least until I figure things out."

To Nick's credit, he didn't get angry. "I don't like to share," he said finally, "and I've got a suspicion Brett would feel the same way."

He stroked my hair once, then released me. "You know how I feel. I'd like to give us a shot. But it's your call, Tara."

"I . . . I just need some time," I said. Time to sort through my feelings, time to evaluate the situation, time to figure out what to do about all of this.

Nick stared intently at me for a moment, then released a long breath. He looked down at his boots then. "All right."

We walked back to the car. Josh stirred as we opened the doors. "Are we there yet?" he asked again.

"Almost," Nick and I said in unison.

CHAPTER THIRTY-TWO

*B*ed and Breakfast

It was two A.M. when we pulled up the gravel drive to my parents' Victorian farmhouse. Mom had saved the soon-to-be-condemned house years ago and, with my father's help and a grant from the local economic development office, she had fixed it up and turned it into a beautiful showcase. She'd furnished the place with antiques she'd snagged at yard sales, secondhand stores, and antiques shops, spending hours restoring the pieces herself. She financed the costs of upkeep by renting out the bottom floor on occasion for bridal and baby showers, rehearsal dinners, that kind of thing.

Nick parked Josh's car next to my father's pickup, and we helped our coworker out of the backseat. One of the barn dogs trotted up, wagging his tail but barking, too, as if unsure whether to welcome us or warn us off.

"Hey, Cooter," I said, giving the shepherd-mix mutt a quick pat on the head. "It's me, sweetie."

He gave my hand a quick swipe with his warm, wet tongue, then headed back to his blanket on the porch.

Josh swayed as we led him up the steps.

"Where are we?" he asked.

"My parents' house in Nacogdoches," I told him. "We'll crash here for the night and head back to Dallas tomorrow."

While Nick held on to Josh, I fumbled in my purse for my keys and opened the door.

My mother, apparently alerted by the barking dog, flipped on the light in the front hallway and stepped to the door, her expression alarmed. "Tara, honey! Is everything okay?"

"Everything's fine."

She pulled her white terry-cloth robe tighter around her and tied the belt when she noticed Nick and Josh behind me. "Hello, again, Nick. Good to see you."

He dipped his head. "Nice to see you again, too, ma'am."

I told her where we'd been, what we'd been doing, and apologized for waking her up.

"Nonsense." She waved a hand dismissively. "You know you're always welcome home no matter what time it is." She eyed Josh. "He sure looks worse for the wear."

"He's drunk," Nick said.

"And a virgin," I added.

"Tara!" Mom scolded. "Watch your mouth."

"'Virgin' isn't a bad word."

Mom shot me her don't-make-me-get-the-wooden-spoon look. She gestured for us to follow her. "We'll put Josh in your brothers' old room. Nick can have the guest room."

We led Josh through the living room, up the stairs, and into the bedroom my two older brothers had once shared. The walls still sported their Faith Hill and LeAnn Rimes posters, along with high school team pennants. We deposited Josh onto the bottom bunk of the bunk bed.

"Bunk beds. Cool." He looked up at Nick. "Want to hang a sheet from the top and make a fort?"

"Dear Lord," my mother said. "No wonder he's still a virgin."

Nick gently pushed Josh down onto the bed. "Go to sleep now. We'll make a fort in the morning."

"Okay." Josh rolled onto his side, facing away from us.

While I pulled off his shoes, Mom inserted the bed rail she used when my young nieces and nephews came to spend the night. "Can't have him falling out of bed and hurting himself."

She turned and looked up at Nick. "I'll show you to the guest room."

"Thanks."

Nick slid me one last look before following my mother out the door and down the hall.

I washed my face and brushed my teeth, grabbing a new toothbrush from the supply Mom always kept in the medicine cabinet for guests. I left it on the counter for Nick.

I stepped to the open door of the guest room, lit dimly by the bedside lamp. Nick sat on the end of the brass bed, pulling off his boots. He stood and unbuckled his belt, easing it out through the loops. My girly parts clenched in agony. His unintentional striptease was pure torture to me. Water-boarding would have been less cruel.

I rapped on the door frame to alert him to my presence. "Bathroom's all yours. I left a clean towel and toothbrush on the counter for you."

He ran a hand through his hair, looking tired now, defeated even. "I appreciate it."

I wanted to say something, anything, but given my state of uncertainty anything I might say would only complicate things further. I finally settled for a simple "good night" and went to my room.

I pulled my charger and cell phone out of my purse, wanting to ensure my mobile had plenty of juice for the drive home tomorrow. The voice mail icon indicated two messages. I punched the button and listened to them. Both were from Brett. The first asked me to return the call as soon as I got the message. In the second, he said he'd called my home number but got a message that the service had been disconnected. Oops. I'd forgotten to tell him I'd had my home phone shut off after all the hate calls I'd received. Brett also mentioned he'd stopped by my town house but I wasn't there.

Brett was in Dallas? He hadn't told me he was coming home for the weekend. If he had, I wouldn't have agreed to play spy on Fischer.

Why was he home? And why hadn't he given me advance notice?

I wasn't sure if he'd still be up this late, so I texted him instead of calling. *At parents' house in Nacogdoches. Let's touch base in morning.*

I slid out of my clothes and into a soft pair of shorts and a T-shirt. I climbed into bed and pulled the covers up.

I had two men in my life, but none in my bed.

Damn, but it felt awfully lonely.

When I woke the next morning, I heard a murmur of voices from the kitchen downstairs and breathed in the inviting aroma of fresh-perked coffee.

I checked my cell phone. No response from Brett yet. He must be sleeping in.

I went to the guest room and peeked inside. No Nick. The guy was an early riser. To be expected of a farm boy, I guess.

I took a quick shower, dressed in an old pair of jeans and one of my volleyball T-shirts from high school, and headed down to the kitchen. Nick, my mom, and my dad sat around the oval table, chatting and drinking coffee. Mom and Dad were in their bathrobes. Dad had the newspaper sports section spread out in front of him. Some things never change.

"Mornin', Miss Merry Sunshine," Mom said, getting up to pour me a cup of coffee.

I grunted in reply. I hadn't slept well, tormented alternately by feelings of guilt and images of Nick undressing.

Nick looked up and gave me a soft smile. He wore his jeans and boots, along with one of my father's Dallas Cowboys jerseys. "Your mother's washing my shirt."

Mom set the mug of coffee in front of me. "I'm not sure if the bloodstain will come out, but I put some hydrogen peroxide on it, gave it my best shot."

I half wondered if Mom offered to wash his shirt just so she could see his bare chest when he took it off.

"How does huevos rancheros sound?" Mom asked Nick.

He put a hand on his taut belly. "Very *bueno*."

Mom went for the can of grease she kept in the cabinet.

Nick raised his coffee mug to his mouth, drawing my eyes to his lips. Those warm, soft lips. The lips that had almost kissed me last night. The lips that I longed to *actually* kiss.

I snapped out of my trance to find Nick's gaze on me. I turned to my father. "What are your plans for the day, Dad?"

"Taking a load of hay to Lufkin," he said, referring to a town a half hour down the road.

"Could you use some help?" Nick asked.

"Heck, yeah, if you're willin'," Dad said. "My back's not what it used to be."

When Nick looked my way, I mouthed the word "ass kisser." He merely grinned in reply.

I took a swig of coffee and stood to help my mother. While she fixed her homemade biscuits, I dropped a spoonful of grease into the cast-iron skillet and scrambled the eggs, topping them with a healthy dose of fiery salsa. I served up four plates and plunked one down in each of our places.

Josh wandered in, looking a little green around the edges. His blue eyes were bloodshot, his spongy curls flat on one side.

Mom pulled out a ladder-back chair. "Take a seat, son."

Josh fell more than sat in the chair.

I fixed another plate and slid it in front of him. "Have some breakfast." I grabbed one of Dad's beers from the fridge and plopped that down in front of him as well. "And some hair of the dog that bit ya'."

Grimacing, Josh pushed the beer away. He stared at the eggs for a moment as if wondering whether they'd stay down. Eventually he picked up his fork and poked at them.

While we ate, we made small talk about the weather, the neighbors, the latest happenings in town. When we finished eating, Mom and I set about doing the dishes while Josh retrieved his laptop from the car. He returned to the kitchen table to download the photo files from his wristwatch and the video files from the pen.

Nick slid his chair closer to Josh so he could better see the computer screen. "I can't wait to see what you got."

CHAPTER THIRTY-THREE

Caught on Tape

Josh plugged a thin, short USB cable into the side of the wrist-watch, stuck the other end into his computer, and downloaded the photos to a newly created folder. When he finished, he unplugged the cable from the watch.

Mom flung her dishtowel back over her shoulder and picked up the watch, looking it over. "This watch has a built-in camera? How nifty. Did the Treasury Department supply this to you?"

Josh, Nick, and I exchanged glances.

"Not exactly," I said.

She put a hand on her hip and frowned at me. "It is legal for you to use it, right?"

"Sure," I replied, though in all honesty I wasn't entirely sure. I didn't think it was illegal to take photographs in public places. Still, legal or not, I assumed those up the chain at the IRS might not approve. Following Fischer around could be considered harassment, abuse of authority. Which was precisely why we'd have to send the photos out anonymously.

The dishes now done, I hung my towel on the stove-mounted rack and pulled my chair up on the other side of Josh so that I could see the laptop screen, too. He opened the folder and clicked on the first thumbnail image to enlarge it.

The photo showed Fischer at the blackjack table, cards in one hand, a highball in the other. The next showed him pushing a stack of chips forward to place a bet. The third showed him pulling an even bigger stack of chips back toward himself, a wide smile on his face.

"He won?" I asked. Looked like I wasn't the only one who'd struck it big at the casinos last night.

Josh nodded. "A couple thousand, at least."

As if the guy needed any more money. He had the Arc's overflowing coffers at his disposal. How greedy could one person be? I bet none of his winnings were going to charity.

Unfortunately, the photos weren't the highest quality. Despite all the bright lights on the slot machines in the casino, the overhead lighting was dim. The thick haze of cigarette smoke didn't help, either. Add that to the disguise and it was questionable whether Fischer could be identified from the photos.

"What do you think?" I asked, leaning forward to make eye contact with Nick, who sat on the other side of Josh.

He shook his head. "They're not the best. Fischer'd have plausible deniability."

I nudged Josh. "What about the video?"

Josh reached into the breast pocket of his wrinkled blue button-down and retrieved the recorder pen that was still clipped there. He plugged the loose end of the USB cable into the pen now. A few clicks later, the video image popped up on the screen.

The clip showed Fischer, cards in front of him, slugging back a drink. The image captured half of the woman seated next to him, a grandmotherly type with dark gray helmet hair. The video quality wasn't much better than the photos.

Given all the noise of the slot machines in the background, the audio wasn't all that clear, either.

"Damn," Nick muttered.

The granny leaned in slightly, enabling us to see all of her now. Her thin lips were clenched tightly around a cigarette that had burned dangerously short. I was reminded of Lu, of her cancer treatments, of the promise I'd made to find her a strawberry-blond beehive wig. I might have to try eBay or Craigslist or pay a personal shopper an astronomical finder's fee. But whatever it took, I'd find the right wig.

The woman tapped a finger on the felt-covered table. The gravelly words "hit me" could barely be heard above the slot-machine din.

We could see Fischer's mouth move a moment later, but the audio didn't pick up what he said. Crap. Since the dealer placed another card on top of Fischer's stack, it appeared Fischer had requested another card, too. The dealer continued around the table until he reached Josh.

Given that the pen was situated just a few inches below Josh's chin, his voice came through loud and clear. "No, thanks."

"What are you doing, dude?" A young man's voice barked from off camera. His voice was also clear. He must've been sitting next to Josh. "You've got a two showing, man. The best you can have is twelve. You're not going to win with that hand. You should've taken another card."

"But I might go over," Josh whined.

The reply bore unveiled disgust. "Whatever, dude."

Yep, a boy doing a man's job.

The dealer went bust and Fischer won again with nineteen. Damn him.

The granny slid an irritated look at Fischer as she took a final drag on her cigarette and stubbed it out in a glass ashtray on the table.

Fischer won the next round, too. After scooping the chips into a pile in front of him, he raised his hands. This time, his voice came through loud and clear. "To God go the glory!"

His catch phrase.

If anyone had doubts whether the man at the table was Pastor Fischer, there'd be no doubt about it now. Nick and I had known Pastor Fischer was a fake and a fraud. Now the world would know it, too.

Nick leaped up from the table and pumped his fist. "We got 'im!"

Josh beamed. He might not know jack about playing blackjack, but he knew his high-tech spy gadgets.

The video played on, cutting from the casino to an image of Fischer sitting on a tall stool at a table in the Hustler Club. A barely legal topless woman performed a personal lap dance for him, moving in and out around him, shaking what her mama gave her. Her mama had been generous. The girl's ta-tas had to be at least double Ds.

Josh leaned forward to get a closer look. Nick rolled his eyes and put out a hand, pushing him back. "Don't drool on the keyboard. It might short out."

On the screen, the girl swung her long, auburn hair, moving so that it draped over Fischer's shoulder as she sidled around the back of his chair. She danced her way back in front of him and motioned for him to spread his knees. When he did, she eased in between them, gyrating, pumping, and grinding to the beat of the rock music.

"Well, well," Nick muttered. "Noah Fischer's got a type."

"What do you mean?" I asked.

He jerked his head at the screen. "Who does that girl look like to you?"

I thought a moment. "Amber Hansen?" They both had long, straight auburn hair.

He nodded. "A little like Marissa Fischer, too. Our naughty boy has a thing for redheads."

On the screen, we saw Noah tuck a bill into the young woman's G-string. With this fresh encouragement, she turned her back to him, lifted her hair above her head with her hands, and let it fall, the tresses cascading over his face, which bore a horny grin.

"He really seemed to like that stripper in particular," Josh said. "He kept putting large bills in her panties."

Nick's gaze sought mine. He raised a brow. "Looks like Fischer may have another plaything in Shreveport."

I wasn't nearly as sure as Nick whether Fischer had anything going on with the stripper or with Amber Hansen. Regardless, though, he was clearly not the pious paragon of virtue he purported to be.

On the screen, the woman backed toward Fischer and began bumping her butt against his crotch. He tucked yet another bill into her G-string.

"You think she's reporting all those tips?" I asked.

Nick responded with a snort.

"She's really hot," Josh said dreamily, his eyes still locked on the screen. "She has one of those sexy moles on her upper lip. Like Cindy Crawford."

I suggested we send the photos from a computer at one of the public libraries in Dallas where the communication couldn't be traced to us. One of the tax evaders I'd recently nailed had done the same thing, sending e-mails from public computers at libraries and hotel lobbies. Made them darn difficult to trace.

Nick ruffled Josh's curls. "We couldn't have done this without you, Josh. You done good, kid."

Josh offered a weak smile in return. "Thanks. Can I go back to bed now?"

"Sure."

Dad returned to the kitchen dressed in his work clothes. "Ready?" he asked Nick.

"Yes, sir."

Mom stopped my father before he and Nick headed out the door. "What time will you be back from Lufkin?"

"Around one," Dad replied.

"That gives me just enough time to whip up chicken-fried steak for lunch," Mom said. She pointed a finger in Nick's face. "Best in the world. You'll see. I'll make a believer out of you yet."

CHAPTER THIRTY-FOUR

$\mathcal{P}$astor or Poser?

While Josh dozed and my mother began preparations for lunch, I drove Josh's car out to the Baptist church my family had attended as long as I could remember.

I had to admit that, like most kids, I didn't pay a lot of attention in church growing up. It was difficult to sit still in a hard, uncomfortable pew for a full hour, especially for a young tomboy who'd rather be climbing trees, wading in the creek, or shooting root beer cans with her BB gun. Still, I'd come away with a general sense of what the Man Upstairs expected of us.

Pastor Beasley's sermons had contained the standard fare. Count your blessings. Respect your parents. Don't lie, cheat, or steal. Don't do nothin' to nobody that you wouldn't want them doin' back to you. It ain't right.

While Pastor Beasley's sermons lacked the glitz and glamour of the Ark's services, he'd offered our rural small-town community precisely what it needed. A practical, pragmatic form of spirituality.

I pulled into the church's lot, glad to see the pastor's pickup truck in place at the parsonage out back. He was an avid angler, one of the Bait Bucket's best customers. I hadn't been sure he'd be around on a Saturday morning when the fish might be biting.

I stepped inside, my eyes taking a moment to adjust. The lights were off, but soft, colored light streamed through the stained-glass windows that lined the sides of the chapel. I glanced up at the large cross mounted at the front of the church, wishing the thorn-crowned Jesus would speak up and tell me if what we planned was the right thing to do. But since that wasn't likely, I looked around for Pastor Beasley.

I found him sitting halfway down a pew in the section where the youth group normally congregated. He was a short, increasingly stout man, with thick salt-and-pepper hair. He'd left his slightly-too-tight Sunday suit in the closet today, opting instead for jeans and a comfortable knit shirt. He had a stack of Bibles next to him and was going through them one by one, erasing notations and unfolding dog-eared pages back into place.

"Good morning, Pastor Beasley."

He looked up and gave me a genuine smile. "Well, if it isn't Tara Holloway. How are ya? Still working hard for Uncle Sam?"

"Yep." *I'm his whore.* "You got a minute?"

"I've got all the time in the world." I wasn't sure whether he meant that literally or figuratively. Perhaps both. He patted the pew. "Come take a seat and help me out. The teenagers keep marking the naughty parts in the Bibles. I have half a mind to tear these pages out."

I sat, picked up a Bible from the stack, and opened it to the first dog-eared page. Someone had underlined a reference to "spilled seed." Ew. I grabbed a pencil from the rack mounted on the back of the pew in front of me, erased the line, and smoothed the page as flat as I could.

"So," Pastor Beasley asked, "what brings you by?"

I was hesitant to broach the subject of Noah Fischer. I didn't want to sound accusing and distrustful. Still, I needed some guidance. I wanted Fischer to get his due, but I wasn't sure that's what God had planned. The Big Guy seemed to be smiling down with favor on Fischer. Who was I to push fate? But surely Pastor Beasley had heard far worse confessions than what I was about to tell him.

I smoothed another page. "Everything I tell you is confidential, right?"

"I love conversations that start this way. It always leads to something juicy." He chortled and rubbed his hands together. "Did you embezzle from the government? Lie under oath? Maybe kill someone and bury the body in your backyard?"

"Sorry to disappoint you," I replied, "but no. Nothing that exciting."

"Shucks."

I folded another page back. "Have you ever met a minister that you thought was a phony?"

"Dozens," he replied, nonplussed.

"How could you tell?" I asked.

"It's the shoes," he said. "If they're wearing expensive shoes, they're a phony."

"That simple, huh?"

He shrugged. "Surprisingly, yes."

I looked down at Pastor Beasley's shoes. Cheap canvas sneakers, worn through on one toe, the tip of a white sweat sock visible through the hole.

I told him about our case against Fischer, how we'd lost in court, how we'd tracked him to the casino and topless bar in Shreveport.

"I've met Noah Fischer," he said, a sour expression on his face.

"And?"

He dropped a Bible into the rack with a resounding *thunk*. "He was wearing the most expensive shoes I've ever seen on a preacher."

His words were as close to a go-ahead from God as I'd get.

"People deserve to hear the truth," he said, his tone matter-of-fact. "Whether they choose to accept it will be up to them. But step lightly, Tara. Give him a chance to do the right thing, to come clean and make amends himself. The man's made some mistakes, but he's still one of God's children. God loves him, even if the rest of us think he's an arrogant, self-righteous snake oil salesman."

Great advice. My heart felt lighter already. "Thanks."

"Be careful, too," he warned, giving me an intent look. "He's not a man who likes to be crossed. He's terminated several of his associate pastors when they didn't agree with him."

That might be true, but I didn't see how Fischer could be a threat to me. I didn't work for him.

I offered to finish the Bibles for Pastor Beasley so he could enjoy his day off.

He stood and put a hand on my shoulder. "You, my child, are an angel. I'm off to find me some bass."

My cell phone chirped as I left the church a half hour later. I checked the readout. Brett.

I pushed the button to take the call. "Hey."

"Hey."

"What are you doing back in Dallas?" I asked. "I thought you'd be gone all month."

"It's raining cats and dogs in Atlanta. They expect it to keep up through the weekend."

The weather had given Brett an unanticipated break. Can't do landscaping work when it's wet outside.

"I'd like to see you," he said. "When were you planning on coming back?"

"This afternoon," I replied. "After lunch."

"Great. Let's get dinner somewhere. Maybe that Cuban place Alicia told you about?"

"Perfect."

"Sorry about the Ark case," he said.

"So Trish gave you the news, huh?" I'd expected her to do as much. Still, it got my ire up.

"Yeah."

I wondered what else she'd give him if given the chance.

We ended the call and I slipped the phone back into the side pocket of my purse.

Weird. I actually felt a bit nervous about my date with Brett. Silly, huh? He'd only been away a few days, yet it seemed as if he'd been gone a very long time. So much had happened, so much had changed.

I felt so far from him now, but it had nothing to do with the actual distance between us.

Dad and Nick returned to the house at lunchtime, both sweaty, both ravenous. Loading and unloading hay was hard labor.

Mom and I met them at the trailer with full tumblers of iced sweet tea. Nick pulled off his work gloves, took the cup from me, and downed it in just a few gulps. Dad did likewise.

While Dad and Nick cleaned up, Mom and I set the table for lunch. In addition to chicken-fried steak, she'd made corn bread, green beans, and blueberry pie. We set everything out family style.

I woke Josh and soon the five of us were seated around the dining room table. Mom had gone all out, covering the table in her best lace tablecloth, using her fine china. All eyes were on Nick as he cut into his chicken-fried steak. He skewered the bite with his fork and lifted it to his mouth. He closed his lips and his eyes and began to chew.

"Well?" my mother asked. "What's the verdict?"

After a few seconds, a slow smile spread across his face. "Mmm." He opened his eyes and looked at my mom. "If you tell my mother I said this, I'll be forced to deny it. But, boy howdy, this is in fact the best chicken-fried steak I've ever eaten."

Dad held a huge chunk of battered meat aloft on his fork. "Told you so."

Josh, too, was digging into his steak, apparently feeling better now.

Nick ate another bite. "What's your secret, Mrs. Holloway?"

"That's for me to know," my mother replied saucily, "and nobody else to ever find out."

I knew what her secret ingredients were—lemon pepper, buttermilk, and a tiny spoonful of finely chopped fresh jalapeño. But I wasn't about to share that information. Mom would disown me if I ever revealed what she put in her batter.

After we'd eaten lunch and followed it with big slabs of blueberry pie, we packed up our meager things and headed out to Josh's car. Nick had changed back into his own shirt. The bloodstain had come out. I wasn't surprised. My mother could do just about anything.

Mom and Dad each gave me a hug.

"Come back soon," Mom said. "You can help me with the canning."

"I'm busy that weekend," I replied.

She shot me a pointed look. "I didn't say when I planned to do it."

"Oh. Right." I hated canning and my mother knew it. While I respected her domestic skills, I'd inherited none of them. Slaving away in a hot kitchen wasn't my idea of fun, even if it would provide an opportunity to spend time with Mom. If we wanted to engage in a female bonding ritual, I'd rather go shopping for antiques or get our nails done. "How about we drive into Jefferson some weekend?" I suggested instead. "Maybe have lunch at the tea room?"

"You're on." She gave me a kiss on the cheek before raising a hand to wave good-bye to Nick and Josh. "Y'all take care, now."

CHAPTER THIRTY-FIVE

*R*eunited

The ride home was uneventful. I sat in the backseat, staring out the window, trying to sort through my feelings, figure out what I should do. It wasn't easy to think straight with Nick sitting three feet away in the front seat. If I was ever going to work through this mess, I needed to put some distance between us so that I could think rationally and reasonably. This close, it was too easy to be influenced by his roguish grin and those whiskey-colored eyes and that crisp, clean smell of soap that, ironically, made me want to do very dirty things to him.

But should I even be trying to think rationally and reasonably? Attraction wasn't about logic, was it? It was about feelings, emotions. Maybe I should be listening to my heart rather than my head. Problem was, my heart was just as confused as my head.

Josh dropped me and Nick back at the office parking lot where we'd left our cars the day before.

"See you Monday," he called before motoring off.

Nick and I were alone again. I felt I should say something, but what? I was at an emotional impasse. My relationship with Nick was in limbo.

"Still on for dinner at my mother's tomorrow?" he asked.

How could I back out now? It would be rude. Besides, the dinner would be her way of thanking me for bringing her son back from Mexico, nothing more. It wasn't a date.

"Sure," I said.

He rattled off the address and I entered it into my cell phone's notation app.

"See you tomorrow." He turned and headed for his truck.

"Yeah. See ya." I climbed into my car, closed the door, and rested my forehead on the steering wheel, my eyes closed. I was tempted to start the engine and drive far away, away from all of this turmoil. I could start a new life somewhere else. Like Boise. Or Walla Walla.

But, no. I couldn't do that. I'd be leaving two great guys behind, one of whom I could very well be happy with. Which one, though, I wasn't sure. Besides, Tara Holloway didn't run away from her problems. She confronted them, worked through them, resolved them.

Even when the thought of doing so scared her shitless.

I rounded the corner onto my street to find Brett's Navigator parked in front of my town house, a flatbed trailer attached to it, a few random pieces of white PVC pipe scattered across it. Brett stood in my yard, tamping down fresh sod with a hoe. Judging from the new grass stripes across my lawn, he'd installed an automatic sprinkler system for me.

I pulled into my driveway and hopped out of my car. Brett's sandy hair was mussed, his forehead smudged with dirt, his shorts and T-shirt dark with dust and sweat. He leaned on the hoe, grinning at me.

Damn. Even covered in sweat and dirt he looked adorable.

Installing a sprinkler system was no small job. He must've been out here working for hours. Not only had he

put in the sprinklers, he'd also replaced the dried-up bego-
nias under my redbud tree with an abundance of bright pink
petunias and Mexican heather, surrounding them with fresh
cedar mulch. He'd trimmed and shaped the pink rosebushes
and even added a white stone birdbath to the flower bed. My
yard was absolutely beautiful.

I rushed over to him and gave him a tight hug. He'd done
all of this for me, and I hadn't even had the foresight to offer
to water his plants and collect his mail when he'd headed off
to Atlanta. To make matters worse, I'd been fantasizing
about Nick. Heck, I'd almost kissed the guy last night!

At that moment I felt completely selfish, totally unde-
serving of Brett. Sure, he'd flubbed up a bit when he'd
phoned me about my pulling a gun on Trish. But everyone
makes mistakes in relationships, right? The fact that he'd
spent the day toiling in my yard in the extreme Texas heat
told me more than words could ever say. He was crazy about
me. And I'd be crazy to risk losing him. Right?

I released Brett and stepped back, looking around the
yard. "Wow! The flowers are beautiful, Brett."

"They were grown in one of the greenhouses at the nursery," he said, pride evident in his voice.

"How'd you get them to grow so big?"

"Pig manure."

Urk. "Remind me not to ask next time."

"We've been experimenting with organic stuff," he said.
"It's better for the environment."

He had me there.

Brett put the final piece of sod in place, and I helped him
round up his tools and load them onto the trailer. As we
headed to my front door, I noticed an envelope posted there,
firmly affixed to the glass with duct tape. I stepped onto my
porch, yanked the envelope off the glass, and unfolded the
piece of paper inside. It was another notice from the Lone
Star Nation. This one featured the same ridiculous photo of
me they'd put on the Facebook page, with the word WANTED

underneath. Apparently the Nation was offering a five-hundred-dollar reward to anyone who could bring me in.

So they'd offered a bounty for me, huh? I wasn't sure whether to be worried that they'd put a price on my head or insulted the reward was so little. At least they hadn't said "dead or alive." The fact that whoever had posted this on my door had directly defied the restraining order gave me further cause for concern.

I refolded the paper and shoved it back into the envelope.

"Advertisement?" Brett asked.

"Yeah." Apparently my freedom was for sale. Cheap.

We headed inside. While Brett took a shower, I fed my cats and changed my clothes. I was tempted to call Nick, to tell him about the notice, but decided to wait until later.

Once we'd freshened up, Brett and I headed outside to his SUV. He helped me in, then climbed in on his side. But he didn't start the car. Instead, he turned to me. "I'm glad I was able to see you this weekend. Lately things between us seem . . . I don't know . . . weird?"

Gee, ya think? "Giving another woman a key to your house can do that to a relationship." As long as he was being honest, I should be, too, right? Too bad honesty sounded a lot like suspicious and bitchy. Stupid Lone Star Nation. Their bounty notice had spoiled my good mood.

Brett gave me a long-suffering look that, frankly, pissed me off. "Trish was just picking up my mail, Tara."

"And watering your plants." I recalled Nick's words. *Plausible deniability.* "How would you feel if I gave another guy a key to my place?"

His eyes narrowed. "It would depend on who the guy was."

I was tired of pussyfooting around. Time to get things out in the open. "Look, Brett. I don't like you being around Trish. I think she's got a thing for you."

"She's just friendly," he said. "She flirts with all the guys on the projects."

"So you admit she's been flirting with you?"

"Well, yes, but not any more than she does with the other male volunteers."

Trying to get Brett to see the problem here was like trying to get an alcoholic to acknowledge he drank too much. "The first step to resolving this problem, Brett, is you recognizing that there *is* a problem."

He let out a breath and looked out the side window for a moment before turning back to me. "You know how I feel about you, Tara. You're making too much of this."

Maybe I was. But maybe he was making too little of it, too. "Regardless," I said, "it bothers me that you two are so chummy. If the shoe were on the other foot and you were upset about me spending time with a male friend, I'd stop doing it."

I would, wouldn't I? Of course, Nick was a coworker. There'd be no way I could totally avoid him, even if Brett asked me to.

"Is that what you want, Tara? For me to avoid Trish?"

It sounded petty, childish, distrusting. But, yes, it was what I wanted. "Yes," I said, looking down at my lap, embarrassed by my neediness and insecurity.

In that moment, I realized his response would be critical. I'd essentially asked him to put my needs before his own, to do something for me even if he felt that what I was asking of him was ridiculous. If he agreed, it would mean he was committed to me, committed to making our relationship work. If he didn't, well, then I'd have to reconsider my commitment to him, maybe give Nick a shot.

I had another epiphany then, too. I realized that I was wimping out, issuing ultimatums so that he'd make the decision for me. I just hoped he'd have more conviction than I did.

Brett cupped my chin and turned my face to him, gazing into my eyes for a moment. "Consider it done."

He leaned in and gave me a soft, warm, reassuring kiss.

In that moment, all seemed right with the world again.

* * *

The food at the Cuban restaurant was delicious. I bypassed the chicken—still couldn't face cooked poultry after the encounter I'd had with August Buchmeyer's hen—and opted for the tilapia with Cuban spices instead. Brett had the *ropa vieja,* a dish of shredded beef and vegetables served over white rice. The menu noted that the name, when translated, meant "old clothes." Brett offered me a sample and, fortunately, it tasted far better than its name would imply. Both of our meals came with fried plantains. Yum!

After dinner, we returned to my town house. Both my tummy and my heart felt full now. I'd made my decision. I'd stay true to Brett, see where our relationship went. He was a great guy and I was lucky to have him. Every relationship went through trials and tribulations. This thing with Trish was nothing more than a minor footnote on what was otherwise a perfect relationship record. And what I felt for Nick, really, it was nothing more than a crush, right?

We went upstairs and undressed for bed. I slid on a red satin nightie, while Brett simply stripped down to his blue boxer briefs.

He swept a hand over the pillowcase on his side of the bed, brushing off pet hair. "Looks like Henry's been sleeping on my pillow."

The reddish hairs belonged to Nick's dog Nutty, not Henry. But I wasn't about to tell Brett that fact. He wouldn't like it one bit if he knew Nick had stayed at my town house again. We'd just managed to get our relationship back on track, no sense derailing it again so soon, right? Besides, Nick had simply been helping out a coworker, nothing more.

Yeah, right.

Great. Now I was thinking of Nick again. Just when Brett and I were about to climb into bed. Damn.

I slid under the sheets. Brett turned off the lamp, flopped onto the bed, and rolled over to me, nuzzling and nipping playfully at my neck as he tugged my nightie upward and slid a hand under it. "I've missed the heck out of you," he said, his fingers going straight for my breast.

My body responded as if on autopilot, my back arching to meet his touch, my leg curling up around his back. But while my body was going through the motions, my mind didn't fuzz into oblivion like it normally did when we engaged in foreplay.

I was thinking. Thinking that maybe I'd been too hasty in reconciling the love spat we'd had, that maybe I should have given things more thought. Then he pulled my nightgown off and put his warm mouth to my breast and I thought that maybe I was thinking too much.

He wasted no time, removing my panties and his underwear and sliding on a condom in record time. If my mind had any hesitancies, it hadn't sent the memo to my body. I wrapped both legs around him, taking him in hard and fast, not giving myself time for second thoughts.

The sex felt divine, but it felt desperate, too, the two of us going at each other like our lives depended on it, as if trying to prove something to each other—or perhaps to ourselves. Though Brett and I were sharing the most intimate of acts, a part of me was elsewhere, thinking of someone else, refusing, even then, to entirely let go.

An image of Nick played through my mind and I imagined what it might be like to make love to *him,* to have *his* hands on me, to have *him* inside me.

Nick, with his rock-hard pecs.

Nick, with his chipped-tooth smile.

Nick, with his whiskey-colored eyes.

Nick, with his take-charge style that both frustrated and titillated me.

I rose to meet Brett's forceful thrust. *Nick.*

Again. *Nick.*

Once more. *Nick.*

I cried out as a shudder built and exploded, rippling through me.

When I settled back against the pillows a moment later, Brett nuzzled my ear. "I was that good again, huh?"

"Mm-hm," I moaned softly, though inside I mentally grimaced.

The cry hadn't been for Brett.

It had been for Nick.

CHAPTER THIRTY-SIX

$\mathcal{D}$inner Date

First thing the next morning, I took a long shower, scrubbing my skin raw with my rough loofah.

I felt dirty. Silly, I know. I hadn't actually cheated on Brett. But Nick had been in my mind the entire time Brett was making love to me. Though there'd been but two physical bodies in the bed, I'd engaged in a mental ménage à trois.

But thinking of another man during sex wasn't anything unusual, was it? Of course not. People did it all the time to keep things fresh. Heck, I bet half of the women who'd had sex last night were picturing George Clooney when they'd climaxed. Some couples even engaged in role play, purposely pretending to be someone else when they did the deed. And then there were those people who dressed up like animals to have sex. Furries. How bizarre is that? There was nothing for me to feel dirty about, really.

Then why didn't the shower help?

Brett and I curled up on the couch with two bowls of cereal. I picked up the remote and turned on the television, surfing through the channels until I found the station broadcasting the Ark's service.

Pastor Walters stood at the altar today, dressed in a basic blue suit with a plain green tie. Though a spotlight shined on him, the colored lights and jumbo screens were turned off today. All that Vegas showiness wasn't Walters's style.

He delivered a simple sermon on the concept of giving to God through charitable service, the exact opposite of Fischer's focus on tithing as an expression of faith. Walters had invited representatives of several local charities that were in need of helping hands. Each was given a few minutes to speak on their organization's needs and volunteer opportunities. There was something for everyone, from painting over graffiti in the disadvantaged parts of town to visiting lonely elderly people in a nursing home.

Walters's focus was one hundred eighty degrees different from Fischer's. Walters didn't feed the parishioners' egos, though he didn't condemn them, either. There was no fire, no brimstone, no threat of eternal damnation or locusts or scourges. He simply invited them to experience the joy of sharing God's love by helping others.

I squinted at the screen. "Can you tell what kind of shoes the minister is wearing?"

"Black ones," Brett said.

That wasn't much help, though, really, what had I expected? My television was neither a big screen nor hi-def.

Brett looked puzzled. "Why'd you ask about the shoes?"

I told him what Pastor Beasley had said about phony preachers wearing expensive shoes.

Brett gestured to the screen. "You think this guy's a phony?"

"Not him, necessarily," I said, "but I suspect Noah Fischer may be just going through the motions."

"What makes you think that?"

"Besides the fact that he hasn't paid the taxes he owes?"

Hmm, maybe the fact that he was playing blackjack and ogling bare breasts in Shreveport two nights ago? But I didn't want to let Brett in on that information. He'd want to know all the details. It would be opening a can of worms I'd rather keep closed, at least for the time being. I settled for "Just a hunch, that's all. Fischer seems much more fashion conscious than any minister I've ever met. And he's got that limo and the big house. He seems self-absorbed."

"I guess it's a moot point, though, since the judge ruled in his favor."

"Don't remind me." A thought crossed my mind then. "You're not going to tell Trish that I asked you not to see her, are you?" It would be embarrassing if she knew I was jealous and I didn't want to give her the satisfaction of knowing I perceived her as a threat to my relationship with Brett.

"No," he said. "But it's going to be a little awkward. She'll wonder why I'm ignoring her calls and texts and e-mails."

Sheez. Was she in constant touch with him? "Just be slow to respond," I said. "Tell her you're busy. She'll get the hint eventually."

"She's still got my key."

Grr. "Tell her I'll be checking your mail and watering your plants now that the Ark case is over." I had half a mind to change his locks, maybe rig a booby trap for her. Perhaps I could get some of that organic pig poop and put a bucket over the door in case she stopped by. The thought of Trish covered in pig manure caused me to snigger.

"Did I miss something?" Brett asked.

I rubbed my nose. "Just stifling a sneeze." *As if.*

I drove Brett to the airport that afternoon. We lingered at the curb, holding each other until airport security grew suspicious and told me to move my car.

Brett gave me a kiss and put his forehead to mine. "Miss me," he whispered.

"Miss me, too," I whispered back.

He went through the glass doors and they slid closed behind him. He turned and gave me a final wave. A sense of emptiness descended on me as I waved back.

"Move it," the security guard ordered. "Now!"

I held up my hands. "Okay, okay!"

At six o'clock, I arrived at Nick's mother's house. I'd been there once before, when I'd brought Nick home after his three-year forced exile in Mexico. But it had been late at night and dark and I hadn't wanted to intrude on their reunion. I'd waited at the curb until she'd opened the door for him and then driven away.

Her house was a modest brown brick model, single story, with ivory shutters. Nick's truck was in the driveway. I pulled in next to it, parked, and took a deep breath before climbing out and making my way to the porch.

I knew I shouldn't, but I felt nervous again, the same way I'd felt when I'd met Brett's parents for the first time. Of course my trepidation then was understandable. Brett and I were in a serious relationship. The Ellingtons could potentially be my future in-laws and our initial impressions of each other were thus significant.

Today, though, was nothing more than a friendly dinner, an expression of thanks from a grateful mother to someone who'd done a favor for her son. There was no reason for my pulse to be pounding and my hands to be sweating. Unfortunately, neither my heart nor my hands seemed to understand that.

A cheerful wreath of silk sunflowers decorated the front door. I wiped my hands on the skirt of my white sundress and lifted the knocker. *Clack. Clack.*

A moment later, Nick's mother opened the door. She wore a women's western shirt in a navy, green, and tan Navajo print, along with jeans, boots, and a welcoming smile. She was tall like Nick, with the same shade of brown hair, though hers was pulled back in a braid and streaked through with hints of silver. Her eyes were blue. Nick's whiskey-colored irises must have come from his father.

Nick stood behind her, Nutty to his side, tail wagging. *Woof! Woof-woof!*

Mrs. Pratt stepped forward, offering her hand. "I'm Bonnie Pratt," she said. "Pleased to meet you."

When I gave her my hand, she used it to pull me toward her, wrapping her long arms around me and enveloping me in a bear hug, not bothering to ask permission first. I could see where Nick got his gumption.

"Oh, Tara!" she cried. "I could just squeeze you to death!"

Nick chuckled and pulled on his mother's arm. "I think you are, Mom. Give her some room to breathe."

She pulled back, holding me by the shoulders, still smiling a wide, bright smile. "I can't even begin to tell you how grateful I am for what you did for my baby."

Her baby? Ha! So Nick was a mama's boy. Who would've known? My gaze flicked to Nick. He rolled his eyes but let his mother slide. I had a feeling he'd fought a battle over the pet name before and lost.

I looked back to Mrs. Pratt. "I was happy to do it," I said. "Besides, I needed Nick's help on the case."

She shook her head. "You're being too modest. You took a lot of risks going down there and I darn well know it." She waved a hand for us to follow her into the kitchen. "Come on in. I've made my chicken-fried steak. Best you'll ever have."

I raised a brow when Nick cut his eyes my way. "Don't sell me down the river," he whispered.

Mrs. Pratt glanced back. "What'd you say, baby?"

"Nothing," Nick replied.

Dozens of framed photographs of Nick hung in the hallway, chronicling his life, beginning with him as a chubby infant lying bare assed on a fluffy white rug, to photos of him in his high school football uniform, to him in a cap and gown at college graduation.

"Only child?" I asked him.

"Yep."

That fact must have made it all the harder for his mother when he was stuck in Mexico.

We stepped into the kitchen. Although she lived in the city now, it was clear Bonnie Pratt hadn't left the country behind. The room was decorated in old-fashioned blue and white gingham. The cookie jar was shaped like a red barn, the salt and pepper shakers like black-and-white Holstein cows. The place settings included white china with blue forget-me-nots around the rim.

Nick pulled out a chair for me at the table and I took a seat. He sat down next to me.

Nick's mother opened the refrigerator and removed a glass pitcher filled with a dark red liquid. Orange and lemon slices floated on top. "How about a glass of homemade sangria?"

"That sounds wonderful."

Bonnie poured two tall glasses, setting one in front of me and the other on the table across from me. She took a bottle of beer from the fridge and plunked that down in front of Nick.

I took a sip of the sangria. Sweet, fruity, refreshing. "Mmm. Good stuff."

She set a basket of dinner rolls on the table, as well as a heaping bowl of mashed potatoes and a gravy boat filled to the brim with cream gravy. The pièce de résistance was a platter of chicken-fried steaks covered in a thick, light-brown batter.

Once his mother had taken a seat, Nick handed me the serving fork. "Help yourself."

I chose one of the smaller steaks, then scooped up a large spoonful of potatoes, smothering both of them with gravy. Nick and his mother served their plates, then seemed to watch me with anticipation.

"Try it," Bonnie said, an expectant look on her face. "I can't wait to see what you think."

I picked up my steak knife and sawed off a bite-sized chunk of meat. I speared it with my fork and put it in my mouth.

I thought I'd never taste a chicken-fried steak better than my mother's. But I'd been wrong. I savored the bite, closing my eyes and chewing slowly. Finally, I opened them. "This is fantastic."

She smiled. "It was my grandmother's recipe."

"What's in it?"

She wagged a finger in the air. "Nuh-uh-uh. Family recipes are top secret."

"But I brought your baby back to you, remember?"

She crinkled up her nose. "Truth be told, he's a pain in the ass."

"Tell me about it," I said.

Nick stood. "I don't have to put up with this."

His mother gestured for him to sit back down. "Yeah, you do. Sit your butt down."

I liked this woman. She was down-to-earth with a sense of humor.

I ate another bite of steak. "I'm guessing there's some chili powder in your batter."

Bonnie pointed her steak knife at me, but her good-natured grin told me she was all bark and no bite. "You best stop that guessing right now if you know what's good for you."

Nick's mother and I chatted casually and comfortably during dinner. We discovered that we shared a love of gardening, though I grew flowers and she grew vegetables. I learned that she was the one who'd taught Nick how to dance, just in time for the high school prom. While she'd been jovial throughout our conversation, her face and voice grew somber when she talked about the years Nick was in Mexico.

"He'd call me every few days, but we had to be careful what we said. We never knew if our conversations were being monitored." Her eyes grew misty but her jaw was firm. "I had to play along, pretend to believe that he'd taken a bribe and fled the country. As if my baby would do something like that. I didn't raise any thieves!" Her voice rose in pitch. "I was worried sick the entire time. I feared that one day he'd just up and disappear and I'd never know what happened to him." A short, involuntary sob broke from her chest.

Nick put a hand on his mother's shoulder. "It's okay now, Mom."

I moved to sit beside her, taking her left hand in both of mine. She gave my hand a squeeze.

"I'm sorry. I still get myself worked up now and then." She dabbed at her eyes with a napkin, then closed them for a moment as if to refocus herself. When she opened them again, she smiled. "Who's ready for dessert?"

I smiled back. "I am."

Dessert featured strawberry shortcake with homemade whipped cream. "I grew the strawberries myself," Bonnie said.

"It's delicious." I scooped up another oversized bite.

After dinner, she took me out back to show me her vegetable garden. The space took up half of the backyard. In addition to the strawberries, she'd grown corn, peppers, zucchini, yellow squash, okra, and tomatoes. Many of the plants appeared to be struggling after the hot summer we'd experienced.

Lording over the garden was a tall, broad scarecrow wearing a lopsided straw cowboy hat. The scarecrow had hay for hair and a stuffed feed sack for a face. He was dressed in a pair of long-legged jeans and a blue and white-striped long-sleeved shirt. Given that three birds were pecking at the ground in the garden, the scarecrow appeared to be ineffective, more for show than substance.

"Nick's clothes?" I asked, fingering the shirt.

"His dad's," Bonnie said softly.

"Nick must take after him," I said.

She glanced back at Nick, who was wrestling a tennis ball out of Nutty's mouth across the yard. "The two of them were practically identical," she said. "Same height, same broad shoulders, same eyes."

So she'd once been taken in by those eyes, too.

"Nick's dad was a hardheaded son of a bitch," she said, looking up wistfully at the scarecrow. "Lord, I miss him."

She looked at me now. "Life wasn't easy with Nick's father," she said, "but it was never boring, neither."

She'd filled my stomach with chicken-fried steak and strawberry shortcake, and now she'd given me food for thought.

When the night was done, Nick's mother sent me out the door with two steaks wrapped in foil, a plastic bag full of her homegrown strawberries, and her sangria recipe.

Nick walked me to my car. "Thanks for coming."

"I had a nice time."

We stood in awkward silence for a moment. If we'd been dating, this would be the point at which we'd give each other a good-night kiss. If we were mere coworkers, this would be the point we'd say "see ya" and turn away from each other. Given that we were less than lovers but more than business associates, I wasn't sure what to do. Nick didn't seem to have a clue, either.

"Guess I'll see you in the morning," I said finally.

He merely nodded and stepped back a couple feet. He stood in the driveway, a lonesome expression in his eyes as he watched me back up and drive away.

CHAPTER THIRTY-SEVEN

Smiting a Sinner

When I arrived at work Monday morning, I faxed a copy of Judge Trumbull's order to both the county clerk's office and the mortgage company. I received a call from the loan officer not ten minutes later.

"Your loan's good to go now," she said. "Of course, interest rates went up a quarter point over the weekend."

Damn. Would this run of bad luck never end?

Josh and Nick appeared in my doorway. Josh held up a jump drive. "Ready to go to the library?"

"Oh, yeah." I'd been screwed over by everyone and their dog lately. I was looking forward to screwing back.

Viola eyed us as we waited at the elevators. "You look like three cats that swallowed three canaries."

Eddie looked up from Lu's desk behind Vi. "You guys aren't getting yourselves in trouble, are you?"

"Of course not," I said.

The elevator doors opened and we climbed on. I stuck my head out and hollered to Eddie. "You only get in trouble if you get caught!"

We walked the five blocks to the central library and stepped inside. I led the way to the bank of computers. We grabbed chairs and pulled up to a computer at the end of the row.

Josh inserted the flash drive into the tower, then logged in to Google Mail. "We'll need to set up an account. What e-mail address do you want to use?"

"How about Jesus H Christ?" I suggested. It might be smart-assed and sacrilegious, but if we were going to go to all this trouble to give Noah Fischer some hell, we might as well take it all the way, right?

"Jesus' middle initial is *F*," Nick said.

"Shhh!" A woman three seats away frowned at us.

"No it's not," I insisted in a whisper.

"It doesn't matter," Josh whispered, clicking keys on the keyboard. "Both of those are taken anyway."

"What about just 'God'?" Nick asked.

Josh typed again. "Not available."

"Shhh!" said the woman again.

We ran through a litany of choices. Jehovah. King of Kings. Abba. The Man Upstairs. All were taken. We finally settled on Yahweh@yahoo.com.

"What do you want the e-mail to say?" Josh asked.

Nick and I exchanged glances.

What would God say if he could speak directly to Fischer? "How about this?" I suggested. " 'You've been a naughty boy, my son. Repent now or I'll cover your pecker with boils.' "

"Works for me," Nick said.

Josh typed up the e-mail and attached the photo and video files. He logged on to the Ark's Web site, located Fischer's e-mail address on the contact page, and dragged the mouse across the pad to copy it. Returning to the e-mail screen, he pasted it into the address line.

Just one more step and the implosion would begin.

I put a hand out to stop Josh from sending the e-mail. "It was Nick's idea to spy on Fischer Friday night. Let's give him the honors."

Josh waved a hand, palm up, over the keyboard, inviting Nick to press the key.

Nick rotated his shoulders dramatically, then interlaced his fingers and stretched them out in front of him, cracking his knuckles. He lifted his index finger high in the air, made a whistling sound like a bomb dropping, and lowered his finger to jab the enter button. "Kaboom!"

"Shhh!" the woman hissed one last time.

With Fischer now in self-destruct mode, I could turn my attention to my other cases. Unfortunately, none were nearly as a big or interesting. I had a nursing home administrator who'd failed to issue himself a W-2 or report his income for the past eight years, a lumber wholesaler who'd taken significant amounts of cash under the table, and a freelance photographer who'd claimed a sizable net loss several years in a row despite the fact that he'd actually turned a nice profit. The photographer tried to claim he'd simply made math errors on his return and hadn't realized it. To the tune of two hundred grand? Not likely. Adding up deductions wasn't exactly advanced math.

The end of the Ark case meant I also had spare time on my hands. I invited Alicia and Christina over for dinner on Tuesday. I desperately needed both girl time and advice.

Over delivery pizza and a pitcher of Bonnie Pratt's homemade sangria, I told them everything. Well, almost everything. No need to tell them I'd thought about Nick during sex with Brett last Saturday.

"Be careful," Christina warned. "Guys get really pissed when you cry out another man's name during orgasm. It's hard to come back from that."

I choked on my wine. When I could finally breathe again, I asked, "Did I do the right thing staying with Brett?"

Christina fished another slice of pizza out of the open box on my kitchen table. "I think you should be honest with

Brett. Tell him that you're crazy about him but that you've got feelings for Nick, too, and that you owe it to both of you to explore that, to make sure you're choosing the best match. If you don't, and you end up with Brett for the long term, you'll be wondering 'what if' for the rest of your life. That won't be good for either one of you."

Christina made sense.

I toyed with a piece of crust. "But what if I tell Brett I want to give Nick a shot and then things don't work out with Nick? Brett might refuse to take me back."

Brett wouldn't like playing second fiddle, but I'd feel the same way if I were him. If things were reversed, and Brett were the one telling me he wanted to give Trish a try, I doubted I'd ever take him back. It would be too humiliating. Like being awarded an honorable mention or winning a consolation prize. I wouldn't want to be someone's lifetime supply of Rice-A-Roni.

"There's always the risk Brett could refuse to reconcile," she agreed, taking a sip of her sangria. "But you need to trust fate. If you and Brett are meant to end up together, then you'll end up together."

I wasn't sure I trusted fate. Fate had been awfully generous with Noah Fischer and he certainly didn't deserve it.

"I disagree with Christina," Alicia said. "Brett's done what you asked. He agreed to avoid Trish. You owe it to him now to see things through."

Two good friends. Two different opinions. Both equally valid.

I was right back where I'd started from. Confused. When I wasn't sure about a tax question, I consulted the Internal Revenue Code for the answer. Too bad there wasn't a Dating Code to consult.

I was leaning the same way as Alicia, though. It wouldn't be fair that I'd demanded Brett stay away from Trish if I were going to change my mind now and keep my options open with Nick. Still, what had seemed resolved on Saturday night didn't feel resolved now. As hard as I tried, my feelings for Nick refused to be completely pushed aside.

Christina swallowed another bite of the veggie supreme and eyed me. "You're staying with Brett, aren't you?"

"Yeah." I sighed.

"You need to give Nick a heads-up," Alicia said. "It wouldn't be right to keep him on the hook now that you've decided to stay with Brett."

"She's right," Christina said.

They both agreed I had to tell Nick. Damn. That wasn't a conversation I was looking forward to.

Early Wednesday evening, Josh, Nick, and I parked once again between two cars in the Ark's lot.

Josh had run by the library twice to see if we'd received a response to the e-mail, but so far Yahweh@yahoo's in-box remained empty.

"Could our e-mail have ended up in Fischer's spam folder?" I asked.

Josh shrugged. "There's always that possibility. Or maybe he just hasn't read it yet."

That could be the case. As pastor of such a large church, he probably received a high volume of e-mails.

Fischer's white limo pulled to the curb thirty yards away. The driver climbed out to open the back door for Noah and Marissa. The two stepped out, looking as much like a Hollywood celebrity couple as ever. She wore a shimmery satin dress in pale mauve with another pair of Jimmy Choos, these a metallic suede espadrille wedge. Four hundred and ninety-five bucks at Neiman's. I should know. I'd coveted that pair also.

Fischer wore tan slacks with a short-sleeved white dress shirt, along with the gold bracelet and Cartier watch.

"Whose shoes are on Fischer's feet?" I asked.

"His," Josh replied. "Duh."

"No, I mean which designer made them?"

Nick and Josh exchanged glances.

"We don't know, Tara," Josh said. "We're not gay."

"You're a virgin," I said. "That's close enough."

A pang of guilt stabbed my gut when Josh's cheeks flamed a bright red.

"I'm sorry, Josh," I said. "That was a low blow."

Nick cocked his head, eyeing Josh. "Maybe you should do something about that."

"About what?"

"Your virginity," Nick replied. "Virginity is curable, you know."

Just after the couple had vacated the limo and turned to head up the ramp into the boat, Amber Hansen drove by in her silver SUV. Noah Fischer glanced back at her car, his gaze lingering just a fraction too long.

Nick sat up in his seat. "Did you see that?"

"Sure did." I shouldn't have doubted Nick's instincts. Maybe there really was something going on between the two of them. Then again, maybe he just found her attractive. But my instincts were buzzing now, too.

Fischer turned his focus to his wife now, putting a hand on Marissa's back and guiding her up the ramp and into the Ark. The doors swung shut behind them.

I'm not sure what we expected, but again it felt anticlimactic. We'd hoped to see Fischer quaking in his expensive shoes and all we'd gotten was him staring a little too long at a parishioner.

"Let's call him," Nick said. "Tell him to check his e-mail."

Josh started his car and we motored out of the lot, making our way down the adjacent road. We stopped at three gas stations and two convenience stores before finding a pay phone. The things were as rare as white rhinos these days.

We decided Josh should make the call since Fischer might recognize my voice or Nick's.

Josh held the receiver in one hand, two quarters in the other. I held up my smartphone so he could read the Ark's phone number I'd pulled up on the screen.

Josh fed the quarters into the slot and they fell into the hopper. *Cha-ching, cha-ching.* He dialed the number, then followed prompts until he reached Fischer's voice mail.

"Thisss is Yaaahweeeh," Josh said, drawing out the words in a deep, quavering voice that was supposed to sound like the Almighty Creator but instead sounded more like someone telling a ghost story at a slumber party. All that was missing was a flashlight shining under Josh's chin. "I sent yooou an impooortant eee-mail. If yoooou don't see it in yourrr iiin-box, cheeeck your spammm folderrr."

Josh hung up the phone. "What now?"

"We attend the Sunday service," Nick said. "And watch Fischer's empire crumble."

Josh drove Nick and me back to the parking lot at the office.

After our coworker drove away, I looked up at Nick. "Nick, I . . ." *Oh, God. This was going to be even harder than I thought.* "I . . . need to . . . um . . . tell you something."

He stared down at me. "What is it?"

I looked away. I couldn't do this if I was looking into those whiskey-colored eyes. "Um . . . I decided . . . well . . ." I let my words trail off, hoping he'd pick up where I left off, fill in the blanks for me. Shit, I was being a wimp again.

"You decided what?" Nick snapped.

He knew.

He knew exactly what I was trying to say. But he wasn't going to make this easy on me.

I looked down at my loafers. "I . . . uh . . ."

"You 'uh' what?" He crouched down, looking up at me with those eyes. "You look me in the eye, Tara," he demanded, "and you tell me!"

Tears clouded my vision. The only good thing about them was that they obscured my view of Nick, of his face, his eyes. "I'm going to . . . to keep seeing Brett. I just think—"

"I don't give a rat's ass what your reasons are."

He stood and, when I looked up at him, the tears rolled from my eyes, leaving my vision clear.

"You're making a mistake." He took a step toward me.

Instinctively, I took one back.

"A big mistake." Another step.

I took another step, too, my backside connecting with the rear fender of my car. If he came at me again, there'd be no place for me to retreat to.

He took a half step this time, not touching me but putting his body so close to mine that a sheet of paper would have a hard time fitting between us. I could feel his heat, smell his scent.

It was torture for me. Pure torture.

He knew that, too.

He chuckled a mirthless chuckle. "You're hot and bothered, Tara. I have that effect on you. Doesn't that tell you something?"

He stared down at me for a few moments and I stared right back. He said nothing. I said nothing right back. He'd challenged me, told me I was making a big mistake. That was equivalent to calling me stupid, which made me angry. The good thing was, I knew how to handle anger. It was love and romance and attraction that got me all discombobulated.

Finally, he took a step backward. "Good-bye, Tara."

He put the white hat I'd bought him on his head, climbed into his truck, and drove off, taking my anger with him and leaving me, now a puddle of blubbering goo, all alone in the parking lot.

CHAPTER THIRTY-EIGHT

$\mathcal{C}$losed Doors

Nick's door was closed when I arrived at the office Thursday. I kept mine closed as well. Best to avoid each other if we could.

I felt miserable. I'd hurt Nick. That was the last thing I'd wanted to do. Hell, I hurt, too. My heart ached with a raw, edgy pain, as if I'd gone through a really bad breakup. Strange, since we hadn't actually been involved. I supposed I'd been much more emotionally invested in Nick than I'd let myself think.

With my heart in jagged shards in my chest, I couldn't concentrate on my work. And why should I have to? Why the hell should I have to bust my ass figuring out how much goddamn money these cheating deadbeats owed to the fucking government? Why the hell didn't we just shoot the assholes? Why, huh? Tell me why!

I picked up a file and hurled it two-handed at my door. *Thunk!* Papers flew everywhere.

Aaaah. That felt good.

I was about to send another file after it when there was a knock at the door. "Come in if you dare!" I hollered. Sheez. I'd really lost it.

The door opened. It was Josh. He stood in the doorway, looking at the file in my hand then down at the papers at his feet. "Is this a bad time?"

I ignored his question, laid the file back on my desk, and took a deep breath to calm myself. "What's up?"

He stepped over the mess and handed me a printout. It was an e-mail response from Noah Fischer. *Thou shalt not bear false witness against thy neighbor.*

"False witness?" I asked. "What's that supposed to mean?"

Josh shrugged. "I have no idea."

As much as I wanted to avoid Nick, I knew we needed to discuss Fischer's e-mail response with him.

I stood, stepped over the puddle of paper I'd created, and walked across the hall, rapping twice on Nick's door.

"Come in," he called.

I opened the door to find him sitting in his chair, his laptop angled in front of him, three leather-bound ledger books open on his desk. He glanced up at me, then at Josh, then at the mess on the floor behind us. "What happened there?"

"Something exploded," I said.

"What was it?" he asked.

"Me."

He gave me a look that said, *What are you doing, Tara? If you are this upset that you can't be with me, then for goodness' sake, be with me! Dump Brett and give me a shot. Come on. You know it's what you really want. Why—*

He looked down at the paper Josh handed him.

Okay, maybe I'd read too much into the look.

" 'False witness'?" Nick said, looking back up now. "What does he mean, 'false witness'?"

"We were hoping you'd know," I said.

Nick shaded his eyes with his hand for a moment, thinking. "Is this his way of claiming that the person in the video and photos isn't him?"

"I don't see how he can claim that," I replied, "what with the watch and the bracelet and him saying 'To God go the glory' and all." Surely he'd realize that everyone would recognize him by his catch phrase.

Nick shook his head. "It's a mystery to me. What say we meet at that burger place by the Ark Sunday morning and head over to the service together? Maybe that would give us a clue."

Last time we'd attended the Ark's service Nick had picked me up at my town house. I suppose I couldn't expect perks like that now that we were merely coworkers and not potential lovers.

Josh and I agreed and headed out of his office.

"Could you shut my door, please?" Nick called after me.

I turned around and stood in his doorway for a moment, mentally willing him to meet my gaze. But he didn't look up at me. His head was down, his finger running over a line in the ledger.

Slowly, sadly, I closed his door.

CHAPTER THIRTY-NINE

Wigging Out

"You want a prescription for an antidepressant?" Ajay asked as he used a pair of tweezers to remove the last stitch from my thigh.

"Yes," I replied, shifting on the exam table, the white paper crinkling under my butt. "The rooster attack left me with post-traumatic stress disorder. I need Prozac. Zoloft. Paxil. Any of them would be fine."

"I'm not a psychiatrist," he said. "And this is a minor-emergency clinic. It would be unethical for me to prescribe one for you."

"How about a painkiller, then? Maybe oxycodone? Vicodin? Percocet?"

"No."

"Can you put me in a medically induced coma?"

"No."

"Party pooper."

He leaned back against the counter. "Is this about Nick?"

I sat bolt upright. "You know about Nick?"

"Yes," he replied.

"That's the last time I'll tell Christina anything."

"Don't worry," he said. "I was rubbing medicated lotion on her feet when she told me so it's covered by doctor-patient confidentiality."

Okay, so maybe asking for drugs was overkill. But the heartache I was suffering was unbearable. I thought it would ease after a day or two, but it had only grown worse. It wasn't just in my heart anymore. It had spread throughout my entire body cavity, engulfing my kidneys, my pancreas, and three quarters of my large intestine.

I hopped off the table, using my elbows to hold the soft paper cover in place over my abdomen while I put my pants back on.

"Christina and I are meeting for dinner," he said. "Why don't you join us?"

"Thanks." Eating out sounded much better than the bowl of Fruity Pebbles I had planned.

I followed Ajay's blue Viper to Rosa's, a small mom-and-pop Mexican restaurant in a nearby strip center. I parked in front of the shop next door. It was one of those seasonal Halloween specialty stores that crop up a couple months before the holiday, hold a clearance sale the first week of November, then disappear until the following year. People milled about inside, unloading boxes, hanging costumes, and decorating the walls with fake spiderwebs.

I met Ajay on the sidewalk in front of Rosa's. We stepped inside, the bell that hung from the door handle jingling as the door swung shut behind us. Christina was already there, sitting at a booth, a basket of tortilla chips and a frozen margarita in front of her.

We weaved our way around other diners to the booth.

"Tara came to my office all sad and pathetic and whining about her broken heart," Ajay told her when we arrived at the table. "I had to invite her."

I slid into the booth across from her. "Your boyfriend wouldn't give me drugs, either."

She looked at me. "I work for the DEA, remember? I can get you all kinds of drugs."

"Really?"

"No. I was being a smart-ass. And even if I could get you drugs you wouldn't do them anyway."

She had me there.

She slid her margarita across the table to me. "Here. Try the legal stuff."

I stuck the straw in my mouth and took a deep draw on her margarita. Mmm. Feeling a little better already.

I stuffed myself silly with spinach enchiladas, rice, and beans but still felt empty inside. An order of sopapillas didn't fill the void, either. I suppose that's too much to ask of Mexican puffed pastries covered with sugar and honey. I felt as hollow and broken as a piñata after a birthday party.

When we were done eating, we stepped back outside. Next door, a young woman was wrangling a mannequin into place on the sidewalk. The dummy wore a sexy French maid costume, complete with fishnet hose and a tickly feather duster.

"Why don't you try that costume on?" Ajay suggested to Christina, waggling his brows. "Then you can dust my knick-knacks."

"Behave," Christina admonished him. She turned to me. "Want to take a look?"

"Why not?" It was over two months until Halloween, but I suppose it couldn't hurt to take a look at the costumes. The good ones sold out quickly, especially in the smaller sizes.

The three of us went inside. The shop was divided into thirds, with men's costumes to the left, women's to the right, and unisex costumes in the middle.

We wandered through the men's section first. Ajay picked up a caveman costume, complete with a brown plastic club. He held it in front of him. "What do you think? Is it me?"

Christina crinkled her nose. "Nah."

"What about this?" He held up a Batman costume, the chest stuffed to look like muscles.

She shook her head again.

"This?" It was a doctor's costume, including a white lab coat, an oversized toy stethoscope, and a brown pill bottle filled with pink, pill-shaped candy.

"There you go."

The unisex section contained a wide assortment of costumes, ranging from a banana suit, to a clown, to a neon-green alien. We bypassed these selections and entered the women's area.

Hundreds of options presented themselves. Slutty witch. Slutty saloon girl. Slutty pirate wench. Slutty fairy. Slutty black cat. Slutty Indian squaw. Heck, they even had a slutty zombie. As if there's anything sexy about rotting flesh. They had a Dallas Cowboy cheerleader costume, too, though it was no more slutty than the actual uniforms worn by the real squad.

"Let's try some on," Christina said.

I was in luck. The store had a good selection of small sizes. I went for the saloon girl, the pirate, and the fairy, while she opted for the cat, the squaw, and the cheerleader. Neither of us wanted to be a sexy zombie. Just the thought of zombies engaging in intercourse was disgusting. What if what went *in* never came back *out*?

We made our way to the makeshift plywood dressing rooms in the back corner of the shop to try on our selections. When I had the saloon girl outfit on, I stepped outside to look at myself in the slightly warped full-length mirror. Not good. The fabric cups on the chest hung limp and empty.

Ajay stepped up next to me. "It looked sexier on the hanger."

I punched him in the arm. Not because what he said was untrue, but because he'd said it out loud.

He was right, though. It was hard to be sexy in anything with my 32As. Which made it all the more meaningful how much Nick wanted me. Any woman with large breasts could grab a man's attention. But for a flat-chested woman to keep a man interested, there had to be more to it. Which got me thinking. Would I be yearning as much for Nick if he didn't have the rock-hard pecs, six-pack abs, and quarter-bouncing ass?

Yes. I would.

His awesome body was merely the icing on the cake . . . a cake I longed to taste.

I could be myself with Nick, completely, without feeling judged or embarrassed or ridiculous. I could be completely honest with him, too. He was an old soul who'd seen a lot, perhaps too much. I loved that he let me see his vulnerabilities, even if he didn't want to acknowledge he had them. And, heck, it was fun kicking ass together on behalf of Uncle Sam.

Had staying with Brett been a bad decision?

Christina came out of the dressing room, dressed as a sex kitten.

"Ooh, daddy like." Ajay stepped toward her, wiggling his fingers. "Here, pussy, pussy."

"For the love of God," I told Christina, "take him to the vet and get him neutered."

We went back into our dressing rooms, emerging a minute later in our next selections. Despite the low neckline and short skirt on the pirate wench costume, I failed to look like a "yo, ho, ho, and a bottle of rum."

Ajay took one look at Christina in the Pocahontas costume and groaned sensuously. "Me pay lots of wampum to make papoose with squaw."

She looked in the mirror, turning first one way, then the other. "I don't know," she said. "Does the fringe make my butt look big?"

We tried on our final costumes. The pink and green fairy costume looked cute on me, and at least it wasn't obvious that I was supposed to look sexy in it but had fallen short. Plus, I liked the sparkly wand. It made me feel powerful, as if I could simply swish it through the air and make everything right. If only.

"Wow," Ajay said when Christina emerged in the cheerleader costume. "I'd like to put my balls between your goalposts."

Where's a penalty flag when you need one?

As we made our way to the cash register, we wound through a display of assorted odds and ends. Colored makeup. Plastic vampire teeth. Glow-in-the-dark necklaces. Wigs.

I stopped, Christina and Ajay slamming into my back.

Oh, my God.

I'd found it.

The holy grail of wigs.

Perched in front of me, on a black Styrofoam head, was a pinkish-orange beehive, complete with a yellow and black bumblebee tucked among the locks.

I grabbed the head and held it in front of me. "This is it!" I cried. "Christina, look!"

She stepped around me. "It's perfect," she agreed.

Lu would be thrilled.

Maybe the wig was a sign. Maybe things were starting to turn around.

CHAPTER FORTY

$\mathscr{B}$ullshit from the Pulpit

Lu squealed with delight as she took the wig from me. "You found my hair!"

"I promised I would," I said. "Surely you didn't doubt me."

The Lobo smiled, her lips quivering and tears forming in her eyes. "I can't tell you what this means to me, Tara."

I was glad to have brought some brightness to Lu's day. She looked like death warmed over. Her skin bore the same sickly shade as the zombie masks in the costume store and she had much more scalp than hair these days. She'd lost more weight, too. The belt on her robe wrapped twice around her now.

She gave me a quick hug, stepped to the mirror in her hallway, and slid the wig on. She squealed again, clapping her hands in front of her like an excited child. "Look! It's me!"

When she reached for her can of hairspray, I backed away and pulled up the neckline of my shirt to cover my mouth and nose. She pushed the nozzle, thoroughly coating the wig from all directions. I had no doubt the spray would live up to its claims to "make big hair not move" and provide "much strong extra hold."

She took one last, happy look at herself in the mirror and turned to me. "I'm feeling great! Let's go out for breakfast."

Half an hour later, Lu and I sat at a table at a nearby IHOP. She'd gone all out, dressing in a groovy purple minidress and her cork platform heels, putting on her orange lipstick, blue eye shadow, and false eyelashes. She'd ordered the Rooty Tooty Fresh 'N Fruity breakfast. I hoped she'd be able to keep it down. I'd opted for a Belgian waffle with blueberry goop on top.

"Lord, it feels good to get out of that house," Lu said between bites of pancake. "Those walls were closing in on me."

"I can imagine." I took a sip of my orange juice.

"Nick came by my house last night," she said.

I involuntarily froze for a moment, then took another sip of my drink, trying to appear casual. "He did?"

"Poor guy," she said. "He must be awfully lonely if he's got nothing better to do than spend time with an old woman like me." She scooped up a forkful of scrambled eggs. "He needs to find himself a woman. I told him so."

I chewed a bite of waffle, having a hard time swallowing. "What did he say to that?"

"He said he'd get right on it."

I feigned taking another sip of my juice. My throat had entirely closed now. When I looked up, I caught Lu watching me.

"What's the matter?" she asked.

"Nothing." Nothing other than the mere thought of Nick going out with another woman made me want to burst into tears.

She took a sip of her coffee. "You ever thought of going out with Nick?"

I tried not to gag on my waffle. "Where's that coming from?"

She shrugged. "You two are a lot alike."

"We are," I replied. "Too much alike. We'd drive each other nuts."

"You don't know until you try."

"You're advising me to date a coworker?" I replied. "Doesn't that go against everything you've been taught in HR training?"

"Of course," she said. "But some things are worth breaking rules for. You know that as well as I do." She shot me a pointed look. It was no secret I'd violated dozens of laws when I smuggled Nick out of Mexico. Luckily for me, nobody seemed interested in punishing me for it. Sometimes Uncle Sam went easy on his whores.

"I can't go out with Nick," I said. "I'm dating someone exclusively."

"Brett?" she replied. "He's a nice boy." She shot me another pointed look. "You weren't made for a nice boy, Tara."

I let my fork clatter to my plate and crossed my arms over my chest. "Excuse me?"

She barked a laugh. "Don't get your panties in a wad. I'm not insulting you. I'm just saying that nice boys are boring. You need someone who will bring some excitement to your life."

"My job brings me plenty of excitement, thank you very much." I picked my fork back up, stabbed a piece of waffle, and angrily ripped it from the utensil with my teeth.

Lu continued to eye me. "You've given me several reasons why you shouldn't date Nick," she said, "but not one of them was because you weren't interested."

Lu'd only had her hair back for an hour but already her attitude had returned full force.

"I liked you better when you were bald," I said.

"Tough toenails," she said, lifting her coffee cup in a salute to herself. "The bitch is back."

The rest of the week sucked. Nick continued to keep his door closed. I caught a glimpse of him pulling out of the parking lot Friday afternoon, but that was it.

I was half tempted to ask Eddie to assign Nick to work with me on another case, just so I could spend time with him. But that wouldn't be good for either of us. Besides, all of the pending cases I had now were small, simple ones that an agent could easily handle alone. Eddie would be suspicious if I asked for help.

I spent Friday evening on my couch, eating Spaghetti-Os straight from the can and watching reruns with my cats. How pathetic is that? Saturday wasn't any better. I only left the house for an hour, to water Brett's houseplants and check his mail. I stacked his bills on his kitchen table, but tossed the Victoria's Secret catalog in the trash. Stupid supermodels with their big breasts and skinny waists and vacuous *I'm-beautiful-and-boinkable-so-I-don't-need-a-brain* expressions.

Brett and I Skyped that afternoon. He updated me on the progress of the landscaping job, his latest golf scores, the delicious peach flambé the club's chef had asked him to give his opinion on. I told him about the Spaghetti-Os and the reruns. Riveting conversation, huh?

I called Christina and Alicia to see if they wanted to get together for dinner, but both had dates planned. I ended up spending a second night on the couch with my cats, though I was too depressed to eat another meal of canned pasta and ordered Chinese delivery instead. After a lonely dinner of lo mein noodles, I cracked open my fortune cookie.

You will have an unexpected visitor.

Hmm. Did that mean the possum would return? My parents would drop in unannounced? My period would be early this month?

Nothing better to do on a Saturday night than ponder the meaning behind a silly strip of paper. Was this what my life had become?

On Sunday morning, I dressed in a teal-colored shift and heels, pulling my hair back in a twist. I put on far more makeup than usual, too. I didn't want anyone at the Ark to recognize me. They just might rip me limb from limb.

I met Josh and Nick at the burger place. Nick had gotten his hair cut short and sported quite an impressive goatee considering it was only three days' growth. He wore a standard navy business suit today, leaving his western-cut suits back home. He looked quite a bit different, but, dammit, still as sexy as ever.

We ditched my car and Nick's truck at the restaurant and headed over to the Ark in Josh's car.

"You think we've torpedoed this ship?" I asked as we parked.

"Hell, yeah," Nick said. "I wouldn't be surprised to hear Pastor Fischer announce his resignation today."

"What about that whole 'false witness' thing?" Josh reminded us.

"I bet he was just blowing smoke," Nick said.

We still hadn't figured out what Fischer had meant by the comment.

Nick and I kept our heads ducked and cowered behind Josh as we walked through the parking lot and entered the building. Nick and I didn't want any of the church staff or parishioners who might have been in court to recognize us. The only one who might recognize Josh would be Fischer himself. Since the pastor was likely already backstage preparing for the service, there was little risk we'd run into him.

Once inside, I grabbed a bulletin off a side table, opened it, and pretended to be reading it as we went up the stairs, though I was actually using it to obscure my face. We made our way to the back of the upper balcony where we'd be less visible.

Nick stopped at the end of the row, holding out an arm, inviting me to enter the row first. "After you."

I stepped in. Josh followed behind me. Nick's gesture was chivalrous, but when I took my seat, realizing Josh would be situated between me and Nick, I wondered if Nick had also been trying to avoid sitting next to me. I tried not to be disappointed there'd be no wrangling over the armrest this time.

The service began the same way it had before, with the

choir singing along with the full, modern orchestra followed by Pastor Walters making preliminary announcements and leading the congregation in an opening prayer. Everything seemed to be business as usual. But surely Pastor Fischer was running scared now, right? Surely the photos and video we'd sent had put the fear of God in him.

Once the opening acts were completed, it was time for the real show. The drum roll kicked in and the colored spotlights began to chase each other over the walls and crowd. The same game-show-emcee voice gave Noah Fischer the same cheesy introduction. "Ladies and gentlemen, boys and girls, put your hands together for the Ark Temple of Worship's very own Pastor Noaaah Fischerrr!"

A large, white spotlight shined on Fischer as he made his way up the center aisle, doing his usual glad-handing. He wore a gray suit today with a pale blue shirt underneath, a gray tie a shade darker than his suit, and what were no doubt extremely expensive dress shoes.

He stepped up to the podium, picking up the clip-on mic Walters had left there, fastening it to the lapel of his suit jacket. He raised a hand in greeting to the crowd. "Good morning, folks! God and I are glad to see you here today."

The crowd erupted in fresh applause.

He offered a broad smile. "It's nice to have the ladies back with us this week, isn't it, fellas?"

The men whooped and applauded.

Fischer continued to lay it on thick. "We missed your pretty faces while you were gone on the retreat. Missed your cooking, too."

This comment was followed by shouts of "Amen!" and tittering from the crowd.

What a suck-up. And I doubted he missed Marissa's cooking. She probably never raised a finger in the kitchen. Why should she when they had a full-time cook on staff?

"As you may recall, over the past few weeks we've been working our way through the seven deadly sins. Two weeks ago we covered pride. Today's sin?" He flung a hand in the air, pointing up at the trio of jumbo screens mounted high over his head. "Greed!"

The word "Greed" appeared in glittering green letters on the screens.

Nick leaned forward and looked past Josh to me. He gave me an expression that said *Can you believe this guy?*

I shook my head in response. Fischer, who had woken this morning in a mansion, arrived at the church in a chauffeured limo, and now stood at the pulpit in an eight-hundred-dollar Hugo Boss suit considered himself qualified to preach about greed?

His hypocrisy was unbelievable.

"Let's talk candidly, folks. Proverbs 15:27 tell us 'A greedy man brings trouble to his family.'" He shook his head and looked down as if in sorrow and pity before lifting his face again to address the crowd. "I saw this very trouble myself only a few nights ago."

The image on the jumbo screens changed to the photo Josh had taken of Noah Fischer raking in the chips at the blackjack table.

"What the hell?" Nick muttered. A woman in front of him turned and shot him a dirty look.

Fischer pointed up at the screens. "You all may not recognize that man in the picture," he said, "but take a closer look."

The image zoomed in until only Fischer's face showed.

"Believe it or not," he said, "that's me."

Puzzled murmurs sounded throughout the crowd.

"What's he doing?" Josh whispered to me.

"I have no idea."

Fischer emitted a soft, calculated chuckle. "It's not what it seems, folks. Just as Jesus spoke to the prostitute, I, too, went directly to the sinners. How could I talk to you good people about greed if I didn't learn something about it myself?"

As if the guy needed a lesson. What a bunch of BS. Fischer was already an expert in materialism and self-indulgence.

Around us, parishioners leaned forward in their seats,

eager to hear about Fischer's dance with the devil. Would Fischer's sheep be so easily led to slaughter?

"As you know, thanks to your generous contributions, the Ark Temple of Worship will soon be spreading the Lord's word to the people of Shreveport, Louisiana."

More applause followed this announcement.

Fisher leaned an elbow on the podium. "When I was in Shreveport earlier this week on church business, I had an epiphany. Right there in town are a number of casinos. What better place to learn firsthand about greed?"

He shook his head in exaggerated sorrow and softened his voice. "It was pitiful, folks. Downright pitiful. Men and women gambling away their hard-earned wages, money needed to feed their families, keep a roof over their heads. They hoped to beat the odds and hit big. Didn't happen for most of them. They left with empty pockets."

But Fischer didn't.

He stepped away from the podium. "Let's take a look at some other verses about greed." He invited the parishioners to open their Bibles to Luke 12:15 and read the verse aloud. "'Watch out! Be on your guard against all kinds of greed; a man's life does not consist in the abundance of his possessions.'" He moved on to Psalms 119:36, reading that verse aloud also. "'Turn my heart toward your statutes and not toward selfish gain.'"

He expounded on the sin of greed for the next twenty minutes, waltzing back and forth across the stage, melodramatically shaking his head and throwing his hands in the air, his voice ranging from a mere whisper at times to an outright roar at others. I had to admit, the guy had flair. He even went so far as to claim that he'd tried to witness to the gamblers at the casino, attempted to save their poor, pitiful, greedy souls. Nick and I eyed Josh for confirmation. He shook his head. Nope, Fischer hadn't tried to save any souls. The guy was as full of shit as a septic tank due for pumping.

The video clip played now, showing Fischer seated at the blackjack table, winning big and raising his hands in the air, proclaiming, "To God go the glory!" Fischer looked up at himself, the image now frozen on the screen. "God sure smiled on the Ark that night. He blessed me with beginner's luck at the blackjack table."

Beginner's luck, my ass. Fischer played like a pro.

Fischer's e-mail about false witness made sense now. The guy was trying to play things off as if his trip to the casino had been purposely planned as research for this sermon rather than what it really was—the indulgence of a greedy man who wouldn't be satisfied until he owned the whole world.

"I've put the winnings in a special fund," Fischer announced. "Once the Shreveport Ark is up and running, we'll use the funds to minister to those who suffer from gambling addiction."

The crowd applauded again.

"An interesting thing about greed," Fischer noted. "It's not just limited to man. As we recently learned, the government gets a little greedy sometimes, too." He pointed up at the jumbo screen again. This time it wasn't Fischer's image on the enormous display. It was Uncle Sam's. But rather than "I Want You for the U.S. Army" it read "I Want the Ark's Money."

The crowd roared with laughter. Some of those around us hooted and whistled. When the crowd finally settled down, Fischer chuckled. "We showed Uncle Sam, didn't we? Those silly folks at the IRS learned an important lesson. You don't mess with God's people."

The crowd roared again, this time with applause.

Silly folks? Molten anger welled up in me so hot I'm surprised it didn't cook my internal organs. I glanced over at Nick. He'd turned so red he appeared to have a third-degree sunburn.

Fischer centered himself on the stage to wrap things up. "I'll leave you fine folks with one last thought from Mark 8:36. 'What good is it for a man to gain the whole world, yet forfeit his soul?' "

I'll be damned. The parishioners rose from their seats and, once again, gave the guy a standing ovation.

All Nick, Josh, and I could do was sit there, stunned.

The guy had managed to best us, yet again.

When the congregants finally retook their seats, Fischer wrapped things up with a preview of next week's sermon. "Next week we'll cover lust," he said. "That's a *touchy* subject." He gave an exaggerated wink at the camera. The audience tittered.

No doubt he'd use the photos from the Hustler Club in next Sunday's sermon.

I glanced over at Nick. His eyes were narrowed to mere slits, his jaw clenched so tight he was likely to break a tooth. A vein in his neck bulged and pulsed.

When the collection plate came by today, I was tempted to empty it into my purse and apply the funds to Fischer's outstanding tax bill. Instead, I contributed a coupon for fifty cents off Cajun blackened fish seasoning. I wondered if Pastor Fischer would see the irony.

When the service ended, we exited the church, swept out in a sea of people buzzing about the inspiring sermon. It was all I could do not to hop up into the bed of a pickup like a roadside preacher and scream, "Are you people idiots? Don't you see what's going on?"

Were these people so desperate for someone to believe in that they'd ignore reason?

We piled into Josh's car, the guys in the front, me in the back.

Nick opened a Bible on his lap.

"I didn't see you bring a Bible in earlier," I said.

Nick's lip twitched as he glanced back at me. "I didn't."

"You stole that Bible from the church?" I looked out the window for lightning bolts and locusts. "You're going to hell for sure."

"I'm just borrowing it," Nick replied. "I'll give it back. Besides, if I end up in hell, it'll damn sure be for something a whole lot bigger and more fun than stealing a Bible."

Heaven help me, but I'd enjoy doing things with Nick that

would secure us an eternal waterfront property on a lake of fire.

He flipped through a few of the pages, then handed the Bible to me, pointing at a passage. Jeremiah 6:13. "I noticed Fischer conveniently forgot to mention this verse."

I read it aloud. " 'From the least to the greatest, all are greedy for gain; prophets and priests alike, all practice deceit.' " So true. I handed the Bible back to him.

"Fischer can spin bullshit into pure gold," Nick muttered.

"What now?" I asked.

"I don't know," Nick spat. He looked from Josh to me. "Either of you got any bright ideas?"

I wished I did. But I didn't. Fischer had managed to use both the law and our incriminating photos for his own purposes. No matter what we threw at him, the guy came out smelling like a rose. I was beginning to wonder if he'd sold his soul to the devil.

But maybe us nabbing Noah Fischer wasn't what God wanted. Didn't God say "Vengeance is mine"? Perhaps we should leave things up to Him.

"Look, Nick," I said. "I'd like to see Fischer get his due. But the fact of the matter is we can't get every tax cheat. Some of them are going to skate by no matter how hard we try." Fischer kept making fools of us. Frankly, I'd had about as much humiliation as I could endure. "Maybe we should just move on."

"No!" Nick boomed, banging a fist on the dashboard.

I was surprised the windows didn't shatter. Josh instinctively shrank back against his seat.

Nick glanced toward the building, where Noah and Marissa Fischer had finally finished shaking hands with the parishioners and were now descending the ramp to their limo. He turned and looked me in the eye. "Fischer may not be a murderer like Marcos Mendoza was, but he's cut from the same cloth. Power hungry. Greedy. Arrogant. Thinks he's above the law. We can't let people like that get away with it."

Nick's obsession over nailing Fischer suddenly made

sense. To Nick, this case was about much more than collecting some overdue taxes and bringing one man to justice. It was about evening the score between the forces of good and evil. Clearly, the emotional wounds he'd suffered at the hands of Mendoza were not yet fully healed. Knowing my rejection may have opened new wounds for Nick gave me a sick feeling. The guy had suffered enough. The least I could do was keep this case open.

"You're right, Nick," I said. "Whatever it takes, we'll get this guy."

CHAPTER FORTY-ONE

$\mathcal{P}$ositioning

On Monday, Nick left his office door open a few inches. I took that as a good sign. He was no longer shutting me out completely. Of course it could also mean he was getting over me. I knew that shouldn't hurt, but it did.

Bad.

I spent the better part of the day sorting through the bank records of a couple who operated a flooring store. Nothing on the statements matched the information in the store's bookkeeping records. More than likely, the couple had a second set of books, the real ones, hidden away somewhere. How was I supposed to figure out from this jumbled mess how much they actually owed in taxes? Oh, well. If they weren't going to help me come up with a good number, I'd pick one out of the air. Or maybe pull one out of my ass. How's six million dollars sound?

At four o'clock, Josh popped his head into my office.

"Fischer's on the move." He held up his cell phone, aiming the screen my way.

As if I could read the tiny display from eight feet away. I waved him in and held out my hand for the phone. The screen showed a feed from a GPS app, a small red dot on Interstate 20, heading east from Texas across the Louisiana border.

I'd all but forgotten about the GPS device I'd placed on Fischer's car.

I stood. "Let's show this to Nick."

We stepped across the hall and I rapped on Nick's door.

"It's open," he called.

Josh followed me into Nick's office. Nick wore navy pants and a white shirt today, the colors tied together by a red, white, and blue belt buckle designed to look like the Texas flag. I handed Nick the phone. Nick glanced down at the readout, then back up at us.

"Fischer's heading back to Shreveport," Josh said.

Nick's brow quirked with interest. He held up the phone, pointing at the screen. "How accurate is this detail?"

"It's good to within a hundred yards for a moving vehicle," Josh said.

"What about a car that's not moving?" Nick asked.

"It'll pinpoint a location for a parked car."

"Good to know." Nick pulled open one of his desk drawers and retrieved a manila file. He held it out to me.

"What's this?"

"I've done some more digging. Looks like our boat captain has a girl in every port. Or at least one in Shreveport."

I took the file from him and pulled one of his wing chairs up to his desk. Josh tugged the other chair over. I opened the file and began looking through the paperwork, laying each paper aside when I was finished so Josh could see them, too.

The records included printouts of tax data for the Hustler Club, including a list of the club's employees. Nick had apparently used the data to search for the stripper Noah Fischer had plied with his gambling winnings. The file contained a printout of a Facebook photo of a young woman with long red hair, along with Louisiana driver's license information identifying her as Leah Michelle Dodd.

"That's her," Josh said when he saw the photo. "She's got the lip mole."

Sure enough, the woman in the photo had a beauty mark. Small, but big enough to be visible in the picture. She also had the double Ds we'd seen in the video. She'd generously displayed them in a tight, low-cut top for her Facebook friends. No wonder she had over four thousand of them, according to the printout. The vast majority were male. No big surprise there.

Still, nothing in the file directly linked the woman to Fischer.

When I mentioned this fact to Nick, he pulled out another file, a thick one I immediately recognized as part of the Ark's financial records. He also pulled out a sheet he'd marked with a sticky note. It was a copy of a statement for Fischer's business credit card account, which was paid each month by the Ark's bookkeeper. He pointed to an entry on the bill. A sixty-four-dollar charge at a gas station in Shreveport.

"So?"

"See the address for the gas station?"

The statement indicated it was on Blanchard Street. "Yeah?"

He pointed to the address on Leah Dodd's driver's license. Apparently she lived in an apartment on Blanchard Street. *An apartment located on the same block as the gas station.* Hmm . . .

"You don't think he'd be stupid enough to go see her now, do you?" I asked. "He knows someone followed him around Shreveport last weekend and took photos. Surely he's being careful."

"Oh, I'm sure he's being careful," Nick said, leaning forward, his body tensed. "But guys like him think they're smarter than everyone else. Especially us 'silly folks' here at the IRS. He's probably looking over his shoulder. But it's not going to stop him from getting what he wants."

"What do you think he wants?"

"What all men want," Nick said. "Sex. As much as physically possible."

I suppose I could've been angry at Nick for his comment, but I suspected he was merely being crude for effect. After all, if Nick wanted just sex, he could muster up a dozen willing partners in the federal building alone. I'd noticed the female deputy who ran the metal detector downstairs routinely took him aside for an extra frisk.

No, Fischer might be looking for sex-without-strings, but Nick was after something more.

And he'd likely soon find someone else who could give it to him. After all, we lived in a metro area of over three million people, half of whom were female. Surely I wasn't the only woman in town who could make Nick happy.

Was I?

"Road trip?" Josh asked, looking from me to Nick.

Nick retrieved a black camera case from his credenza and stood. "Let's hit the highway."

Since Fischer was surely being more careful, we figured we should be extra careful, too. We snagged a rental car for the trip, a sand-colored minivan so plain it was virtually invisible. Luckily for us, the thing had darkly tinted windows that would make secret surveillance easier.

On the drive to Shreveport, we kept a close eye on the readout for the GPS gadget. The data indicated Fischer had stopped at the convenience store near the Ark's construction site.

"Think he's getting gas?" I asked.

"My money's on condoms," Nick said.

Josh giggled in the driver's seat.

"Condoms," Nick repeated, eyeing Josh.

Josh giggled again.

"Dude," Nick said. "You so need to get laid."

After the convenience store, the little red dot continued down the block to the location of the future Ark Temple. It remained there for the three hours it took us to make the drive to Louisiana.

We circled the block in our soccer mom car, passing by the construction site. We could see Noah Fischer's Infiniti parked inside the fence, but there was no Noah Fischer in sight.

"Think he's in the trailer?" I asked, gesturing to the small prefab building erected at the back corner of the site.

Nick shook his head. "I doubt it. It looks dark inside."

I glanced around the area. In addition to the convenience store, there were a few other shops nearby. A nail salon. A pet supply store. A barber shop. None seemed like the type of place Noah Fischer would venture into, though.

We drove slowly around, looking for Fischer. There was no sign of him.

"Let's go by Leah Dodd's apartment," Nick suggested. "But take me to the convenience store first."

"For condoms?" I teased.

Josh giggled again. Sheez. Nick was right. The guy really needed to get laid.

"No, not condoms," Nick said. "For a newspaper."

"What, you want to read the comics?" I asked.

Nick shook his head. "You'll see."

Nick stepped up to the newspaper machine on the sidewalk in front of the convenience store, stuck two quarters in the slot, and purchased the daily edition of the *Shreveport Times*. He climbed back into the car and unfolded the paper, perusing the front page. Today's cover bore a large full-color photograph of a schoolteacher who'd snatched her elderly neighbor's schnauzer from the hungry jaws of a rampaging alligator, along with the bold headline "All Bark, No Bite."

"Perfect," Nick said.

"Perfect for what?" I asked.

Again he said only, "You'll see."

We made our way across town to Leah Dodd's apartment complex. Just after the station where Fischer had bought gas, we turned into the development.

The place consisted of five buildings, each of which was

three stories high and contained four luxury apartments. The buildings were painted gray with white trim. Garages comprised the first story of each building. A separate staircase with a black iron banister led up to the front door of each apartment, located on the second floor of each unit.

The landscaping was well maintained, as was the expansive pool area in which several residents relaxed on padded chaise longues. The speakers mounted on the corners of the small poolhouse filled the air with the sounds of soft jazz, presumably Kenny G. Wouldn't he be the perfect spokesman for Preparation H?

My random thought for the day now thunk, we located Leah's unit, which was at the left end of the central building. Black metal numbers affixed to her door identified her apartment number, 3D.

"Pretty swanky place for a stripper," I noted.

"Those girls make a shitload of money," Nick said. "You should've seen their W-2s."

I glanced down at my 32As. If I tried stripping, I'd starve to death. Good thing I had a brain in my head.

Josh circled the lot, searching for a spot from which we could surreptitiously keep an eye on Leah's front door. We finally found one in the shade along the side of another building in the complex.

Nick handed Josh the newspaper. "Go lean this against the wall by her garage," he instructed. "Make sure the front page is showing."

I shot Nick a puzzled look.

"You ever see that movie *Proof of Life* with Meg Ryan?" he asked.

And Russell *the-walking-orgasm* Crowe? Of course I'd seen it. "Yeah?"

"Well, we're going to get a proof of life," he said. "Or, more precisely, a proof of lust."

"You think Fischer's in her apartment?"

"Let's just say it wouldn't surprise me." He grabbed his camera bag and unzipped it. "Leah could have picked Fischer up at the Ark site, or he could have taken a bus or a cab over here."

"Wait." I put a hand on Josh's arm before he exited the car. "Give me the ads before you go."

Josh pulled out the colorful advertising section and handed it to me before climbing out of the van.

"Do you think Leah knows who Fischer is?" I asked Nick. "I mean, what kind of woman would fool around with a married minister?"

Nick shot me a *duh* look. "Maybe the same kind of woman who'd take off her clothes and shake her breasts in men's faces for money?"

He had a point. Still, there had to be a special place in the lower circles of hell for people like that.

"Besides," Nick added, "I noticed a pattern in the financial records. Fischer always made a significant cash withdrawal a day or two before his trips to Shreveport. Usually in the four- or five-thousand-dollar range. I have a hunch Leah's being compensated for her services."

"You think she's a hooker?"

"More or less," Nick said. "I think Fischer's making it worth her while to spend time with him."

And for five grand he was probably getting more than standard sex in the missionary position. My guess would be something kinky involving spurs and a riding crop.

Josh weaved between cars and tiptoed up to Leah's garage door, glancing around him to make sure there were no witnesses. He crouched down and leaned the newspaper against the wall between the bottom stair and the garage door. Luckily for us it wasn't a windy day so we wouldn't have to worry about the paper blowing away. Once the paper was in place, Josh walked down to the end of the row of buildings and carefully cut down the side of the parking lot before sneaking back to the van.

Nick began assembling the camera, pulling pieces from the bag and laying them on the dashboard. The camera was a fairly intricate model with interchangeable lenses for zoom and wide focus. When he finished, he rested the camera on his lap for quick access.

Then we waited.

And waited, and waited, and waited.

I looked through every ad in the paper, tearing out a few coupons and jotting down a shopping list. No Spaghetti-Os, though. I was sick of the darn things.

Everyone had long since left the pool area and the night had grown dark. Crickets chirped nearby and an occasional mosquito flew into the open window of the van in search of dinner. I swatted the nasty bloodsuckers away with the Target circular.

Leah's porch light remained dark. Around the edges of her drawn curtains, however, we could see soft lights on in the apartment, along with an occasional flicker, probably from her television. Too bad we couldn't tell whether she was alone or with someone.

My bladder began to feel full. "I need to use the bathroom."

"You'll have to go to the gas station."

"Ew."

Nick shot me a look of irritation. "If you don't want to use the gas station, go try the poolhouse."

I hopped out of the car and made my way to the pool area. Unfortunately, the gate required a key. I glanced around quickly and, seeing no one, pulled myself up and over the fence. Unfortunately, the poolhouse was locked, too. Looked like it was either the gas station or crouching behind a tree. I was seriously considering the tree until I remembered the mosquitoes. Not sure I wanted to bare my ass with a swarm of insects ready to sink their probosces into it.

I used the gas station bathroom, buying and using a full box of antibacterial wet wipes on my hands afterward. I bought a box of Hot Tamales, too, as well as a beer for Nick and some Twinkies for Josh. I returned to the van a hero.

Two hours later, the night was fully dark. The sugar high from the candy had peaked and I was now in the throes of a sugar crash. I yawned.

Nick glanced back at me. "Stay with us, Tara."

I sat up straighter in my seat. "I will."

When he turned his head away again, though, I slouched. Surveillance is unbelievably boring. I had no idea how full-time spies and private detectives could do this type of work day after day.

Another yawn escaped me. Then another.

Shortly after midnight, the clicking sound of Nick's camera woke me. I sat up and looked out the window, having trouble seeing much across the dimly lit parking lot. Leah still hadn't turned on her porch light and my eyes, which had been closed for who knows how long, hadn't yet acclimated to the darkness.

A cab waited at the bottom of the stairs that led to Leah's front door, the headlights on and the engine idling. Fortunately, the taxi driver had pulled up far enough that the newspaper was visible behind the car.

Nick released a soft chuckle. "Well, hello there, Pastor Fischer." He raised his camera to his face and snapped several more shots as a man scurried down Leah's steps. He wore a dark hoodie pulled out around his face, shadowing his cheeks. He looked like a gangster grim reaper. We couldn't see his face, but his build was definitely Fischer.

He rushed up to the cab and yanked the door open. The interior light illuminated Fischer's face for only a split second before he jumped in and slammed the door.

But a split second was all Nick needed.

Click.

CHAPTER FORTY-TWO

Hell Hath No Fury like a Woman Scorned

Just after Fischer's cab pulled out of the complex, we sent Josh up the dark stairs to Leah's door. He knocked three times, loudly and in quick succession, the self-assured knock of someone familiar with the resident. We hoped Leah would assume it was Noah at the door, that perhaps he'd forgotten something and had come right back for it.

She fell for it.

She opened the door wearing only a skimpy black satin robe. Her long red hair appeared tousled and tangled, as if she'd just climbed out of bed after a rousing bout of sex. When she found Josh on her doorstep, the expectant look on her face quickly changed to confusion. Nick shot several photos of Leah in rapid succession, the apartment number 3D clearly visible on the opened door behind her, while Josh apologized for the unintended intrusion. He pretended to have mistaken her unit for another inhabited by a friend.

After Leah shut the door, Josh descended the stairs and made his way back to the minivan. "Did you get the pictures?"

"Oh, yeah," Nick said, a broad smile spreading across his face as he reviewed the photos on the camera's screen. "Noah Fischer isn't going to know what hit him."

First thing Tuesday morning, Nick and I left the federal building and walked to the downtown post office. Nick had loaded the photos he'd shot last night onto a flash drive. The twenty-six shots showed a quick but telling chronology of events.

A cab arrives. A man, clearly trying to obscure his face with a hooded sweat jacket, emerges from a doorway marked 3D and dashes down a flight of stairs. Said man steps past a newspaper strategically positioned against the building to establish the date, opens the taxi's back door, and climbs in, his face illuminated for one brief moment before he yanks the door closed.

Thanks to the zoom lens, the clarity of the photos was exceptional. The identifying image contained only part of Fischer's face and what was shown was in profile. But it was enough for our purposes. Someone close to him, someone who'd been intimate with him, could certainly recognize him from the photo.

The photos of Leah followed, the final shot being a wide-angle picture taking in both Leah at the door and the newspaper positioned at the bottom of her staircase. Nick had cropped Josh out of the photo.

Though we hadn't managed to get a shot of Leah and Noah together, the message was clear. Both of them had been inside the same apartment last night.

We had no intention of sending the photos to Fischer this time. He'd find some way to spin them in his favor. Instead, we decided to disarm him with the element of surprise and take an entirely different tack.

Hell hath no fury like a woman scorned.

Given Noah Fischer's flagrant indiscretions in Shreveport, my doubts whether he'd sired Amber Hansen's son had been all but eliminated. Obviously, the guy couldn't keep it in his pants. Besides, if Amber was still engaged in a sexual relationship with Fischer, she had a right to know what he was up to. The guy could expose her to venereal disease, genital warts, crabs, or some other kind of crotch cooties.

Once inside the post office, we slid the flash drive and the copy of the *Shreveport Times* into an express mail envelope along with a typed note to Amber suggesting she ask Noah what he was doing at a stripper's apartment Monday night.

Tossing his net, perhaps?

I wrote Amber's name and address on the front of the envelope. For the sender's name and address, I wrote: *Your Guardian Angel, 1 Fluffy Cloud Way, Pearly Gates, Heaven 00000.* Luckily for us, the postal employee paid no attention to the return address, last decade's anthrax scare only a distant memory.

We paid the astronomical overnight delivery fee in cash and headed back outside.

I looked up into the sky. *It's up to you now, Big Guy.*

Per the U.S. Postal Service's online track and confirm system, the mailman left the package at Amber's house at 3:48 P.M. Wednesday afternoon. Hopefully she'd open it before heading out to the evening's choir practice.

At a quarter after six, Nick, Josh, and I parked yet again in the Ark's lot. We watched as members of the choir streamed into the building, along with parents bringing their children to the Wednesday night activities.

The white limo pulled up to the curb but only Marissa Fischer emerged tonight. Her husband was nowhere to be seen. Amber Hansen, who'd seemed a devout churchgoer, failed to show, too. The choir would be short one soprano tonight.

Operation Iceberg appeared to be moving full steam ahead.

Nick turned around from the front seat. "Shall we see what's up at the parsonage?"

"Why not?"

Nick instructed Josh to take the long drive to the mansion. Josh circled along the right side of the fountain and pulled to a stop at the closed gate.

The three of us looked through the iron bars. There were no telltale piles of clothing on the front lawn, no bonfires fueled by bed sheets. Still, something told me that, behind the closed doors of the parsonage, all hell was breaking loose.

Nick must have had the same gut feeling. When Josh began to drive away, Nick stopped him. "Wait a few more minutes."

Sure enough, ten minutes later, the garage door rose, revealing the back of Noah Fischer's Infiniti. The white reverse lights came on and Fischer backed out of the driveway at warp speed, turning too soon and taking out a potted hydrangea with his back bumper. He zoomed up to the closed gate, his car packed full of clothing and personal items that appeared to have been loaded in haste.

When he spotted Josh's car in the drive, his face flashed alarm.

My gaze met Fischer's through the black bars as the gate slowly slid open. Pure hatred burned in his eyes, along with something else.

A promise of retribution?

Nick jabbed the button to roll his window down. "Why, hello, Pastor Fischer," Nick called loudly over the sound of the gate, waving his hand in a mock-friendly manner. "How's tricks?"

Fischer didn't respond. He didn't wait for the gate to finish opening, either. He gunned his engine and pulled through the too narrow space, the metal lock mounted on the brick gate support gouging the driver's side of his car from fender to fender as he forced the vehicle through, the contact giving off a tinny, earsplitting *screeeeeech*.

Tires squealing, Fischer circled around the fountain and roared off.

"This is the day the Lord has made!" Nick hollered after him. "Rejoice and be glad in it, asshole!"

CHAPTER FORTY-THREE

The Fires of Hell

Viola appeared in my doorway Friday, just before noon. She gestured for me to follow her. "There's breaking news about Noah Fischer on TV."

Nick looked up from his desk across the hall and leaped to his feet, too.

This was the moment we'd been waiting for.

We grabbed Josh as we passed him at the copier and dragged him along with us.

Minutes later, everyone on our floor was gathered around the television in the break room. Nick had his stress ball in his hand, squeezing the heck out of it in anticipation.

According to the anchorman's introductory sound bite, Amber Hansen had contacted the media outlets, identifying herself as Fischer's long-term mistress after receiving incriminating photographs of Noah Fischer from "an anonymous source."

Eddie eyed me, Nick, and Josh, a brow cocked in question. "You three wouldn't happen to know anything about this 'anonymous source,' would you?"

Nick diverted his eyes to the ceiling, innocently whistling "This Little Light of Mine." Josh and I followed suit.

The anchorman noted that Trish LeGrande had been dispatched to interview the iconic pastor's jilted lover and had negotiated an exclusive. Okay, so I had to admit Trish wasn't as dumb as she looked. And it would be nice to have the persistent bitch on our side for a change. If anyone could dig up the dirt on Fischer, it was Trish.

The image on the screen changed, now showing the two women seated in armchairs angled slightly toward each other. Both women wore suits, Trish in lavender and Amber in white, microphones clipped to their lapels. Trish's hair was pulled into a professional yet feminine upsweep. She sat primly on the edge of her seat, her head cocked at an attentive angle as she launched into the interview questions.

"Miss Hansen, when did you begin your relationship with Pastor Noah Fischer?"

"Four years ago," Amber replied. "My husband was deployed overseas for several months and I became very lonely."

"Oh, boo-hoo," I said to the television screen. "You could've gotten a cat." It's what I'd done when I was lonely.

Amber continued her story. "I had car trouble after choir practice one evening. Noah came out to the parking lot to help me. One thing led to another and, well, that's how we became involved."

Trish nodded. "It's my understanding that you and Pastor Fischer share a child?"

"A son," Amber said. "He'll be two years old soon."

Trish steered the conversation to more recent events, including the revelation that Fischer had been dallying with a stripper.

"When I received the photos," Amber said, "I confronted Noah." The pastor claimed to have been ministering to the woman. But, much like items in a clearance bin, Amber didn't buy his crap. She went on to say that Fischer offered to buy her silence for a half-million-dollar bribe, funded, no doubt, by the Ark's contributors. To her credit, she hadn't accepted the hush money. The poor girl had actually been in love with the fraud. Although she'd refused the bribe, she planned to pursue child support. "It's the right thing to do for my child."

Trish leaned toward Amber, her voice soft and sympathetic. "How did learning about Noah's relationship with Leah Dodd make you feel?"

Amber stiffened. Her feelings were written all over her face, from her narrowed eyes, to her rage-flushed cheeks, to her tightly pursed lips. Although she'd been perfectly happy to serve as Noah Fischer's mistress, she was none too happy to learn she wasn't the only cookie Fischer'd been nibbling on the side. "I was disgusted," she spat. "I felt totally betrayed."

There's some irony for ya.

When the interview concluded, Viola shooed everyone back to their offices. "One tax cheat down, thousands to go."

So much for savoring our victory.

As I lay in bed that night, I was awakened by a loud and unmistakable creak. My third stair.

I sat bolt upright. Was someone in my house?

Henry trotted into my room and hopped up onto the bed, his tail whisking back and forth as if annoyed. I exhaled in relief. It had only been my cat.

Henry glanced back at the doorway.

That creak had only been my cat, right?

I glanced at my digital alarm clock to check the time. Silly, I know. It's not like there's a rule that burglaries only happen between midnight and five A.M.

The clock was dark. I glanced into the bathroom where I normally left a night-light on. It was dark, too. The electricity was off. Odd, since there wasn't a storm.

Uh-oh.

Had someone cut my electric lines? Without electricity, my security system wouldn't sound the alarm.

Surely I was just being paranoid, right? The power could have gone off for any number of reasons. Maybe a transformer had blown. Or maybe a drunk driver had taken down a pole nearby. It had been known to happen.

Another sound came from the stairs, another creak. Whoever had stepped onto my third stair had just stepped off it.

Oh, God! OhGodOhGodOhGod!

What if it was one of those crazy Lone Star Nation kooks? They'd had plenty of time to replace the weapons we'd seized from them. And they knew where I lived. Heck, they'd tried to sell this place out from under me! Maybe one of them had come to kidnap me, to drag me back to Buchmeyer's place and collect the bounty on my head.

I slid out from under my covers, unsure what to do. There was only one way out of the room. Down the stairs. And I couldn't go there. That's where the intruder was.

The window wasn't an option. It was a fifteen-foot, ankle-shattering drop to my concrete patio. Plus, the window always stuck. There wasn't time to wrangle it open. Stupid shifting foundation.

Blind terror seized me and I began to hyperventilate, the fireflies flitting in and out of my vision once again.

Then my special agent training kicked in, giving me a sense of calm and direction.

Step one—prepare to defend yourself.

With what? I had my Glock on my night table and a virtual arsenal of guns in my closet, but I was entirely out of ammunition. That's what I got for showing off for Nick at the gun range this afternoon. Ammo was on my shopping list, between entries for cat treats and tampons, but I hadn't had time to run by the store.

So much for step one.

Step two—call for backup.

How? I'd had my landline disconnected after the Ark members left all those nasty messages on my machine. Without a landline, no break-in signal had been transmitted to the security company, either. My cell phone was in my purse downstairs. Argh!

Step two was a bust also.

Step three—be prepared to launch an offensive if necessary.

With what? My bare hands? Unless the intruder was ticklish, my hands wouldn't be much help. I wasn't exactly a black belt at karate.

I quickly glanced around, looking for anything I could use as a weapon. Henry stood on my bed, his tail still twitching. I supposed I could have launched the furry beast at the burglar, but that just didn't seem right. Even if he was an ungrateful, spoiled brat, I still loved the darn cat. I wouldn't want him getting hurt.

A lamp? No. The cheap lamps I'd bought were lightweight and not likely to do much harm.

And then I spotted it, the metal gleaming like a beacon in the dark.

Sitting there on my bathroom countertop was the can of Lu's extra-hold hairspray.

The spray wouldn't stop the intruder in his tracks, but it could blind him momentarily, allowing me the chance to escape.

I scurried into the bathroom, snatching the can off the countertop. Instinct told me to grab the lighter I used for my scented candles, too.

I climbed into the tub and cowered behind the shower curtain. With any luck, the guy would just take my laptop and television and leave. But I had a hunch that whoever was in my house wasn't here to rob me. I had little worth stealing.

No, whoever was in my house was there *for me*.

In the bedroom, Henry let loose with a short, insistent hiss and jumped to the floor with a thump. I hoped he'd run under the bed with Annie to hide.

I peeked around the edge of the shower curtain. I could see the dark silhouette of a person stepping into the bathroom, a gun in his hand, the unusually long barrel indicating he'd attached a silencer.

No sense waiting for the inevitable, right? The element of surprise had worked once. It could work again.

In a continuum of motion, I swept the curtain aside, flicked the lighter into a flame, and hit the nozzle on Lu's noxious hairspray, creating my own personal flamethrower. There was a crackling sound and the room exploded in brightness.

Tara said "Let there be light." And there was light.

The stream of flame reflected in the mirror as it snaked through the air and ignited the front of the intruder's black hoodie.

"Welcome to hell!" I shrieked.

The man screamed and reflexively jerked back, his gun discharging with a muffled bang and a flash before clattering to the tile. Fortunately, the bullet missed me, lodging instead in the floor. He turned and ran into my dark bedroom, his movements serving only to fan the flames. Blinded, he ran into my dresser, then a wall, the flames beginning to engulf his sleeves now.

Hadn't he ever heard of "stop, drop, and roll?"

I grabbed his gun from the floor and scampered after him. He'd fallen back onto my bed now, catching the patchwork quilt my grandmother had made me on fire. I grabbed him by the back of his jacket and yanked him to the floor, as much to prevent him from igniting my entire condo as to save his life. Down on the carpet now, he instinctively rolled one way, then another. I grabbed a pillow from my bed and smothered the flames on the mattress. Then I turned to the intruder and whopped him with the pillow in an attempt to put out the flames engulfing him. The guy better hope I'd win this one-person pillow fight.

The fire was finally extinguished, but the man continued to roll side to side on the floor, shrieking in agony.

His gun still in my hand, I ran downstairs and grabbed my cell phone from my purse. Luckily for the charred man upstairs, the phone had a charge. Plugging the damn thing in wouldn't have done any good with my electricity cut.

I dialed 911, requesting both police and an ambulance.

Henry and Anne had followed me into the kitchen. Before they could protest, I scooped them both into the dark pantry where'd they'd be safe. I felt around in my purse for the furry handcuffs Nick had bought me, grabbed them, and ran back upstairs. The guy was hurt, sure, but adrenaline made people capable of virtually superhuman feats. I wasn't going to chance him gathering his wits and getting away.

Putting my foot on his ass, I tried to force the screaming man onto his belly, but he fought me, kicking and flailing his arms. I took a hard kick to the shin before I was able to grab one of his wrists and secure it to my brass footboard with the cuffs. *Click-click.* Unless he dragged the entire bed with him, he wasn't going anywhere. I ran down the stairs, threw open my front door, and dashed into the driveway where I could flag down the cops and EMTs.

My door hung open, the wails of the barbecued burglar drifting out into the night. His sounds were soon joined with the wailing of sirens.

The EMTs arrived first. There were two of them in the ambulance, the driver and an attendant.

"Where's the injured party?" the driver asked as he hopped down from the vehicle.

"Upstairs," I told him. "He's cuffed to my bed."

The medics exchanged glances.

"Must be one of *those* situations," the attendant said. He turned to me. "He's not wearing your panties, is he? 'Cause if he is, I need some warning. I got written up for laughing at the last guy we found chained to a bed wearing women's underwear."

"No! It's not one of *those* situations and he's not wearing my panties!" I told them the person upstairs had been in my house uninvited and had been armed. "He must've cut my wires. My electricity is off."

Fortunately, a pair of cops arrived and escorted the medics safely upstairs, lighting the way with a pair of heavy-duty flashlights. I remained outside where I wouldn't get in the way. Besides, the smell of fricasseed flesh in my town house had me feeling nauseated. The air was much fresher outside.

My next-door neighbor emerged from her unit in her pajamas and stepped over to me. "What's going on?"

"A burglar broke into my place," I told her.

"You shoot him?"

"No. I'm out of ammo. I set him on fire instead."

"That works, too." She raised a hand to another neighbor who'd been roused by the commotion and come outside, too. "You know, when I first heard those shrieks coming through the wall, I figured you were getting some really good sex."

If only.

"But then they went on and on and on," she said. "No sex is that good."

A few minutes later, the medics carried the intruder out of my house. His right arm hung off the side of the stretcher, the furry handcuffs dangling from his wrist. The streetlights provided some illumination, but the man's face was burned and blistered beyond recognition.

Who was it? And what was he after? Was it a bounty hunter from the Lone Star Nation? Five hundred bucks hardly seemed worth risking a felony kidnapping conviction.

I stood in my driveway as they loaded the stretcher into the back of the ambulance.

The last thing I saw before they shut the door was the man's shoes.

They looked expensive as hell.

CHAPTER FORTY-FOUR

Ashes to Ashes

I stood in my driveway, shivering uncontrollably. The shaking had nothing to do with the temperature and everything to do with the fact that I'd almost bit the dust tonight. If not for my creaky step, I'd be lying dead in my bed right now.

That would have really sucked.

My intruder had no ID on him, but given his pricey shoes I suspected it was Noah Fischer. My suspicions were confirmed when one of the cops found his scraped-up Infiniti parked just around the corner.

The officers collected my statement for their report and called a tow truck to haul Fischer's car away. Before the tow truck took off with the vehicle, I scurried over to remove Josh's GPS from the undercarriage.

Then I was all alone in my dark house. I'd have to call an electrician tomorrow to come repair my lines.

I lit a candle downstairs and freed my cats from the pantry.

Annie appeared traumatized, though Henry had taken advantage of his time in the lockup to chew through the bag of kitty kibble and help himself to a midnight snack. He'd also peed in my potato bin to punish me. Like I said. Ungrateful brat.

After the night's events, I was too wound up to sleep. Without electricity, I couldn't watch TV. Without sufficient light, I couldn't read a book or even clean up the mess in my bedroom. And without someone here with me, I just might fall to pieces.

I checked my cell phone. The charge was rapidly waning. But there was just enough juice left for one final call.

I called Nick, told him I needed him.

He came right over.

And, there in the dark, on my lumpy guest room bed, he held me tight against him until I finally stopped shaking.

Amber Hansen's fury proved more effective than we could have ever imagined.

Over the next few weeks a media circus ensued, the likes of which had not been seen in years. Leah Dodd saw the situation as an opportunity to cash in. In short order, she landed high-dollar gigs on *60 Minutes*, *The View*, and *The Jerry Springer Show*, not to mention interviews with *People* magazine and the *National Enquirer*. If she played her cards right, her days of dancing around a pole could be over.

I'd expected Marissa Fischer to be humiliated and avoid the limelight, but instead she seemed to enjoy the attention she received as the poor, unsuspecting wife. She, too, played her role for all it was worth, landing similar remunerative gigs with tell-all tabloids and television talk shows. Rumor had it she was being considered for a role on a new television show called *Do Over*, essentially *The Bachelorette* for divorced women. I had mentioned she'd filed for divorce, right?

Noah Fischer's burns turned out to be mostly superficial, thanks to my quick action with the pillow. Still, once reports of me broiling Fischer with my improvised flamethrower hit the newspapers, I received a "Revocation of Bounty and

Declaration of Trooce" from the Lone Star Nation, the document signed by August Buchmeyer, Jr., who'd succeeded his father as president. The Nation even took up a collection and paid the Buchmeyers' outstanding tax bill in full. I wouldn't have to worry about those kooks anymore.

A white-blond hair from Fischer's comb confirmed him as the father of Amber's child. The attorneys worked out a settlement of the child support, taking a significant chunk from Fischer's savings. He pleaded guilty to a variety of charges and was sentenced to fifteen years in prison.

The parishioners who'd been so quick to defend Fischer were just as quick to turn on him when they learned they'd been duped. Michael Walters took over as head pastor of the Ark and made sweeping changes. Although he moved his family into the parsonage, their doors were always open. As soon as they'd settled in, they hosted a pool party for the youth group and several backyard cookouts for Ark members, invitations extended regardless of the size of their contributions. They opened a wing of the house up to traveling missionaries and those who ministered at inner-city churches unable to provide a livable wage to their pastors.

Walters even extended an olive branch to the IRS, inviting Nick and me out to meet with him and the Ark's staff, ensuring us he'd run a much tighter ship than Fischer had and would comply with tax requirements. I had no doubt he'd be true to his word. On our way out, Nick left the Bible he'd borrowed on the table in the conference room.

Forty days and forty nights after Fischer had tried to kill me, it was late September and my life was back to normal.

Brett had returned from Atlanta, the country club's landscaping completed. Though things between us picked up where they'd left off, at times I found myself feeling a bit restless. Maybe even bored?

I still yearned for Nick. As hard as I tried, I couldn't completely shake it.

Lu received the green light from her oncologist to return

to work. She'd beat the cancer. Boo-yah! Her hair hadn't yet had time to regrow, so she was still sporting the beehive wig when she stepped off the elevator her first day back. So were the rest of us in Criminal Investigations. I'd stopped by the costume store and purchased two dozen of the wigs, cleaning out their inventory.

Lu found the hallway lined with her agents and administrative staff, all wearing pink beehives and tossing confetti. Overwhelmed by the reception, she began to blubber. One of her false eyelashes broke free and floated on a stream of happy tears down her cheek.

Once she'd received her welcoming hugs, she brushed her tears away and put her hands on her hips. "Get back to work! Those taxes aren't going to collect themselves!"

I'd never been so glad to have someone barking orders at me.

Lu had replaced her cigarettes with Slim Jims, so it didn't take long for her pear-shaped rump to return. I supposed we'd have to worry about her developing heart disease next.

With the Lobo back at the office, Eddie was demoted to a mere agent again. No more migraines.

He and I were assigned to partner on a big new case, one involving the CIA, Homeland Security, and a slew of terrorists. But, heck, I was one of God's chosen people. A few terrorists weren't going to scare me.

Then I read the file and nearly wet myself.

Read on for an excerpt from

Death, Taxes, and Peach Sangria—

the next Tara Holloway novel from
Diane Kelly and St. Martin's Paperbacks!

On a Monday morning in late September, Eddie Bardin and I donned our ballistic vests, slid our Glocks into our ankle holsters, and headed out of downtown Dallas in a plain white government-issue sedan that smelled faintly of French fries.

Eddie leaned toward the door and checked himself in the side mirror. "How do I look?"

What my response lacked in decorum it made up for in sincerity. "Like an idiot."

"Then it's the perfect disguise."

With the shiny gold chains, sagging jeans that exposed polka-dot boxers, and untied hi-top tennis shoes, he looked like a hip-hop singer or a wannabe gangster. The disguise was a far cry from Eddie's usual attire of classic business suits and silk ties. I, too, wore a disguise, though mine was far more subtle. In blue jeans, sneakers, and a Dallas Mavericks T-shirt, I was undercover as a retail sales associate from a sporting goods store at a nearby mall. As a final touch, I'd pulled my chestnut-brown hair into a ponytail and topped it with a Texas Rangers baseball cap. Go team!

We were two IRS special agents on a mission. Today's mission would be taking down a tax preparer who called herself "the Deduction Diva." According to her glittery red advertising flyer, she provided clients with massage chairs and a complimentary glass of champagne while their returns were prepared. Hoity toity, huh?

With tax law growing increasingly complex, more people were turning to professional tax preparers. Entrepreneurs looking for a niche figured tax prep would be a good way to cash in on the trend. Unfortunately, too many had jumped on the bandwagon. Tax preparation services had become a crowded market and preparers had resorted to gimmicks to grab the attention of potential clients. But where these people came up with the gimmicks God only knows.

After merging onto the freeway, I glanced over at my partner, slapping his hand away as he attempted to eject my Tim McGraw CD from the stereo and slip in some John Mayer. "Don't you dare touch that stereo."

Yep, in many ways Eddie and I were polar opposites. He was tall and black, a father of two who'd grown up and was now raising his family in the affluent north Dallas suburbs. I was a petite white woman, a recovering tomboy who'd grown up climbing trees, shooting BB guns, and swimming in the muddy creeks of the east Texas piney woods.

Dig a little deeper, though, and you'd find Eddie and I shared quite a few similarities. We'd both kicked academic ass in college, graduating at the top of our classes. We'd both taken jobs as special agents in IRS Criminal Investigations when we'd discovered that sitting at a desk all day didn't suit us. And we both wanted to see tax cheats get their due. Especially the Deduction Diva. She'd been cheating the government for years. The Diva's due was long *overdue*.

Twenty minutes later, I pulled the car into the lot of the suburban office park where the Diva's business was located and took a spot on the second row. Eddie opened the door and climbed out, a phony W-2 clutched in his hand. I sat in the car, snickering as he shuffled across the parking lot in his saggy jeans, and entered the glass-front office space.

The audit department had referred the Diva's case to Criminal Investigations after audits of several of her clients revealed a disturbing pattern. Each of their returns showed a significant loss on a vague "consulting" business. Suspiciously, the loss in each case was just enough to offset the client's actual income, resulting in a refund of all taxes the client had paid in. When questioned by auditors, the clients pointed fingers at their tax preparer, claiming the Deduction Diva had devised the fraudulent scheme.

Though the Diva's clients were hardly innocent, as long as they made good on the taxes owed we'd let them slide with a stern warning. Criminal Investigations was more interested in nailing the preparer who'd perpetrated the fraud on a wide-scale basis. Besides, we'd need the clients to testify against the Diva should she plead *not guilty*. But just in case our potential witnesses decided to assert their Fifth Amendment right to remain silent, we were here to collect direct evidence of the Diva's fraud. Catching tax cheats red-handed was always a hoot. There's nothing quite as satisfying as seeing that *oh-shit-they-got-me!* look in their eyes.

The Deduction Diva wasn't the only abusive preparer in the Dallas area. There were dozens of them on the IRS radar—so many, in fact, that the agency had recently enacted a number of measures intended to crack down on preparer fraud, including background checks and competency testing. Whether these new measures would reduce fraud remained to be seen.

Our boss, Lu "the Lobo" Lobozinski, had decided that the most efficient and effective way to deal with these cheats was to do an intense, concentrated sweep. She'd paired up all of the special agents in the office and handed each team a list of preparers to arrest. Eddie and I were halfway through our list. We'd already taken down a moron who called himself "the Weapon of Mass Deductions" and advertised on TV, wearing combat fatigues and army boots in his cheesy commercial. We'd also arrested "the Tax Wizard," an older man who wore a long white beard and a pointy hat and claimed he could make taxes magically disappear. Clearly, he'd read a little too much *Harry Potter* and *Lord of the Rings*. Or perhaps he'd been snorting fairy dust.

With the October fifteenth extension deadline rapidly approaching, the summer lull was over. Tax preparers were busy dealing with clients who'd requested more time to file their returns, some because their finances were extensive and complicated, others because they couldn't get their act together by the April deadline. I suspected most of the Diva's clients were of the latter variety.

While the Deduction Diva prepared my partner's tax return, I sat in the car playing Scrabble on my cell phone and tried not to think of the major case Eddie and I had pending. We'd dealt with some pretty nasty people in our investigations, but these guys were by far the nastiest we'd ever faced. They were heartless, cruel, and extremely violent, killing hundreds, perhaps thousands, in their attacks, with no thought to the lives they'd ruined, to the innocents maimed and killed as collateral damage.

Terrorists.

Just the thought gave me acid reflux.

A half-hour later, I'd just earned a triple score with the word FUNGUS when Eddie emerged from the Diva's office, walked around the corner of the building, and sent me a text.

4K refund.

The Diva had done it again. Eddie'd gone into her office with a decoy W-2 showing thirty-five thousand in earnings from a purported job as a DJ at a local nightclub. Given the amount of tax withholding on the W-2, Eddie should have owed $38.76 in additional tax had the Diva properly prepared his return.

Busted.

I tugged on the hem of my jeans to make sure my ankle

holster wasn't exposed, slid my phone into my purse, and headed inside with my false W-2. Mine showed I'd earned twenty-eight grand, with just enough withholding to cover my income taxes. If the Diva prepared my return correctly, I'd be due a whopping fourteen-cent refund.

I pushed open the glass door and stepped inside.

Whoa.

The office looked like a brothel. The walls were painted a deep scarlet. The cushy black velvet massage chairs featured red satin pillows. A pole lamp with a red fringed shade stood between the chairs. Over the gray industrial carpet lay a large, fluffy red rug. A Barry White CD played softly from a boombox in the corner.

A young African-American receptionist sat at a desk chewing on the end of a yellow highlighter, a college textbook open in front of her. Accounting 101, an introductory class. She wouldn't have learned enough yet to know her boss was up to no good. The girl's casual coed attire clashed with the seductive office motif, but for ten bucks an hour, who wanted to suffer in heels and panty hose? On the corner of her desk was a silver champagne bucket that contained partially melted ice and a half-empty bottle of champagne.

Behind the receptionist were two doors. The one that read "Diva" in sparkling red paint was closed. The other one, which was unmarked, was cracked open a few inches. Through the open door, I could see a trio of young girls seated at long portable tables, buds in their ears as they input data into computers. The Diva's production staff, no doubt.

The receptionist removed the highlighter from her mouth. "Can I help you?"

I held up my W-2. "I need to have my tax return prepared."

"Fifty dollars per form," the girl recited. "Ten-percent discount if you pay cash."

"Great. Can it be done while I wait?"

"No problem. It'll just take a few minutes." She reached into a small cabinet behind her, retrieved a plastic champagne flute, and poured me a glass of bubbly. "Enjoy."

"Thanks." I traded my W-2 for the champagne. As I took a seat in one of the massage chairs, the girl carried my W-2 through the open door.

I looked down at the magazine offerings on the coffee table. *Ebony. Essence.* Oprah's magazine *O.* I picked up the *O* magazine. I had a lot of respect for Oprah Winfrey. She was a ballsy yet classy broad, fighting for justice and fairness and generally making the world a better place. Though I shared her admirable aspirations, I could never be as classy as Oprah. I find it hard to be consistently well-behaved.

I jabbed the button on the chair control and the entire seat began to vibrate. The movement made it a little difficult to sip the champagne without spilling it on myself, but I wasn't going to let that stop me from enjoying the stuff.

"This is g-g-great," I told the receptionist, my voice quivering along with the chair.

She smiled. "Sometimes clients fall asleep there."

I could see why. Between the effects of the champagne and the gentle rocking, I was tempted to take a nap myself. The Diva was definitely onto something here.

I was halfway through an article on the merits of regular colonoscopies when one of the girls from the back room came out of her door with a piece of paper in her hand. A draft of my return. She rapped softly on the other door. A husky woman's voice called "Come in."

The coed stepped inside for a moment, then came back out, closing the Diva's door behind her. She returned to her spot at the portable table.

Not long after, the receptionist's phone buzzed. A voice came over the speaker. "Miss Henry's return is ready."

Yep, my alias was Anne Henry, a combination of the names of my two cats. I'd wanted to go with something more clever like *Gwen Down,* a veiled take on *Going Down*, but Eddie'd feared it might be too obvious.

The receptionist slipped into the Diva's office and returned with my tax return.

I turned off the chair and looked over the paperwork she

handed me. The return showed I was due a refund of fourteen cents. *Damn*. The Diva had computed my taxes correctly. I felt cheated that I hadn't been cheated. Silly, huh? But it didn't matter that she'd prepared my return accurately. We had more than enough evidence of her large-scale fraud to take her in.

"That'll be fifty dollars for the preparation service," the receptionist said as she slid back into her chair. "We can e-file it for you for another twenty-five."

"No thanks."

I stood, pulled out my phone, and texted Eddie. *Fourteen cent refund.*

He texted back. *U want a big refund, u gotta ask for it.*

So that's where I'd gone wrong.

I'm coming in, he added.

The receptionist stared up at me, waiting for me to pay my bill.

"You said fifty dollars, right?" I asked, stalling for time as Eddie returned to the office.

The girl nodded.

I reached into my purse, but instead of removing my wallet I pulled out the leather holder that contained my special agent badge. Eddie opened the door and came back inside, his badge at the ready.

"We're from the IRS," I told the receptionist. "We need to see the Diva."

"Uh . . . okay." The girl's expression was equal parts confused and surprised as we knocked on the Diva's door.

"Come in," the woman called.

We opened the door and stepped inside. The Diva's office was just as gaudy as her foyer. Red wallpaper with thick gold stripes graced the walls, her windows covered with red satin curtains. She sat behind a shiny black lacquer desk in a high-backed red leather chair.

The Diva was a light-skinned black woman, with shiny swirls of dark hair swept into an elegant updo on her head, like a pile of chocolate shavings. Her make-up was heavy yet impeccable, from her perfectly lined crimson lips to her glimmering burgundy eyelids. Her long acrylic fingernails were painted a shiny ruby color. Her voluptuous body was packed into a low-cut red dress, the bust line around her double D's trimmed with black faux fur. She looked like a movie star on Oscar night. But she wouldn't be going home with a bag of pricey SWAG or a gold, man-shaped trophy, her photo featured on the cover of *People* magazine. Nope, the only things she'd get today would be a mug shot, a body cavity search, and a one-size-fits-nobody jumpsuit.

Neener-neener.

At our unexpected intrusion, the Diva stood from her chair, her expression as surprised and confused as her receptionist's. "May I help you?"

Eddie and I flashed our badges.

"We're from the IRS," I said. "Criminal Investigations Division."

Now her expression was only surprised. The confusion was gone. She knew exactly why we were here. But that knowledge wasn't going to prevent her from feigning innocence.

"What do you want with me?" She put one hand to her chest, pointing to herself. The other hand went for her bulky electric stapler.

At point-blank proximity, I wasn't able to fully avoid the stapler she hurled at me. I only had time to duck. The device bounced off my back and onto the floor. Thanks to the padded Kevlar vest under my Mavericks tee, I hardly felt the impact.

She flung a box of paper clips at Eddie. He batted them away with both hands.

I reached down my leg and unholstered my gun. I really didn't want to draw on the woman, but the way she was acting left me no choice. "Put your hands up!"

She yanked open her desk drawer and pulled out a metal letter opener, clutching it in a loose fist, her long fingernails preventing her from fully closing her hand.

I aimed my gun at her. "Drop it, Diva!"

"No!" She swung the blade around as if she were a Jet and Eddie and I were Sharks. But this was east Dallas, not *West*

Side Story. And I certainly hoped none of us would end up dead like Riff, Bernardo, or Tony. I prefer happy endings.

In a move that would make Chuck Norris proud, Eddie stepped forward and brought up his right arm, knocking the letter opener out of the Diva's hand. The blade sailed through the air, bouncing off the wall and falling back to the floor. Before she could retrieve it, Eddie ran around one side of the desk, I ran around the other, and together we tackled the Diva to the ground. On her back now, she kicked and rolled side to side, trying to loosen our hold on her.

"You touched my breasts!" she shrieked at Eddie.

It was kind of hard not to touch them given that there was so much fur-trimmed cleavage heaving to and fro. She raised a knee and rammed it into Eddie's groin. He rolled aside, retching and grabbing his crotch in agony.

Poor guy. Looked like his wife wouldn't be getting any for a while. It also looked like I'd have to handle the Diva by myself now.

The woman spun away from Eddie. Once she'd gotten herself up on all fours, I grabbed her right wrist from the back and yanked it out from under her. Ha! Roughhousing with my two older brothers as a kid had taught me some good moves. The Diva fell onto her face on the fluffy rug, sputtering and spitting fuzz out of her mouth. I climbed onto her back, straddling her as I grabbed her arms and pulled them up behind her.

"Let me go!" she yelled, squirming under me.

"Yeah," I said, "that's not gonna happen." Two *click*s later, I had her hands cuffed.

The Diva's four employees stood in the open doorway, mouths hanging open.

"OMG," one of them said.

"Totally," said another.

The third nodded her head in agreement. "Totally OMG."

"Does this mean we won't get our paychecks?" asked the receptionist.

The Diva had ripped off the IRS, but I didn't want these

hard-working college kids to get ripped off, too. It hadn't been all that long ago that I'd been a starving student, eating ramen noodles for dinner three times a week. "I'll let her make out your checks before we go. But cash them immediately. We'll be freezing her accounts later today."

Realizing she was now in deep doo-doo, the Diva switched tactics, boo-hooing and promising to be a good little girl from now on if we'd only let her go. "I'll pay back every penny!" she cried. "I swear!"

Eddie shot her a pointed look from where he stood, hunched over, hands on his knees. "You should've thought about that before you busted my balls."

Was it just my imagination, or was his voice an octave higher?

I removed the right handcuff so the Diva could make out her employees' paychecks, clicking the cuff onto the arm of her chair lest she attempt a last-ditch effort to escape. Once she finished, I cuffed her wrists back together and handed out the checks.

"Sorry about this, girls," I said. "But let this be a lesson to you. Keep your noses clean."